995

COPY 1

Fiction Yasar Kemal, 1922-
YASAR   The legend of the thousand bulls.
By Yashar Kemal. Trans. from the
Turkish by Thilda Kemal. London,
Collins and Harvill Press, 1976.
        288 p.

        I. Title.
0002614529   0042609

The Legend of
the Thousand Bulls

by the same author

Memed, my Hawk
The Wind from the Plain
Anatolian Tales
They Burn the Thistles
Iron Earth, Copper Sky
The Legend of Ararat

YASHAR KEMAL

The Legend of
the Thousand Bulls

Translated from the Turkish by
Thilda Kemal

COLLINS AND HARVILL PRESS
London, 1976

This book was first published under the title of
BIN BOGALAR EFSANESI by Cem Yayinevi, Istanbul

© 1971 Yashar Kemal
© 1976 in the English translation by
William Collins Sons & Co. Ltd, London

ISBN 0 00 261452 9

Set in Monotype Imprint
Made and Printed in Great Britain by
William Collins Sons & Co. Ltd, Glasgow
for Collins, St. James's Place and Harvill Press
30A Pavilion Road, London, SW1

I

*Beyond Aladag Mountain is a long valley, densely wooded,
with hundreds of springs bubbling forth everywhere, bright
cool pebbly springs bedded in mint and heather. It is light
that flows from these springs, not water, but a tinkling brightness. Since time out of mind this valley has been the summer
pasture of the wandering Turcomans, the Yörüks and the
nomads of the Aydinli tribe. Just as the Chukurova plain has
always been their wintering place, so the long valley beyond
Aladag has been their summer pasture. Take the Yörüks
away from their pastures or their winter quarters and they
would die. The Yörük of Aladag is like a plant growing on a rock, its roots clinging tenaciously to the granite
stone.*

Haydar, the Master Blacksmith, stopped dead in his tracks. His
right hand went to his long copper-red beard and grasped it
firmly under the chin. The other hand followed. Another two
faltering steps and he stood quite still. He lifted his head and
looked around, craning his neck as though he smelt something
in the air. Then he went blank, lost in his thoughts. Only when
his hands fell to his sides like two huge sledge-hammers did he
move on, walking more and more swiftly. He wore nut-brown
shalvar-trousers of homespun wool and a waistcoat cut from an
old silver-embroidered jacket or *aba*. On his head was a tall
golden conical coif of goathair, woven by his own hand, that
made him look twice as imposing. His bushy eyebrows hung in
tufts and suited the broad forehead, the tall golden coif and the
rolling copper beard.

On and on he pressed, very quickly, breathing hard. Then his
feet dragged to a standstill again and he grasped his beard once
more, weighed down by some terrible thought. His shadow,

equally grim and thoughtful, fell over the purple earth. From a wooden spout nearby water spirted down the rocks, smashing to shivers even before it reached the ground. His mind rushed on, quick as the gushing water.

'Oh great Allah, all-powerful Allah . . . Give me a place to winter on the Chukurova plain. Grant me a pasture up on Aladag. You did so before. Why have you changed? Why do you deny me now what you always gave me? Hey green-robed Hizir,[1] come to me on your white horse, come to my aid! Tonight we are honouring you. Tonight I'll entreat you to help us when I see your bright hazel eyes.'

He felt tired. Clambering on to a rock, he sat down and leant against an ancient pine-tree that grew out of a crevice. The tree was as old as Haydar the blacksmith. Its trunk was grooved and cleft, its boughs bent and sagging.

'I know I'll see him tonight. I know! I'm sure. I shall be able to honour him face to face. I'll give him the sword I'm making, a sword fit for kings. Yes, I'm sure. Sure!'

He clutched at his beard again. In the noonday sun the copper beard, the tufty eyebrows glistened beneath the golden coif. His moss-green eyes flashed and darkened, then sparkled again.

'Listen,' he said, 'great Allah, my beautiful, brave Allah, my friend, my lion, didn't you make the earth and the heavens, spirits and sprites, myself, yourself? Well then brother! . . . I told them already, you see, I said to those godforsaken nomads that I'd speak to you this year on *Hidirellez*[2] night. Come what may. No, I didn't exactly promise, I just gave them some hope. As if I've nothing better to do than plead for summer pastures and winter quarters for those good-for-nothing rascally wretches . . . As if I've nothing better to do than worry you Allah, and hurt your exquisitely delicate feelings . . .'

[1] Hizir: legendary figure who attained immortality by drinking the water of life. He is frequently invoked for help.
[2] Hidirellez: the 40th day after the vernal equinox, May 6, popularly considered as the beginning of summer.

6

He raised his head to the sky and fixed his eyes on the distant depths beyond a drift of white cloud.

'Well, speak!' he said suddenly. 'Will you give me what I want?' Then almost in the same breath: 'No no, of course you won't, my lion. Never. Don't I know it? You've deserted us. You've deserted the skies and the stars, the forests and the streams. You never come out of your mosques now. You've built huge bright cities for yourself. You've made birds of iron to fly in the sky. You've created monsters that devour the earth with a roaring noise. You've set up houses one on top of the other and multiplied the seas. So if I ask you now for a place to winter in the Chukurova and a summer pasture on Aladag, why should you give it to me? . . . Well then, I won't ask. I won't plead with you tonight. Let the tribe go to the dogs because of you. Let them waste away and perish. All because of you . . .'

The Chukurova rose before his eyes. On an autumn night . . . The darkness of the plain dotted star-like with lights . . . Great stars of iron rolling through the fields with a roar. Huge iron fireflies . . . Flowing rivers checked like bridled horses . . . And the roads, with their never-ending stream of horses all of iron, swift as the lightning, enough to make a man's head whirl . . . The dust and the smoke, the heat and the sweat, the fever and the misery . . . The strange parched men . . . The half-naked sunburnt women . . . Especially the women . . . Naked . . .

The whites of his moss-green eyes seemed to expand.

From below came the sound of footsteps. A stone rolled down the deep ravine. Gathering other stones on the way it plunged on with a loud rumbling. The delicate scent of a crushed sun-drenched flower reached his nostrils. He was vexed with himself. Here he was sitting on this rock dreaming of days long gone, seeing the Chukurova again, Adana city and Mersin port and the town girls with long sunburnt legs. Here he was ready to delve even further back to that time when gazelles roamed free through the empty plain like flocks of sheep.

He looked up at the footsteps and let go of his beard. It was

7

his friend Müslüm who was coming up the slope. His hair, beard, eyebrows, whiskers, hands, all of him was quite white. He flowed up like a ball of cotton.

'Brother, brother! Hey cousin Haydar, I've been looking for you all day!'

Still spinning the wooden spindle in his hand he hurried up and slumped down breathless at Old Haydar's side. He took off his sandals and shook out the little snails that had got into them. Then he tied them on again firmly. He was a tiny roly-poly man, this Müslüm.

He fixed his eyes on Haydar's and stared hard. 'You'll do this for the tribe this year, Haydar. That's enough wishing you've done for that grandson of yours. This year you won't forget us, the tribe, when Hizir and Ilyas meet. We've had as much as we can bear of this misery. If the great Allah doesn't come to our aid now we're finished, Haydar.'

Clutching at his beard the Master Blacksmith put his elbows to his knees and thought. Then suddenly his moss-green eyes widened and flashed. 'What's the use, Müslüm?' he asked. 'Hasn't Allah abandoned us? Hasn't he deserted our mountains and gone down to the big cities? We must go too, Müslüm. We must go down to where Allah is now.'

'Ah cousin,' Müslüm cried, 'your breath is powerful. If you ask something of the great Allah on Hidirellez night he will grant it. Only make your wish for us this year and not for your grandson.'

They rose and made for the path, the blacksmith leading the way and Müslüm following. Spring had only just opened her eye. The flowers were half in bloom, half in the bud. Birds and bees floated languidly to and fro under the warm sun, half asleep. The earth was stretching itself. Rocks and trees and streams, insects, deer, foxes, jackals, sheep and lambs all were stretching themselves sleepily in the morning haze.

It was three days now since they had put up here, in this valley. The tribe consisted of sixty tents and went by the name of Karachullu. Its oldest member was Haydar, the Master Blacksmith. This winter they had suffered hell in the Chuku-

8

rova plain. Never in anyone's memory, never since the tribe had gone wintering down in the Chukurova had the people there shown them so much hostility and given them such a terrible time. They were still staggering under the shock.

The Karachullu tribe was run-down, sapless, impoverished now, but it still retained some of its ancient traditions. As soon as they had reached the valley and pitched their tents, they had set up the meeting-pavilion as well. The meeting-pavilion was not long like the other tents. Meeting-pavilions are always round and their dome-like top is covered with kilims and felt rugs. Over the doorway hangs a kilim with unusual designs and the inner walls are all lined with old embroidered hangings. The floor is spread from one end to another with orange felt rugs. To the right of the entrance is set a stone hearth filled with embers. For the past thirty years the Karachullu meeting-pavilion has always been erected on this same spot.

In the middle of an encampment at the bottom of the valley was a flat white marble-like slabstone, broad as three threshing-floors. Since morning the nomads had been carrying rugs and kilims and cushions and spreading them over the white stone that shone now in a riot of colour under the warm sunlight. Fragrant smelling food had been put to cook in huge cauldrons and the older women were busy emptying the food into large platters and filling up the cauldrons again, vanishing and re-appearing in the swirling smoke. Everyone was joyfully making ready for the big feast. And if only, ah if only Old Haydar did what they wanted, then their joy would be unalloyed. The feast would really be a feast then.

'Please, Haydar, Master . . . Just this once . . . Wish for us just this time. Aren't you the oldest of the tribe, the father of us all? Do this for us this year, just this one year and then you can do what you like. All God's years, what are they for, eh? Come, Haydar, Master . . . Dear Haydar . . . Look, a whole tribe, young and old, everyone is hanging on your lips. Come, what do you say, Master?'

'Now look here, where did you get this idea that Allah will do anything I ask him?'

9

'He will, he will!'

'How d'you know, for heaven's sake?'

'We know. Allah won't refuse you.'

They had him surrounded, the whole tribe. Old Haydar stood in their midst clutching at his beard that gushed from his hands and flowed down his breast in a coppery shimmer.

'Stop it, will you, you worthless wretches,' he cried. 'Stop it! You'll make me a laughing-stock for all the world, and for Allah as well. Stop it, d'you think Allah is at my beck and call?'

The tents were faded and tattered . . . The children's faces were drained of blood, their eyes dull. Never in all his long life had Old Haydar seen such wretchedness, such a disaster as the winter they had just gone through.

'Ah,' he moaned, 'if there was anything I could do . . . Aaah, if I really could . . .'

'You can,' came the answer from all sides.

'Nobody must sleep tonight. No one at all. If even one person sleeps then the spell will be broken, the magic . . . And as soon as I see it, if I do . . .'

'You will,' they all shouted in one voice, and the deep long wooded craggy valley of Aladag resounded from top to bottom.

'All right then, if I see it I'll wish for you. Whoever sees it this year must wish for the tribe . . . Are we agreed?'

'Agreed!' they cried.

'If anyone cheats and wishes for something else, then everything will be spoiled. We mustn't be selfish, hard-pressed as we are. If we don't find somewhere to winter this year, we're finished, done for.'

'Finished! Done for!' they echoed.

The pipers had arrived. They sat cross-legged on the orange felt rugs, very straight, silent, never saying a word, never moving, tall copper-skinned men, with moss-green eyes, come from the unknown, from the sun or the moon or some strange far land. Everyone looked at them with wonder and reverence and a kind of fear. They waited, as firm and still as the rocks about them, waited for some magic spell to come true.

And the feast began. Flowers were strewn over the orange

meal-cloths, beside the yufka-bread. Fragrant yogurts and ayrans . . . Whole roasted sheep and goats, lambs and kids on large copper platters . . . Piles and piles of white rice-pilaff . . .

The *gülbenk*[1] invocation was recited and hymns were sung and songs of praise in honour of the prophet of bounty, Halil Ibrahim. And then they fell to the feast. Men and women, old and young, children and infants, the whole tribe settled about the spread. A wave of gladness rippled through the valley, over the white slabstone, around the orange felt rugs woven with the traditional motifs of sun-disks and goose-feet.

And then a drummer stood up, a single drummer, and began to whirl as he beat his drum, now lifting the huge drum high above his head, now crouching over it. Round and round he went at a furious speed, his arm beating a vibrating staccato, drawing an incredible variety of sounds from the drum, pleading, weeping, laughter, anger, mockery, defiance, revolt . . .

Suddenly the drumming stopped and the drummer knelt to worship. Bending down he kissed the earth three times. One by one they rose from the feast and came to kneel before the drummer, to kiss the earth as he had done, three times, and to pray, every single one of them, even the sick and crippled and the little children.

Just before sunset a big fire was lit below the feasting place. The blaze flooded the whole valley, setting the dusky forest aglow.

Then the pipers struck up. As one man, they piped away, distant thousand-year-old strains that made the nomads forget their troubles and float into another world. After the pipers came the *saz*-players.[2] It was an ancient long-forgotten whirling *semah*[3] they were playing, that nobody would have known how to dance to now, for the leading *saz*-player was the centenarian sheikh, Koyun Dédé, the Father Sheep. Old Haydar's eyes gleamed. He rose and began to turn to the music. For a long time he whirled on alone, round and round, nearer

[1] gülbenk: a special kind of prayer chanted in unison.
[2] saz: a stringed musical instrument especially used in folk music.
[3] semah: a kind of whirling religious dance.

and nearer the huge heaped embers, a mountain of a man, his broad beard covering his chest and glimmering in the firelight. Then a tall willowy girl with huge eyes and long hair rose to join him, and together, the old man and the young girl whirled on as though in a trance. The drum joined in again and the pipers took up the tune. The nomads rose and entered into the *semah*, two by two. Soon the whole tribe from seven to seventy was up and the ritual *semah* expanded into a long crowded *mengü*.[1] The sun set. Beating his drum all the time, the drummer circled the fire like a surging torrent. Colours, lights, the forest, the streams, sounds and stars and people, the whole valley was awhirl in mad frenzied motion.

From time to time everything would stop. All would be silence and the crowd would prostrate itself in worship to the fire and to old Koyun Dédé who sat on the edge of the pile of embers. At the *yatsi namaz* prayer, two hours after sunset, the *mengü* ended. Koyun Dédé stood up on a tall rock and entoned the *gülbenk* prayer.

'Allah, Allah, Allah . . . Sairi Selman,[2] blessed be Solomon, cursed be Mervan.[3] Our deliverers the Twelve Imams . . . Receive our prayer, O Lord. Grant us your blessing . . .'

'Receive our prayer, O Lord. Grant us your blessing,' the crowd repeated in one voice.

'May our offering find grace . . .'

'Grace . . .'

'May the Twelve Imams and Selman the Pure safeguard and protect us always . . .'

'Always . . .'

'Ya Allah, ya Muhammed, ya Ali!'

'Ya Ali . . .'

'For the sake of the Twelve Imams who abide in brightness . . .'

[1] mengü: a collective dance of worship.
[2] Sairi Selman: an early Shiite figure also called Selman the Persian.
[3] Mervan: a seventh-century caliph execrated by the Shiite sect of Islam.

'In brightness!' the crowd shouted ecstatically, raising long echoes all through the valley.

'For the sake of Sultan Hatai who was spirited away . . .'

'Spirited away . . .'

'Forgive us our sins in your holy mercy . . .'

'May your strength protect us. May our blasphemy turn to faith, our help and guide the Twelve Imams. May we always follow in their steps and look upon their bright countenance for ever and ever. Allah, hüüü! Hüüü to the truth. Hüüü to divine truth . . .'

'Hüüü to the truth,' came the moaning echo from the surrounding crags.

Koyun Dédé clambered down the rock and walked to the crowd, speaking to them in his hoarse voice.

'This world has everything . . .' he said. 'Trees and birds and earth and many scents . . . So many many blessings . . . The earth is bountiful. It gives a thousandfold, a millionfold. A thing of wonder . . . The waters, the stars . . . And all created for man alone. This night you will cleanse your heart and make it pure. If you harbour scorn inside of you for anyone, know that no man is to be despised. If you think evil of anyone, know that the man has not been born yet of whom evil should be thought. Evil does not exist. It's we who have invented it. There is only goodness in this world, two kinds of goodness. Take a staff of light, a long staff . . . One end of the staff will be very bright and the other just a shade less bright. That is the only difference between good and evil, and you must never forget it. Mervan was not evil originally. We made him so. We created his evil . . . So tonight you must purify your heart and trust in Allah and the truth. Hüüü, my friends! Hüüü to friendship among men . . .'

Old Haydar embraced him, kissing him on the shoulder. Koyun Dédé laughed. 'You too must purify your heart, friend,' he said. 'This night is your night. Tonight it's you who will save this tribe.'

'I?' Old Haydar was taken aback. 'You too, Dédé?'

Koyun Dédé clasped his hand. 'By what stream do you plan

to keep watch, my sultan?' he asked.

'I'll wait up at Alagöz.'

'Go with my blessing,' Koyun Dédé said, and they each went their way.

Slowly the crowd broke up, everyone making for the springs and brooks of the forest.

This is the night that links the fifth to the sixth of May. To-night, Ilyas, the patron saint of the seas, and Hizir, the patron saint of land, will meet, and so it has been ever since Creation once a year on this night. Should they fail to do so any year, a deathly change would strike the world. The seas would dry up, bereft of waves and light and colour and fish. Flowers would not bloom, birds and bees would not fly, crops would not grow, waters would cease to flow, the rain would not fall and women, mares, all the creatures of this earth would stop giving birth. Should those two fail to meet . . . That will be the harbinger of Doomsday.

Each year Hizir and Ilyas meet in another part of the world and wherever it is, spring explodes that year with a lushness never seen before. The flowers are never so large, so profuse. The bees are bigger, brighter. The milk of cows and sheep is more abundant and fatter. The sky is purer, a different blue. The stars are larger, more sparkling. The stalks can hardly bear the grain, the trees are weighted down with fruits and flowers. People are healthier. No one is sick that year. No one dies, no one, not even a bird, an ant, a bee, a butterfly.

Just as Hizir and Ilyas are about to meet two stars rise up, one in the west, one in the east, and glide towards the meeting-place, and when Hizir and Ilyas hold hands they too join together and become one single star that bathes the two saints in its light. At that very moment, as Hizir and Ilyas hold hands and the two stars merge, everything stops in the world. Flowing streams are arrested as though suddenly frozen. The winds cease to blow, the turbulent seas are still, not a leaf stirs. Birds do not fly and the quivering wings of bees are inert. Everything stops, down to the flow of blood in men's veins. Nothing stirs in the world,

14

nothing at all. Even the fleeting light and the coursing stars are held up. For that one moment the world is dead. And then it awakes in a fantastic resurgence of living.

And that is why on this night people stay awake till morning. They flock to high places, roofs, minarets, hilltops or mountain-peaks, so they can better catch a glimpse of the two stars joining together. Some choose to wait beside a water-source, a spring, a fountain, a brook. All through the night they keep their eyes fixed on the water, without stirring.

For whoever sees the joining of the stars in the heavens can make a wish that instant and it will come true, whatever it may be. It is said that a farmer who went by the name of Slave Hüseyin was waiting up once for the stars and, as he tells it, he suddenly saw two stars streaming through the sky towards each other and uniting in one large blaze. Slave Hüseyin was so flustered he simply could not recall what he had been going to wish for. 'Ya Allah . . .' he could only stammer, his tongue twisting, his legs and hands shaking. 'Ya Allah, ya Hizir . . . Ya Ilyas . . .' There was no time. He had to make his wish quickly or . . . But his mind was quite blank. 'Ya Allah, ya Hizir, ya Ilyas . . . Take this hill with me on top of it and carry us to the other side of that river . . .' Then he remembered his real wish but it was too late. So Slave Hüseyin just went to sleep there on the hill and when he opened his eyes in the morning, what should he see! He had been transported to the flatland below the river together with the hill he had been lying on.

Old Haydar made his way up the valley to Alagöz spring which sprouted at the foot of a red flint rock. He spread out his felt cloak and sat down. With him was his twelve-year-old grand-son, Kerem. He took Kerem by the hand and drew him down beside him.

The spring had formed a little pool that spread into the hol-low of the rock. Under the starlight, in the frozen luminance of the night, the pebbles at the bottom of the pool shone brightly. Tiny ripples circled the surface and died away on the edge of the pool. The rough-hewn pinewood spout that had been fixed to the mouth of the spring was overgrown with moss and beneath was a thick bed of watermint. The tall towering red rock, the water, the night, the stars, the earth were all impregnated with the scent of mint. From deep down, as though coming from under the very rock, a rolling sound spread through the night. The forest soughed, muffled and far off. The smell of the pines, of the many flowers, of the newly sprouting grass mingled with other scents carried by the warm breeze, fresh delicate pleasant scents.

'Grandfather, look!' Kerem cried in a thrilled voice. 'Look, look in the water. How the fish sparkle, how quickly they swim. One, two, three . . . Three fish! Like three lights . . .'

The fish sparkled into view at one end of the pool and darted swiftly to the other, vanishing into the hollow under the red rock.

The old man had been silent for a long while, lost in his thoughts. At last he raised his head. 'Kerem,' he said softly. 'Grandfather's own, I have brought you along with me tonight on purpose. Listen, my own, this night is the most important night of the year. Many things may happen tonight. Tonight Hizir and Ilyas will meet. They're both of them saints who have attained immortality. If it ever happened that they should not meet one day a year, on this very night, then the whole world would cease to breed and produce. D'you understand, grandfather's own?'

'I understand,' Kerem replied. 'Besides I know what Hidirellez is. From last year, and the years before too . . .'

'Then listen to me, grandfather's own. You see the water gushing out of that spring? Well, it'll stop suddenly, frozen in its fall. And up on high two stars like bright suns will be joined into one . . . And then a light will descend upon us. Listen, grandfather's own, you must watch the water without falling asleep, without even blinking an eye. And I will watch the stars.'

'All right, grandfather, I won't bat an eyelid.'

'And then, Kerem my child, when you see this gurgling spring frozen dead you will make your wish and Hizir will grant it to you. Whatever you want, whatever you wish for at that instant when the water ceases to flow, will be yours. Now tell me, grandfather's own, what are you going to wish for?'

Kerem held his chin just like his grandfather and thought. 'I don't know, grandfather,' he said at last. 'I don't know at all. What shall I wish for, tell me grandfather?'

'My own Kerem,' Old Haydar said, 'you will have the chance to watch many springs and stars in the years before you. You will make many wishes. So this year as soon as you see the water stop flowing, if you do, pray to Hizir. Ya Hizir, you will say, give us a wintering place in the Chukurova and a summer pasture on Aladag . . . Will you do that?'

'All right, grandfather. But will I see the water stop and the stars join?'

'It isn't given to everyone, my child. Only the innocent, the virtuous, the pure are able to see them. Such things never appear to evil people, to those who are cruel to men and birds and beasts. They will appear to you, my child. And perhaps to me . . . That is why the tribe trusts me. They think I am sinless, a saint. I'm not a saint, but I have sinned very little in my life and I never hurt a living thing. Three times I have seen the meeting of the stars and three times my wish was granted by the good Lord Hizir.'

Kerem fell silent and stared at the gurgling spout and at the water dashing itself in white foam over the pebbles. Oh dear, oh dear, he kept saying to himself in silent dismay.

'Why don't you speak, my little falcon?' Old Haydar said at last. 'Eh, my little falcon?'

Lost in thought Kerem kept his eyes on the pool and the fish. Are the fish that fall out of the spout dashed to death over the pebbles, he wondered? Who knows, perhaps they're not hurt at all. Otherwise there would be no fish in the stream down below, would there? Kerem believed that this spring was the source of the fish as it was the source of the brook.

I want no summer pasture or wintering places, he was thinking. What do I care about land? If I see the water stop, then I'll wish for a baby falcon. Hizir will give it to me and I'll raise it.

Like an arrow I'll teach it to dart into the sky, like an arrow! And it'll catch all kinds of birds, partridges, stock-doves, hoopoes, starlings and wild ducks, and bring them back to me. Rabbits too . . . But no, it's a sin to touch rabbits . . . And the eagle-owl too . . . The blind eagle-owl . . . The falcon is a small bird, with greenish feathers, but hard and heavy as a stone and its beak is long and steely . . .

'What are you thinking about, Kerem?'

Kerem started. He muttered something that Old Haydar did not catch. 'What's the matter, my Kerem?' he asked. 'Is anything wrong?'

'Dear grandfather,' Kerem blurted out suddenly, 'I'll never, never be able to see the freezing of the water or the joining of the stars. Ah, never never!'

Old Haydar was surprised. 'But why, Kerem? What makes you say that, my little falcon?'

'Because . . .' Kerem faltered. 'Because, grandfather . . . Because I . . .'

He was almost in tears at the thought of losing this golden chance of having the baby falcon he had been longing for all these years. If only he hadn't done that bad thing . . . He had first asked his grandfather for a baby falcon. His grandfather promised to find one for him, but he never did. Then Kerem asked his father, his elder brother and also the hunter Bald Kamil and the piper Musajik. They all promised to get him his falcon, but nothing came of it. There was a boy called Kemal from that other tribe, with his nose always peeling and yellow hair stiff as a hedgehog's spines . . . Well, that Kemal owned a falcon. It was his grandfather, old as he was, a hundred and fifteen years old, who had caught one for him, clambering up the steep crags to do so. A tiny little bell, no bigger than a chickpea, was tied to the falcon's leg, and on Kemal's right wrist was a leather bracelet. The falcon would come and perch there. It would soar into the air, into the depths of the sky and always it would come back again, drawing circles in the air, and alight on Kemal's arm. Kemal would call it, as if he were calling you or me, and wherever the falcon might be, however far up in the sky, it would come swooping down at the sound of Kemal's voice. And then Kemal had another trick. He could make the falcon fly over his head as he walked. Wherever he went the falcon would accompany him, circling above him at a man's height. How marvellous, ah ah ah ... If only he hadn't done that bad thing ... Aaaah!

'Why are you sighing, my darling, my little lion?' Old Haydar said. 'What is it?'

'Nothing,' Kerem said.

'But tell me, my child.'

Suddenly Kerem burst out. 'I'll never see the stars meet and the waters stop, grandfather! Never. It's a waste of time my waiting up here with you, a waste of time.'

'But why, my little bull?'

'I just won't.' Kerem could not bring himself to confess.

'Tell me the reason. Perhaps it's not as you think.'

Kerem was silent. Suddenly a large fish leaped out of the pool and dropped back with a plash. As it sank to the bottom its silvery belly flashed. Kerem was fascinated. 'Grandfather,' he said absent-mindedly. 'I once spoilt a swallow's nest. I killed the three young swallows and tied a string to the mother swallow's leg and made her fly like that for three days, and she died too. So how can I see the stars? How can I see the water stop flowing?'

'Of course you can,' Old Haydar asserted.

'But you said that those who have committed a sin could never see them. Isn't killing swallows a sin?'

'Yes, it is,' Old Haydar admitted. 'It's a sin but ... Maybe Allah hasn't marked it down as a sin. Did you beg Allah to forgive you afterwards?'

'I didn't.'

'Oh ... Then that's different ... Quite different.'

They both lapsed into thought. A flight of birds alighted on to a huge planetree before them. Then another ... Wave after wave of birds flowed through the darkness to cluster in the tree until its boughs sagged under their weight.

At last Old Haydar spoke. 'Listen grandfather's own, if you

19

look at it that way then there isn't a single sinless human being in this world. Even Hizir whom we're all waiting for now has sinned, that saint without whom the earth would not be the same. If Hizir didn't exist there would be no spring, mothers would not give birth. Everything in the world, the stones, the earth, birds and beasts and insects, snakes and crawling creatures, the fish in the water, the stars in the heavens, human beings on earth, everything would be asleep. The whole world would be plunged into deep sleep. For Hizir is the blood of this world. He is the leaf on the tree, the flower, the scent. He is the light and warmth of the world. And yet he too must have sinned, even if it was only by stepping on an ant as he walked or by killing an insect without knowing it. That's why a childhood sin doesn't count as a sin, grandfather's own. Now you be careful and don't fall asleep. And don't take your eyes off the water coming out of that spout. It won't do to be caught off your guard. If your mind wanders for a minute, for a second even, and if they choose that instant to meet, then it'll be all over. Keep your ears on the spring and as soon as the gurgling stops . . . Those birds, see, clustering on that tree, all astir and a-twitter, all that noise they're making will be cut short, just like that. And then . . . But no, never mind the birds, they might fall asleep . . . You keep your eyes on the spring and your ears on its gurgle.'

'All right,' Kerem said.

Since killing a swallow didn't count as a sin, then he might see the stars unite, the waters arrested, frozen. He felt elated. Tomorrow, very early, he would go up to the crags and catch the baby falcon with his own hands. But had the chicks been hatched already? Who cared! Hizir would see to it that they were hatched. After all wasn't he bound to make wishes come true? Wasn't that what his grandfather had told him?

It was on the tip of his tongue. 'Grandfather,' he nearly asked, 'can Hizir give me a falcon that has not yet been hatched? Or will he wait for the chicks to break out of their eggs?' But he stopped himself in time. His grandfather would understand that instead of winter quarters in the Chukurova and summer pastures on Aladag he was going to wish for a falcon and he would raise hell. Well, not that exactly, but he'd be sore. He could be frightening, his grandfather, when offended . . .

'I won't sleep a wink, grandfather. I'll watch the spring without blinking. And my ear will be on the gurgling water. And you, grandfather, you mustn't take your eyes off the stars.'

'I won't,' Old Haydar assured him.

'You'll tell me if you see the stars joining, won't you?'

'Of course I will, grandfather's own. How could I not tell you? It's a beautiful thing to see the meeting of those two stars. A man feels different at that moment, as though he had entered Paradise. Light fills his whole body and he trembles with joy. A man can never forget that moment, not for a lifetime. A whole lifetime he will recall that single intoxicating moment. Would I ever not tell you, my Kerem!'

'Grandfather . . .'

'What is it, Kerem?'

Kerem had been about to confess his intention of wishing for a falcon instead of land, but he thought better of it. 'Nothing,' he said. 'My eyes are fixed now on the flowing water and my ears on its sound.'

All was silence down in the camp below. Only the sounds of nature filled the night. Maid Jeren was the only girl among three brothers. Tall and tanned, with large hazel eyes, she always wore the old traditional Turcoman costume. Now she was sitting up by Tashbuyduran spring, the spring that freezes the stones. It spurted from the middle of a steep wall of blue crags and formed a deep well-like pool among the rocks below. From a stone spout the water then expanded into a level stretch overgrown with pennyroyal. Jeren had settled herself in a hollow between two rocks. She was dreaming, her eyes fixed on the water-spout. Last year and the year before she had also waited here, in the same spot by Tashbuyduran spring on Hidirellez night with the silent Maid Pembé beside her, but she had never had the luck to see the stars join and the water freeze. It's because of my sins, she had said. I have so many sins to account for. Still she had waited till morning without blinking an eyelid, for if she did catch the meeting of the stars, the sudden freezing of the water, then she would wish to see Halil again, just once.

'Let me see the miracle tonight, please Allah,' she prayed. 'Just this once . . . It's only a drop in the ocean of your bounty.' Her eyes fixed on a large sparkling star in the south, she kept on pleading. 'Pretty star, let me see you meet with your companion. Just this once. So I can ask the Lord Hizir for my Halil . . .'

The tribe had decided that anyone who saw the stars or the water should wish for land in the Chukurova and pastures on Aladag, but Jeren, battling with herself as she made her way to the spring, had decided otherwise. 'What do I care about land and such! I want my Halil. If I do get this chance, this chance in a million, I can't lose it just for the sake of a little bit of land. It's no use deceiving myself!'

A long thin golden-coated greyhound lay beside her. It had been Halil's greyhound and when Halil had gone away it had come to Jeren's tent and never left it since. It had sorrow-laden eyes, sad and human. It wept and laughed, felt hope, boredom or longing, just like a human being.

'Please Allah, let me catch that moment. Give me the chance to see Halil again, just once, even from a distance. Just once . . . Even if it's for the last time . . .'

The water babbled on over the blue crags. In the starlight the night was bright as day. Was she deceived? Had the sun really gone down? All through that year, every single day Jeren had lived with the hope that Halil would come. With searing impatience she had waited for Hidirellez night. Many were the miracles that had been wrought when Hizir met Ilyas, many were the longings that had been assuaged. Enough that the watcher should see the stars join . . . That he should not be distracted . . . That he should keep his heart pure . . .

There, with the streams and the lights about her, the towering mountain, now bright now dark, growing larger and larger, exhaling a wealth of scents, there, wrapped in her loneliness, a burning desire gripped her, a frightening maddening yearning for Halil that made her heart beat faster and set her whole body on fire. She stretched her burning limbs.

'Pembé,' she cried, 'I'm burning.' She rose and rushed from rock to rock. 'I'm burning, burning!'

Hurriedly she threw off her clothes. Her body shone in the starlight, fresh, shapely, fecund. She plunged into the pool. The water was cold. Pembé undressed too and got into the pool after her. In the water Jeren was not afraid of missing her chance to make her wish. Wouldn't she sense it if the spring stopped flowing about her?

When she came out she felt cleansed and pure, as if reborn. She would see the meeting of the stars. She would be able to wish for Halil.

But Halil knew nothing. All these years she had not dared look him in the face or come eye to eye with him. At his sight her whole body thrilled with ecstasy, and she was afraid of losing all control, of dying of rapture should their eyes meet. No, Halil knew nothing of her love for him. And even if he did, would he care? Halil was so handsome! You could gaze on his countenance for a thousand years and still not have your fill.

'Just once, please Allah, let me see him even from far off, and then let me die.'

'Let me die too,' Pembé said. 'That's my wish too.'

Halil is as handsome as Joseph, Jacob's Joseph . . .

'Isn't that so, Jeren?'

Jeren sighed.

Stars were streaming about the sky, endlessly. Some fell streaking over Aladag. The peak of the mountain was bright with stars. At every star that darted into view Jeren's heart trembled and she followed it with her eyes until it had trailed out of sight. And then a wave of despair swept over her.

Suddenly a large star glided out of the west, shooting sparks as it whirled. Jeren's heart leaped to her mouth. Now blue, now orange, ever brighter the star kept up its spinning coruscating

23

course through the sky. And then from the east a whole bevy of stars irrupted, and then another . . . Each one a source of light, they blazed along their different trails. Spellbound, Jeren tried to keep her eyes on them all. The light of the stars struck the water and the rocky spring boiled over in a bubbling frothing ferment of stars. The sky was teeming with them now, masses of stars, thousands, shooting, tossing in all directions. They flooded the pool and swarmed over the mountain and the forest.

'I want Halil!'

Jeren's head was whirling. Before her eyes stars and water burst into a blaze and boiled over, and the rocks about her cracked.

'I want Halil!'

The trees, the sand, the birds and beasts and ants, all was now a darting tossing mass of stars. All the flowers, all the eyes in the world.

'I want Halil . . .'

Müslüm's back was bent. His hands trembled. His mouth was quite toothless and now he was cutting second teeth. He sat there alone by the Sazlik spring and watched the star-spangled water. He felt very hungry. Since early evening he had performed his ritual ablutions five times already.

'Time's running out, my beauty, running out . . .' he kept muttering to himself. 'I know it too well. All my contemporaries have been dead these twenty years. Here today and gone tomorrow but long live Halep town, as they say . . . Those stars, this spring, that planetree even, are better off than we are. Ah great Hizir, ah almighty Allah, you've made yourselves immortal, then why not me, us, everyone? What have we done? Here I am and gone tomorrow, a hundred years I've lived and it's over, gone in the twinkling of an eye, like smoke in the wind . . . It's now I'm alive, now only, this instant . . . I want you to make me young again like Selman the Pure. O Allah, I want you to make me immortal like Hizir. Today's the day, now's the

24

moment. What's life, an instant's breath. It's the water flowing out of this spring. Only one moment it'll stop its flow. I'll look at the sky and see the stars meet. Ah, a whole lifetime concentrated in this one instant.'

Think of Lokman the Physician who gained immortality and became a saint by dint of trying. Sixty years he roamed the world, leaving no stone unturned, no mountain unexplored. He talked to the flowers, the plants, the grasses, and they revealed to him their virtues and properties, and he wrote it all down in his book, what each flower told him in its own particular language. Every flower holds the cure to some illness or other and Lokman discovered them all. Only the flower that is the cure to death he could not find, but he kept on looking for it. And one day . . . One day Lokman the Physician learned that the flower of life, the water of life, the plant of life were to be found somewhere on this mountain, in one of the valleys of Aladag. So he came here and made Aladag his abode. He talked to the grasses and flowers of the valleys, to the springs and streams of the mountain, to its birds and beasts and insects. He questioned the blowing wind, the dawning day, the flowing light, the falling rain. And in the end he found the remedy for death.

'Tonight I'll see the light darken, the rain held up, the bird arrested in flight, the stream frozen in its flow, the meeting stars, and I'll say, ya Hizir, give me Lokman's cure . . . And if he doesn't . . . If he retracts, then I'll show him what's Hizir! I'll make him sorry he was ever born. He'll rue the day he became a saint and wish for the next seventy-two thousand years that he wasn't immortal.'

Müslüm, brother, for thirty years now you have waited up on Hidirellez night and watched the stars and the springs . . . I can't, I won't say it. I won't complain. All my wasted efforts . . . No, I won't say it.

'Waiting up on mountains, under the stars . . . Watching the flow of springs and streams . . .'

It's not to everyone that the flowers will speak. The flower of life will speak to no one, not even to Hizir or to Lokman the

Sage, nor even to that saint of saints Tashbash.[1] Only once did it speak to Lokman, this flower that holds the cure of death, and Lokman went up to it and smelled it. And all at once lights burst out before his eyes, spring bloomed in a riot of flowers, the world was changed into a different world. Bathed in joy, lost in a rapturous dream, Lokman attained immortality. At that moment the world was so sweet, oh so sweet that Lokman fell to his knees and prayed to Allah. Ya Allah, he said, let me smell that flower once more and I will give up my right to immortality. For that is how it is, breathe of the flower once and you become immortal, but breathe of it a second time and you turn mortal again. Lokman knew this very well, but he could not forget the blissful sensation the flower had given him, whatever that sensation might be . . . It's a giant of a flower, as they tell it, with petals of light, the colour of the sun, each one as long as three poplars. If a man happens to stop in its shade he will live to be a hundred and if he smells it, then he will never die. At the foot of the flower is a spring and whoever drinks of its water is made well on the spot, however sick he may be.

'And it's here, this flower,' Müslüm said. 'Here, somewhere in this valley beyond Aladag . . . Invisible . . .'

Why, if they had the slightest hope of seeing it they'd all come flocking here, all the peoples of the world.

'O powerful Hizir, you have shed the flower's shadow over me, you have favoured me with a hundred years of life. Let me also breathe the flower. Death is Allah's will, but I'm afraid. I'm afraid of death, afraid, afraid! I don't want to die. I don't want to die!'

'I don't want to die,' the echoes in the valley repeated. The words shattered against the rocks and died away.

'Don't you hear me? I don't want to die, to be no more, to be nothing. Nothing! Like a weed, an insect. No one will know that I lived in this world. And even if they do what good will it do me? I shall be blotted out in an instant as though I had never been. I don't want to die.'

[1] Tashbash: a character in *Iron Earth, Copper Sky* by Yashar Kemal, who was worshipped as a saint by his fellow villagers.

The water-spout beside which Müslüm had taken up his station issued from the body of a huge planetree with a trunk so thick that five men could not have joined hands about it. The bed of a stream behind it had been deflected so that the stream now flowed into a hole bored through the trunk of the tree and out of the spout.

'Look, great Hizir, here I am waiting by this lonely spring and I've laid bare my heart to you, I've told you I don't want to die . . .' He rose, the bones of his knees cracking. His back ached and his hands and feet were numb. 'I want immortality, yes, but I want youth as well. What good will it do me to live on like this?'

He felt as though this was his last day on earth. He lay down on his back, his eyes on the stars and one hand under the water-spout. It froze in the water. He drew it back and concentrated on his sight and hearing.

'Damn it, I'll see you joined, stars! I'll see you coupling, bees. I'll see you . . .'

Once he had spent a whole summer down in the Chukurova and had almost died from the heat and the mosquitoes. It was there he had seen those hard, gilt-shelled beetles swarming over each other, coupling, an iridescent mass, the shells flashing greenly, red, black, mauve, yellow, silver and gold, dotted with a million tiny sparks . . . Insects don't die, flowers and grasses don't die either. They join together like this in a long chain, insects, flowers, grasses, close together, one after the other and they don't die, not till Doomsday.

'They fall asleep and wake up again each spring. They never die.'

But human beings die. They die because man is unique. He is born alone and dies alone, not like insects who are born all together, all the time, in masses, and never die.

'Only one creature dies in the whole world. Only one living thing is doomed and that is man . . . Man! Man!'

He was shouting, waking the echoes in the craggy valley.

What kind of flower can it be, this flower that can make a man immortal? And yet be quite invisible, even to saints? Or is it? . . .

27

Can it be that? . . . No no, of course the flower exists. Otherwise how could Lokman the Physician live on through the centuries? And Hizir and Ilyas for whom all the world is waiting tonight? No no, of course it must exist somewhere.

His eyes spotted a star hurtling through the sky in a meandering course, hitting at this star and that.

'Can it be? . . .'

The branches above him hid part of the sky from his view. He moved further off and lay down again.

'This is my last chance. Tonight I must see it all, the stars, the flower of immortality. When a man's a hundred, how much longer can he expect to live . . . I can feel death's breath on my neck, cold, snake-like, disgusting. I don't want to die.' He sighed. 'You're my only hope, all-powerful Hizir,' he repeated, keeping his eyes steadfastly on the stars. Despair took hold of him. He felt himself drowning, the world about him grew black as pitch, the teeming sparkling stars were wiped out. Then he took hope once more. The stars were whirling about the sky again in a frenzied tumult and Müslüm was lost in rapture as though he had already breathed of the flower of life.

Maid Yeter was waiting for Yunus who had been absent sixteen years now. After they had plighted troth Yunus had gone off to make money for the marriage portion. He had never come back and no one ever heard from him again.

'Life is a living grave now for me, Yunus. Come back. Come quickly. I want no winter quarters in the Chukurova, no high pastures on Aladag. I want you. I'm getting old without having been young. Come quickly! If you stay away much longer it'll be too late, life is passing us by. Come back . . . Quickly, oh quickly . . .'

She was waiting up beside a pool as large as a threshing-floor. Its blue surface held lambent gleams of red and yellow. It was deep too, the height of two men. A number of springs flowed into it from all sides.

'Sixteen years! Easy to the tongue . . . If you don't come today . . . Then tomorrow morning . . . If I don't see the stars join and the waters freeze tonight . . . If I can't make my wish, then I know what I'm going to do.'

Stars dropped into the pool, one by one, and on its edge huge giants of flowers bloomed, exhaling a strong scent. The surface of the water was paling now, its brightness was reflected on the slopes of the valley. It was getting lighter and lighter.

'I know what I'm going to do!'

Of the three boys Hüseyin was seven, Veli nine and Dursun eleven.

'I don't want any land,' Hüseyin declared. 'I want to go and work in that city of lights with my sister's husband, Fahrettin. I . . . I . . . I'm going to buy one of those cars. So if I see anything I'll ask to be taken straight to that city.'

'All right,' Veli said. 'All right, you ask to go to the city. And I . . . I wish to sleep for one night in that big house I saw on the road. The hotel. I don't want anything else.'

'I want my father to get out of prison,' Dursun said, and told the others how his father had killed Bekir in spite of his screaming and begging. 'If my father comes out he'll give me anything I want. So when I see the star I'll wish for him to be released.'

'I'm sure he will,' Hüseyin said.

Then they made plans to go to a nearby village in the morning. Then they played a game. Afterwards they fell to weaving dreams about the towns of the Chukurova plain, towns they had never set foot in, which they had only seen from a distance as they passed by on their camels, and donkeys, with their sheep and goats . . . Towns where people swarmed like ants. Towns bright with lights. Towns where there were all sorts of things you would not even dream of . . . Towns . . . Towns . . . Towns, frightening, as magic as the depths of that forest. The heart of the forest, the towns, fairies, crystal palaces . . . Giants . . . Jinn . . .

The fell asleep as they talked.

Bald Osman was fishing for trout in the stream. Every time he put his hand into the water he hit upon some trout under a

29

stone or in a hollow. When he looked up at the sky he saw that it was getting light and that the stars had faded away. The red-speckled trout which he had strung up on sticks shone palely in the dawn light.

'It doesn't matter,' Bald Osman said. 'Hizir has sent me all this fish. Next year I'll ask him for a wintering place in the Chukurova. Now, I'll take these fish and sell the half to the villagers down below. The other half I'll cook over a fire and eat myself. Good for old Hizir.'

Meryem was waiting. Her seventeen-year-old daughter was a bed-ridden cripple. If she ever saw the stars she would wish for a cure for her. The youth Alish was waiting. Each day in the afternoon he was seized with a fit of malaria. He would ask to be made well. Süleyman Dédé was waiting. He was sick of tents and of moving all the time from one place to another. Grant me the right to die in a house like a human being, he would say. Sultan Woman wanted a grandson. Her family had all died except for one daughter and if she did not bear a son their hearth would be extinguished. More than anything in the world she yearned for someone to keep up the family line.

In the town on the steppe down below everyone had climbed up to the roofs to scan the sky. Villagers and wandering nomads all watched the streams and running waters. Tonight people everywhere were waiting, eager, expectant.

Mustan was waiting. Last autumn when they had gone down to the Chukurova the people of Yeryurt village had driven them away from their winter quarters. A violent fight had broken out. The Karachullu tribe had left four dead and the Yeryurt villagers six. Beside himself with rage, Mustan had killed Osman Agha's son Fahri on the threshold of his house. Many people had been arrested, but Mustan had escaped into the mountains. He knew only too well that if caught and thrown into jail Osman Agha would have him killed there by his men.

He was alone now by the Kozpinar spring. Six armed men had been trailing him wherever he went, up hill and down vale, never losing track of him for one moment. No one could hide and give the slip like Mustan, but still he was afraid. Osman Agha would never rest until he had him killed. Even if he sheltered under the wing of a bird, in the hole of the serpent, anywhere, he would be killed in the end. With all the police of the Chukurova on the lookout for him. And the things the newspapers were writing . . . It was his friend Murat from the town who saved all these newspapers and read them out to him whenever they had a chance to meet. Mustan could scarcely believe it. How could they make up all this? One of the stories that enraged him most was about how he had held up a bus in the Gülek Pass and after having robbed all the passengers had abducted four women into the mountains and raped them for a whole week. He who had always been on the run, without even stopping for a breather! As if he had time to abduct girls or commit highway robbery or kill anyone . . . It made him mad. He could not bear the burden of all the crimes that were laid at his door.

Did Jeren know all this that was being written about him? Had she heard, did she believe it? She had never looked upon him with any favour, and now she never would. And yet it was for her, with a deep revulsion of inner feeling that Mustan had killed the Agha's son. He had borne all, insults and gibes, being trampled under Fahri's horse and whipped and chased by him among the tents. His body running with blood, he had put up no resistance at all until he had come eye to eye with Jeren and read her look. I or Halil, I or Halil? Halil, Halil of course, would Halil ever run away and be humiliated in this way? After this Mustan had lost himself. He had jumped onto a horse and, gun in hand, had pursued Fahri right up to his doorstep. There he had shot him, slashed off his head and returned to throw it in front of Jeren.

The Kozpinar spring rushed out of a hole in the middle of a wall-like rock somewhere near the peak of the mountain where the pine trees ceased to grow.

'I won't say a thing,' Mustan muttered. 'You can see for yourself what a mess I'm in. If I don't see your star tonight . . . If the water here doesn't freeze over this rock, then it's all up

31

with me and you know it. There's no need for me to tell you, to say anything.'

Over the crest of Aladag the stars shone brightly and beneath them thousands of eagles were swirling in endless motion.

'There's something special about this night,' Mustan said. 'Or how could so many eagles come together like this?'

Suddenly he saw figures looming out of the darkness down below, seven or eight men. A stone rolled from under someone's foot. Above him he heard a rustling noise and there too he could make out a group of armed men. Right and left he felt movements, heard whispers and muffled coughing. Here and there a tinder was struck and cigarettes glowed in the night. Mustan knew he was encircled.

He smiled. 'Yes, there's something special about this night, Hidirellez night. All those eagles . . .' He grasped his gun firmly. He had been on the run for nearly a year and had not yet fired a single shot. 'Tonight I'll give my first fight,' he laughed. 'Tonight . . . Hidirellez night . . .'

Up to now the mere sight of a policeman would be enough to make him go limp all over. Now he felt no fear at all and the thought of death never crossed his mind.

He looked up at the stars, so many of them, immobile, as if nailed in their places. A group of eagles broke away from the whirling mass and flapped over to Kozpinar spring. Mustan waited for the first shot to burst out.

'Something's going to give tonight, Mustan, brother. Who knows, maybe the great Hizir is going to help me.' He looked at his cartridge-pouch. It was full to the brim. Suddenly he was filled with pity for himself. 'So many many times I got away and it's here, on this mountain top that they have to find me.'

His hand on the trigger he waited for the first move from his pursuers. He could see the glow of their burning cigarettes.

'Don't go to sleep, Kerem.'
'I'm not sleeping, grandfather.'
'Look, Kerem!'
A deer with long spreading antlers was standing at the spring.

32

It raised its head sniffing warily at the air, then bent down to the water and all in the same instant jumped and flowed swiftly out of sight.

'He saw us, Kerem,' Old Haydar said. 'He took fright.'

'What a pity,' Kerem exclaimed. 'And what a pity it's so dark, who knows what a beautiful deer he was . . .' I'll wish for a deer too, he thought.

After a while a fox drew near the spring flourishing its huge tail and sniffing at every tree root and trail and stone. It went away and then a mountain goat appeared, then a pack of jackals and a whole lot of other animals they could not identify.

'Don't sleep Kerem. Keep your eyes on the water.'

'All right, grandfather.' A fox too, he was thinking. And . . . And . . . That insect of iron with eyes of light that ploughs the fields and smells so strange. I'll wish for that, and also . . .

There were so many things he wanted that he was ashamed. He toyed with the idea of giving up some of his wishes, then changed his mind.

It was surely past midnight. Old Haydar thought he heard the crowing of cocks from the steppe below.

'Look, great Allah, this is not a way to come to you, I know, and if it were just for me I would never have waited up like this on Hidirellez night. Now look, let's talk this over man to man, the two of us. The tribe is really hard-pressed. And hasn't this valley on Aladag been our summering place since time out of mind? So why did you go and put in our way things like the police and forest guards that won't let us breathe, that make us sick of our lives? Look friend, haven't we gone down to winter in the Chukurova since the world was made? And now we can't even find a scrap of land to pitch a tent on. Where are we to live? Up in the sky? Look my lion, please! The tribespeople trust me, they've sent me to you as their envoy. They're not all perfect, we know that, they've got their share of twisters and scoundrels among them. But they have no land. And tomorrow morning they'll look to me for an answer to that. Don't shame me before those rascals. It won't do any harm to show me those stars. It's only to have our land back, this land that was ours long long ago. Now what d'you say? Don't turn an old man down . . .'

He rumbled on interminably, his eyes on the stars. There were so many, shooting out from right and left, north, south, east, west, that he could not keep up with them all. 'How am I to find your star, Hizir,' he complained, 'in all this medley?'

An excited voice cried: 'Grandfather, grandfather look!'

A fish leaped out of the water. Its silvery belly glinted palely as it plopped back.

The dawn began to break, slowly silvering the edge of the clouds, and a widening strip of light spread in the sky about the brightening clouds and the mountain peaks.

Bayram the *abdal*[1] took his drum and climbing on to the white stone slab began to beat the dawning rhythm, a deep slow sound at first that speeded up as the day lightened.

Then the tribespeople drifted back into the valley, weary, the light of their eyes snuffed out, their faces long and dull and yellow. Huddling behind their lost hopes they came one by one to squat around the white slabstone until they were all gathered there, the whole tribe, old and young. The only absent ones were Maid Yeter, Mustan the fugitive and Old Haydar and his grandson. After a while the old man appeared leading his grandson by the hand and smiling. The abdal's drum was beating half-heartedly now. The crowd was still and silent, as though turned to stone. Everyone's head hung low.

'No need to worry any more,' Old Haydar said, still smiling. 'No need at all.'

'No need indeed!' Müslüm retorted, rising. 'Who's to worry if not us? When we haven't got a scrap of land to live on this winter? When we'll have been hounded all through the summer here on Aladag by the forestry guards and the gendarmes . . . Who's to worry, who's to die of misery if not us?'

'Not us!' Haydar said sternly, his voice ringing with confidence. 'I have news for you. Good news.'

---

[1] abdal: a member of a nomadic tribe who plays the drum at weddings and on ritual occasions.

Life flowed back into them. Their faces brightened and in an instant they had breasted the wall of despondency.

'Say it, quick!' Müslüm cried in a sudden fever. 'Say it, you've seen the stars, haven't you? Did you have time to make our wish?'

'It wasn't I who saw them,' Haydar replied. 'I must have fallen into a doze when Kerem roused me. He was shouting for all he was worth, look grandfather, look! But it was too late. The moment of the meeting of the stars had passed. So I asked Kerem quickly, did you make your wish? And Kerem said, yes grandfather, I did . . . Tell them about it, Kerem.'

Kerem hung his head and closed his eyes. 'I never slept a wink,' he began. 'Not a wink. And I didn't take my eyes off the stars for one moment. It was towards morning. The dawn was about to break . . . Yes indeed, it was growing light already. All of a sudden I saw a huge flaming star shoot out, as big as my head, a star that gave out blue sparks . . . And then from the other side of the sky I saw another star, just like the first one, shooting out. They glided on towards each other until they came together just above us. And then the water stopped flowing just like that. It just froze still. Then a light burst out, a light . . . The world was drowned in light. My eyes were dazzled. And I made my wish as quickly as I could.'

'What did you wish for?' Müslüm asked. 'It's just like that they appear. The child's telling the truth.'

They were all excited now, on their feet, hanging fervently on Kerem's lips. The boy was embarrassed. His hands trembled. His face worked as though trying to remember something. 'I wished,' he said, 'just like grandfather told me to.'

'But how?' Müslüm persisted wistfully. 'What did you say?'

Biting his lips Kerem could only repeat 'I wished for that', as though he were strangling. They pressed all around him. 'What? How?' they kept asking.

Kerem was thoroughly disturbed now. 'Well, I wished for . . . I wished for . . .'

'What would he wish for?' his grandfather spoke for him. 'What would Kerem wish for except what we all wish for . . .

Land in the Chukurova and pastures on Aladag? Isn't that so, Kerem?'

'Yes,' Kerem said very low, 'yes . . . I wished.'

They were not convinced. Dispirited, they slumped down again. The haunting thought of the coming autumn was preying on everyone's mind. Again they would find no place to winter in the Chukurova. Again the inhabitants of the plain would attack them with their dogs and horses wherever they happened to pitch their tents. Again they would be killed, their daughters abducted, their caravans driven over the muddy roads under the rain. They had no hope left now. This night of Hidirellez they had waited for so impatiently, the meeting of the stars, the freezing of the waters, all had failed. No one but the boy Kerem had seen anything at all . . .

Kerem had slipped away from the crowd and with all the children about him was telling his tale. 'My grandfather said . . . Don't sleep Kerem, he said. It won't do to miss the stars this time. My grandfather said . . . Kerem, he said. This time . . . This time . . . And I saw the stars moving, gliding, fleeting . . .'

Old Haydar could not bear to see the tribe so depressed. 'Look here,' he said gruffly, 'if Kerem's wish isn't granted then I'll find you winter-quarters myself. I will, you'll see. My sword's nearly finished. I'll give it to Ismet Pasha[1], to Menderes[2], to Temir Agha, and I'll get land for you in exchange.'

There was no response from the gloomy crowd. But Old Haydar would not give up. He felt he must do something to raise their spirits. 'Look friends, listen my brave people, you mustn't despair. Despair is bad. It doesn't become a man who calls himself a man. Despair is good for the dead . . . Why, that sword I'm making is almost finished.'

They listened to him in silence. They had heard the story of Haydar's sword for the past thirty years. At first the sword was intended for Mustafa Kemal Pasha,[3] then for Ismet Pasha,

---

[1] Ismet Pasha: Ismet Inönü, hero of the War of Independence and second president of Turkey.

[2] Menderes: Prime Minister of Turkey from 1950 to 1960.

[3] Mustafa Kemal Pasha: Atatürk, founder of the Turkish Republic.

then for Menderes . . . In the end Haydar decided to give it to Temir Agha in exchange for land. But the engraving of the golden calligraphy on the sword had turned out to be an unending task. Haydar was making an exact copy of the calligraphy on an ancient broken sword.

In the time of the Padishahs, the Chebi tribe had grown tired of the nomad life. The tribe's blacksmith, Rüstem, was a master-craftsman. No one surpassed him in making swords and engraving them with gold. This Rüstem had worked on a special sword for fifteen years. Its handle was engraved all in gold. Ah, where would Old Haydar find that much gold! Well anyway, Rüstem the Master Blacksmith went to the Padishah and presented him with this sword. How pleased the Padishah was! 'Wish me a wish, Master,' he said. 'I wish your health,' the other answered. 'What use is my health to you?' the Padishah said. 'Wish me a wish.' Bashful, embarrassed, the blacksmith at last gave tongue to his secret wish. 'Our tribe's weary of this miserable nomadic life, and yet we don't own a scrap of land to step on.' And so the Padishah issued a firman and Rüstem the blacksmith's tribe was given a huge plain all to themselves to settle there at leisure or to leave when they felt like going up into the mountains . . .

'Kerem's seen the stars, that's sure. But say he hasn't . . . There's still my sword. I'll go now and melt some more gold . . . Why, Ismet Pasha will give us a whole plain, see if he doesn't . . .'

Old Haydar talked on, but the crowd was breaking up, drifting away one by one. Only Abdal Bayram was left asleep on the white slabstone, his head resting on his drum. Haydar looked about him sadly. Then he too made off for his tent.

Next morning black news reached them from up in the mountain. The police and Osman Agha's men had surrounded Mustan as he was watching for the stars by Kozpinar spring. After having wounded eleven policemen, Mustan had managed to escape, but he too was badly wounded.

As for Maid Yeter she was found drowned in the pool of the many springs.

37

2

*In 1876 a battle took place between the Turcoman nomads
and the Ottoman rulers. The Ottomans wanted to settle the
nomads, to tie them to the earth, to make them pay taxes and
enroll them in the army. The Turcomans refused to be yoked.
They resisted fiercely, but were beaten in the end and com-
pelled to settle. The bitterness of this defeat, the ignominy of
their forced settlement, have ever remained a raw wound in
the heart of every Turcoman. Many there were who would
not bow to this fate, who ran away from the settlements, who
evaded exile and persevered in their old nomadic ways. But
this grew more difficult with every passing day. And nowadays
it was well-nigh impossible.*

The sound of cannon was coming from the south, from Iskenderun and Payas and the Gavur Mountains. It was almost
spring. The February winds had long driven away the cold
winter draughts. That winter, from Yozgat and Sivas, from
Kazova, Tokat and Gündeshliova, from Haran and Kamishli
and Aleppo, from all over the land of Anatolia and from other
lands too, the people of the black tents had gathered and raised
the standard of revolt against the Ottoman. At their head was
the chief of the Taurus Varsaks, Kozanoglu. Down south on
the plain near Payas fortress the Ottoman army was met by
the Beys of Küchükalioglu and Payaslioglu and behind the
Gavur Mountains by the tribes of Barak and Elbeylioglu. The
Gülek Pass was held by the Menemenjioglus. The Beys of the
Jadioglu, Chapanoglu and Sunguroglu tribes also entered the
fray.

In the fighting that broke out on the Gavur Mountains the
Turcomans were defeated. They fell back, leaving many killed
behind them. The Ottomans had cannons and guns, while the

Turcomans possessed no firearms save a few flintlock muskets. For two months they suffered defeat after defeat. The Ottomans had sent an army over the highlands through Hachin, Féké and Göksün and cut off all the roads of retreat into the mountains. They were forcing the Turcomans down into the plain and trapping them between the Mediterranean Sea and the mountains. At last the Turcomans stopped fighting. They lay low, waiting . . . Waiting for the night that links the fifth to the sixth of May. That night they would set up watch by water-heads and on top of hills and trees for the meeting of the stars and the freezing of the waters and then they would make their wish . . . 'O Allah, sharpen the Turcoman's sword. Blind the Ottoman's eye. Look at us, see what we've come to. Yet grant us even this life, this day, O Creator . . . Let the land of the Chukurova be theirs, O Lord, and allow us to keep our own nomadic ways. Don't deprive us of our cool mauve-flowered springs, O Creator . . .'

That night the crowds of nomads massed on the Chukurova plain did not sleep. Desperately, they watched for the stars and gave prayers to the Lord Hizir. And as dawn broke the last big battle with the Ottoman began. Many were the dead among the Turcomans . . . Those who survived surrendered. Nomad tribes all over Anatolia were rounded up and herded into the Chukurova. Unused to the heat and mosquitoes of the plain they died like flies or were struck down by malaria. The dead lay about, stinking, for there was no one to bury them. Their sheep and camels, their noble horses were also decimated. In those days the Chukurova plain was only an empty expanse of bogland and marsh.

And yet one morning, sick and wounded as they were, the Turcomans rose up once more against the Ottoman soldiers only to suffer their final crushing defeat. They knew it was impossible for them to survive a summer down in the Chukurova. They had to think of other ways to get out.

Now, at that time Haydar the blacksmith's father was the smith of the Karachullu tribe as had been his father before him. There had always been smiths in the family, going way back to when the nomads had lived in the land of Khorassan, and they had always forged swords, sturdy, beautifully engraved swords that were reputed to bear a charm. Haydar's father had just finished a sword of Egyptian design. It lay there like a drop of water, luminous, long and slim. He took it and went straight to the Ottoman major, Ali Bey. When he saw this sword, Ali Bey's eyes opened like saucers and his tongue flowed down his throat. 'Major, take it,' the blacksmith said. 'Take this sword and let us go up into our mountains. We'll all die in this Chukurova before the month's up. Save us . . .' The major thought awhile, then he kneeled down in awe and spoke: 'A race of men who can make such swords does not deserve to be treated like this. Go to your tribe and tell them to set out for the mountains up this road here.'

This tale was a constant source of pride to Haydar the black-smith. ''Tis a sword saved those who escaped the sword,' he repeated. 'My father's sword!'

But others of the tribe differed. 'Curse that sword,' they said. 'If only it had never existed! We would have been settled by now, living like human beings on the rich fertile Chukurova plain. We would have had our own land and homes. Certainly, many would have perished, but the remainder would have grown used to the heat. Not all the nomads who were settled died . . .'

Though no one dared say this to Old Haydar's face, he knew well what they were thinking and saying, so he would throw out off-handedly: 'Let it be our turn to take a sword to the Ottoman, and this time we'll ask for land, so that'll make up for our fathers' error.'

The story of the sword and Major Ali Bey got around and the Turcomans loosened their purse-strings. Shiny bright gold pieces came to light and flowed into the palms of Ottoman officers in exchange for freedom from the prison of the Chuku-rova plain.

Beautiful nomad maidens were also offered to Ottoman

soldiers. One girl could open the road to the mountains for a whole tribe. Many are the ballads and laments of these Yörük maidens married off against their will to Ottoman soldiers. They are still sung among the nomads, along with the bitter epic of their defeat. But for the gold and the girls there would have been not a single nomad left to wander the mountains and pitch his tent nowadays.

The Turcomans still think back on the time before the settlement as the age of gold.

3

*That spring and summer a thousand troubles assailed the
Karachullu tribe on Aladag Mountain. The forest guards
gave them no quarter. They had but to see a stray goat and
they would raise hell. A broken bough off a tree and the
police would be upon them like black thunder. The many
bribes, the lamb-feasts offered to the guards were of no avail.
This could not go on. The headman of the tribe, Süleyman,
sent telegrams to Ankara. 'Kill us straight off or give us a
plot of land to settle on . . .' Sheep-rot set in, decimating the
flocks. Because of the runaway Mustan the police raided
their tents five times and all the men were made to run the
gauntlet, even Old Müslüm. A young boy was found shot as
he was pasturing the lambs up on Ortabel ridge. It never came
out who shot him and he died coughing up lumps of blood.*

Old Haydar was worked up. 'It won't do not to finish this
sword before the winter,' he muttered. 'Our Yörüks will have
nowhere to go. They'll either have to freeze up here under the
snow or be hounded all over the Chukurova plain.' So he set
off for Adana town, driving five well-fed sheep before him.
Having obtained a good price for them, he thrust the money
into his waistband and made for Altinbüken's jewelry shop.
There he asked for a gold leaf, and after driving a hard bargain,
he bought the leaf and went back to Aladag, where he lost no
time in summoning the youths of the tribe.

'Come lads,' he said. 'Come help me put up the forge.' And
a few days later the forge was ready with its bellows at the foot
of the mauve crags. It had been tough work nailing the anvil to
the rocky ground.

Old Haydar clutched at his beard with both hands and looked
around to see if anything was missing. 'Well done,' he said at

last. 'Now get along and let me start working. Kerem, stay with me.'

Those who saw Old Haydar and Kerem some days after could hardly recognize them, especially Old Haydar whose face was black to the eyes, and whose hands and beard, equally black, were stuck with specks of gold. He was meticulously copying the verses of the Koran from the ancient sword on to the one he was making and then filling in the engraving with gold. However long he worked, however much he hurried, still he made slow progress. And before he knew it autumn had come, and the huge planetree down below with branches that stretched up into the heavens was yellow with glints of red among its leaves, a sure sign that it was time to trek down to the Chukurova again.

Old Haydar had been working non-stop from dawn to sunset, even sleeping in the forge. When he noticed the yellowing tree he gave a cry. 'Oh dear, oh dear, I'm late. I'll never finish it in time . . .' He tried to step up the work. 'Kerem,' he kept saying, 'Kerem go and take a look at that planetree. Is it shedding its leaves? Are they still reddish?'

Kerem would go and look. 'No, grandfather,' he would reply. 'The tree's just as yellow as ever. It has red leaves too, fluttering here and there, grandfather.'

One morning the elders of the tribe with Müslüm at their head appeared at the entrance to the forge.

'Haydar, Master,' Süleyman the Headman called out.

Old Haydar came hurrying up. 'What is it, Headman?' he asked.

'Autumn's come and drawing to a close too. Winter'll be upon us in no time. The lambs are beginning to sicken and to die. Your sword's not ready and never will be at this rate. And even if you do finish it, is it likely that anyone will even look at a sword these days, let alone give us land for it?'

'Not look at my sword?' Old Haydar was shaking with wrath. He rushed in and returned with the sword in his hand. It flashed brightly as he held it up. 'No one look at this sword, eh? This pure gem of a sword! Not look at it, hah! Why Süleyman, a blind man would feel its beauty. Madmen, idiots would see it. If it had been in my father's time that I'd made it, if I'd taken it to the Vali, the Grand Vizir, the Padishah himself, why they'd have given us the whole of the Chukurova in exchange. The sword my father made was not one hundredth bit as beautiful as this one. So stop there Süleyman, and don't talk through your head! I know where I'm going to take this sword. I know someone who'll appreciate it. Yes cousin, just you wait a little and let me finish. There's not much left. If this sword doesn't bring us a home in the Chukurova, then I . . . Then I . . .'

'Well, you can go on with it, Haydar, but the tribe will have to strike tents tomorrow.'

Old Haydar paled. 'Don't do that, Süleyman, I beg you. Let me be the dust under your feet, let me be your slave, but don't do it. Give me another three days. Perhaps I'll be able to finish it by then. There's so little left. Anyway, what's the good of going down to the Chukurova like this? Will we find a stitch of land to settle on, a hilltop, a knoll, a tussock that isn't already tilled and sown? Where will we go, Süleyman? Only another three days. Perhaps . . .'

Süleyman bowed his head. What Old Haydar was saying was only too true. Where were they to go? Last year already there had not been an acre of untilled land in the Chukurova. These iron machines ate up the earth, swallowed it in great lumps, and in one day a huge tract of land was ploughed and sown. 'Well all right then,' he said, 'we'll wait another three days. Though what good it will do . . . How this sword you've been sweating over for a thousand years will be of any use.'

Old Haydar's face brightened. 'Now go away, all of you. I've got to work.' He went inside at once. 'Kerem! Kerem, bring me the bowl with the gold!' they heard him calling as they left.

The Headman was smiling bitterly. 'Poor old chap,' he said. 'Thinks he'll get anything for that sword. That was a hundred years ago, but he still imagines he'll get land for it.'

Old Müslüm bristled. 'You're talking nonsense, Süleyman,' he said. 'It's you who don't know anything of the world.

44

Wasn't it a sword saved us in the past from settlement, death and tyranny? What are you talking about? People will be struck dumb when they see Haydar's sword, they'll be dazzled, amazed. No one's seen such a beautiful thing since the world began. Just let Ismet Pasha set eyes on that sword and he'll give all he has to possess it. He'll give us not only the Chukurova, but Amik plain too. Yes, just like that! You're wrong, Süleyman. Wait till that sword's finished and you'll see. Why that sword's an Egyptian sword, worthy of the Shah and the Padishah!'

The Headman and those with him smiled bitterly at the stubborn faith of these old men. Yet they found themselves sharing it too against their better judgement. 'Perhaps,' Rüstem was saying. 'Maybe . . .' He was a man about thirty who had been at the Dardanelles and Gallipoli for his military service and had been discharged with the rank of sergeant. 'Who knows? Perhaps Old Haydar knows something. There might still be someone in this age who would understand that sword's value.'

For the past thirty years they had grown familiar with this crazy business of the sword. They would laugh at the old blacksmith and pity him, but deep down inside and hidden even from themselves, a hope, though not as strong as his, yet near to it, had taken root. Thank heaven this sword was being finished at last. It would have been finished long ago if Old Haydar had only worked for two summers like he had worked this summer. It seemed to them the blacksmith was stretching hope too far.

They went to the meeting-pavilion and sat down.

Süleyman the Headman was a fleshy man of medium height with a grey beard and green eyes and a cheerful face. He wore shalvar-trousers of homespun wool tucked into knee-high embroidered stockings. 'In three days we'll be going. Now let's decide where to stay in the Chukurova.'

'Isn't Akmashat our winter home?' Rüstem asked. 'Hasn't it been so since time out of mind?'

'It is, it is,' the Headman replied. 'But the title-deeds to the land are now in the hands of Dervish Bey. He's not a bad chap, but his sons and brothers are terrible.'

'Terrible!' Müslüm echoed. 'Time's running out. You'd better look out for yourselves.'

The meeting-pavilion had been filling up. The nomads came in and sat down, each one according to his age.

'Call Haydar the blacksmith too,' the Headman ordered Mustafa who was sitting next to him. 'This is important.'

With Old Haydar's arrival almost all the elders of the tribe were gathered now in the meeting-pavilion. The old men were silent, spinning the black goathair and other multi-coloured wools on their spindles.

The Headman spoke again: 'We have to move in a few days. It's cold already and it'll be snowing soon. We can't stay up here any longer but there's not an inch of land for us to move down into except perhaps some village pastures, and those are not enough for the villagers themselves because even pasture-land is being cultivated now. There is still some empty land on the large estates, a few hilltops, some bogland and the rice-paddies. Where are we to go? And with the people there so hostile too . . . They can't bear the sight of a goathair tent any more.'

'Akmashat's our winter home,' repeated Rüstem. His yellow whiskers sagged mournfully. 'Since ever. We must go there and let Dervish Bey do his worst.'

'Rüstem's right,' Sakarjali Ali affirmed. 'Let's fight it out. Either we win our winter home back by force or we are wiped out, all of us. Let them kill us . . . It'd be better than living like we're living now.'

'Tyranny,' Müslüm broke in. 'Time's running out. I'm warning you.'

Tanish Agha began to speak. He was a tall man but bent like a bow. His long face was quite smooth save for a few strands of beard hanging from the tip of his chin. He wore an embroidered cloak that never left his back, winter or summer. 'The long and the short . . .' he said. 'The long and the short is that we've got to buy back Akmashat, the home of our fathers, with money. There's no other way out. They've set up a government, but it's their government. The soldiers, the police are theirs. They have

46

aeroplanes that fly in the skies, tractors that rend the earth, trucks, fire-eyed trains, palaces, cities where a man can lose his way, they have cannons and guns. They have everything. We'll never get the better of them. The only thing is to find enough money by hook or by crook and buy Akmashat, since Dervish Bey is willing to sell.'

'We tried that last year, and the year before,' Old Murat objected. 'We've tried buying land in the Chukurova many times, but our money was never enough. We couldn't have put up two tents on the land they offered us for it. Even if we sold all our women's gold trinkets, our camels and sheep, our tents, our cloaks, everything we own, it would still not bring in the price of land.'

'He's right,' Rüstem said.

'What about renting some land?' Sakarjali Ali suggested.

'As if they'd rent it to us . . .' Old Murat said.

'Then what shall we do?' Mustafa said.

'Time's running out,' Old Müslüm quavered again. 'Look to yourselves, my friends.'

On and on they argued with no result, and then night fell and they were tired. Food was brought in from the tents, but the morsels stuck in their throats and the food tasted like poison to them.

It was getting on for midnight when Bald Musa spoke. 'Hassan Agha's son was in love with Jeren and Hassan Agha owns a hundred thousand *dönüms*. His son said to me, "Give me Jeren and I will find a place for you on my father's estate so you can set up a village there. You'll pay my father back a little every year for twenty years." I came and told you, but you refused. As though your precious Jeren was the Virgin Mother, or the holy Fatima or Hatije . . . Why didn't we do it? We'd have been safe and in peace by now.'

Abdurrahman rose, a thick-necked man with a child's full-lipped mouth. He spoke in clear decided tones. 'My daughter'll marry whom she wants, whom she likes. Didn't I tell her before? Look, daughter, I said, why don't you marry this Oktay Bey and save us all from want and misery? Didn't she refuse in

47

front of you all? Didn't the whole tribe beg her to change her mind? What more can I do?'

'You can do a lot more,' Bald Musa retorted. 'After all she's only a girl-child. One doesn't ask girls whom they wish to marry.'

'What,' Abdurrahman cried, 'force the girl into marriage and settle on the land only to wake one morning and find she's run off to someone else? Or killed herself? Won't Oktay Bey kick us off his land that minute? We can't do such a thing.'

'No, we can't,' the Headman agreed. 'It's stepping on a rotten bough to marry a girl off against her will.'

The argument lasted till daybreak. Then they summoned Jeren's mother and Süleyman the Headman put the matter to her, stressing the danger they were in and how Jeren was now their only hope. 'Jeren wouldn't want to be the cause of our death,' he said. 'And Oktay's quite a handsome lad. He may look a bit like a woman with those soft hands of his, but you'd find that much fault even in the Padishah's son. Half the Chukurova belongs to him too . . . What do you say, sister?'

The Headman's voice was sad as a lament. Jeren's mother began to cry. 'I'll tell her,' she said bitterly. 'I'll tell Jeren she must kill herself to save us, she must give herself to that womanish fellow.'

The sun rose and still nothing was decided. Old Haydar remained there till morning, thoughtful, his hands twisted about his beard. He got up. 'Don't worry,' he said. 'The sword will be finished in three days and after that we'll have nothing to fear. Only that sword can save us.' He made his way to the forge and started up the fire.

Camels, horses, donkeys, sheep, goats wandered about outside. In front of some tents, perched on a tree, secured by a strap, were a few falcons and eagles with little bells tied to their legs. Huge sheepdogs, each one as large as a horse, prowled through the camp.

Old Haydar's purebred Arab horse neighed.

'Kerem,' the blacksmith said, 'did you water my horse?'

48

'I didn't,' Kerem said, rushing out. He loved the horse. When the Lord Hizir gave him his falcon he would go riding on it to hunt with the falcon on his arm. Many years ago Haydar the blacksmith had bought this horse from a Turcoman bey. It was a young colt then, but the blacksmith had given three camels, eleven rams and two sheepdogs for it. And the horse had been worth it. It flew like the wind.

Things had come to pass that Old Haydar could not understand and never would. The land of the Chukurova, its people had changed as though at the touch of a magician's wand. White had become black and black white, and all without warning. Nobody knew anybody else any more. Even the streams, the trees, the hills and woods were not the same. Instead of a vast lake, where before all had been bogland and marsh, a roaring forest would suddenly spring into being. And those giant insects harvesting, threshing the crops in the twinkling of an eye and throwing the sheaves all ready-made into the middle of the fields . . . Iron insects that fed on fire . . . God protect us. God be praised!

He drew the molten gold out into long thin threads. The glow of the furnace lit up his tawny beard and made it redder still. His thoughtful eyes, sunk in a dark hollow, flickered alert, then grew dazed.

He was thinking of the Turcoman bey, Ali the Kurd . . . Unspoilt, pure as the water of Kozpinar spring. If he had been alive now wouldn't he have given them some land, just enough to pitch their tents and keep alive? He visualized him, the slim willowy body, the large sad eyes of a gazelle, the long, sparse pointed beard, the silk shirt, the shalvar-trousers, the coat, the gold watch and chain that must have weighed nearly three pounds.

His eyes filled and he sighed. 'He would, he would,' he said. 'He owned so much on the nether bank of Jeyhan River, beyond Jeyhan Bekirli village . . . It takes a good man to measure other men. Aaah . . .' The more he thought, the more the injustice of it all sickened him.

Süleyman the Headman was thinking too. The son of Ali

Pasha, way over in Tarsus, had so much land that he did not even plough or sow it. Suppose they were to go to him and say, give us some of your land so we may cultivate it and earn a living and we'll pay you back year by year . . . Would he accept? Perhaps . . . 'Abdurrahman,' he said, 'do you remember Rahmi Bey, the son of Ali Pasha?'

'How could I forget him! We used to go hunting together.'

'D'you think he's alive?'

'A traveller from Tarsus last year told me he was alive and thriving. He's married and has six grown-up children. He owns five farms and two textile mills left over from the Armenians, with three thousand people working in them. But he lives in Ankara now. He's become a big man, a pasha.'

Years ago Rahmi Bey had left his home and town to join the Yörüks, with the firm intention of leading the nomad life. 'I'm going to make myself a tent,' he declared, 'with seven posts. I'll buy camels, horses, sheep and marry a pure virtuous nomad girl. I want nothing else.' For a whole year he stayed with the Headman Süleyman who spared no effort to make him feel at home. He taught him to ride and shoot and hunt and even toyed with the idea of marrying him to his sister Senem. And then one morning they woke up to find Rahmi Bey gone. He had got bored with the nomad way of life too and left just like that. Worried about him Süleyman sent men to enquire at the Pasha's mansion. Rahmi Bey was there, but when the men said they came from Süleyman he only stared as though trying to recapture some vague recollection. Then he turned away without a word and left them standing there.

'Suppose we were to go now, would he know us if we showed him this watch?' He drew out a gold watch that glittered on its gold chain. 'Would he give us a little patch of land? He was weary of his life once, and came to us. And now we too are weary of our life and would seek refuge with him.'

Abdurrahman's hands trembled with excitement. 'He would, he would!' he cried. 'Such a good man he was, and sensible too. He'd give us some land.'

'I had a friend during my military service,' Rüstem said.

'From Kargili village in the district of Yenidje. Crazy Ibrahim. Such a generous man the world has never seen. If he has the slightest bit of land to spare, he'll let us settle on it.'

'Yes,' Süleyman said. 'You've always spoken to us of him since you came back.'

'And I,' Old Müslüm said, 'I'm a man who's played the pipe before the great Ramazanoglu himself. Time's running out. I'm done for. Look, I'm even growing second teeth. Ramazanoglu listened and listened as I played and tears fell from his eyes. Wish me a wish Müslüm, he said. I thanked him and refused all his gifts. Nothing would I ever accept when I played my pipe. It's a thing you do for the love of God, for the pleasure of the heart. Like the thunder in the sky he was, the great Ramazanoglu . . . When we go down to the Chukurova, I'll go straight to Adana town and find him. Give us back our winter home, I'll say. Let me see him refuse!'

Everyone was racking his brains to find some way to avoid being chased about ignominiously from place to place as they had been the year before in the Chukurova plain.

4

*How to live this winter in the Chukurova and not be hounded
about like dogs? What can they do? They rack their brains
and still Maid Jeren seems to them the best answer. It has
been done so often in the past. A nomad gives his beautiful
daughter to a landowner and his whole tribe is allowed to
settle on the land. If Maid Jeren will only consent they will
find a home at last. From seven to seventy they all beg her to
do it. But it is Bald Musa who in the end hits on the most
effective way to force her hand.*

A fine sand . . . Not the bed of a torrent but of a little brook . . .
The brook has gone, vanished, not even deflected elsewhere,
but stanched, sunk underground, even its source quite drained,
its moss-grown pebbles dry and filmed over with a thin silvery
crust of mud. The wellspring is smothered with dead leaves.
They lie over the pebbles, shrivelled, red, purple-streaked, or
stuck flat on to the sand, like the imprints of large red hands,
purple-veined. And here, right beside this planetree leaf is
another track, like a bear's paw, maybe larger. A little further
the tracks become even larger, and then they break out into
three, side by side, leading to a shrub of flowering heather, one
of its slim stems broken. The shrub is parted in two as though
some weighty object had crashed into it.

From the flatland a rill oozes over the yellow earth and all
about it are thousands of large and small prints. Here the large
tracks are arrested in an agitated turmoil, as if the thing had
gone round and round blindly, a whole day, a whole night. Here
the soil is glinting gold, clean and bright, washed by the water,
and as the moonbeams strike it, shimmering gold, sparkling.
The huge frame has lain itself down here and wallowed on its
back, the big long furry body burrowing its mould into the

golden fine-filtered earth, every particle of which seems to have been scoured clean. Beside the mould is the print of a single rawhide-sandalled foot, just one. There is no trace of the other foot. A one-legged man. His other leg snapped off . . . by a beast no one knows nor has ever seen. His sandal pinching, hurting his single foot, he goes seeking for his lost leg, blood-dripping in the jaws of the beast.

And all of it sprung out of some old very ancient nomad tale. The black tents, very black, of goathair, spun in long strips spread close to the ground, the very blackest goathair. Long black tents, the best ones with seven domes. A green-tinged black. Slow-moving, nomadic, going from one never-to-be-known, never-to-be-discovered place to another, stranger still, like sleepwalkers. The lambs and camels, the grasses, the huge sheepdogs, deep-mouthed, commanding obeyance, well-trained, sensing in their bones how to pitch their bark, weighing the effect and aiming their muzzles unerringly. The long slim-waisted well-sprung greyhounds, dark, pink, purplish, their feet white-socked, their foreheads and backs spotted.

A very ancient crossbow – maybe a thousand years old, its engraved stock worm-eaten, the worm holes weaving another superimposed pattern – is hung to the tent's carved pole with its silver-nielloed roundel, no bigger than the palm of a hand. Beside it a *saz* with only two chords left, but not mute. Then a flute, then a drum, its skin shrivelled, crackling, flaking off at a touch. And then the white silk standard. Of pure silk. Two span wide, seventeen span long. It bears the imprint of a red hand. Or maybe it was not a hand steeped in red or purple dye that was pressed upon it . . . Maybe it was some other thing. The silk is half yellowed. Like a talisman it is, this standard, to which the tribesmen turn when in trouble. It has its legend too, never voiced these hundred years or so, for shame. Only one line is left of those days, of that glorious epic: the great Ottomans were nephews of ours.

The Ottomans should never have done this to us. From Khorassan we came, long lances on our shoulders. Long spears. Over the long long roads, pitching our long black tents. Long black eagles overhead. The Syrian desert, the plain of Harran, its ancient ruins, the slant-eyed somnolent people of stone . . . The long-drawn-out songs, passionate, angry, plaintive, bitter. The fugitives, the blood . . . And the traces. No, the Ottomans should never have done this to us, who overflowed the boundaries of Khorassan, to us who stood guard at the gates of seventy-two cities . . . The tall long-necked men with brindled oval eyes, cloaked in silver-threaded coltskins, long conical felt coifs on their heads. The long spears, the long long roads . . . The long-drawn voice of the flute. The darkness of the night . . . The fertile plain of Harran. The Lord Abraham. The mosque named after him, with the sweating stamping black horses tied to its gate. A black tent held up by seventy-two poles. Seventy-two! A seventy-two-domed tent. As vast as the covered bazaar at Marash. All gay in green and red, its one wing spanning the world. The noble nomad beys of the Aydinli tribe, of the House of Ahmet the Haji, with their fierce hawks on their arms . . . And now only Hüseyin . . . The tribes, big and small, the flocks of sheep, the trains of camels, all a riot of red and green. The carved oak chests with little mirrors. The copper coffee-pots with folding handles, engraved, red, glowing bright. The golden cups . . .

From Khorassan we came, and all in our train Persian Palaces, the drama of the Turcoman Shah Ismail, battles, broken spearheads, Dadaloglu, poet of the revolt against the Ottomans, captivity, exile, the Chukurova, the fear . . . The long long fear. The thraldom of the Chukurova . . . A cruel arrow has struck me, has broken my back. Look at me, what is left of me! A tiny white puff, only Old Müslüm! From Khorassan we came. Spanning whole countries from Khorassan to the land of Canaan, to the plain of Harran, seat of the Lord Abraham. Long long flocks of sheep, long trains of camels, herds and herds of Arab horses. A part of us still in Khorassan, a part of us wasting in the heat of the Chukurova, captive to the yellow death and the fever. A part of us still in Khorassan, in the Turkmenistan. A part of us . . . With broken swords . . . Our craftsmen dead. Sparks are flying. And one man only, his

54

long red coppery beard, his long long sword, Haydar, the master-craftsman. His long shrivelled neck. Whirling in a *semah* dance, on his toes since last night, whirling still, never slackening, whirling in the bursts of coruscating sparks shooting from the forge, worshipping . . . From Khorassan we came, bearing our long lances. Ya Allah, ya Muhammed, ya Ali! Ya Ali, O Ali . . . Our long spears. Our long swords, each one a crucible of blood, objects of worship, life-giving, death-striking. The eighty thousand sufis of Anatolia, the ninety thousand pirs of Khorassan. The holy *tekke*[1] of Ahmedi Yesevi,[2] that bright-faced ancient, long-bearded, tiny, sitting on his golden fleece. Ya Allah, ya Muhammed, ya Ali . . . A lofty tree uprooted whose branches used to spread the whole world over.

Beware the treacherous man! Oh to lie in the shade of the rocks were it not for the big serpent, oh to kiss a pretty maid were she not fickle . . . Bald Musa did not come from Khorassan. Short, squat, runty, a mangy goat that had strayed into the flock from no one knew where.

The trail of the single foot led past the white planetree, past the Seven Brothers and stopped at the Three Sleepers. There was nothing at all after the Sleepers Rock.

'Hey there, shepherd! Have you seen Halil? Or Mustan?'

A fire is smoking in the distance, long, tapering into the sky. 'Uh-uh.'

No other word. 'Don't you know me, shepherd? I'm Musa. Bald Musa . . .'

'Uh-uh.'

'God damn you . . . Mustan! Mustaaan! Can you hear me? I'm Musa, Bald Musa . . .' The valley echoed 'Bald Musa', wave after wave.

A faint moaning rose from the foot of the long sharp speckled blue rock. A shot was fired. Musa rushed over. Mustan was lying there on the pine needles. One of his legs was bloated the

---

[1] tekke: a dervish lodge.
[2] Ahmedi Yesevi: twelfth-Century central Asian Turkish poet and sheikh, founder of the oldest Turkish mystical order, the Yeseviya.

size of a man's body, crawling with worms, stinking. He himself was nothing but skin and bones.

'I'm dying Musa. I can't move. How did you find me? Did that shepherd tell you? But no, it can't be.'

'Nobody told me,' Bald Musa said. He was thinking. The fellow's done for, dying. 'I found you by myself.' If I can save him, he'll do what I want. Halil trusts him. And then one night, when he's asleep . . .

'Ah, that shepherd . . . He comes every day, stands there before me. I'm going to kill you, he says, just you wait . . . He plays with me, makes me beg to him. Then he gives me half a bowl of milk. You're my prisoner, he says, I can do what I like to you.'

With his upturned nose, his stubbly yellow hair, his peeling nose and face, his large grey-streaked eyes, bloodshot, stubborn, evil, he comes to Mustan every day, a half-filled bowl of milk in his hand. Beg, Mustan, he says. Say I kiss the soles of your feet, shepherd boy . . . What can Mustan do, he says just that. And then the shepherd asks, Who is king of these mountains? Shepherd Resul. Who is the bravest of men? Shepherd Resul. Shepherd Resul, the giver and taker of life. All this Mustan repeats quickly in one breath, and then he holds out his hand and begs: 'Give me the milk.' The shepherd places the bowl on his head and slowly, very slowly, taking half an hour to cross the space of ten steps while Mustan is watching, his eyes starting out of his head, his heart in his mouth for fear he will trip and fall, he draws near and holds out the milk which Mustan swallows at one draw. 'Today I'm sparing you because you've spoken well,' the shepherd says. 'I'll kill you tomorrow.' And off he goes. An orphan, brought up by strangers, victimized, never slept on anything but the hard earth or a bed of grass, everything he ever wore spun and woven by himself, never saw a friendly hand, never heard a pleasant word . . . And suddenly here is Mustan, all at his mercy.

'Make me well, Musa brother, and I'll do anything for you.'

One by one Musa explained to him the difficulties besetting the tribe.

56

But Mustan knew it all too well. 'What d'you want of me?'

'If I make you well, will you kill Halil?'

'I'll kill him.'

'Jeren will be yours then. First we'll give her to the son of that Chukurova agha and after a few months all you'll have to do is to run away with her.'

'All right, but first you've got to take care of my wound.'

'Get on to my back. My! How that wound of yours stinks!'

'That shepherd mustn't know where I am. He'll go and give me away to the police straight away. If he hasn't up to now it was only so as to torture me. That's why he gave me a little milk, just to keep me alive.'

Only let me get well, Mustan was thinking, and I'll kill this mangy, dirty son-of-a-bitch. Not Halil. Never! All these many years, nobody can tell how many, that tent has been raised of which Halil is the last Bey. Nobody dares enter it. Inside is the standard that came from Khorassan, and the horsetail too, and the big drum, the ancient coins, the halberd, the two crowns of iron . . . No one would dare touch a hair of Halil's head. I can't do what you ask, Bald Musa, my lad. Just because I bore Halil a little grudge look what happened to me! Yes indeed, Baldish Musa . . . Baldy baldilicks . . .

He was burning with fever.

Bald Musa was gloating at his good fortune. A harvest moon shone in the sky as he lifted Mustan on to his back. The flies infesting the noisome leg came after them, thick and fast. The wound was itching unbearably, driving Mustan mad.

As day broke they came to the cave at Göktash, and Musa laid out a bed of wormwood for him. 'You stay right here,' he said. 'I'll go back to the camp and get some ointment for you. And food too.'

In the evening he was back. Cleaning the wound carefully of the worms and pus and putrefied flesh, he applied the salve and made a bandage. He had also brought bullets for Mustan's gun. 'This is for Halil,' he muttered as he loaded the gun. 'Right into his heart . . . This one too, for Halil, for the middle of his forehead. This one too, Halil's, his right eye . . . This

57

one . . . Into his mouth.'

No one suspected that Musa, this bald puny little man bore Halil such bitter enmity. Halil had always been kind to Musa, as he was to everyone. Why then this deadly hatred? Mustan simply could not understand it.

It was in one of the many fights arising from the problem of wintering in the Chukurova that Halil had got into trouble, and for five years now he had been a fugitive in the mountains. Yet he had never touched a hair of another man's head. No one knew where he hid, what he did. Very rarely, when the tribe moved to Aladag, he would turn up for a short while to visit the empty tent of his ancestors and pray before the white silk standard. And that was all.

Everything had begun when the villagers attacked them one day in the Chukurova. A few policemen were lending a hand too as they pulled down the tents and even set fire to some of them, laughing uproariously all the while. When they came to the torn worn-down ancestral tent, Halil, Old Müslüm, Haydar the blacksmith, Headman Süleyman, and even Mother Döneh and Jeren stood before them, barring the way.

'Over my dead body,' Halil said.

The Agha's son spurred his fiery horse straight at them and on to the tent. It collapsed and he rode on. Halil just stood there, frozen, drained of colour.

That night Arif Agha's village was burned to the ground. 'I did it,' Halil said. 'No one else . . .' But the whole tribe was bundled off to the town and herded into the mosque, and for a week every single one of them, young and old, was flogged mercilessly. Old Sultan, Halil's grandmother, had her backbone broken, and she died, after uttering shrill bird-like cries for a whole night and a whole day. Halil was beaten to pulp. Black and blue all over, his mouth, nose and ears swollen, a monstrous bloat of a man, they had to put him in hospital. It was six months before he recovered. And then he escaped. Maid Suna was raped. She went up to the top of the minaret and cast herself down, and for two days her body lay sprawled and broken there, in the middle of the market-place.

58

From Khorassan we came, long lances on our shoulders, long Egyptian swords in our hands, steel-crested spears . . . Proud, honoured, unconfined, nomadic, surging on like a flood that knows no dam, scaling unsurmountable peaks, crossing impassable lands, routing armies, storming castles. In gold mortars was our coffee ground . . . Knee-deep were the carpets we spread for our guests to step on.

From Khorassan we came . . .

One day on the road nearabouts the Gülek Pass, on an upland plain where a boundless forest of rocks reaches up to the sky, vast as the sky itself, long, far-ranging, sharp, flinty blue rocks, a deep blue with tiny golden sparks . . . And red too, with scarlet pimpernels rooted in flaming clusters redder than the red rock . . . And yellow too, gold-spangled. And green. And mauve, a vivid knife-edged mauve, sheeny bright . . . Where the waterfall sounds among the mauve crags, on the green, well-watered highland plain . . . One day as the tribe was preparing to pitch their tents, Bald Musa brought a blood-stained shirt to Halil's mother. With him were Rüstem and Süleyman the Headman. They did not speak. Without a word they handed her the bloody shirt and turned away, slowly, their heads bent. She understood at once and uttered a piercing cry. The news spread in an instant. The women gathered around the bloody shirt and keened dirges all through the night. The passionate accents of Jeren's keening laid her heart open for all to see. Nobody had suspected the intensity of her great love for Halil. Now they feared she might take her life, and where would they be then.

She did not kill herself, but she turned her back on people, on the world. Like a sleepwalker she was, mute, half-dead, soulless . . .

Duran Ali had given his daughter Esheh to the agha of a village down in the plain, near Léché. She was a real beauty. Three years later they hauled her corpse out of a well. She had thrown herself in quite naked. Her breasts were small and pointed like a very young girl's. The Chukurova women marvelled at this, and even more at the snow-white pureness of her body. There

59

was nobody to weep at her death, to sing dirges for her. She was buried without ceremony in a far corner of the graveyard, all alone, beside a ditch. And there she lies, away from her people, in the scorching heat of the Chukurova.

Zeliha, the daughter of Ibrahim, lost her heart to a plainsman called Mazlum from Chukurköprü and ran away to live with him. Two years later she had fled, a crazed creature, who can still be seen wandering through the Chukurova from village to village, crying for her mountains, 'Aladag, Aladag, Aladag . . .'

Haji Salman had no qualms when he gave his lovely daughter Yeshil to Salih Bey, the miller down in the town. He took his tent too and pitched it near the mill. Less than a year afterwards Yeshil was dead of the wasting sickness. Many are the nomad girls that have gone as brides into Chukurova homes, many are the dead with bridal wreaths and veils still fresh.

But there is also the Haji Kerimli tribe who married off one of their daughters to a rich landowner from Imran. They became kin to the plainsmen and had a place to winter in. Then slowly they stayed on longer, first until the middle of May, then until the end of May, till July, till August, getting used by degrees to the heat of the Chukurova, to its mosquitoes, its poisonous air, to the dust and the smell of gasoline and petroleum. And so they settled at last. Now they own tractors, harvesters, trucks, motor-cars. Their tents are mouldering, cast away in a corner of their red-roofed houses. All this through one single girl! And not half as beautiful as Jeren.

As for the Tanishmans, the son-in-law they hit upon in the Chukurova turned out to be a powerful man, and used his influence to settle the whole tribe on the Agba plain. There they were happy. Every household owned one of those earth-devouring, fire-spitting iron machines, and their tents were not left to rot away either. Each summer they moved up to the Gülek highlands and pitched them above Tekir.

Over Jeren's head the eagles of death are hovering. Now that Halil is dead, what is there left for her in this world?

'For God's sake, keep an eye on Jeren . . . For pity's sake . . .

She's our only hope now. It's Jeren or nothing. Thank God for her.'

From Khorassan we came. Oh, the sages of Khorassan . . . The halberds, the brave songs, the herds and herds of horses, the golden saddles, the Egyptian swords. From Khorassan we came. Oh, the silver-embroidered cloaks of tiger-skins, of colthides . . . From Khorassan we came . . .

5

*Deliboga, the Mad Bull Knoll, is bounded by marshes on
every side. And beyond the marshes are dense scrubs of
blackthorn. The land hereabouts belongs to no one, neither
the knoll, nor the marshes, nor the blackthorn scrub, and the
limits of the nearest village are a long way off. Nomads have
never had graveyards, they must bury their dead anywhere as
they move from place to place, but Deliboga Knoll is dotted
all over with graves for it has been a wintering place for the
nomads since time out of mind. This is where the Karachullu
tribe finally decided to settle for the winter until they could
find something better. But what befell them here was worse
than they could ever have imagined.*

They pitched their tents on the sunwise slope of the knoll.
Beyond the blackthorn scrub a dry gully extended right up to
Jeyhan River. It was bordered on each side by barren thistle-
ridden land or uncultivated fields, dry and fissured after some
recent floodings. This they planned to make do for pasture. It
was better than nothing. And if hard-pressed they could always
drive their sheep and goats on to the nearby hills of Hemité,
Bozkuyu, Jiyjik and Köyyeri, so arid that nobody ever went
there. All the same, Süleyman the Headman was afraid. What if
the Chukurova people should pick on them even here? They
knew the nomads were reduced to straits and would be sure to
put the screws on. If we can just get through this winter, he
thought, we'll find something next time with God's help . . .

The peak of the Gavur Mountains began to glow. In a far-off
field the stubble had been set afire during the night. Smoke
was rising with intermittent bursts of flame.

The cries of lambs and kids and young camels sounded
across the plain. Fresh young girls in red aprons and red

scarves tied over their golden hair had started milking and a wholesome steaming odour of milk and of sheep spread through that morning of early autumn. So pleasant, so heart-warming . . . All in the gentle dawn breeze that wafts you into some paradise, that brushes your face so softly your whole body is soaring, flying, that fills you with joyousness, whatever your sorrows, whatever your troubles. And in the prime of autumn too, and in the Chukurova, with Jeyhan River lolling lazily on the plain, relaxed in the first rays of the sun, and the fresh milk, and the scorched whiffs of sundried, sunburnt flowers and grass mingled with chaff and dust. Dead flowers, dry stalks in the dust at dawn, and the autumn leaves over the dew-wet earth. The thin layer of dust on the autumn leaves, on the autumn grass, on the yellow mullein, on the camelthistles turning to mud in the dew. The long deep bark of the big sheepdogs, resonant in the morning stillness . . . On the Chukurova plain . . . The sound of churns, the smell of butter, of sour yoghurt, of milk, all blending with the odour of the scorched Chukurova earth. And the long-necked mournful Arab horses, sad-eyed, old now most of them.

The fear is there in Headman Süleyman's heart and gives him no rest, a creeping fear like a repugnance, a nausea, a dread of some unknown, some trouble, some evil that may break upon them any minute.

A thousand and one scents wafting in warm waves as the morning haze thickens, cloud-like . . . The tall handsome sun-burnt copper-skinned men, sorrowful . . . The women all in bright blue, and here and there a flash of red or green or yellow. Golden glints in their mauve embroidered fezzes. Gold and coral noserings. Anklets of gold and precious stones, black, green, yellow. In the vaporous dawnlight, afloat in the haze with the grass, the trees, the earth, the dustwhirls, alike to large graceful dewy dusty flowers . . . The firm imprints on the earth of long tapering feet. And the shepherds playing age-old tunes dating back to ˙Canaan, to the Prophet Abraham who bred noble horses at Urfa and had many many sons. A voice im-memorial from Khorassan and the steppes of Central Asia, centuries old, singing the fortunes and the thousand-and-one adventures of a people, telling of a generous tradition that knows no evil, chivalrous, humble, sorrow-laden, a tradition of love and friendship. The voice of a happy life that has conquered all the cares of this world. The voice of mankind in harmony with itself, with the waters, the mountains and the sounds, with grief and joy and the stars above, that has felt nature to the marrow, warmed to her, loved her, known her for a friend, a part of its own tradition . . . Songs that are the finest testimonial of man's fellowship to man.

An old black Arab horse was tethered before Haydar the blacksmith's tent. It stood there motionless, its right hindleg drawn up to its belly. Inside, perched on a stake fixed at the head of Kerem's pallet was a peregrine falcon, an eyas, its eyes spinning in their sockets. Kerem would wake up half a dozen times in the night to look at it and speak a few words to it before falling asleep again. The bird was already familiar with him. It was Mad Aptullah who had caught it. Mad Aptullah spent his days and nights scrambling up the high crags to observe eagles, falcons, hawks and kites. Yet he never harmed the birds nor did he touch the nestlings and the eggs. He knew about Kerem's passionate longing. Haydar the blacksmith, whom he loved more than anyone else in the world, was his uncle. All the tribespeople were in one way or another related to each other. For no one else but Old Haydar's grandson would Mad Aptullah have taken an eyas away from its mother. There are two birds that nest in the steepest, sheerest, most inaccessible crags, one is the eagle and the other the peregrine falcon.

Headman Süleyman wandered on from tent to tent. The whole tribe was up and about, everything was as usual. But still he could not overcome his uneasiness. Could it be that they would be left in peace on this piece of land they had found for themselves?

The sun was up the flight of a bird and still no one had appeared. He looked at the road going from the foot of Hemité Mountain to Anavarza hill, and then towards Hürüushak. There was nothing at all, not a car or a tractor, not even a horse.

Suddenly, down Karabajak way he saw a jeep moving through the fields. His heart sank. The jeep was coming straight towards Deliboga Knoll. He summoned Müslüm, Rüstem, Old Haydar, Zekeriya and a few others and they all went down to the foot of the knoll to meet the jeep. It stopped right in front of them and out of it stepped a wiredrawn, long-necked man in a white suit with a red kerchief stuck into his collar. Two button-like eyes without any whites at all in a tiny thin face stared at them from under a large straw hat.

'I am Dervish Hassan,' the man said with a swagger, 'the eldest son of Harun Bey who is the Bey of the Beshoguzlu tribe and owns all the land around here. Where is the Headman, Süleyman?'

The Headman stepped forward, bracing himself. 'What can I do for you?' he said humbly.

The other stretched out his hand. 'Good morning to you,' he said and turned to the two men who had just emerged from the jeep after him. Both had large pistols dangling at their waists. Both were thin with wrinkled sunburnt faces. 'This is Flower Durmush, you know, who was just as famous a bandit as Brokenfoot in his time. He works for us now, our armed bodyguard he is. Because, sir, we took him from his mountain lair and made it worth his while. And his honour safe, he accepted to be our gunman, our knight. And this, sir, is Mad Muzaffer, who can shoot the flying bird in the eye and the fleeting hare in the hindleg. Yes, that's how I have come to you, in state, with the two best of my fifteen braves. All because my father, the late Zal Tahir Agha, who was as you know, Headman Süleyman, a friend of your father's, always said to me, Son, he said, this is my last will and testament to you, be kind to the Karachullu tribe. And so I kept his will and never touched a hair of your heads, not up to now, did I?'

Nothing could be clearer. Headman Süleyman's lips quivered with anger. 'Come up to the tent, Dervish Hassan Bey,' he said. The smile, the goodwill and kindness of his face that made Süleyman such a pleasant person, were frozen now.

In the tent Dervish Hassan stared hard at the hangings on

the walls, at the delicate woodwork of the central pole, at the embroidered orange felt rugs on the ground. They must be very rich, he thought.

Coffee was served. It smelled good and its aroma hung in the air for a long while. After he had drunk his coffee, Dervish Hassan's countenance went black, the lines of his tiny face hardened.

'You, Süleyman Bey, without even consulting me, you've come and installed yourself on my land. That's a wicked thing to do. I resent it. It riles me. After all if you descend from the noble Nine Oguz race, we come from the Eleven Oguz . . . We live only for our religion and our traditions . . . The Democrat Party, our very own party! has fashioned a state out of a tribe, out of the Nine Oguz and the Eleven and the Seventeen . . .' He was speaking as though at an electoral meeting and Süleyman and the others stared dumbfounded at this strange gesticulating creature. 'We . . . We three, Celal Bey, Adnan Bey[1] and I, we have fashioned a state out of a mere wandering tribe. Therefore and consequently, and since with Allah's blessing I am one of the great men of this great state, what you've done has hurt me to the core . . .' He raised his voice. 'Yes indeed, but I, and Celal Bey and Adnan Bey too, in spite of your intrusion, your shameful behaviour, I will pardon you, yes, pardon you!' The cords of his neck swelled out the size of a rolling-pin. 'But on one condition.' He dropped to normal. 'How long are you going to stay here? Till the spring, eh? Till May at least.' He ticked off on his fingers. 'Eight months . . . Well, for this, for each month you stay here you will pay me a thousand liras. That adds up to eight thousand and not a penny less will I take.' Suddenly he was shouting again. 'And if you don't hand it over now, on the nail, then you can pack up right away and get off my land. Right away, sir! It's only because of my father's honoured will and testament that I'm being kind to you, a real friend.'

The whole tribe from seven to seventy had gathered behind

---

[1] Celal Bayar: former President of Turkey. Adnan Menderes: former Prime Minister of Turkey.

the big tent, listening aghast to this terrible voice.

'From anyone else, Süleyman Bey, I'd have requested a clean hundred thousand, and with Allah's blessing. Because, I'll have you know that ever since the time of my great ancestor, the Lord Sultan Halid, son of Talat, son of the Shah, all my ancestors have built their palaces on this very land.' He stamped his foot. 'Dig here, dig anywhere just a little bit and the bones of my brave deceased will come to light, their relics . . . Here, right here lie the foundations of the palace of my forefather the Shah, sprung of Talat, son of Yektaza, son of Halid, son of Zülal . . . Never on this hallowed land, we . . . we . . . Never shall we allow a single tent to be set up. And if it is, if people make unclean with their horses and their dogs this sacred land, holy for the past thousand years, then . . . Theeen we . . . weee . . . meet sons of our forefathers, we shall shed blood. Bloood!'

His henchmen's hands went swiftly to their pistols, and this did not escape the nomads' eyes.

'Dervish Hassan Efendi,' the Headman said, his voice quite calm, as though nothing untoward were happening, 'let's talk it over among ourselves. We'll come back in a little while.'

The nomads went out and the three men were left in the tent waiting anxiously.

'Just let them refuse,' Dervish Hassan said. 'Let them and they'll see . . . This place is like tinder. The scrub, the dry grass, the whole mound is just asking for a fire. Only set a match to it tonight and the job's done. They'll be burnt to cinders with their tents and sheep and all . . . Like tinder this place is,' he repeated to put heart into the others.

'Let them just try to give us less than eight thousand,' Muzaffer said. 'Let them . . . They'll find the whole world on fire about them and not a hole to slip through . . . Just let them.'

'Just let them,' Flower Durmush echoed. He stopped, then went on, not to be outdone by his companion. 'Let them . . . I'll set fire here, I'll set fire there . . . I'll have them in a circle of flames. Trapped in the fire! And then . . . Then I'll tell you

67

what I'll do, I'll shoot those who try to escape, every man of them.'

Kerem came running to the Headman, his falcon still on his arm. 'I heard them talking,' he blurted out, trembling. 'They're going to burn us, all of us, if we don't give them the money. Burn us alive . . .'

'We'll be careful, my Kerem,' Süleyman said. 'You go back now and listen some more. And come and tell me everything afterwards.'

'I will,' Kerem panted, rushing off.

'I know this man,' Süleyman said. 'He's been living off the nomads for the past fifteen years, extorting money from the tribes from Adana to Tarsus, from Amik plain to Islahiye and Marash. According to him all the land this side of the Mediterranean is his. We'll give him a thousand liras. Two thousand if he insists. And if he doesn't accept that, he can go to hell.'

'But you mustn't!' Haydar the blacksmith protested. 'Throwing away all that money when I've nearly finished my sword . . . It's a shame. I'll have that sword ready tomorrow or the day after, or . . . And I'll take it to Ismet Pasha . . . And he'll give us land.'

But the Headman was already leading the way back to the big tent. Dervish Hassan was waiting in suspense, sweating, his eyes starting from their sockets. 'We're going to give you a thousand liras,' Süleyman the Headman told him. The other leapt to his feet as though actioned by a spring and began to shout. The police, he threatened, the Government . . . I'll bring fire upon your heads, he said. This holy land, the palaces, my ancestors' bones, my father's testament . . . He ranted on, but Süleyman simply said, as though he had heard nothing: 'Won't a thousand do? Well, you know best. There's nothing more to be said.'

Dervish Hassan tried again. He roared and blustered, but Süleyman held good. One thousand liras, he repeated.

Suddenly Dervish Hassan crumpled up. 'Everyone's against me,' he whined. 'And I have nothing left but this place here.

If I can't get rent out of it, I'll die. I'll die for sure.' He pleaded and threatened all in the same breath. 'I'll die. I'm dead already. And what has a dead dog to fear? Nothing! Nothing, you hear? So I warn you, I have nothing to fear.'

Repulsion, nausea settled on Süleyman's face like the dirt of a great black fly. 'That's enough Dervish Hassan,' he said. 'Here, take these two thousand liras and go away.' He turned quickly and left the tent, retching as though he were going to vomit.

A fortnight later, when Dervish Hassan entered the town club, all the gamblers gathered around him rubbing their hands. Eagerly they enquired about this year's hunt. Rumour had it that his spoils amounted to a hundred or two hundred thousand liras. A million even, some said.

Dervish Hassan sighed. 'They're getting poorer every year these nomads,' he said. 'Twice they tried to kill me, just for a matter of a paltry sum. When, as everyone knows, the whole Chukurova all along the Mediterranean is the land of my noble ancestors. But that made no difference to them. I had a narrow escape, I can tell you. Savages they are. But I'll show them. One of the tribes has its account settled already, such a trick I've played on them they'll never recover till doomsday. But they asked for it. What we want from them is only our due after all, the rent of our own land . . . Come on, let's get down to our poker game.'

'How much did you get?'

'I can't tell.'

'How much?'

'A hundred and twenty thousand. I told you, they're getting poor. Next year, God knows, I won't even get fifty thousand out of them. And the year after . . . You'll draw a real blank, Dervish Hassan, that's all. Now come, let's get to work.'

His hands were shuffling the cards rapidly, machine-like.

69

6

In the summer of 1876 the commander of the Firkai Islahiye,[1] Jevdet Pasha, entrusted Major Mustafa Ali Bey with the task of guarding the roads leading into the Taurus Mountains from the Chukurova plain. Not a soul was to be allowed to pass either from the plain into the mountains or from the mountains down into the plain. And so the huge plain became a death-trap for the Turcoman nomads.

Ali Bey first accepted the gift of the sword. Then he began to feel quite sorry for the Turcomans. 'Dying like flies, the poor beggars,' he said, and allowed some of them to migrate up into the high pastures.

At this time Ali Bey was busy setting up the new villages and towns. Measuring, calculating, he decided where the town's square would be and aptly delineated its streets and avenues. For his sites he selected the traditional market-places of the wintering Turcomans or the ruins of ancient Greek, Roman or Armenian cities. His new villages were also happily located on the well-tried wintering quarters of the nomads.

But malaria was rampant. Mosquitoes gave the people no quarter. That summer unheard-of epidemics ravaged the countryside. The Chukurova was strewn with skeletons of men and animals and all through the summer the stench of carrion infested the plain. Ali Bey was a humane man. This was too much for him. He knew also that it would not be possible to enforce the settlement. The Ottoman government could not

---

[1] Firkai Islahiye: the Reform Division, a military force sent by the Sultan to southern Turkey in the nineteenth century to subjugate independent feudal lords and tribal chiefs, destroy the power of the bands of brigands and Turcoman nomads and thus prepare the way for agricultural settlement.

keep up a huge division in the Chukurova for ever. In a couple of years the police posts would have to be reduced, or else their vigilance would relax. He was a clever man, Ali Bey, a man of experience. Tall, blond, with blue eyes, he looked not a day older than thirty. He was ambitious. Born into an indigent family in a poor quarter of Istanbul, his one goal was to make money and rise in the world. Already the nomads had found ways to break the encirclement by his soldiers and to escape into the mountains, and with the increase of fever, epidemics and deaths, the trickle of fugitives was turning into a flow.

One morning he made up his mind. The Turcomans would be allowed to move into the mountains, but under his own supervision. He had done what he could to tie them to the Chukurova. In the villages he had given them land and space for commons and mills, and in the towns houses and building lots. The rest he would leave to time and to gradually changing circumstances.

He summoned the Bey of the Bozdogan tribe, one of the largest tribes that always wintered where Enderin Köyyeri is now situated. The Bey made his appearance, shivering with the fever.

'I shall allow you to migrate into the mountains, Bey,' the major said. 'And will provide you with a firman to that effect. Only, in exchange for this, how many gold pieces are you prepared to give me?'

The Bey was delighted. 'I'll give you anything you want,' he said.

'With this firman you'll have no trouble. The land here that I gave you, the villages will still be yours. You will stay permanently settled in the plain, but you'll be free to go up into the mountains whenever you like.'

He accepted five hundred gold pieces from the Bey of Bozdogan. He did not approve of bribery, but what could he do? The firman he gave the Bey came to be known as the 'Major Ali Pasha Firman.'

'Yes, the Ottoman State has grown weak,' he said. 'It needs as much gold and silver as it can find. Think of all this

71

gold lying in the dirty pouches of the nomads, to no use at all!'

The other Turcoman tribes heard of this and their beys fell into line to obtain a 'Major Ali Pasha Firman' too. The major soon found himself in possession of countless pouches filled with gold coins.

Eventually, the Firkai Islahiye was withdrawn and Ali Bey left with it for Istanbul. But the validity of the 'Major Ali Pasha Firman' held good for many long years after his departure. As for him, he built himself several stately mansions in Istanbul with the Turcomans' money, and rose to the rank of Pasha.

Still, his judgement turned out to be correct. Once the Turcomans had got the feel of a settled life they were less inclined to take up their old nomadic ways again. In time they started setting up homes on the village lands assigned to them. They made houses out of the *jilpirti* bushes and the reeds and rushes that abounded in the Chukurova. They would cut down the *jilpirtis* and weave them into walls like a sheep-pen and then daub them with mud. Their houses had one door and small windows on each side. For the roof they laid reeds first and then covered them with thick sheaves of rushes, the whole securely bound with rushes again. The villages were in fact nothing but clusters of heaped grass.

At the first sign of spring the Turcomans would hasten up into the mountains, returning to their huts only in the winter. Even then they erected tents in their yards and slept in them. Only gradually did they get used to living in the huts. In the summer not a living soul remained in the Turcoman villages and towns, save for a few shopkeepers. Then they learned to sow the land. So when spring came the women and children were sent up into the mountains while the men stayed on until they had reaped the harvest. Later, when cotton cultivation caught up with them, the women stayed too. And so by degrees they grew accustomed to the heat of the Chukurova.

Until the Second World War there were hardly any stone or brick houses in the Chukurova. After the war, as though at the stroke of a magician's wand, an astonishing change took place. In the space of a few years the reed-huts disappeared to be replaced by houses of stone and brick with zinc roofs. This was because there were no marshes or uncultivated land left where reeds and rushes and *jilpirti* bushes could grow. The Turcomans were making money out of the produce of their land. They had long forgotten the nomadic life they had led in the mountains and clung jealously to their land. Quarrels over land ownership were rife now.

Only one group of tribes, called the Aydinlis, pursued their nomadic ways, living in the black goathair tents, winters in the plain and summers in the high pastures, according to the sanction given them by the 'Ali Pasha Firman'.

But in the winter of 1949 they were in for a shock. When they descended into the plain there was not a strip of land left untilled and they could scarcely find a place to pitch their tents, let alone graze their stock. They had been feeling the pinch for some years now, but had never dreamed it would come to this. The 'Ali Pasha Firman' was no longer of any use at all. Their hearts burning for the carefree days of old, they bitterly regretted not having settled in the Chukurova like the other nomads. With the years their regret and bewilderment increased as they wandered about wretchedly, beating their heads against obstacles from Aladag to Mersin, from Antalya to Gediz plain, from the Chukurova to Amik plain, tossed about like flotsam on the sea. The embroidered kilims, the palatial tents grew faded and worn and mouldy. Customs and traditions, the age-old songs and laments were forgotten under the continued blows of fortune. They tried putting up a fight to regain their former wintering places, but the land had long ago been cultivated by others and settled with farms. Their blood was shed in vain. For some years they managed to camp on village pasture-land, paying fortunes to the villagers for the right to stay there one winter. Then pasture-land too began to be cultivated. And in the mountains they were harassed by forest guards who made life impossible for them up there too. They damned Ali Pasha and his firman many times and called

73

down curses on his bones.

In the village of Kösejik, Muhtar Fehmi had built himself a palatial forty-room mansion on two floors. Up to ten years ago Fehmi had been proud of his grandfather, a Turcoman bey, and would boast incessantly of the noble Arab horses he used to keep. 'Horses that could catch up with the fleeting gazelle,' he would say. Then he began to fill the houses with modern furniture bought in Adana, with carpets and refrigerators, and to throw out the old Turcoman kilims, the carved oak chests, the firkins, the embroidered pouches, the harnesses, all things that the peasants snapped up eagerly. The fine Turcoman coffee-pots with folding handles, the trays, the ewers, the basins, the carved wooden mortars in which Turcoman women pounded the coffee, making up bewitching songs to the rhythm of the pestle . . . Fehmi would screw up his face in disdain. 'Throw it away,' he would say pointing at this or that old Turcoman relic with his foot. 'I don't want to see it.' And he would run his hand proudly over the new gilded armchairs and the lacquered beds. His grandfather's purebreds, the old Turcoman traditions were put out of mind. If anyone so much as mentioned them he squirmed and at once took a strong dislike to the speaker. It was his tractors he boasted of now, his combines, his private car, his trucks, his farm. He was muhtar of Kösejik, now, the agha of the village, the president of the local branch of the party. He bragged about his friend the minister who when Fehmi went to Ankara would rush to visit him at his hotel, of his sons and daughters who were all being educated in private schools and universities. He was toying with the idea of inviting his important friends in Adana and Ankara, government officials and party bigwigs, so that they should see in what a palace he lived. This house had cost Fehmi considerably more than he could afford. He was a man who made a lot of money, but somehow it was never enough.

Catty Veli was one of his most trusted men. His father, his grandfather, had always been close to Fehmi's family. It was this Veli who now jumped out of the jeep, sweating. 'The

74

Yörüks have settled on Deliboga Knoll and Dervish Hassan's already sponged them. But when I asked for money they hummed and hawed. Tell me Agha, what shall I do?' He was red with fury.

'You know what to do,' Fehmi said.

'Good!' Catty Veli rejoiced. He checked his pistol, mustered five men, all of them armed, and set off.

The Karachullu tribe had been expecting some fresh calamity. With Süleyman at their head, their eyes wide with dread, they watched Catty Veli, small, dry, vindictive, as he shot out of the jeep like lightning and came bouncing up to their tents with his men at his heels.

'I give you twenty-four hours, Fehmi Agha's orders, to get off our knoll. Or . . . Or you'll take those gold shiners out of your pouches and put them before me. I've had enough of you. Is this your father's property, this knoll, that you come and settle on it without so much as a by-your-leave? All high and mighty you are, eh, efendis? Spending your summers up in the mountains, by cool springs scented with pine and mint . . . And look at us here, with the fever, the mosquitoes, the yellow heat, the water like hot blood . . . Look at me and look at you. A flick on your cheek and the bright red blood will spurt out! Aren't we human too? I've got three children and they're all sick. The wife's been laid up for the past two years. Our bellies bloat like balloons with the muddy infected waters we drink. As though we're not human beings like you! Twenty-four hours you have, that's all. No more!' He turned away and made quickly for the jeep. 'That's all. Enough . . .'

Süleyman the Headman hurried after him while the others stood staring, too numb to move. 'Wait,' he cried. 'Wait, Agha, listen!'

Veli clambered into the jeep. 'Twenty-four hours I've allowed you. No more. We haven't bred and raised this land for your enjoyment. And shed our blood too. Twenty-four hours, and if you don't loosen your pursestrings, you go. Fehmi Agha's orders. Not a word will I hear from you.'

The jeep spurted off in a cloud of dust and was soon lost to

75

sight. Headman Süleyman was left standing there helplessly.

'I used to know this Fehmi Agha's father very well,' Old Müslüm said. 'And his grandfather too. We were good friends. Once I made his father a gift of a three-year-old purebred colt. This Fehmi Agha was only a child then. He would sit on my knee and play with my watch-chain. And one day I strung the chain over his neck and gave it to him. Old Circassian work. I'll go to Fehmi Agha and talk to him.'

Old Müslüm asked Haydar the blacksmith for his horse. It was the only good one left in the whole tribe and, though old, a handsome noble beast. They decked it out with the best saddle available, a silver-threaded bridle and worked stirrups. Old Müslüm produced from his pack his most beautiful silver-embroidered shalvar-trousers, bought long ago in the Marash bazaar. He put on his *jepken*[1] and rode away with two young men, one flanking him on each side.

They came to Fehmi's mansion in the afternoon, and Old Müslüm looked about expectantly for somone to hold the reins and welcome him in. Hadn't he come as a guest? Weren't these the age-old rules of hospitality? But he waited in vain there at the door, his back breaking from the effort to sit upright on his horse. No one appeared. What was he to do? He had never suffered such an indignity in all his life. The only answer to this was to leave at once, but that he could not do.

'You go in,' he ordered one of the youths accompanying him, 'and ask for Fehmi Agha. See if he's there and then tell him that Müslüm, an old friend of his father's and grandfather's, has come to visit him.'

The youth went in and Old Müslüm waited, struggling to keep up his dignified seat on the horse. After a little while the youth returned but his face was pale. 'He said you were to come up,' he said.

Stiffly, his bones creaking, Old Müslüm dismounted. His body was numb. Breathing laboriously, he climbed the flight of new marble stairs with the help of the two youths. At the head of the staircase, afraid to step on to the thick new carpets, he

[1] jepken: a jacket with slit sleeves leaving the arms free.

stopped and took off his sandals, fumbling with the laces for a long time. Then he stepped shrinkingly into the drawing-room. Fehmi Agha was there, sunk in a gilt armchair and puffing on a huge cigar. He looked at Old Müslüm and began to laugh.

'What's this costume, this rig-out?' he derided. 'It's too funny! Too ridiculous.' And he sent out peal after peal of laughter.

Old Müslüm stood rooted in the middle of the room. His eyes went dark and the world started whirling all about him. Trembling, he sank to the ground. Then, with a desperate effort, he pulled himself together. He saw a lot of people, men and women, laughing uproariously.

'I'm a friend of your father's,' he blurted out. 'It's not because . . . The horse I gave . . . I wouldn't remind you . . . And . . .' He strangled.

'But why are you decked out like this?' Fehmi Agha asked in between bursts of laughter. 'Like something out of history, come from two thousand years away . . . What's that tinselled thing on your head?'

Old Müslüm tried again. 'I'm a guest at your door, come with a plea. Allah's guest . . . I was a friend of your father's when you were only a child. You used to like watch-chains . . . Gold ones, you remember?' His hurried words were almost unintelligible.

Fehmi Agha stopped laughing. He turned to his guests with an expression of pity on his face. 'I suppose that's how our ancestors looked,' he said. 'But surely not as funny as this . . . The poor beggars.' And he went on to expatiate on the ignorance of their forefathers and their benighted traditions. 'I seem to remember this man. A pity they're so backward, so very ignorant. It's people like these make the Europeans think we're a backward country. Ah, when will we see the last of them?' He looked at the old man who was still huddled on the floor, his hands fluttering, his face as white as his beard. 'Is there anything you want?' he asked.

'Your grandfather used to love our people. And your father too,' Old Müslüm said. 'They were related to our tribe.'

Fehmi Agha flushed crimson. 'Never!' he shouted. 'God forbid.' He felt terribly humiliated before Sabahattin Bey, the manager of the Ford agency, who was present among the guests. 'The whole world tries to invent some kind of kinship with me, God forbid. Speak, old man, what is it you want?'

'Only this, nephew. If you will only allow us to spend this winter on Deliboga Knoll . . .'

'That's impossible,' Fehmi Agha said. 'Quite impossible, my poor ridiculous fellow. I've spent hundreds of thousands this year on this house. Open your pursestrings for once in your lives. It won't hurt you!' He turned and began to talk to his guests without another glance at Old Müslüm. The two young men lifted the old man up and supported him down the stairs. With difficulty they heaved him on to the horse and held him on each side to prevent his falling off.

'Aaah, aaah, strange times, ah!' Old Müslüm moaned.

All the way back he kept up a mournful wail like a lament.

7

*As the Yörüks gradually settled in the Chukurova they fell
prey to countless ills. They suffered from the heat, the
mosquitoes, the fever, the epidemics, and, even worse, from
Government officials. Some incidents were never forgotten,
and one was the burning down of their huts by the Vali of
Adana. And the wars . . . And the plagues . . . The Tripoli
War in 1911 . . . And then the French occupation . . .*

'What haven't we seen, what!' Beardless Ali Agha said. 'What
haven't we gone through! When did we ever live like human
beings in this Chukurova plain? You see that railway that
comes piercing through the mountains? That pair of iron rails
stretching on and on, which the Germans laid? Well, every foot
of it holds a human life . . . What haven't we seen till we reached
this day, what! What haven't we suffered, what haven't we gone
through!'

Beardless Ali Agha was launched now.

'I don't have the heart to look back on the past. Not ever!
Not one of us old Turcomans has the heart to remember.
Before we came to live this sedentary life, the whole world was
a paradise for us, everywhere, the Taurus Mountains that we
call the Thousand Bulls, with their many peaks, Aladag, Düldül,
Kayranli, Berit, and also the Gavur Mountains, and all the
region of Payas and Dumlukalé, and the whole of the Chukurova
plain . . . But all this came to an end with the settlement. And
now these Aydinli nomads come to us and complain! After
living like princes for a hundred years, they complain! Well, let
them. While we were dying like flies down here on this bloody
plain with the heat, the mosquitoes, the fever, the pestilences,
the wars, the taxes, they were taking their ease up in the highlands beside the cool springs, among the blue hyacinths and

pennyroyal, in the dappled shade of the pines. Did they ever trouble about us? Did they once ask how we were faring? No, they've parted company with us, they've become a separate people. It's they who've broken the old tradition, who've caused this division among the tribes . . . Get me my horse,' he shouted suddenly from the window of his mansion. 'I'll go myself and give them a piece of my mind.'

Two menials at once brought the horse to the door. The aged Ali Agha descended the creaking wooden staircase and was lifted on to the saddle by them. His villagers crowded into a tractor and set out after him.

In those days, the Vali, who was a pasha, had issued an order . . . How could one live in these grass huts? It wasn't human. With walls that were nothing but brushwood and reeds! And even the roofs made of rushes! Piles of grass, not villages at all! The Vali Pasha ordered the villagers to build themselves houses of bricks and mortar and stone and tiles, and to keep their villages spick and span. Very stern orders the Vali Pasha gave . . . A year later he went on inspection and what should he see? The grass huts were there the same as ever. And so were the young men, sallow-skinned, wasted, but otherwise not a soul in any of the villages. The Turcomans had gone up into the mountains as usual, leaving a few youths behind, a prey to the heat, the fever, the sickness. Indeed, they had no choice. Each Turcoman household must keep one of its sons down in the Chukurova to reap the harvest. When they went they left the youth a shroud. What else could they do? It was impossible to live without the produce of the Chukurova, the wheat, the cotton . . . A handful of lads, each with his shroud in readiness . . . Like a dirge was the departure of the nomads for the highlands, and like a dirge their return. They went leaving their hearts and their minds behind, and coming back they found some dead, some incurably sick and some gone for ever. Many were the young men who fled the Chukurova in those years, never to return. Later, mothers, sisters, sweethearts refused to abandon their loved ones for so long and braved the yellow heat of the

Chukurova to be with them.

The Vali Pasha went from one village to another. 'Why haven't these huts been pulled down?' he asked the young men he found there. Trembling with fever, too weak even to answer, they stood helplessly before him like so many trees or stones. The Vali Pasha was enraged by their silence. They were defying him, these dirty nomads, they were making a fool of him with their passive resistance. His anger knew no bounds. 'Set fire to the villages,' was his mad, furious order. 'Burn all these grass huts.'

That summer many villages were set on fire. The young men fled and took refuge on hills, in marshes or streams. From there, they watched the Chukurova go up in flames, as the fire spread from the villages to the fields, from the fields to the thickets and from there to the woods. The whole Chukurova was burning and a cry of lamentation swept through the plain.

There was a great confusion after this, but things did not change much. New huts were built, but again of reeds and rushes and *jilpirti* bushes. There was nothing the Vali Pasha could do. Who knows what became of him? Maybe he died of impotent fury, maybe he went mad. Maybe the Government had him posted elsewhere. But the grass huts lasted on until the Second World War.

Beardless Ali Agha reined in at the foot of Deliboga Knoll. The tractor had preceded him and the villagers riding it had announced his arrival to Headman Süleyman. The Yörüks rushed up to hold his horse while he dismounted. Then they ushered him into the big tent. A lamb was killed in his honour and he was treated with the greatest deference. Beardless Ali Agha was highly gratified by this show of respect. He spoke to them of the old days, of the big fire, of their tribulations.

'That's the way the world goes,' he kept repeating. 'Settling on the land was the only solution for us.' On and on he expatiated, and always he came back to the time before the settlement, the Turcoman age of gold . . . 'You've been living in a paradise,' he said, 'while we were having a hard time of it here, dying like flies. But you'll have to settle too in the end. You'll have to go through what we've gone through. That's the way it is . . .'

The others who had come with him from the village never said a word. They sat still, listening respectfully, a sly knowing look on their faces.

'It was nearly dawn. I was asleep in the *chardak*[1] beside my hut when I woke up to find myself surrounded by flames. The whole place was on fire. I darted this way and that in my underclothes, but there wasn't a hole to slip through. I was going to be burned alive. The flames were drawing in upon me when I saw a gendarme. Tears were running down his face. He pulled me out somehow. He saved my life. Our village at that time was on the plain of Yüregir. After the fire we moved here. This knoll that you see, the marshes, the scrub all around have been ours since that time. Yes, our very own property! And now, Aghas, you the elders of the tribe, I've come to you so that . . .'

And the bargaining began. It lasted three days.

'The party leader in the town, the Kaymakam, our member for Parliament . . . Both the Government party and the opposition stand in need of us. The formalities for turning Deliboga Knoll over to you will be done in no time. You'll be given the full title-deeds. Now, what do you say?'

At first Beardless Ali Agha insisted on a hundred and fifty thousand liras.

'Good God!' Headman Süleyman exclaimed. 'Why, we couldn't put that sum together even if we sold our flocks and all we have. Ten or fifteen years ago it would have been possible, but now . . .'

'Ah, but you don't know!' Beardless Ali Agha broke in. 'Aaah, what do you people know! We know, we who have survived all these plagues and calamities . . . If I'd been in your place I'd have given half a million to possess this Deliboga Knoll. Look, even the name of the place is a pretty one. Deliboga Knoll Village! D'you think the Chukurova was like this when we came to settle? Such mosquitoes we had! With

[1] chardak: a summer shelter built of branches and set on stilts.

bones for stings. And the marshes! And the scrub reaching up to the heavens, so thick you could not see the sky as you walked through . . . Well then, since you've no money, let's make it a hundred thousand.'

In the end Beardless Ali Agha was persuaded to accept fifteen thousand, and three thousand were to be paid to him right away on account.

'Are you sure this knoll belongs to your village?' Süleyman asked hesitantly as he was about to pay. 'Are you sure it's included in the title-deeds?'

'You give me that money and don't trouble yourself about the rest,' Beardless Ali Agha admonished him in confident tones. 'Just pay over . . . As though I was asking for the earth! Why, when I divide this money between the villagers, there won't be ten liras a head. As though I was asking for the earth . . . Why, I wouldn't sell a quarter of an acre for this sum. Every inch of land is worth its weight in gold in the Chukurova today. I'm selling this cheap to you. And why am I doing this? Tell me, why? Why? No, you wouldn't know. Don't rack your brains, you'd never guess why . . . Such a thing's never been written in all history. But it's written here in my heart, the reason why. Yes, like you I've suffered, I've endured wars and fires and many calamities, and I've a heart here that burns for you like Blind Memet's limestone quarry. Yes, brother Headman, a heart that burns and sizzles too . . . That's why! Nobody'd sell you this priceless land for such a sum, nobody!'

'Nobody!' the villagers agreed, speaking for the first time.

Headman Süleyman wavered. What if these people didn't own the title-deeds? What would they do then? The nomads conferred for a long while, but they had no choice. In the end they counted over three thousand liras into Beardless Ali Agha's hand, and it was agreed that they would meet in town a week later for the transfer of the title-deeds.

That night a delirious mood of joy swept through the tribe. Old Müslüm was licking his lips. 'Good, good,' he said. 'Very good, very! When I die you'll dig my grave here, at the foot of this white inscribed stone. And you'll cover me with myrtle shrubs before you throw the earth in, won't you?' It was an old Greek marble slab half buried in the ground. The knoll was strewn with such stones. One had only to dig a little and another inscribed ancient block would turn up.

The pipers played their pipes and the maids and youths sang songs. Nobody slept that night. Everyone was weaving a dream of this land that was to be theirs. They saw houses with bright window-panes, tractors, motor-cars, rich clothes . . .

A week later Süleyman and a group of elders went to the town on the appointed day at the appointed hour. They waited there till evening, but there was no sign or news of Beardless Ali Agha. Somebody advised them to go to the public scribe, Blind Kemal.

Blind Kemal was a tall lank youth who looked as if he would topple over at the slightest puff of wind. He listened as they poured out their troubles, and then he told them the bare truth. Beardless Ali Agha had been selling Deliboga Knoll to various nomads for the past fifteen years.

'But what are we to do now?'

'Nothing, that's that.'

'There must be a way . . .'

'On the whole, he hasn't been too hard on you,' Blind Kemal said. 'Took pity on you this time, Beardless Ali did.' And then he explained all that was yet in store for them. This was the fate of every nomad group who had come to rest on Deliboga Knoll these last fifteen years.

'What shall we do? What?'

'Has Dervish Hassan come yet?' Blind Kemal asked.

'Yes.'

'Zalimoglu Veli?'

'No . . .'

'He'll come too. Yozoglu Osman?'

'No.'

'He'll come . . . Anyone from Bozduvar Village?'

'No.'

'They'll come, never fear!'

'What are we to do?'

'What about that longterm corporal from Yalnizagach police-station, Nuri Daglaryolu? No? You can expect him too.'

'What shall we do?'

'Goldtooth Riza?'

'He hasn't come . . .'

'He'll come yet.'

'What are we to do?'

There was nothing the scribe could say to help them, no way out that he could advise.

'But who does that knoll belong to?' Headman Süleyman asked.

'Nobody,' Blind Kemal said. 'Or at any rate everybody but you.'

They could make nothing of this. 'Write us a petition then, Kemal Efendi,' Headman Süleyman said. 'Make it so that people will realize what a plight we're in.'

'It's no use,' Blind Kemal said.

'Why not? You've got to. Write that this can't go on.'

'I can't.'

They begged and pleaded with him.

'But to whom am I to write? Where?' he said. His only eye, large and sad, shone with pity. 'Where, to whom?'

'Anywhere . . . To Ankara, to the big Pashas, to the Padishah in Istanbul. To the Vali in Adana. To anyone you like. But write.'

They would not budge before they had made him draw up a petition.

8

The autumn rains began. Long peals of thunder rolled in the distant skies. Torrents of water irrupted all over the place. Deliboga Knoll and the fields around it were turned to knee-deep mud. The long-legged rains pelted down over the tattered, faded, mouldering tents, drenching the kilims and the felt rugs. Many ills befell the tribe, but they clung to their knoll and would not let go. No power on earth could drag them away from there. After Blind Kemal, they went to other public letter-writers, to Teloglu and Haji Ali. Eight times they obtained an audience with the Kaymakam in the town and offered him some of their fresh butter. They solicited the lawyer, Murtaza Bey, and paid him an enormous fee. They appealed to the Party leaders too . . . But no one had an answer to their problem. Under the driving rain they wandered about the town market-place, sheltering their petitions under their felt cloaks, and would not lose hope. They were forced to sell many of their sheep and goats, their orange silver-embroidered rugs and carpets, and also butter and yoghurt and wool . . . But the worst was what befell the boy, Kerem.

It was past midnight. That morning the rain had let up and they had had a sunny day. They woke up to the sound of shots . . . Bullets were raining on the encampment from the gully down below. Dogs began to yelp, children howled, and the women shrieked and wailed.

'Don't move from your beds,' Headman Süleyman shouted. 'You, lads, take your guns and go to the top of the hill. But keep low. I'm coming too.'

A little later sixteen men were crouching in a hollow on the hilltop and in their turn they opened fire into the gully. The exchange of shots went on intermittently until dawn.

As day was breaking the men in the gully retreated to their jeeps. 'We'll be back tonight,' they shouted as they went.

Dogs barked, sheep bleated, horses neighed. The baby peregrine falcon was wet. Kerem looked at its ruffled feathers, its closed eyes, its drawn-in neck and he felt something choking in his throat. Down below the laurels were in flower, full-blown and bright pink in the sun. And the camelthorns . . . The bells tied to the goats and mules tinkled on. People and tents, sheep and camels, everything was wet from the dew. Huddled on its stake in front of the tent, greyish green in the morning light, the falcon opened an eye.

The elders of the tribe sat on the ancient inscribed stones and talked.

'We must hide our weapons,' Headman Süleyman said. 'Longterm Corporal will lose no time coming, and he's sure to confiscate them. Let Resul collect all the weapons and hide them in some hollow.'

Some way off a huge sheepdog, as large as a horse, was lying on the ground, its legs stretched out stiffly, as though fast asleep. All around its head, at the foot of an inscribed white stone, was a pool of blood. Hüsné was crouching beside it. She was ashamed to keen. Swaying from side to side she wept quietly, and her weeping had the sound of a dirge.

Kerem drew near. He knew the dog well. A bullet had pierced its neck and come out under its left ear. He sat down before Hüsné. Two tears trickled down his cheeks. He wanted to say something, but try as he would the words stuck in his throat.

'Don't cry, Aunt Hüsné,' he said at last. 'Please, please don't cry.'

But Hüsné went on swaying and weeping, and would not even look up. Then Jeren approached. Her large eyes were only two slits now. 'It's all because of me, Hüsné,' she said. 'Don't cry, my dear, don't. It's I who ought to be dead.' She sank down on to the muddy ground beside Hüsné. The sultry sun of the after-rain beat down upon them ever more hotly. Large green flies began to buzz over the pool of blood, and tiny

87

midge-flies settled on the dog's black eyes. 'Don't cry, Hüsné. The blame is mine. It's my fault all this wretchedness. Oh, if only I could die and be delivered.' She pushed herself up. 'If somebody would only kill me,' she kept repeating. 'If I could only die . . . It's all my fault.'

'No, it's mine!' The words came out of Kerem in a shout. He had been holding himself in check for days now. 'It's my fault! My fault!' Then he stopped short. The elders had all turned and were staring at him. Kerem's face was drawn and drained of colour. The sunlight hit the scorched grass, hotter and hotter. A thick cloudlike vapour rose from the sheep and camels and goats, from the earth, from people's backs. The dead dog, the pool of blood were steaming too.

Kerem turned and rushed down into the gully.

'Why, oh why did I wish for that falcon and not for a wintering place in the Chukurova?' he reproached himself. 'The Lord Hizir who gave me the falcon could have given a wintering place too. But . . .' He hesitated. 'Did I really see the meeting of the stars? . . . But if I didn't would I have got the falcon all at once when I'd been longing for it so long? It must have been in my sleep, half asleep, half awake that I saw those stars . . . And now . . . Curse this falcon, what are we to do now? We haven't a patch of land to step on. These Chukurova people are going to kill us all. They'll take everything we have and kill us. Look what they've done to poor Old Müslüm though he's a thousand years old! He'll never get over it, what Fehmi Agha did to him, and Old Müslüm a friend of his father's too! Now he's sick after all that humiliation, he's on his death-bed . . . Curse that falcon! Ah, I wish I'd never set eyes on it!'

He was wandering along the gully holding his sandals in his hand, when he spotted two empty cartridges on the ground. They had a strange acrid burnt smell. A little further off there were some more, and soon he forgot everything as he searched for the cartridge-cases which were strewn here and there all about the sands. There were marks too on the sands left by birds and men. He walked on, groping in the holes of bee-eaters and inspecting all the bird-nests he came across. Towards noon he looked back. The tents, the knoll seemed to be miles away. This pulled him up. The sun was blazing hot now. His wet clothes were dry, stiff. He scraped the crusted mud off his feet and drew on his sandals. A terrible fear of Deliboga Knoll had got into him. Teeming with graves it was, and so old! Older even than Old Müslüm . . . And then people told things about this knoll. They said it sometimes raised itself up and roamed about the countryside the whole night long, bellowing like a bull. Stalking through the land and bellowing till break of day . . . If angered . . . They say this knoll is really a bull, as old as Old Müslüm, an old bull that was killed right here. The villagers shot him and he fell all in a heap right in this place. So when he sees the villagers, when he sees those who killed him, he wakes up and charges at them with a roar. The villagers bolt their doors, and . . . Yes, in their pants from fear! If he rose now, this bull, mad, furious, and bellowed, and bellowed, shaking earth and sky . . . They'd see those villagers who fired at them last night!

'He'll rise up, he will!' he shouted. 'That bull's biding his time, but once he's roused he'll come crashing down like a mountain upon those villagers. They'll see! They'll see, and tonight too. He'll make a shambles of their village. A shambles . . . Let them come again tonight. Just let them. Let them try to shoot at the knoll again.'

As he drew nearer, the knoll loomed out of the heat-haze and stirred. It was as though a thick hide were twitching in anger. He's our bull, Kerem said. Our grandfather. Would he ever leave us in the lurch! Heheeyy!

He came to the tents. The dead dog was still lying in the same place with a circle of women and children about it. Kerem laughed in his sleeve. If they knew! If only they knew that this knoll would rise up tonight and march upon the villagers . . . If they only knew! He went to his falcon. Its eyes were wide open now. It was trying to fly. Opening its wings it whirled and whirled at the end of the rope that tied it to the stake, then it settled again holding its wings outstretched till it had regained its balance.

'Let them see! I know what I'll wish for next year on Hidirellez night . . . Gububuk, hey Gububuk my lion, d'you hear me?'

All his regrets were gone now. He felt safe in the thought of the bull and of the coming Hidirellez night. Now the falcon appeared more beautiful than ever to his eyes. He untied it from the stake and took it in his hands. The elders were still sitting on the white stones, conferring. They would fall into long silences then start talking again very loudly as if quarrelling.

'Let's move from here,' Headman Süleyman was saying. 'This place is no good for us. Too many people pretend to own it. Who knows who'll be coming next. They'll strip us of all we have and still not let us winter in peace here. Let's get out.'

'Yes, but where shall we go?' someone asked dully.

'Where shall we go?' other voices echoed wearily. And in the end Headman Süleyman found himself joining them. 'Where are we to go? Every place is the same, if not worse . . . There's nowhere for us to stay. Not an inch of land uncultivated, except a few barren hills. What shall we do, where shall we go?'

If you knew, Kerem was thinking, ah if only you knew! You'd be dancing with joy now, uncles! If you knew that the bull's going to rise and march against those villages and wipe them off the face of the earth . . . And tonight too . . .

Suppose he told them, those poor old men who were almost dying of sorrow and fear . . . Why not? He edged up and taking the cartridge-cases out of his pocket showed them to Headman Süleyman. 'I found these in the gully down below,' he said. He was perspiring with excitement and embarrassment.

The Headman turned the cartridges over in his hand. His green eyes rested on Kerem sadly. 'They're from the bullets that were fired last night,' he said as though asking the boy's pardon.

Kerem trembled. The cold sweat ran down his back. 'The bull,' he blurted out at last. 'It'll rise up tonight and it'll attack those villagers . . .' He strangled. Red to the roots of his hair he turned and fled.

Kerem's words were like a knife thrust into Süleyman's heart.

'Aaah,' he sighed, 'ah Kerem, aaah . . . The bull rise for us? Even the Lord Hizir won't come to our help. No bull, no Hizir, not even the blessed Ali will help us any more. They've abandoned us all. Ah Kerem, aah!'

Kerem had disappeared among the tents with his falcon. The women were slowly retiring into their tents, weary and downcast, sad as though returning from a funeral. Not the slightest breeze stirred. The mist hung close to the ground, motionless, trembling in the air.

Suddenly they heard a rumbling noise in the mist and all the dogs began to bark at once. A voice called from below: 'Hey, Yörüks, hold back your dogs.' The voice was deep, authoritative. Then a jeep heaved into sight and Longterm Corporal and his policemen poured out of it and clambered up the slope, talking all the time. There was a man in civilian clothes with them too.

The Corporal halted before the tents. 'Call Süleyman,' he ordered, his arm on his hip, his chest thrown out.

The Headman was hurrying up. 'Here I am, my Pasha,' he said breathlessly.

The Corporal drew himself up still more and took a few steps towards him. 'What's this scandal?' he shouted. 'I'm sick and tired of you people. And so's the Government and the whole country. Sick and tired! Why, you've turned this peaceful Chukurova plain into a battlefield! What kind of a nuisance are you? Robbers? Bandits? I won't put up with this. Bring out your weapons and hand them over. The whole Chukurova was kept awake last night with the noise of your firing. What d'you think you're about? Not only guilty, but playing high and mighty too! Coming and settling by force on people's land and then showering them with bullets! Now, I'll have no humming and hawing from you. I want your weapons at once. Either you give them up or I'll round you all up and take you to the town. Yes, I'm a Yörük too, like you. My father was a Yörük and so was my mother, but there never were such barbarians among us,

91

never! No, never, never . . .'

'Corporal Pasha,' Headman Süleyman interrupted him, 'don't be angry, come and sit down and let's talk. You've been given false information. It wasn't us who fired these shots last night. Two men came in a jeep and attacked us. They fired at us all through the night. We were going to lodge a complaint, then we decided not to bother you . . .'

The Corporal's eyes started from their sockets, the veins in his neck swelled. 'What? What did you say?' He bore down threateningly on Süleyman. 'No villager in the Chukurova keeps arms. Impossible, quite impossible! Are you trying to say that there's no public order in the Chukurova? That we're not able to keep the public peace? Adding slander to everything else, are you? Well, write then, send telegrams to Ankara, complain to anyone you like. Not only guilty but brazen too, eh? Hassan, clap those handcuffs on him!'

The handcuffs rattled. Headman Süleyman held out his hands. 'Handcuff me if you will, but there must be some mistake. How can we mean anything against you, Pasha Efendi? We've always had the greatest respect for your person.'

'Respect! Hah!' the Corporal shrilled vehemently. 'Süleyman Agha respects me! Why, you've drowned the whole of the Chukurova in money . . . But when it comes to us . . . We might just as well be left to starve, with our children and all! And on top of it all, you unscrupulous rascals, you bring a bad name to my district, shooting all over the place the whole night long.' He turned to the policemen. 'Round them all up, every single one of them from seven to seventy, the children and the sick too, and herd them off to the police-station. I'll have you up before the court. Those two men found dead on that road there not so long ago, the poor fellows, you killed them! In my district there's not a man carries even a penknife to commit murder with. And then every night you secretly dig up this knoll for antiquities, for ancient gold coins, and you sell them to the tourists. Think I'm not informed of all your criminal activities, eh? Why, you've drowned the whole of the Chukurova in gold. Dispensing money all over the place . . . But when it comes to us, to the country's guardians of the peace, to those who stay awake night after night to watch over you . . .'

His breath failed him. Breathing hard he pulled out the whip from his boot and began to play with it. 'Yes!' he started afresh at the top of his voice. 'Yes sir! So we're to suffer all the troubles and curses of living down here, and then allow a band of nomads to come and settle on our knoll as though it was their fathers' own property? And let them deal out money to all and sundry? And go shooting at night all over the plain, frightening the whole population out of their wits? . . . No, no, no sir! I won't allow it! Round them up! Arrest them, every one of them . . .'

Haydar the blacksmith intervened. 'My good Pasha,' he said, 'what has Süleyman said to make you so angry? It's in the noble tradition of great pashas to be angry, I know, but wait a minute. Our people love you. Please sit down and drink our humble coffee.'

'Never!' the Corporal roared. 'I can't drink coffee with insolent people like you. We're Yörüks too, but we know how to treat visitors. We'd never insult them like you did.'

Old Haydar threw himself on the Corporal's hand and tried to kiss it. The Corporal snatched it away. 'You must excuse an old man,' Haydar said. 'I'm the descendant of the holy blacksmith's hearth. You'll know since you're a Yörük. I'm asking you to forgive our offence.'

The Corporal suddenly turned pale. 'The blacksmith's hearth?' he said. 'Not the Horzumlu blacksmiths?'

'The very one,' Old Haydar said, breathing with relief. 'Come on in and drink our coffee and forgive us.'

The Corporal stood transfixed. Then he turned to his men and pointed to Headman Süleyman. 'Take off those handcuffs,' he ordered. 'I come from the Horzumlu tribe too,' he said to Old Haydar. 'How did you happen to settle with these Karachullus?'

'It's a long story,' Old Haydar replied. 'Too long to tell here. We made our home with these people a hundred years ago. They're a good honest people.'

'Your's is a sacred hearth,' the Corporal said. 'Feared and respected by all.'

'Yes, so it was,' Old Haydar said. 'But people don't care about that any more. Now they take turns to spit on us . . . But come on in.' And he led the Corporal into the big tent. The policemen and the man in town clothes followed. They all sat down.

The Corporal's mood had changed. 'I'm come home at last,' he kept saying. 'How Allah has scattered us all!'

The coffees were brought in. The man in town clothes was sulking. Old Haydar was delighted. He laughed and joked. The Yörüks told the Corporal of their predicament. 'What are we to do now, Pasha, where are we to go?' Headman Süleyman said. 'What do you suggest, Pasha brother? You've gone through this too. Give us your advice and we'll do as you say.'

The Corporal considered for a while. 'You'd better go to the Vali,' he said. 'He likes us Yörüks. In the meantime I'll try and keep you here, but it's difficult. These Chukurova aghas are cruel, monsters every one of them. There's no escaping their clutches. And for some reason they hate us Yörüks. For heaven's sake, don't go spreading it about that I'm a Yörük and that I'm helping you!'

'Of course we won't,' they assured him only too gladly.

Old Haydar signalled to the Headman to follow him outside. 'Let's put something into that fellow's pocket,' he whispered into his ear. 'Just a little something. He may be one of us, but he's human. He's sucked raw milk like everyone else . . .'

The Headman had never entertained the slightest illusion. He knew that it would all end up as usual and had already made up his mind as to just how much money he was going to give. He went to his tent. When he came back he found the Corporal waiting for him at the entrance of the big tent. He approached him and slipped the money into his pocket.

'Many thanks, uncle,' the Corporal said. 'We're all dragging out a miserable existence in this Chukurova. They've killed us off, finished us all, aaah ah!'

A little further away Kerem was at the front of a group of

women and children who were holding their breaths as they watched the whole proceedings with wide-open eyes.

'Come on, lads,' the Corporal called inside the tent. 'Come on out and let's go.'

As they were starting down the hill the Corporal's eyes fell on the falcon perched on Kerem's arm. He stopped and smiled. 'Hey, you there,' he called. 'The boy with the falcon! Come here.' Kerem ran up to him. The Corporal stroked the bird and inspected its eyes and talons. 'It's a genuine peregrine falcon,' he said after taking long stock of it. Then his eyes lit up suddenly. 'Look, won't you give it to me? What's your name?'

'Kerem,' the boy faltered, a terrible fear gripping him. The Corporal was stretching out his hand. He was going to take his falcon away . . . All at once Kerem was out of the crowd and bolting down the hill. The Corporal stood there looking vexed.

'The little scum,' Old Haydar cried in alarm. Kerem was messing up everything. 'Run after him and bring back that falcon at once.'

'It doesn't matter really,' the Corporal said with bad grace. 'I just thought . . . Since he can always get another falcon up in the mountains, not only one but half a dozen too . . . I just thought I'd take this one to my son. It would make him so happy. And it would help him not to forget he's a Yörük too. But no matter, no matter, let it go.'

He turned to leave, but Old Haydar held him back. 'Wait Pasha,' he said. 'Won't you wait just a little? They'll get that falcon for you in no time. That a guest should ask for something from a Yörük and not have it! You're of the Horzumlus too, Corporal Pasha, and you should know such a thing's never been heard of.'

The Corporal brightened. 'That's true,' he laughed, and then he proceeded to tell them how his father and mother had come to settle in the Chukurova.

Down in the gully three long-legged youths were giving chase to Kerem who ran for all he was worth, tripping, falling, rising, the falcon on his arm wild with fury now, its wings flailing, its claws tearing at his hand.

95

Back on the knoll, the Corporal was rambling on. 'I had a sister who was very beautiful. A real beauty she was, Meryem. We'd come down that year, just like you now, to the Chukurova and found there was nowhere for us to stay. The villagers wouldn't let us camp anywhere, not even for one day. Wherever we went they would be upon us with their clubs and their weapons, with their dogs and their horses, and we would be forced to strike camp. For two whole months we wandered about the plain without being able to stop anywhere. The children, the old people could not pull through, not one of them survived . . .'

There was a place where the flood-bed divided to merge again lower down, forming an island. Kerem was racing round and round this island. Suddenly he spotted a blackthorn thicket and threw himself into it. The young men lost all trace of him.

'And if our sheep and goats happened to pluck off a spike of corn in the fields we were passing by, which was bound to happen as the roads are so narrow, well then, they would at once ask for damages and that meant three sheep for a handful of growing corn! It was drawing near the time when we could return to our mountains, but we found we had nothing left. Our sheep and goats, our horses and donkeys were all gone. One winter in the Chukurova had been enough to leave us destitute. Spring was almost upon us when a fight broke out between the villagers and our people. We lost five men, and three of theirs were killed. But it was during this fight that one of their young men saw Meryem and fell for her. Give me this girl, he said, and you can build yourself houses near mine and have land to sow near my fields . . .'

The three youths finally ran Kerem to earth in the thicket. He took to his heels once again. He was rested now and ran so hard that they could not catch up with him.

'So we told Meryem. But she wouldn't have him. She wept and cried and declared she'd kill herself. We insisted, we begged her, all of us, my father, my mother, my other sisters and brothers. Look Meryem, we said, there's no place in all this

96

wide world for us to go. Shall we die? Even dead no place will have us. Our bodies will be food for the dogs. She gave in in the end. And then her husband let us settle on his land. But Meryem didn't live. A year later she was dead, and after that her husband drove us away. He was a bad man.'

The Corporal mopped his sweating face with a white handkerchief, and went on to tell of their further tribulations in the Chukurova.

Kerem was losing speed. His legs were trembling. How could they take his falcon from him? How could they? How? His eyes went dark, he stumbled and fell. His pursuers came upon him as he lay there in a faint. They untied the falcon from his wrist and carried it off. The bird was in utter disarray, a bedraggled jumble of feathers that looked like anything but a falcon.

When Kerem came to, they were far away. He rose and ran after them, a gleam of hope still in his heart. He saw them go up the slope and hand the falcon over to the Corporal. Kerem looked at the Corporal. A last hope . . . But the Corporal was already walking to the jeep carrying the falcon in his hand. He never even noticed Kerem.

The jeep started off and vanished into the mist. Kerem's knees gave way as though breaking and he sank to the ground.

9

The tribe was feeling the pinch more and more. Who knows who would come next, what more would be exacted from them? They were groping blindly in a dense black night, beating against a dark wall and not a gleam of hope filtered through. There was no place for them in the Chukurova. Deliboga Knoll was still the least of evils and they must cling to it as long as they could, die on it even. Akmashat, their usual wintering place, they could not even approach. Karadirgenoglu Dervish Bey saw to it that they should not so much as pass near it.

A pistol at his waist Fethullah was pacing up and down the three-pillared tent. What had they done to make these villagers so hostile? Hadn't they too been like them in the old days?

'I'll kill them,' he was saying to himself. 'I'll fight them. We must fight. There's no other way. Like a swarm of ants they've fallen upon us, tearing us piecemeal, devouring us, destroying us . . . And all the other ants are getting the scent and coming too.'

He reflected on their condition some years ago, even only a few months back . . . Now, sheep and goats, camels and donkeys, tents and rugs, all their possessions were reduced by half, and dwindling still with every passing day. A couple of years more at this rate and they would be utterly destitute. Nothing more than beggars eking out a miserable existence. Not even that. They would all be dying on the roadsides. For none of them knew of any other way to make a living. They had no special crafts or skills. No one in the tribe had ever been trained for such things. Only Old Haydar, the blacksmith.

'I'll kill them, I'll kill them. The more we flatten ourselves before them, the more they tramp us underfoot. This Deliboga

Knoll now, it's nobody's at all and yet the whole world's claiming it, just to rob us. I'll kill them.'

He despised himself bitterly. The humiliation, the loneliness, the helplessness . . . With difficulty he held back his tears. Once in his life only he had cried. Long long ago. Two whole days he had wept for his dead grandmother. Yet try as he might he could not remember where they had buried her. Where was her grave? A towering planetree . . . The rising land bordering a river with mauve-flowering marjoram, fresh and fragrant in the breeze . . . And large glossy bright-coloured autumn butterflies fluttering down like rain . . . What place was that? How terrible the old nomad custom never to ask after the graves of the dead! A people who did not know where their dead ones were buried, who could never find the place again . . . Horrible, revolting, pitiable.

'Everyone, everyone's got a place under the sun. But we, we're not even suffered to travel along the roads. Ah, father!'

Fethullah was Headman Süleyman's son. For two years when they had wintered down at Telkubbé he had attended a school in a distant village and had learned to read and write.

'Ah, father . . .'

In those days their purses were full of gold and land could be had for a song. They might have bought as much as they liked and settled down. How could they have known? The whole of the Chukurova was empty then and the Yörüks were like mighty eagles. The peasants hardly dared greet them, let alone raise a hand against them. They could have bought land for five villages, even ten. Hadn't the Sarihajis done just that? And today their village was a village no longer, but a large town full of lights. Now they denied their Yörük origin and avoided other Yörüks like the plague.

'It's the rule of might now. One must stand up and fight. Like Halil. Like Mustan. They say Halil's been killed . . . And Mustan wounded. Lamed . . .'

How many young men were there in the tribe? At least thirty. If they were to take up arms, all of them . . . Who were the people who had assaulted them, who had shot at them? Find

99

their village and raid it. . .

But three years ago they had done just that. The Yörüks had retaliated and attacked their assailants' village. And then what happened? The next morning the whole tribe from seven to seventy had been rounded up and herded into the town. The blows, the abuse, the rapings . . . Even the shepherds had been arrested, even palsied hundred-year-old women . . . The tents were left empty. The flocks, the camels, the horses straggled unshepherded all about the plain. Two months later when they were set free, they returned to find their tents broken, beaten flat into the dust and mud, looted down to the last matchstick. Not a bed or blanket, not a pot or pan. The herds decimated, sold away, slaughtered or divided up between the villagers. The Corporal of the district had staked his claim over a whole herd of sheep and sold them. The ten-room house he had bought for himself in the town with the money was still a legend on the tongues of men.

That year the whole tribe dragged itself, halt and sick, from place to place, begging their way along. They went to Adana, to the Vali to plead their cause. The Vali laughed. The Government House laughed at them, the policemen, the clerks laughed, all the town was laughing. The streets were thronged with people. Fethullah huddled close to his father. Bewildered, angry, ashamed, afraid, almost crazed, he stared at this flood of human beings. They were all laughing at them. Night was falling as they left the town behind, all glittering with lights. The town was laughing at them. They fell to the dusty country roads, and even the dust laughed at them. The trees, the birds, the bees, the flowers, everything was laughing at them.

'Father, father, father they're laughing . . .'

Under a tree Fethullah lay burning with fever, writhing, shivering.

'Father, father, father they're laughing at us!'

He remembered his father's wet beard, his sisters' faces, pale as ashes, his mother's eyes, wide, unnaturally large, starting from their sockets. And nothing more. A long blank . . . Then the Bey of Musali tribe rose before his eyes. The long sad face, the deep wrinkles, the grizzling black beard . . . Smiling a gentle, heart-warming smile . . . 'Don't worry, dear Süleyman, dear friend. Our tribe has a few sheep and camels and horses left. And some money too. We'll give you some of what we have, every household will give something to one of your tribe. It's the custom, the old tradition of our people.'

And that is what they did.

Only Old Haydar's horse was not lost. That noble beast . . . While he was languishing away in prison, the horse evaded all its pursuers. It would not be caught. On the way back from town Old Haydar was lagging behind all alone, dragging himself on his lacerated feet. The tip of the sun had appeared and the Gavur Mountains were resplendent with light. Suddenly he felt a warm breath on his neck and turning he beheld his horse. It was trying to help him. He held its head and kissed its hazel eyes three times. The horse bent over, but Old Haydar was unable to climb on to its back. So in the end it seized Old Haydar with its teeth and heaved him up.

'I'll kill them! Kill them, kill them! Aaah, father . . .'

A hectic fire consumed Fethullah. He had so many cartridges. Two hundred perhaps.

Storm the village. Give it to them. Start at one end and go right through to the other . . . The men only. Spare the women and children . . . And, afterwards, the last bullet . . . For you Fethullah.

Lost in his vision he was rounding up man after man and discharging his pistol at their foreheads. When he came to himself he was drenched in sweat as though he had taken a plunge in the river.

The nomads were sitting in scattered groups on the knoll. No one spoke. No one even moved. The sound of bells floated through the air, muffled, broken now and then by the barking of dogs.

And way off in Sandal village, under the huge planetree in Jennetoglu's orchard the villagers had got together and were angrily inveighing against the Karachullus.

'You're right,' Jennetoglu was saying. 'It's the plain truth what you're saying. Deliboga Knoll is ours. It's our wintering place. Only yesterday we were still wintering there as we'd been doing for the past fifty years. So indeed, why is it that Süleyman is dealing out money to all and sundry and not to us?'

'Why indeed?' they asked.

'Because let me tell you, the why and wherefore is that we're not men, that's what! We're not worth a farthing, not even in heathen brass.'

'He's right,' they said.

A very tall man with a dark leathery countenance, tiny eyes and tattered clothes covered with dust and chaff, rose suddenly stretching out a pair of huge hands.

'So we're to live here in this burning hell, working ourselves to death for a morsel of bread, ravaged by fever, devoured by mosquitoes, and then those people are to come from the highlands, from lazying beside cool clear springs and streams, from where the mauve violet and pennyroyal grows, drinking of the ice-cold waters, ice-cold! Think of it, ice-cold . . . They're to come and occupy our very own wintering place, and what's more, they have money . . .' His eyes flashed and popped out. The veins in his neck swelled. 'Pouches full of gold! Bags full! Sacks full! Gold which they dispense all over the place and not even a mite for us! No, no my friends, we can't put up with that! And worse still, they all belong to the *Kizilbash*[1] sect, yes my friends, without even the excuse of being Kurds. Yes my friends, they're just like us and yet Kizilbash too. No, no my friends, we can't put up with that.'

'You're speaking like Halil, the Democrat Party leader,' someone from the group said. 'Just like him. Damn me for a liar if I don't make you a deputy at the very next election . . .'

'Idiot!' the long one said. 'This is no joking matter. There now, you've made me forget what I was going to say, you son-of-a-bitch. It's no use trying to do anything with you people.' He pitched his voice higher. 'No, no, we can't stomach this, my friends. We can't suffer these heathen Kizilbash people to sully our sacred wintering place, the soil where our forefathers are

[1] Kizilbash: a religious sect of the Shiite branch.

buried. And Kizilbash who aren't even Kurds too!'

'That's straight speaking,' several voices approved.

'Of course it is,' he thundered. 'As straight as the arrows of our ancestors. A *jihad*, comrades, a holy war, that's what! against the kafir, the heathen, the Kizilbash! I call for a jihad to exact our rights!'

'Just like Democrat Halil!' the man who had first spoken marvelled. 'But you've forgotten something. You didn't say a jihad against the communists.'

'What communists, idiot?' the long man said as he sat down. 'You find communists in towns, not under tents.'

'That's what you think,' the others rejoined. 'Top communists live in tents.'

They all laughed.

'I've summoned Süleyman here,' Jennetoglu interposed, frowning. 'We'll claim our due from him. And if he refuses then there'll be hell to pay.'

'What will we do to them?' a young man asked innocently.

The long man was still fuming. His breast heaved with rage. 'You wait,' he said breathing hard at every word. 'You just wait and see. I've been preparing for this all the year. You'll all be bowled over when you see what I've thought up to make them decamp.'

'But if we throw them out . . .' Jennetoglu hesitated. 'Anyway, we'll see what Headman Süleyman's got to say. He used to be all right in the past. Never settled anywhere without coming to see me first. His nose is up in the air now, the dog. Doesn't even send a word of greeting to me! And the why and the wherefore is that he's pandering to that Yörük corporal, giving him presents, a falcon, an Arab horse, and gold too! Well, let's see what Süleyman's got to say. Let him come . . .'

With chaff sticking all over their dusty clothes, their faces burnt black and dry by the sun, their cheeks sunken, their eyes fixed on the road, glazed, ruthless, they waited, nursing their rancour.

And on Deliboga Knoll the little group of nomads clung on to the hillside, silent, rock-like, as though they had taken root there. Maybe they had all fallen asleep in broad daylight, maybe they were all dead. In a tent pitched high up a baby was whining away, a sick person moaned. Only that. Nothing else, not a sound. All life snuffed out . . . Down Anavarza way, south-west, the green boundless expanse of a rice-paddy, and behind, the main highway overhung with an everlasting cloud of dust . . . To the south the cotton fields with sparse last groups of pickers, small and far away, plucking a third growth of bolls. A solitary gleaner here and there, like a stork that has alighted on the cotton-field . . . To the east the stubbled fields, teeming with tractors endlessly churning the land right down to the foot of Yassi Hill, fluttering, bustling the whole night long. The strange unfamiliar songs of the tractor-drivers . . . To the north, stubbled fields again as far as the eye can see, and in the middle of the stubble a clump of oaktrees with a large spring gushing forth in the deep stony gully below.

Their sheep, cattle, goats, donkeys, camels were all packed into the small space surrounding the oaktrees. The shepherds could not take a step out of that area. Let a single animal stray into somebody's stubble, two armed men would at once spring into view and seize a sheep, five sheep, a hundred sheep, as many as they could, and bear them off to their village. The confiscated animals would be returned only after they had extracted damages from the Yörüks. All the shepherds' faces were battered and bruised. One had a black eye, the other a broken nose, a gash in his head, swollen feet. Their clothes were in tatters, smeared with blood . . .

'Welcome, Süleyman,' Jennetoglu said dourly without rising to greet him, his long moustache drooping even longer, his sullen face dark with anger. He pointed to a seat beside him. 'Sit down and let's talk.'

The villagers, taking their cue from Jennetoglu, let their moustaches droop and looked daggers at Süleyman. Used as he was to this kind of treatment from the village people, Süleyman still felt a tremor of apprehension. He was in for a bad time. Silently he took his seat beside Jennetoglu. A bitter smile hovered on his lips, like a poignant ache, flurried, strange.

Everyone called out the usual 'merhaba' in greeting. 'Merhaba to you all,' Süleyman said in his turn, and then there was a pregnant silence.

Then Jennetoglu began to speak. 'I'm very offended with you, Headman Süleyman,' he said. 'You've forgotten us.' His voice was sly, crafty, cruel, seasoned, parasitical.

'I'm sorry,' Süleyman said like a timid child, woebegone, tired, helpless.

'Look here, Headman Süleyman,' Jennetoglu continued in the same tone, 'here you come and settle on our very own land, the why and the wherefore is that Deliboga Knoll belongs to our village . . . And then you go on to drown the whole of the Chukurova in money. You give away lambs and rugs and falcons and Arab horses. And not one thought for us! Since when have you begun to turn up your nose at us?' He stopped and riveted his greenish streaked eyes unblinkingly on Süleyman. The four or five hairs of his sparse beard bristled with fury.

Swallowing hard, Süleyman tried to answer. He spoke for some time without knowing what he was saying. 'If only I knew,' he said in the end, 'to whom that Deliboga Knoll belongs! Everybody's laying a claim to it. The ant on the ground, the fish in the water, even the little children . . . The whole world claims it for its own. They've killed us. It's worse than death what they've done to us.'

Jennetoglu blew up. 'You let your own wintering place slip through your fingers,' he thundered, 'and then you come and occupy ours . . . No, no, Süleyman, I won't put up with this. I'm not dead yet, Süleyman!'

Süleyman muttered something. Then Jennetoglu spoke again. The villagers joined in too.

'I could never scrape together the sum you ask for,' Headman Süleyman said at last. 'Not even if we sold all the sheep, camels, horses, tents and rugs we own, not even if we sold our very clothes.'

'Very well then,' Jennetoglu countered with finality. 'You must pack up and go. You'd better think twice about this . . .'

Süleyman seemed to shrink, to melt away. He could not bring himself to say, 'Don't do this, we have nowhere to turn to, nothing we can do'. He could not bring himself to get up and go. He remained sitting there numb and dry. His mouth was parched, his lips cracked. He could not utter another word, not for the life of him. At last he heaved himself up and staggered to his horse. The two youths who had accompanied him lifted him on to the saddle. He slouched over the horse's neck and they led him away.

It was evening by the time they reached Deliboga Knoll. He said not a word to the nomads who greeted him with hope in their hearts. He went straight to his tent, stretched himself out on his bed and buried his head in his arms.

A strong wind was blowing from the north, a desiccating wind draining the marrow from men's bones, dulling the spirits, casting a gloom over the whole world. The Chukurova north wind saps the strength of a man, it makes him ill. Those who are not used to it take to their beds, sick unto death. Some people in the Chukurova have been driven insane when this wild boreal wind is blowing.

During the night, the wind gathered strength. The Yörüks were awake, keeping a gloomy watch, when they caught sight of the first flames flaring up in the north and making rapid headway towards Deliboga. Then, more fires broke out in front of the rice-paddies. The unploughed edges of the fallow cotton fields caught fire too. A circle of flames was tightening in on Deliboga Knoll and a great clamour rose up in the encampment. Dogs barked, sheep bleated and children bawled. Then a volley of shots rang out. Bullets whizzed over the tents. All was turmoil and confusion.

'Strike the tents,' Headman Süleyman cried. 'We're moving. They're going to burn us alive, these people.'

Fethullah broke into a run. With his pistol in his hand he was rushing madly towards the fire.

10

The boy Kerem woke up in the midst of the raging fire. He slipped into his sandals and, without another look about him, fled down the slope. He found a gap in the circle of flames and stumbled through into a rice-paddy. On and on he walked in the night along the fringe of the paddy, with no idea of where he was going. When day dawned he turned and looked back at Deliboga. The knoll was drowned in a mass of black smoke and the fields around it were still burning. They're dead, all of them, was his immediate thought, burnt alive. Aaah grandfather, how brightly his sword shone, and now he's dead and the sword burnt with him. If only I hadn't wished for that falcon, if only I'd wished as grandfather said, all this would never have happened. If only . . . A long flame darted up into the dappled dawn sky and broke away. The horse, he thought, has it escaped? Then he saw the trucks and motorcars in the distance. The big road must be over there . . . It's a good thing I ran away or I would have been burnt too. But what am I to do all alone in this cruel world without my grandfather and his noble Arab horse?

With a mighty crackling roar the fire was closing in on Deliboga Knoll. The shrieking flames swirled furiously high up the slope. Long red snakes, hares, foxes, frogs, birds, insects, fleeing in a frenzied helter-skelter before the fire, were streaming towards the tents. The whole earth and sky were on fire. A deafening clamour of panicking men and beasts rolled through the night. Huge long snakes, flushed crimson, furled into each other, tongues flickering in alarm, kept snarling at the oncoming fire as they scurried away. A horse stretched through the air, black as the night. In one long flying leap it had spanned the flames and galloped out of sight. The rice-paddy gleamed in the darkness. It surged and overflowed. Then it sank back and the whole earth rocked. A flaming iron insect, huge, roaring, with angry gaping jaws, had grabbed the knoll and was shaking it furiously. The rocks splintered into flickering shards. One moment everything was pitch dark, and the next bright as day. The smell of burning flesh and wool was everywhere, greasy, stinking in the nostrils, overpowering, nauseating . . . Writhing snakes flew through the air, burning, and dropped in blazing masses to the ground. Great eagles, birds, sparrows spiralled down, each one a fiery ember.

'It's a good thing the Corporal took my falcon away,' Kerem thought. 'He would have been burnt too now.'

They were loading the camels and horses and the long-eared donkeys, while the sheep in huddling bunches, scrambling one on top of the other, milled about shrinking from the on-coming fire, only to butt against another wall of flame.

'What shall I do now? How shall I get back my falcon?'

Stricken with fear, still dull with sleep, the bullets whizzing over their heads, the nomads hurriedly packed up their tents. Their hands worked mechanically, their one thought was to get away.

'Am I still asleep? Where am I? Where am I going? Where is the Corporal? Would he give me back my falcon if I begged him to? If I kissed his hand . . . He looked kind, he had a pleasant face.'

His feet sank into the dust of the road. Something, some shadowy form loomed before him, growing larger and larger, some angry hurtling thing. What could it be? And all along the road other creatures like wolves, huge wolves, were creeping nearer and nearer. Shuddering, Kerem threw himself into the ditch on the roadside. He drew himself into a tiny heap and closed his eyes tightly.

'Here I am thinking of my falcon when everyone's trapped in the fire, burning . . . Oh, my grandfather, what's happened to him? And mother, and father? Döné, Hassan, Mustafa? Ah, my brother Mustafa . . . Oh, mother . . . I'm no good. I'll never be any good, never! If only I'd asked for land instead of that falcon. The Lord Hizir, blessed be his name, would have given it to me as sure as he gave me the falcon. Wouldn't he? Of course he would. It's much easier to give one a wintering place than a falcon. The whole world's full of land. The whole wide world ... Chock-full. But falcons are rare, hard to get. If he could find a falcon for me, he'd have found land all the more quickly. And we wouldn't all have been burned alive. Aah, aaah, I've done this, I've burned everyone, and the foxes and snakes too ... I could have asked for land this year and waited another year for the falcon, and no one would have been burned. Ah, no one, you stupid head ... And now the land's gone and the falcon too. Now the wolves ...'

He opened his eyes and took a peep at the road. The wolves were there, larger than ever, running, tumbling over each other. Quickly, he shut his eyes again and squeezed himself against the wall of the ditch, trembling with fear, his teeth chattering. Then suddenly his trembling stopped and his body went limp. He felt nothing at all now, neither fear, nor cold. All his senses were dead.

'Feed for the wolves, that's what I'll be ... Oh, oh, mother! Grandfather ... Oh, the horse ... Mustafa ... And poor father ... All burned to ashes.'

The wolves were above him now, leaping one by one over the ditch. A burst of flames nearby and Kerem felt himself burning. The dark shadowy shapes of wolves, huge, their long white teeth dripping with blood ... The flames all about him.

'I'll never get out alive. And there's no water here either ...'

All at once he was up and running in the cold dust of the road. The fire yawned behind him. It was hounding him with a roaring hue-and-cry. The earth rocked beneath him. The fire, the dark, the sheep and bulls, the camels, falcons, children, they were all there after him, a frantic confusion in the night. The long flowing river burst into wild tossing flames. The tents were ablaze. His grandfather stood in the midst of the fire holding his long sword that flashed like the sun. All about him people were burning, the Chukurova aghas with their broad-brimmed hats and their neckties. His grandfather, red beard all aglow, was slashing off their heads with his sword, and the heads of all the corporals too. They ran, screaming in terror, but his grandfather caught up with them, his beard and sword flashing bright, growing longer and longer, dazzling, blinding, and one by one he hacked off their heads. He was in a towering rage, his grandfather, oh God, how terrible his anger . . . The veins in his neck were swelling, he was sweating, his sweating face shining copper bright. Again and again the sword fell. The Corporal, yes the Corporal! The Corporal was running for his life, scrambling up the steep jagged crags. And still the fire raged on, the trees, the forest, the rocks, the streams, the grass, the whole world a mass of flames. The Corporal fled and the flames pursued him. Sometimes it was a huge flame hard on his heels and sometimes his grandfather. The Binboga, the lofty Thousand Bulls Mountain, burst into flame. It blazed like the sun and the stars whirled above its crest. Binboga throbbed, it flared and tossed the coruscating stars far up into the high heavens. It rose and marched upon the Chukurova, an incandescent mass that broke into a thousand bulls of fire as it advanced. At one blow his grandfather had slashed off the Corporal's head and had descended upon the Chukurova plain like a thunderbolt. The thousand bulls, wonderfully huge, beautiful bulls, flashing, wild-eyed, with glittering sword-like horns, were galloping along the burning plain. They charged at the villages, they horned up houses, towns, cars, trucks, trains, they wrecked and gutted, and then they went back to their abode. They became the Binboga Mountain again.

His falcon whirled through the skies, fluttering up, up, growing larger, larger . . .

'Ah, grandfather, mother, father, Mustafa, Hassan! What has happened to them? Were they burnt in the fire? Or did they escape? But where? How am I to find them again? And anyway, wherever they go the villagers will kill them. They won't let them live. They'll take away all our girls too. Those Chukurova men have always been mad about nomad girls.'

A wall of darkness was before him, long, endless, without a break, like a dark forest, a dense reed-bed, a tangled thicket, a tall mountain. He turned and ran to the edge of the water. Somehow, for some reason he ran on, back and forth between the dark wall and water, until his legs failed him. He was bathed in sweat, panting, choked by the acrid odour of smoke. Lights flashed before his eyes, a bright vortex whirled spangled yellow and red, sparkling, dazzling, dizzying.

As the day began to dawn he found himself in the dust of the road. His ears were drumming, he was emerging from a dream he could not clearly remember now. What had happened this night? His body ached as though it had been pounded in a mortar.

'Everyone's vanished. I'm all alone. Where's grandfather? Where's my falcon? What's happened? What?'

For a long while he could remember nothing. Then like lightning it all came back to him. He jumped up in an agony of sorrow. 'The falcon! I should never have wished for it, never! I've killed them all. If they knew . . . Oh dear, if they knew I'd asked Hizir for a falcon they'd break my bones to pulp. If they knew . . . They'd wring my neck, they'd eat me alive. Oh dear, damn that falcon! You fool, you ass, what did you want with that falcon? It didn't even catch a tiny sparrow for you. It didn't even take to the air properly. And then the Corporal came and took it away as though it was his very own. Not even if I die, no, even my bones will never forget this sin of mine. I'm a wicked person, wicked, wicked! I hope a stone as big as the falcon falls on my head and kills me.'

But had there been two stars meeting in the sky? Had the waters really ceased to flow? The flowers, the leaves, the insects and birds and beasts, all the living people of the world, had they really died for a moment and been restored to life again? Was it true? Did the whole universe stop living for one instant every year just when the stars met, to come alive again afterwards? Every single year . . .

'Grandfather says so. Grandfather is Haydar the Master Blacksmith, who makes wonderful swords. He is head of the holy hearth and knows everything.'

Aimlessly he walked along the reed-bed and came to a little

irrigation canal for the rice-paddies. He jumped over it and suddenly Deliboga Knoll reared before him, a pitch-black smoking hulk. All the way south down to Jeyhan River, the land was burnt black by the fire. He took a few steps up the slope, but he was afraid. The dawn breeze caressed him, filling him with a shivering joy, soon replaced by black gloom. Dead snakes lay coiled up all over the knoll, charred black. Dead dogs too, and sheep, foxes, wolves and people too, dead, burnt to cinders . . . A noisome odour of burning blew into his nostrils, and suddenly he vomited. He retched and retched until nothing came out. His stomach ached, he writhed with pain and his eyes went black. He turned and fled. The dead, the burning smell, the charred snakes, the wolves and horses, his people, his grandfather, the Corporal, everyone, the whole world was at his heels. He stumbled, fell, rose again. He ran on until he was at his last breath and dropped down on the roadside.

The sun rose the height of a minaret, the mountains brightened. The knoll was far behind now, a long column of smoke stretched above it, perfectly straight and motionless. Cars passed along the road, a constant stream, smothering Kerem in cloud after cloud of dust. And still he did not move. His hands lay listlessly on the ground. His large eyes had grown even larger. Then he saw the two men. They were walking close together, almost stuck to each other, and talking very quickly, shouting as though in a quarrel. Kerem rose and fell in after them. It was as if he had suddenly been lassoed and was being pulled along. Again and again he turned to look back at the long endless column of smoke over the knoll.

'If they're not dead, if they didn't burn, if they got away, then where am I to find them? Where would they go? There's no place in the whole wide world they can go to, nowhere at all for them to pitch their tents. As soon as they set foot somewhere it's money, money all the time . . . Where are they to find so much money? And all for the right to winter on a patch of dry arid land, on an abandoned knoll!'

He quickened his step and caught up with the two men. 'Selam to you, aghas,' he said.

The men turned and saw a little red-cheeked boy, his cheeks flushed still redder with sweat, his cheekbones high and jutting, his eyes huge and frightened. They smiled, amused at the boy's dignified look, the confident grown-up tone of his greeting.

'Selam to you too, brother,' the long one said. 'Where are you coming from and where are you going? Won't you tell us your name?'

Kerem fell into step with them. 'I'm called Kerem. I'm the grandson of Haydar, the Master Blacksmith.'

'My name's Abdi. And this is Haji . . .'

'I'm going to the Yalnizagach police-station,' Kerem announced. 'The Corporal's one of us, you know . . . So I'm going to see him . . . About how they set fire to our knoll last night.'

'Who did that?' Abdi asked.

'Who knows,' Kerem said. 'The villagers, I suppose. They wanted money from us, but we had no money left because we'd already given it all to some other villagers. So these villagers who couldn't get any money out of us came last night and shot everybody dead, and then they burnt everything. I was the only one to escape.'

He stopped, unable to say another word. There was a knot in his throat choking him. It was all he could do not to break down. He bit his lips until they bled and the unspilt tears scalded his eyes.

'Look, Kerem,' Abdi said, 'you probably had a fright and ran away in the night. The knoll was certainly set on fire, but nothing's happened to the Yörüks, not a hair of their heads singed, you can be sure. They must have packed up and gone somewhere else. They'll soon find another place to pitch their tents.'

'Don't worry yourself at all, Kerem,' Haji urged. 'Why, they're probably settled in some new place already.'

It was at least a crumb of comfort. The knot in Kerem's throat loosened. 'Aah, ah, they'll never find a place to settle, never!' he cried. 'We'll always be like this, driven wretchedly from place to place, dying on the roads . . . Aaah, ah, and it's all my fault, all!'

Abdi and Haji were startled at this sudden explosion of grief. For a long time they found nothing to say. Then without waiting for a word from them, Kerem let himself go. Everything came pouring out, the night of the stars, his grandfather and what he had said to him, how he had wished for the falcon instead of land to winter on, his grandfather's sword, the coming of the falcon. He told it all.

'And so you see,' he said at last, 'it's all my fault. My fault everyone got burnt alive.' He burst into tears. 'They ought to kill me,' he sobbed. 'I want to die. It's all because of my falcon. And the Corporal's taken even that away from me.'

'Don't cry, brother,' Abdi said. 'The Corporal will get his deserts and so will all the tyrants of this earth. Don't cry.'

'Don't cry, brother,' Haji said too.

But Kerem was sobbing his heart out now. 'They're both gone. The falcon and the wintering place. The falcon . . .'

'Look, brother,' Abdi began again. He had caught on to the reason for Kerem's access of woe. 'Look, Kerem brother, this road leads straight to Yalnizagach police-station. Come with us and I'll show you where it is. And then you'll find some way of getting back your falcon from the Corporal, won't you?'

Kerem stopped crying at once. His eyes lit up. 'But how can I?' he asked. 'The Corporal's got a great big gun. What if he kills me?'

'You'll steal it in the night,' Abdi said. 'How can he see you and kill you in the night? In the dark of night, without even the birds and ants having wind of it.'

'Not a soul,' Kerem said joyfully. He had forgotten his grief and everything else now.

All along the way the three of them thought up all kinds of schemes for stealing the falcon from the Corporal. When they came to the police-station Kerem kissed their hands gratefully and they left him.

'Poor boy,' Abdi said. 'I wish to God nothing happens to him . . . Perhaps I shouldn't have put the idea of stealing the falcon into his head. What if that Corporal does shoot the child?'

'Nonsense,' Haji said. 'The child would have found the police-station anyway. He was bent on getting back his falcon and would have hit on the idea of stealing it himself. Don't you worry. He'll filch that falcon as easily as he'd draw a hair out of butter.'

'I hope so,' Abdi said. 'Oh, I hope so. Poor Kerem, what a sweet clever child! Please God nothing bad happens to him . . .'

I I

*By mid-morning the caravan was well away, crossing the
bridge over Jeyhan River. A pall of grey smoke lay over
Hemité village. Mount Hemité loomed above the plain, a
great mauve craggy mass, arid, grassless, sharp and dreary,
its rocks now purpling darkly, now steaming blue and now lost
in a dense haze. The caravan came to rest below the grove of
mulberry trees at Sakarjalik. The smaller children were
strapped to their mothers' backs. The others rode on the
camels and donkeys. As always the camels were adorned with
embroidered rugs and blue and white beads and surcingles of
a thousand-and-one designs, like rainbows. The packs, the
whole caravan were in perfect order as though nothing untoward had happened, as though they had never fled in haste
before the fire. The bells tied to the necks of the camels and
billy-goats sounded their muffled chimes. To put this caravan
into travelling order in the dark, in the midst of a raging fire,
was the fruit of long-ingrained, centuries-old custom. Since
the days when they had roamed the land of Khorassan, this
caravan had been daily unloaded and loaded again.*

The caravan trailed to a halt on the sands of Sakarjalik. Here,
the river Jeyhan, cleaving through the crags higher up, ran a
swift course down into the plain, banking the sands over to this
side. The villagers of Sakarjalik had already spotted the caravan.
They were waiting. The minute the nomads pitched their
tents on the sandbank, they would pounce upon them like birds
of prey and exact the most, money, sheep, rugs, whatever they
could get. The word was whispered around the village: 'The
nomads have come! And it looks like a rich large tribe. We can
get a lot out of them if they settle on the sandbank.'

fight. We've got to find some suitable place and stay there,

The nomads were waiting too, not knowing what to do, where to go. They just stood about on the sands, irresolute. A drizzling rain began to fall. The sheep huddled together in a heap. The donkeys let their ears swag down, and the large sheepdogs prowled about restlessly in their spiked iron collars. The drizzle turned into rain. Over Mount Hemité a mass of black clouds was churning, shot with flashes of lightning.

Süleyman the Headman turned to Old Haydar. 'What shall we do?' he asked helplessly.

The old man could not answer. Only an angry unintelligible mutter came from his lips.

'Why don't you speak, Haydar?' Old Müslüm asked too. 'What shall we do?'

Old Haydar said something again, but no one could make anything out of it. It was always like this when the old man was angry, and he was angry now, a dark formidable anger that made them shrink from him.

'What shall we do, Kamil?'

'I don't know, Headman,' Kamil said. 'That village over there is Sakarjalik. The villagers'll be upon us the minute we settle down. They'll ask for a king's ransom. Remember last year, the fight we had with them? And anyway why should we stop here? There's not a tuft of grass on this sandbank. The flocks will die of hunger.'

'It's raining,' the Headman groaned. 'Look up there at the mountain. There's a bad storm coming.'

Old Haydar had drawn away from the others and stood on the edge of the river, holding his red beard in both hands. They all looked towards him with hope.

'What shall we do?'

'Let's get out of here,' Old Murat said.

'But where . . .' the Headman asked.

'To the pit of hell!' Fethullah burst out vehemently. His eyes were starting from their sockets. 'If we go on like this, cringing before everybody and everything, they won't even allow us to pass along these roads, let alone settle anywhere. We've got to stick fast, all of us from seven to seventy, and never let go until we die.'

'Aah, my son,' Süleyman said. 'Ah Fethullah, if it's death will save us or killing, let's die right away. All of us . . . But neither death nor giving death will do any good . . . Everything's against us, the whole world, every creature, the birds and beasts, even the insects, even the falling rain, the blowing wind. Nothing can save us.'

Fethullah's anger broke all bounds. He was like a madman. 'Father,' he cried, 'father, I can't bear it. It's more than flesh and blood can stand. There's the river flowing right here beside us. Let's all throw ourselves into it and get it over with. Or let's make a stand against those villagers. Let's die fighting.'

Süleyman seemed to shrink to half his size. 'All right,' he said. 'Let's die, let's throw ourselves into the river.'

Just then Old Haydar came hurrying up to them. He was his old self again and they looked at him with renewed hope. The rain came lashing down in a storm. The camels, donkeys, sheep, dogs, children, women all huddled together, merging into one black heap. The sky closed down upon them and everything went dark.

With a slight smile, Old Haydar turned to Bald Osman. 'Get my horse, Osman,' he ordered. 'You're coming with me to Adana.' Then he went up to the Headman and put his hand on his shoulder. 'I'm going,' he said. His voice rang with confidence, his thick eyebrows were lifted, his green eyes gleamed brightly. 'I'll do something. I'll go to Adana and find Ramazanoglu. And if that fails I'll go to Ankara and see Ismet Pasha himself. I'll go all the way to Istanbul if need be. And if that fails too . . . But I won't accept failure. I'll find a patch of land for the tribe. If I don't . . . Farewell. I'll join you wherever you are when I come back. Send someone for Kerem. He's at Yalnizagach. You'll find him right there in front of the police-station, watching out for his falcon. As for you the best you can do is to get out of here and go down to the Mediterranean. You may find some place on the shore there.'

Osman had the horse ready. Old Haydar went and took his

sword from the camel-pack. He kissed goodbye his son, his daughter-in-law and his grandchildren. 'Don't worry about Kerem,' he said. 'He's at Yalnizagach village. I'm going to the great Ramazanoglu of name and fame. Don't be anxious if I'm not back soon. That means I'll have had to go to Ankara to Ismet Pasha or even still further, to Istanbul. But you must all rest easy, we'll have our wintering place in the Chukurova and our summer pastures up on Aladag in the end.'

He returned to the group of old people. There was a thin quivering smile on his shrivelled trembling lips, a sadness deep down in his eyes. 'Farewell to you,' he said again. 'You must all rest easy.'

Two persons held the stirrups for him. With unexpected nimbleness he mounted the horse and spurred it on.

'Wait, Haydar,' Headman Süleyman called, running after him. 'I was nearly forgetting.'

Old Haydar reined in and looked back. The Headman thrust his hand into his belt and tremblingly held out a sheaf of banknotes. 'Take this, Haydar, you'll be needing it.'

'Thank you, Süleyman,' Old Haydar said. 'But I'm well provided for. I've been saving for this day many years. I've got a lot.' He smiled again, a bright smile, with his lips, his beard, the glinting red of his beard, his golden conical cap ... Then he rode away, erect on his horse, with Osman walking in front.

'A child,' Fethullah muttered after him through clenched teeth. 'A mere child. The idea of spending thirty years to make a sword and then to take it to some bey or pasha and expect him to give you land! The idea ... They wouldn't even look at that sword of yours if it was pure gold, much less give you land for it.'

The black storm clouds were moving south towards the Mediterranean. The day brightened and it stopped raining. Soon the sun was shining again.

'What shall we do?' the Headman repeated when Old Haydar was lost to sight.

'We can't settle here,' Tanish Agha said decisively. 'These people are wild, vicious, bloodthirsty, mad for a fight. Even if we only stay one night we'll never get out without leaving at least two dead behind. That Cross-eyed Durmush will be here any minute . . .' He raised his head. 'There he is now!'

They all fell silent, their eyes on Cross-eyed Durmush. Fethullah's face was crimson, his eyes wilder than ever. All his limbs began to tremble.

'Fethullah,' his father told him, 'don't stay here. Go down to the riverside and wait. I'll deal with him.'

Fethullah rushed away.

Cross-eyed Durmush was lashing his tail. He stopped and held his hand over his eyes peering at the Headman. 'Well well well! So it's you, Süleyman, is it? You're welcome, I'm sure. But first fork out the step-on toll. Orders of the Village Council. They've sent me.' Slowly, meaningfully his hand moved to the huge pistol that hung over his hip. 'Three sheep, and see to it they're good fat ones, and a hundred and fifty liras. That is, if you don't intend to spend the night here . . . If you do, that's another matter. You'll have to come with me then, and we'll strike a bargain.'

'We're going,' the Headman replied. 'Right away. I can't give you anything, Durmush Agha.'

'How's that?' Durmush sneered. 'You've been occupying our land since early morning. Who's going to pay for that?'

'This isn't your land,' the Headman retorted. 'It's God's own road. We just loitered a little as we were passing. No passage toll's been invented yet that I know of. So I can't give you a thing.'

'But you will!' Durmush insisted. 'You jolly well will and gladly too. If you stir a step from here it'll be over my dead body. Are you looking for trouble, Süleyman? Go to some other village for that! But I won't let you leave before you give us our due.'

'Let's see you stop us,' the Headman said.

Suddenly a look of alarm suffused the faces of the nomads about him. Süleyman turned and saw Fethullah hurtling towards them. He broke into a run. 'Wait, Fethullah,' he shouted. 'Stop!'

'Let him come,' Durmush cried, whipping out his pistol.

'Let him come and kill me for a couple of sheep . . . All right, say one sheep, not three. Let him kill me for a single sheep.' He advanced towards Fethullah whom Süleyman was holding back. 'Let him go, Süleyman. Let him come and kill me for a sheep. One single sheep . . . That's the kind of people you are, no spark of humanity in you. For one single sheep you go and kill a man. That's how you've made an enemy of everyone in the Chukurova, that's why the whole wide world's too narrow to hold you . . . Does a man kill for one single sheep?' He was near the struggling father and son now. 'Wait a minute! Stop, my friends. What are you doing? Süleyman, leave Fethullah alone. Look here, Fethullah, what are you getting mad about? Put that pistol away. Look, I'm doing the same. There!' He thrust his pistol into his waistband. 'There you are. All I've asked for is one single sheep. If you're going to kill me for that, then here I am. Let him go, Süleyman.'

'It's all right, father,' Fethullah said with weary disgust. 'I won't do anything.'

Süleyman dropped his hands.

'Look, Fethullah,' Durmush went on, 'anyone else would have got a hundred sheep out of you for staying on their land so long. I'm only asking for one. One little sheep! Is that fair, what you're doing, brother? Does a man treat his friend like an enemy?'

'You'll get no sheep from us,' Fethullah said. 'Not so much as a tuft of wool.'

'Oh yes, I will!'

'Let's see you do it then!'

Durmush fell to pleading. 'You've got so many sheep . . . While we here never have a bit of meat all the year round. Only when you nomads come along, God bless you for that, only then our children can eat a little meat.'

'Well, you won't get it from us.'

'I will. You'll give me that one sheep or kill me right here and bring a whole peck of troubles on your heads.'

'I won't,' Fethullah said.

'You will,' Durmush said. 'You don't know me, Fethullah.

And don't take yourself for the prophet Ali either. I was a sergeant in the army. There's not a man in our village would dare to look askance at me. Everyone's afraid of me. I've spent no small time in prison, fourteen years, I'll have you know. Three murders I've got to my credit, and eight pardons. Yes, eight! I'll bet you've never yet even met a man who's been amnestied eight times. Who d'you take me for, Fethullah? D'you think I'm afraid of that pistol of yours? Pull it out then. Come on! I'll do the same and we'll kill each other for a sheep, one tiny little sheep. Come on!' He drew out his pistol again. 'It's touch and go now. Come on, what are you waiting for?'

The whole tribe, men, women and children, had gathered about in a circle. The steam rose from their backs under the hot after-rain sun.

The Headman saw Fethullah's glowering face and starting eyes. There was going to be trouble, and all for nothing. 'Shut up, Durmush,' he warned anxiously.

'I won't shut up,' Durmush said. 'After all, it's only a matter of one sheep.'

'Father,' Fethullah spat out between clenched teeth, 'give the fellow his sheep and let him go. Quick, father.' He was almost ready to vomit.

Durmush laughed with glee and grasped the Headman's hands. 'Thank you, Headman, thank you, Fethullah brother. It's too little, much too little, one sheep for staying so long on our land, but I'll take it, thank you.'

Fethullah was bathed in perspiration. 'Father, please, give the fellow that sheep quickly and let him get out of my sight. Quick father, quick.'

'Now look here, Fethullah,' Durmush stammered. 'What d'you mean? I'm not begging, I'm just asking for my due. This land, these roads, that village, the grass here, the trees, the river, they're ours. All ours, see? You mustn't treat me like a beggar . . . See?'

'Father, father!' Fethullah's voice was almost a moan. 'Please father . . .'

12

How many days, how many nights since they had last pitched their tents and unloaded their belongings? How long driven from pillar to post all over the Chukurova? There was hardly a village in the huge plain they had not clashed with during the past years over winter-quarters or grazing space, with whom there had not been some blood shed. On and on they wandered without respite between the shores of the Mediterranean, the Nurhak Mountains and the Leché barrens. And all the time it rained. Relentlessly. The sheep, camels, dogs, donkeys and horses, the children, everyone, everything was steeped in mud. Their clothes stuck to their bodies, wet steaming. Under the cover of night, they led their starving flocks into the freshly sprouting crops and moved on, leaving behind them crushed, wasted fields and bitter rancour. They had bloody fights with the villagers and many of them were wounded. But they had no choice. They could not allow their flocks to die of hunger. And so the Karachullu tribe, like a dirge, like a grieving lament, groped on in a black night.

As the tip of day showed itself, they passed Telkubbé. The rain had abated with the dawn. The road stretched far into the distance, wet, slippery, glistening, with the speeding cars, trucks and tractors squirting water to right and left under their wheels. Somewhere below Toprakkalé Castle they encountered another nomad group, the Horzumlus, just as bedraggled and muddy as they were. The meeting of the two tribes, both of ancient and noble stock, was like a smarting hurt. They dragged to a stop face to face on the plain, silent and still. Not a sound came out of the one or the other . . . Like a song ended, hushed forever, exhausted, they stood staring, unable to believe the truth of what they saw.

At last the Bey of Horzumlu rode up to Headman Süleyman. 'Selam to you, Süleyman,' he said. His voice trailed away hoarsely as though he regretted having spoken.

'Greetings, Bey,' the Headman said, walking his horse to meet the Bey. They gazed at each other and then smiled, bitterly, wearily.

'They've finished us in this Chukurova,' the Bey of Horzumlu said dully. 'We're finished, Süleyman.'

'Finished,' Süleyman echoed. He could not speak. Another word and he would be crying like a child.

'It's the same with all the other tribes,' the Bey continued. 'They're desperate, dying like flies. There are no children left any more among the Turcomans and the Aydinlis. No sheep left. They've finished us, sapped us at the roots, Süleyman, in this cruel Chukurova land. What are we to do? I'm at a loss. For ten days we've been like this, on horseback, without finding a place to spend a single night. Birds, beasts and men, they hate us all in this Chukurova.'

'They hate us . . .' Süleyman broke down. He began to sob quietly, in silence, and the tears ran down his cheeks straight as cords, into his beard. The Bey of Horzumlu struggled to keep a hold on himself, trembling with the effort.

'What shall we do, Süleyman?'

The Headman could not answer. He could not even look at him again. His eyes were on his horse's neck and he was weeping. And so they stood for a while in the early morning mist, over the muddy earth, not speaking, thinking of the past, of the old and glorious days. Like a bright stream the days of greatness and of happiness flowed through the minds of the two old men.

'Keep well, Headman Süleyman,' the Bey said. 'Keep well.' And he rode away. Süleyman never even lifted his head to look after him. It was all he could do to keep straight on his saddle. Without a sound the depleted remnants of the great Horzumlu tribe, mud-soiled, battered, passed them by and went their way.

Like a swarm of eagles the Horzumlus would descend into the Chukurova plain in days of old, with a thousand brand-new black tents. The Chukurova was too small to hold their flocks of sheep and goats, their camels, their ruby-eyed noble horses. The Bey's tent was a legend on the tongues of men, with its fourteen domes and its thirty rooms. It would take the Yörüks a week, even with their well-practised hands, to put up this tent, and a week too to pull it down. The kilims, rugs and carpets, each one worth a fortune, would dazzle a man's eyes. Every single pole supporting the tent was exquisitely chiselled and chased with gold and silver and nacre. No palace could surpass the splendour of this tent, no monarch the generosity of the Bey of Horzumlu.

Headman Süleyman sat still on his horse, trying not to think of the past, yet unable to resist the heady pleasure of those memories coming to him now in their present days of strife and strain. And when he saw himself as he had been then, he was ashamed. It was as though he were merely boasting. The meeting with the Bey of Horzumlu had released a cataract of old reminiscences.

He turned to his son who had come up beside him. 'We're going to pitch our tents up there, on the flanks of that castle,' he said pointing to Toprakkalé. 'We've got to stop somewhere and bury that dead child.'

Duran's son had died three days ago and they had not been able to stop anywhere long enough to bury him. His mother had been carrying the dead body on her back all this time.

'Think of it, Fethullah, the great Bey of Horzumlu! It made me forget our own troubles to see him like this. The Bey of Horzumlu of name and fame, whom Sultans and Shahs were honoured to visit, whose wealth compared with that of Egypt. All the way from Khorassan castles and pennants would bow before him. And this is what he's come to . . .'

Fethullah's heart was full. 'He was crying, father,' he gulped, 'the Bey of Horzumlu, as he left you.'

The Bey had realized that Süleyman was weeping for him, the great Horzumlu.

'They're even worse off than us,' Süleyman said. 'They've dwindled to almost nothing at all.'

'D'you remember, father, when we came across them five years ago? Three hundred tents they were then. And now . . . I don't believe they make up even forty. What can have happened to them?'

'Nothing more than what's happening to us, son,' Headman Süleyman said, and he spurred his horse on towards the ruins of Toprakkalé Castle that loomed black and grim in the distance, shedding a deathly gloom into men's hearts. He did not stop or look back until they had reached the castle.

The caravan stopped on the slope. In an instant the tents were put up and fires were lit in front of them. Soon the women were busy baking the yufka-bread over the circular iron-plates.

'Father,' Fethullah said, 'we can't stay here on this barren hill. Not even for a day. There's no grass, nothing. The flocks are already weak with hunger. They'll drop dead on us . . .'

'You'll lead them into the fields in the night. The fields of those heathen villagers. Let them graze there, let them lay the crops waste, let them do their worst. We've nothing to lose now but our lives . . . Only see to it that the flocks are divided into five groups and take them to separate and distant places.'

'All right,' Fethullah said. 'That'll keep them going for a few days until we think of some place to make for.'

When the baking was over, the women heated up a little water and quickly washed the body of the dead child. Then Old Müslüm said a short prayer over him and they all went up to the castle and buried the body at the foot of the ruins. Before leaving, the father of the child stuck a long shepherd's staff at the head of the little grave.

Evening came and the sun set. The women were milking the sheep, but Fethullah was in a hurry. He ordered all the bells to be taken off the billy-goats, and as soon as it was dark they herded the sheep and goats down the hill.

After they had left, Jeren's father came to Headman Süley-

man's tent and sat down beside him. The ancient deserted
snake-infested ruined castle above bore down upon them in the
gloom, grim, hollow sounding, booming.

'I've talked to Jeren,' Abdurrahman began. 'I've begged and
begged her. We went on our knees before her, all the tribe, but
she won't do it.'

'Even though she sees what we've come to?'

'I told her,' Abdurrahman went on. 'My daughter, I said, at
this rate we'll die, all of us. Look, I said, Oktay Bey is following
us, he's suffering with us on the roads, under the rain. He's been
with us all these days, mad with love, dying for the love of you.
And what's more he's a good lad, and handsome too. And his
family owns half the Chukurova. If he didn't love you, I said to
her, I'd have died rather than asked you to do this. But he loves
you. If you marry him the whole tribe will be able to winter
on his plantation. You'll save us all from death, from this
misery. We shall live again as in the good old days. You won't
be separated from us. If it's for Halil, I said, he's dead. Otherwise . . . But he's dead.'

'What did she say?' Headman Süleyman asked. 'When you
said he was dead?'

'She said he's not dead, and even if he is, she said, I'll never
marry anyone else.'

There was a long silence.

Then Süleyman sighed. 'So she won't do it, even though
Halil's dead and gone?' he said. 'And where is Oktay Bey
now?'

'He's gone to Adana,' Abdurrahman replied. 'To get things
for the wedding, the ring, bracelets . . . You'll bring her around
by the time I come back, he told me, and then you'll all come
and settle on our plantation, and we'll hold the wedding
there.'

He went on talking, but Headman Süleyman was listening
no longer, wrapped in his thoughts. Suddenly he realized that
Abdurrahman had been silent a long time. 'Well, Abdurrahman?' he said.

'I've come to you because we've talked it over with the

tribespeople and we have something to ask you.'

'Well, say it, Abdurrahman.'

'It's like this . . .' Abdurrahman gulped and then spoke very quickly. He was sweating. 'The tribespeople think that if you talk to Jeren yourself, she won't refuse you.'

A heavy stone came and settled on the Headman's heart. He felt himself sinking into a swamp of shame, dirty, slimy, viscid, like a dark night. Anything, anything but this. Never had anyone in this tribe interfered with their daughters in matters of the heart. No one had ever forced a girl to marry for money or riches or for any other reason. Had they fallen so low, were they lost to all the old values, utterly degenerate? How could they put pressure on the girl by telling her Halil was dead and throwing his blood-stained shirt at her to prove it? Everything was decaying, everything was dying out. I've gone through a lot, humiliation, trials, blows . . . I've been dragged to police-stations, beaten, crushed, spit upon . . . There was nothing I could do about it. But this . . . The breakdown of all the old traditions . . . The tribes dwindling away to nothing. The tents, once so proudly upright, seven-poled, now old and tattered with only a pole or two. Everything was ending, withering away . . .

Abdurrahman's voice jarred in his ears. 'So I said, well then, my girl, you'll marry him by force. And she said, I'll kill myself then, father. And I said, since you're going to kill yourself, why not marry Oktay Bey and be dead that way? And Jeren said, it's a dirty thing to be Oktay Bey's wife, but death is beautiful . . . We all begged her, all of us on our knees. But she only repeated, I'll kill myself, I'll kill myself, and that was all.'

Jeren was standing firm, good for her! So it was not all over with them yet. So the old blood still ran clear in their veins. So they still could . . . 'How many years is it that Oktay Bey fell in love with Jeren?'

'A full six years. It was love at first sight with him, and Jeren knows it. You know it, Headman Süleyman, everyone's witness to how he's dragged on after us all these years. I pity him, really, such a violent passion . . . Ask me anything, he says, ask for my soul, but let Jeren be mine or I'll kill myself . . . You're our last hope, Headman Süleyman. Your word is law in the tribe, nobody will go against you. Jeren will do as you say.'

The Headman smiled bitterly. 'She'll do as I say.'

I can't do it. I can't go to Jeren. I've done much to save the tribe, I've licked people's boots, I've begged and crawled, but this I can't do . . . From Khorassan we came, riding our noble horses . . . And all through the years, through the many turns of fortune, our women and children were ever sacred to us. No one would hurt a hair of their heads. That is our tradition, our lifeblood, our whole existence. If I do this it'll be the end. Everything we have lived for will be lost for ever.

Oh Jeren, Jeren, the women of our tribe . . .

Headman Süleyman looked up. His eyes were frozen and glinted like steel. 'This is one thing I won't do, Abdurrahman,' he said flatly.

'But Headman, there'll be nothing left of us if we go on like this,' Abdurrahman protested. 'Is one single girl to be counted more than a whole tribe?'

The Headman rose on his knees. 'Let's die, but die true to ourselves. Like men. Not after we've killed one poor girl. Even the great Horzumlus are no more. Are we any better than them? Let's die, Abdurrahman, our honour safe, true to ourselves.'

Abdurrahman leapt to his feet. 'But what is there left of ourselves, Headman?' he cried angrily. 'What, that you say we should die like ourselves? After the wretched life we've led all these years? It's too late for us even to be able to die like ourselves. Give us leave to live like other people.'

'They'll never let us live like other people, Abdurrahman. So let's die if only like the crumbs of what we were once. Don't take this last thing away from me. Not at my age . . .' He sank down again where he was. His face was like parchment.

Oh Jeren, Jeren, the women of our tribe . . . They were swimming, crowding in his vision, white kerchiefs and hennaed hair, long soft green eyes and red cheeks, simple silver-trimmed fezzes, full red smiling lips, silver diadems, nose-rings, golden earrings, long flowered gowns, red and blue embroidered woven aprons, silver braided girdles.

Oh Jeren, Jeren . . . And Halil dead! Dead . . .

The serpent, the black serpent is a poignant creature when in the throes of love. Red as a glowing ember it becomes. And it is known to lose its heart to girls too, and to follow them wherever they go, springing suddenly upon them, ruby-red, fiery, bright as the pomegranate flower. At home, on the road, behind a bush, in a deserted ruin, sleeping in a tent, dancing at a wedding, milking the sheep, lulling a child, the girl will find the serpent planted before her, all aglow. It will come to her out of the green grass, the dense forest, the dust, the dark marshes, red as ever, harmless, lifting itself on the tip of its tail, then stretching itself out in all its length at her feet. Try and kill it, the love-lorn serpent, if you can harden your heart. All that is red it loves and above all the pomegranate flower and girls wearing red.

'Flow on, black serpent, get out of my way!'

Meekly the black serpent, the cold serpent, red now, flushing redder still, slithers away. But at night it comes back and slips into her bed. It lies there without hurting her, hardly touching her.

'Black serpent, get out of my bed . . .'

Jeren gazed on the dark walls of Toprakkalé Castle. They were swarming with thousands of black serpents, that gleamed red in the night, turning and twisting, flowing this way, that way, everywhere . . .

'Halil, Halil, Haliiil!'

'Think of it, a large whitewashed mansion! How wonderful! You'll be sitting all day long, not toiling away miserably, barefoot, hungry, dirty under the rain. Five children I've had and all of them dead of the cold and the rain. Your children won't die, think of it . . . At your door a large motor-car. Servants, tractors, land, brightly-lit cities, all will be yours, places we have always passed near and never been able to enter, bright as the sun, dazzling to the eyes.'

A sunny vision in the middle of the wide plain, brightly

vaporous, shining all night long, a forest of lights blazing through the night. Which we can never attain.

'Goathair tents! Damn these goathair tents. All the winds of the earth blow through them, all the rain in the skies rains into them. Not a lump of sugar can we get any more. Oh Jeren, Jeren, Jeren, your children won't die. Think of it, all the babies you give birth to will live. Oh Jeren, Jeren . . .'

'I'll kill myself,' Jeren said. 'I want nothing else.'

No one talks to her, not even the children, not even her brothers . . . Even the sheep, the dogs, the gracile camels are hostile to her . . .

'You killed my child, Jeren, you!'

'I didn't, sister! It's Allah . . .'

'No, it's you. Six years Oktay Bey's been pining away for you. If you'd married him, we'd be living on his land now and my child wouldn't have frozen to death in the rain like this. It's you killed my child.'

'I never killed anyone. You've killed me.'

'Halil too! You've killed him too. If you'd married Oktay Bey six years ago, Halil would never have set fire to that village. He'd never have taken to the mountains. He'd never have been shot and killed, and his bloody shirt would never have been brought to us. You've killed him. You've killed Halil too.'

'Halil isn't dead!'

'And my husband too, who died in that fight at Chukur-köprü.'

'And what about my son who killed a man in the fight we had at Dumlukalé?'

'And Kerem who's run away, lost?'

'And my brother too, hasn't he disappeared?'

'It's all your fault, Jeren.'

'All your fault!'

'All!'

Jeren cannot breathe any more.

Now what's wrong with Oktay Bey? He's tall, he's handsome. He has a moustache and large black eyes. He's the son of a Turcoman agha of ancient stock. You wouldn't count them as strangers. They're of us. They talk exactly like us. After all, they settled only very recently. It's hardly twenty years that they've changed from tents to houses, selling their flocks and gold to buy land. And how right they were! Their manners, their customs are the same as ours. They laugh like us, walk like us. We both come from the same tradition.'

'Oktay Bey will drown you in gold. He'll give you silks and satins and brocades and Lahore shawls, more than you can ever want. Oh say yes, Jeren!'

'If you won't, then go away. Leave the tribe and take yourself off elsewhere.'

'Oktay Bey's gone to make all the arrangements . . . Such a wedding I'm going to hold, he said, with seven big drums, a hundred boy-dancers, a great feast, such a wedding it'll be that the whole Chukurova will gape in wonder. I'm a Yörük too, he said, a true-born Yörük. It's because we had no choice that we settled down . . . They left us no choice, just like you now . . . But we never broke with the old tradition. We kept the faith, we never denied our ancestors, our Yörük origins . . . Oh say yes, Jeren . . .'

'It's his blood that spoke. Blood's thicker than water. No native, no villager, no Chukurova man would ever burn with such a love for a Yörük maiden. It's his blood that's speaking. Oktay Bey is one of us, and one of the noblest too.'

'You've killed us all, you! You've extinguished our hearths, you've destroyed our homes.'

Morning came and with the morning bitter news. During the night, the shepherds grazing the flocks had been surprised by the villagers and there had been a fight. Hundreds of villagers had set upon them, beating them black and blue. Hüseyin had a broken arm. Duran could not walk at all. Fethullah was lying in a field, half dead, with blood spirting out of his mouth and nose. As for the flocks and the rest of the shepherds, the villagers had herded them off to the police-station at Toprak-kalé.

'Jeren, Jeren, Jeren! . . . Curse you Jeren, it's your fault, yours . . .'

132

The long red serpents . . . Their long flickering tongues . . .
The tall, black, mottled walls of Toprakkalé Castle . . . Looming above like death.

'Jeren, Jeren . . .'

13

The paddies stretched all the way from Yalnizagach to Anavarza. The yellow spikes hung in clusters, lush and full. thousands of labourers, their garments tucked up, were gleaning the plants and carrying them to the threshing-floors. Steeped in mud they moved constantly like columns of ants from the paddies to the threshing-floors, from the threshing-floors to the paddies. There were tractors and harvesters everywhere. The harvesters were disgorging grain on one side and stalks on the other. With the curiosity of a cat Kerem wandered through the fields, taking stock of everything, the harvesters, the tractors, the trucks, the threshing, the labourers. And then it was noon and the sun was hot and Kerem hungry. Some children were playing in the shade of a thicket of weeping-willows surrounding a little pool formed by the irrigation canal. With instinctive confidence Kerem walked over to them.

The police-station, a mud-daubed building, squat as an old inn, stood all by itself some way out of the village. In front of it was a small yard in which grew a few withering marigolds smothered in dust. A flag hung on the flagstaff so faded that its red had turned grey and the crescent and star were almost invisible. The police-station was fifty paces off the main thoroughfare, on the other side of which was the village. Some *jilpirti* bushes had survived on the roadside, overgrown with weeds and brambles.

It was raining. Crouching in the bushes Kerem kept his eyes fixed on the door of the police-station. They were bringing a young girl handcuffed to a youth. Her face was wet, her hair all tangled. The youth's head hung before him. The policemen pushed them through the door. And then she screamed. On and on the scream persisted and Kerem was terrified. He wanted to run, to get away from this place. But the falcon . . . In his mind's eye it soared high into the skies and fluttered down again on to the Chukurova plain. The Anavarza crags were glittering in the sun like crystal palaces. That is how he saw them, and then he thought of the serpents that pullulate there. It was said that the king of the serpents lived on the Anavarza crags. He tried to remember the tale about him, but only a few fugitive snatches drifted through his mind. Then he forgot everything as the policemen appeared again. This time they were bringing an old man, very fat, and a tall scraggy woman, both wrapped up in old blankets. The policemen spat on them as they shoved them into the police-station.

Kerem's eyes ached suddenly, his throat went dry. 'Ah grandfather!' he moaned. 'My noble grandfather, who knows where you are now? You may be sick or lying under the black earth . . . Or these rascally Chukurova people may have laid you under the lash in some police-station.'

But my grandfather wouldn't cry. Never! No one saw a tear drop from his eyes in all his hundred years. My grandfather, the Master Blacksmith . . . And I am his grandson . . . I wish they had called me Haydar too. My grandfather's grandfather came here all the way from Khorassan. The powerful Bey of the Avshars who was a vizir with three plumes, waited a whole year at his door to obtain one of his swords. Yes, shahs and padishahs all fought their wars with swords that Haydar, the Master Blacksmith, made. That's how it was.

'And now they drag him to police-stations. They beat him black and blue. They make him piss blood. But he's strong, my grandfather. He's of the old Khorassan earth. He won't die.'

The sacred hearth of the blacksmiths is our hearth. They say that whoever came to lay his forehead on that hearth was forever safe from bullets and swords. Could it be true? Why not, if God made it so? Beys and pashas, brave warriors, shahs and padishahs all crowded to worship at our hearth. And each one of them brought a gift of a noble Arab horse, long-necked and slim-eared and green-eyed. Yes indeed, with eyes as green as emeralds. The noblest horses have green eyes, but they're rare and hard to get, like my falcon. They even fly like my falcon . . . Before our tent there used to be a whole herd of horses of every breed and colour, and my grandfather would ride a different one every day.

'Ah grandfather!'

Ah Jeren . . . Why didn't she marry that Oktay Bey? And when he had been crawling on his knees after her all these years. . .

Oktay Bey rose before his eyes with his drooping lips, his ox-like eyes, his stubby fingers. Suddenly he was angry. Jeren, so beautiful . . . Her auburn hair . . . He sighed. If he were grown-up he would have run away with her. He could do it even now, he could save Jeren from this hell. But the falcon? Aaah, if only he weren't tied to this place by that falcon, he'd have gone and carried her off. Poor Jeren, everyone was against her, even her own father and mother, just because she refused to marry that dirty man and let the tribe settle on his dirty land.

'But I'm not against her,' he muttered.

Then why did I do like the others, why didn't I talk to her? I was afraid, ashamed. What's there to be ashamed about? Now, as soon as I get back my falcon, I'll find the tribe and go straight up to her. How are you, big sister? I'm well, Kerem. But she'll be weeping . . . Aaah Kerem, they've burnt him, your grand-father, the patron of the holy blacksmith's hearth, your noble handsome grandfather. Burnt him alive . . . With his last breath he murmured your name . . . And you weren't there. I've got back my falcon, big sister, and I've come to take you away from this hell, to carry you way off beyond Mount Aladag. Yes, I will! I'll save you from this hell. I'll take you to Halil . . . He stopped suddenly. But Halil's dead . . . Anyway, big sister, I'll stay with you always.

The screams of the girl in the police-station had dropped to a low persistent moaning.

'They've killed her,' Kerem said. 'Aaah, they've killed her.'

He shuddered. Jeren was dead too, burnt that night together with his mother and all the rest of them. What was he to do

136

now, all alone, without a friend in the world, without a soul to know he was of the holy blacksmith's hearth where people came to worship and be safe from bullets and swords? All-healing herbs would be set to boil in huge cauldrons in front of the forge tent, miraculous medicines, a cure to every ill on earth. They would come in streams, the village poor, scrofulous, fevered, wounded, and would be made well. They would leave the hearth reborn, taking some of the medicine with them.

'Ah Jeren! Aaah grandfather . . . It's our leaders that are bad. Headman Süleyman's a timorous old man who hardly ever says a word. The Beys of old, Headman Süleyman's grandfather, were like fierce eagles. Like my grandfather . . . Aaah ah, they've burnt him! He's dead, burnt alive.'

What could he do to get that falcon of his? He had been hiding for three days now in this bush. And he had gone thieving too in the night . . . How could he look people in the face again? He had stolen the bread of those poor mud-soaked rice-pickers. What if they went hungry now? Because of him.

Suddenly he could not believe his eyes. His falcon! His own falcon in the hands of a boy, a thin yellow weakling of a boy . . . He had seen it at last! Now the rest would be easy . . . Holding the falcon the boy went into the police-station from where there still came the sounds of shouts and swearing mingled with the girl's faint moaning. A minute later he emerged again still holding the falcon, accompanied by a policeman this time. They were trying to make the falcon eat something, but the bird didn't want to. A stone-like anguish gripped at Kerem's heart. What if they killed the falcon, what if it died because they did not know how to feed it?

'It's eating!' he cried, jumping up for joy. Then quickly he ducked down into the bush. After a while the boy began to walk away with the falcon. He made for the village and disappeared between the houses.

There was no sound from the girl now. A group of four or five men were approaching the police-station. All of them had their heads bound in blood-soaked white rags and three were limping. They're nomads, Kerem thought, who knows from

137

what tribe . . . Hot on their heels came a whole truckful of howling villagers, breathing fire and fury. They're going to kill the nomads, Kerem thought. They've already beaten them to within an inch of their lives.

'Ah grandfather, I wish my tongue had dried up before I asked for that falcon! Why didn't I ask for winter-quarters instead? Poor grandfather, they're killing him too, like this, in some police-station.'

Then he heard the sound of a reed-pipe. He pricked up his ears and listened. Whoever was playing was doing it very badly. A smug feeling of knowing better spread through him. With serpent-like motions he glided swiftly out of the bush to the road. The piping came from the thicket of willows. He straightened up and walked towards the sound. Four or five boys were there under the willows, trying to produce sounds from a broken reed-pipe. They passed it from hand to hand, but not one of them could get the semblance of a tune out of it.

Kerem crouched down a little way off, at the foot of a clump of reeds. He wanted to go to them, but he hesitated because their faces were so sullen. The tall one, twisted like a rope, was all in a stew, cutting off reeds and whittling away, then trying them to his mouth, but with no success. Kerem smiled as he watched. What bunglers, he said to himself. At last, the children lost all patience. They fell to breaking the reeds into small pieces and hurling them into the water. The tall boy, in a rage, rammed his penknife into the root of a willow and slumped down on the edge of the ditch. The others squatted about him, seething silently. What clods, Kerem thought And they call themselves boys when they're not even able to make a reed-pipe! So these people are going to train my falcon and make it fly and hunt? Aaah, ah, Corporal Nuri, pasha of the police-station! Ah, my grandfather . . . My home . . .

The children sat on, silent, averting each other's eyes, sulking as though they had quarrelled. One of them must have been poor. His shalvar-trousers were washed out and torn. His striped shirt was faded and tattered. Another wore black shalvar-trousers that were shining new, and a shirt striped with

138

red, yellow, green and mauve, which was just as new. He wore yellow shoes too, real city shoes! The others were all barefoot. This one must be the son of the agha. Or perhaps they had some holy hearth too, who knows, maybe theirs too was a blacksmith's hearth.

Kerem got up and walked towards the children. They had seen him long ago, but had taken no notice. As Kerem drew near they turned their heads and looked at him. He took another few steps and stopped. They stared at each other for a while. Kerem was the first to smile. The children smiled too. Then he went and sat down beside them. They took stock of one another for a while, then smiled again. Quietly, Kerem produced a jack-knife from his pocket. The children stared.

'Is it sharp, brother?' the tall boy asked.

Kerem smiled, his warmest, most ingratiating smile. 'Very sharp,' he replied and added, a little ashamed as he said it: 'Our family is a blacksmith's hearth, so the knives we make are always very sharp, very very sharp. My grandfather made this one, Haydar the Master Blacksmith. Have you heard of him? Everyone knows him, you know . . . He makes swords. Now he's made a sword that he's going to take to Ismet Pasha, and Ismet Pasha will give us land.'

'Haven't you got any land?' the dark-eyed boy with the yellow shoes asked.

'They're Aydinli nomads,' the tall boy declared knowingly. 'They never have any land at all. They're always on the move, settling here and there on other people's lands and spoiling their crops with their flocks. They kill people too and steal things. That's why they get flogged in police-stations and their women are always being taken away from them. These people don't even have graves. That's what my father said. They're a people without graves, he said.'

'That's a lie,' the boy with the yellow shoes countered. 'That father of yours lies all the time, anyway! How can people not have graves? It's impossible. And as for being beaten up in police-stations, it's because they have no one to defend them. No government, nothing. That's why! If they have no graves as you say, then where are their dead buried? Eh, where, where?'

'They just leave them to rot on a rock, that's all. Up on the high mountains. And the eagles eat them up . . . My father said just that.'

'What does your father know about it? Didn't he mess up our tractor that day? And before my eyes too! And then my father sacked him. Your father doesn't know a thing. Would anyone ever let his dead ones be devoured by eagles?'

'Yes, they would,' the other persisted, though slightly deflated.

In the meantime Kerem's knife was being passed from hand to hand.

'Look, look!' a small boy shouted. 'It can even cut a hair! Look!' His eyes were wide with excitement. One after the other they all tested the knife again and Kerem's credit took a turn for the better. But he was still smouldering at the tall boy's allegations.

'We do have graves of course,' he said. 'But as we never stop in one place, we don't know where they are. And we don't steal either, not in our tribe. But for some reason they beat us cruelly in police-stations. And three days ago they set fire to our tents on Deliboga Knoll. Everyone was burnt, my grandfather, my mother, everyone. The horses, the donkeys, all the flocks were burnt too. So were all the children. And Jeren . . . Even the dogs. Only I got away alive.'

The children were silent now. Their eyes filled with tears.

'You're not cross with me, are you,' the tall boy said, 'because of what I said?'

'No, not really,' Kerem replied.

'My father's always mad at everything and everyone. That's why he says things like that. Isn't that so, Hassan?'

Hassan was the boy with the yellow shoes. 'It's true,' he said. 'But my father says he's not a bad man . . . So they burnt you all, did they?'

'Yes,' Kerem said. 'The whole tribe was burnt to cinders.'

'What are you going to do now?' Hassan asked.

'I don't know,' Kerem said.

'What's your name?' the tall boy asked.

'Kerem . . . They called me Haydar at first, then my mother changed it to Kerem. My poor mother, she's dead now, burnt alive . . .'

'But where will you go, what will you do?' Hassan asked again.

'I've no idea,' Kerem said. 'I've no one left in the world. They're all burnt . . . How should I know?'

'All burnt!' the tall boy repeated. 'What a shame! It's a bad thing to be all alone in the world.'

'All burnt!' Hassan echoed.

The two other boys wanted to say something but the words were choking in their throats. At last the smallest one spoke. 'Burnt alive!' he uttered hoarsely. 'Who knows how they screamed as they were burning! And those who were beaten up at the police-station . . . They were burnt too . . .' He broke down and huge tears rolled down his cheeks.

'Don't cry, Osman,' Hassan said. 'One doesn't die with the dead. It's a bad thing to get burnt. A terrible thing . . . And now Kerem's all alone. And hungry too, I bet.'

Osman jumped up. 'I'll go and get him something to eat right away,' he cried.

'Stop, Osman!' Kerem ran after him. 'Wait a minute, brother.' Osman turned back. 'Listen, come here, all of you,' Kerem said in a low voice. The children all huddled up apprehensively. 'You mustn't breathe a word of this to anyone,' he said dropping his voice still further. 'That they burnt us . . . If the grown-ups hear of it, they'll go and tell our enemies who'll find me and burn me too.'

'He's right,' Hassan said. 'They'll burn him. We mustn't tell anyone.'

'I won't even tell my father,' the tall boy promised.

'Nobody must know,' the other small boy whose name was Dursun, said. 'Or they'll burn Kerem too.'

'They're after me now, this minute. A man on a horse, all in black, gave me the chase for three days and three nights. He had a torch in his hand and was burning everything on his way. I jumped into the water and escaped. And another time I hid in a clump of fennel and he set fire to it, but I escaped again. If one single grown-up knows I'm here, he'll tell the other grown-ups. My enemies will hear of it and the black horseman will come and this time he'll burn me to ashes.'

'To ashes!' Hassan cried. 'Osman, go quickly now and get something to eat from your house, cheese, bread, tomatoes, anything. But be careful no one sees you. We'll all eat here with Kerem.'

'But where will he sleep?' Osman asked.

'We'll think of something,' Hassan said. He assumed an important grown-up air. 'As if so many of us can't hide one single boy!'

Kerem was elated. He would wait until they were really friends and open the matter of the falcon to them. They would surely find a way to steal it back if they put their heads together. The thing now was to be sure no grown-up got wind of his presence.

'And then there's Oktay Bey too,' he said, 'who wants to kill me. He's the one who fell in love with our Jeren. But Jeren loved Halil. So Oktay Bey killed Halil and brought his bloody shirt back to show Jeren. And Jeren wept and wept. She tried to throw herself down from the top of the crags, but they held her back. So she went to Oktay Bey and said, kill me like you killed Halil for I'll never marry you. And Oktay Bey pulled out his pistol and began to shoot all over the place. They said he'd gone mad with love. My grandfather said . . .'

'But why did Oktay Bey want to kill you especially?' Hassan asked.

Kerem was disconcerted. Why indeed? He could not think of anything. 'He just wants to, that's all,' he replied, confused. 'He's mad, you know. Love made him mad. Crazy people always kill.' But he saw that Hassan was not convinced. He read the doubt in his eyes. Now he had gone and spoilt everything!

'Look, Hassan,' he said. 'Come here a bit.' He leaned to his

142

ear. 'I'll tell you why, but no one must know except you.'

Under the curious gaze of the others he led Hassan behind the willows. 'My father,' he began in a whisper, 'has killed Oktay Bey's brother. You see, they killed Halil first and Halil was my father's friend, like you're my friend now. So to avenge Halil, my father caught Oktay Bey's brother and . . . You see those crags on Anavarza? He laid him down up there and cut his throat, like you'd do to a sheep. You won't tell anyone, will you? But after my father got burnt Oktay Bey decided to take his revenge on me. If he catches me, he'll take me up there, on those steep crags, and he'll throw me down and cut my throat and my blood'll spirt all over the place. Don't tell anyone, will you, but that black horseman, the one who chased me for three days, that was Oktay Bey. He was really going to burn me alive, but he didn't because what he really wants is to cut my throat.'

The others were crouching behind the trees, their eyes wide, straining their ears. Hassan looked at them. 'Kerem,' he said, 'we must tell the others too. It's not right to keep it from them. They'll never tell. We never tell our secrets to grown-ups. And Süllü's a good chap, that tall one . . .'

'All right,' Kerem assented. 'Since they're your friends and you trust them.'

'Children!' Hassan called triumphantly. 'Come here, he's going to tell you too.'

Kerem began again, embroidering his story a thousandfold, and told them about Oktay Bey and Jeren, his father and the slaughtered man. The children were chilled with fear.

'Don't be afraid, Kerem,' Hassan said. 'Nobody'll kill you here, or burn you either. Not while we're with you . . . Eh, Süllü?'

Süllü drew his lanky frame up importantly and his face grew dark and obstinate. He took Kerem's hand and held it tensely in a warm grasp. 'Don't you be a bit afraid, Kerem,' he said stoutly.

Kerem's face was a mixture of fear, despair and remorse. He was on the point of bursting into tears. The children noticed this. 'You must trust us,' Süllü said confidently. 'We'll hide you from all your enemies. No one will find you, not even the Vali, nor the Corporal, nor the Kaymakam. Not even Hassan's father!'

'Not even my father,' Hassan boasted. 'Never fear. We'll get burnt ourselves before we let them burn you.'

'We'll never let them get you,' Süllü said.

A wonderful feeling of importance, heroism and self-sacrifice was swelling inside them all.

Kerem's face brightened. He laughed and took his knife from Hassan's hand. 'All right then. Let me make you a reed-pipe while we're waiting for Osman. And I'll teach you to play on it, too.'

He walked over to the reeds and selecting a good thick one he slashed it off, sat down and began whittling away at it expertly.

14

In the valley up on Aladag Mountain, Mustan's wounds were healing with the poultices Bald Musa had brought him. Bald Musa also brought butter, honey, yogurt, meat and bread to the cave on Mordelik crags. Mustan was his only hope. Why was Musa so set upon killing Halil? Only for Jeren, only for land? No. Was there some secret understanding between him and Oktay Bey? What had Oktay Bey promised him that he pursued Halil with such a deadly hatred? Or was it some grudge dating back to their childhood? A mystery. But one thing was sure, Musa would never have nursed Mustan back to health were it not for the hope that he would kill Halil. I'd swear to that on the holy book. You just wait, Bald Musa, I'll get even with you . . . So Mustan was able to get up with not even a trace of his wounds. He had gained flesh and had let his moustache grow to a fine curl. In short, he felt better than ever before.

'Well, well, well! Look who's here! The great Resul Agha!'

The shepherd was startled out of his wits when he saw Mustan right there in front of him. His eyes darted to right and left to see if he could escape. His mouth, his throat, his nose went dry. A cold sweat broke out all over him and his knees gave way.

'Come here, don't go away, Resul Agha. Aren't you king of these mountains, braver than the bandit Köroglu himself?'

The shepherd let out a moan. Mustan was holding his rifle plumb on his brow. His finger was on the trigger and he was laughing.

'What's that, Resul Agha? You're not afraid!'

Resul was crouching on the ground, his head on his chest, stock-still, as though a part of the earth beneath him. Mustan stopped talking and stood there over him, his hand on the trigger. A long time passed. Then, still silent, Mustan settled himself on a stone. All of a sudden he gave a yell and pressed the trigger. The shepherd sprung up like an arrow and fell back. Mustan kept on showering bullets all about him, and at every shot Resul jumped into the air and dropped back again.

'So, my lord Resul Agha, there isn't another one like you in all the Taurus Mountains, nor in the Chukurova, nor in the sunny lands of Anatolia, eh? And how are you going to pay for torturing me, for holding me captive, eh?' He fired at a limestone and the exploding fragments fell over Resul who jumped again. Only this time he did not fall back. He took a few steps towards Mustan and looked him full in the face, unblinkingly. His eyes were blazing. Mustan was unnerved. It was as though a corpse had suddenly come alive. He pulled himself together and shouted angrily: 'Answer me, you wretch, how are you going to pay for all those insults and tortures?'

'Not by begging and grovelling like you! If I pay, I pay dying,' the shepherd cried in ringing tones, already accepting the worst.

Mustan was deflated. He had not bargained for this. Never had he dreamed that the shepherd would take such a stand. 'So that's how it is, my lord Resul? A real lord you are, to be sure! So you won't beg like me, eh?'

'I won't,' Resul defied him. 'I did bother you a little, but I also saved your life.'

'So you won't beg, eh?'

'I won't,' Resul repeated stubbornly. His voice was indifferent now, ready for everything, even death.

Mustan whipped out his dagger and leapt to his feet. Like a madman he hurled himself at Resul and plunged the dagger into his hip. Resul did not even wince. Not a cry of pain came out of him.

'Strip!' Mustan howled. It was as if the shepherd had not heard him. He was quite still. But the fleeting tremor that ran through his body did not escape Mustan's eyes. 'Strip, you cur,' he repeated jubilantly. And still the shepherd stood impassive before him with only that very slight quivering of his body.

'Strip! Strip, strip, you wretch.' And he began to rip up his clothes. In an instant the shepherd was left stark naked, his body trembling uncontrollably and blood oozing down his leg. 'Go to that tree,' Mustan ordered. 'So you thought I was simply going to kill you? Come on, walk, damn you!' He grabbed Resul's hand and yanked him along. Then he uncoiled a long goathair rope from his waist and lashed the shepherd to the tree-trunk so tightly that the rope sank into his flesh. 'Let's see you not beg now!' he flashed.

Resul raised his head. There was no trace of fear in his eyes. They had not changed at all. 'I'll never beg you,' he said. 'I'd never beg anyone simply to save my skin. Not like you.'

'All right,' Mustan said. 'We'll soon see how brave you are.'

He broke a huge thistle off its stalk and set at the shepherd's body with slow deliberate strokes until he was bleeding all over. Then, taking his gourd from his waist he filled it at the spring and poured the water over Resul. He went to the sheep, milked one of them and smeared the milk all over Resul's body.

'Let's see you not beg now! I'm going, leaving you to the flies. I'll come back tomorrow morning.'

He got no answer. So he put on the shepherd's thick felt cloak, and herding the flocks before him, he led them to graze lower down in the valley.

'Damn that boy,' he muttered. 'I never saw such a thing. He's a monster. If he lives, if he doesn't die after this, he'll never rest until he gets even with me. I must go back and set him free right away or I'll have to kill him. What a boy! He doesn't even turn a hair. I've never seen such a son-of-a-bitch.' He was beginning to blame himself. He shouldn't be doing this. 'I should have let him go when he defied me, when he said he would not beg like me, not even for his life. When a man shows such courage, you forgive him. You even kiss his hands. Well, what a lion you've turned out to be, Resul!' He had almost forgotten all that he had suffered at Resul's hands. 'But why, how could such a valiant fellow torture me like he did?' Suddenly it flashed on his mind. 'He was just playing, that's it! Like a child, I'm sure of it. He doesn't know about torture and things like that. He was lonely and he just found me to play with. Still . . .' he thought, 'what kind of game is that? No, it's that the child's an orphan. He was victimized, as all children are, especially orphans. And so he found me and took it out on me. I ought to go back and release him.'

Evening fell and a bitter wind sprung up from the north, ice-cold. If I leave him up there this night, Mustan thought, he'll freeze to death.

'Let him freeze,' he shouted out loud. 'Let him die, the cruel brute, the dog! Let him freeze to death.'

He had learnt from Blind Ali that Halil was here in these mountains and had clashed with the police only a couple of days ago at the place they call the Three Brothers. 'If only I hadn't shown myself to Blind Ali,' Mustan chided himself. 'I thought I'd find that shepherd and get rid of him at once. Now what shall I do? If Halil sees what I'm doing to a mere boy, what will he say, whatever will he think of me? I must let him go. After all he's only a miserable child.'

But then why didn't he plead, the son-of-a-bitch? No, he didn't care if Halil saw him. He didn't care if anyone saw him, not even Ismet Pasha himself. He'd tell him, he'd explain . . . And anyway, by the time Halil arrived the shepherd would be well out of the way, dead or otherwise. But the owners of the flock? Wouldn't they look for him? . . . Who would go looking after a mere shepherd boy? Not for months they wouldn't, especially a boy like this one, a rebel, a thorn-in-the-flesh for everybody.

The flock was there before him, still grazing. The moon was up, a full moon, and the night was growing colder every minute. He was chilled to the bone. Let me sleep, he said, let me not keep thinking of that boy all the time. But he couldn't. Again and again the shepherd rose before his eyes, his head held high, streaming with blood, yet laughing, his eyes like two nails, glinting. Come, Resul, Mustan entreats him, beg me, just once, only a little bit. Come Resul, please . . . And Mustan finds himself begging the shepherd again, just as he was begging him for milk.

What's the matter with me? Why are we doing this to each other, he a mere chit of a child, and me a grown man? Why do we take such pleasure in hurting each other? For days and days he tried to humble me by making me beg for a bowl of milk, and with no reason at all too. How he trembled with joy every time I had to beg him, the bastard . . . And I, what do I do, I go mad with fury because I can't make him do the same. Why do people do such things to each other? Why, why, why? Men are always itching to hurt their fellow-men. Who knows what the Chukurova people are doing now to our people! What new tricks to humiliate them, to hurt their pride, to degrade them! And yet isn't a man degrading himself when he does such things to others? Doesn't anyone realize this? If a man honours other men, even the lowliest, if he values and respects all creatures, even the birds and beasts, the crawling ant, even the trees and streams, isn't he himself the better for it? Why aren't people a little wiser, why aren't they stronger? Why Mustan, why? A child no bigger than a finger, a stubborn child won't be humbled before you, and there you go and get all mad. Why, why, why Mustan? Is it because everybody's always looked down on you, everybody, Jeren, Halil, the whole tribe, even the flying bird above? Are you trying to get even with them all by taking it out on a small child? Is that it, Mustan?

It was nearly noon when he went back the next day. Resul was frozen to the tree-trunk, not a trace of life in him, not a breath in his body which was all shrunken and dry and blood-stained and swarming with flies. Mustan stopped at a distance, watching for some little movement, unable to draw any nearer. Then with a superhuman effort he closed his eyes and rushed forward. Quickly, he loosened the rope. The boy rolled to the ground. Mustan put his hand to his heart. It was beating. Faint with relief he picked Resul up and laid him over a mound of soft grass. Then wetting his neckerchief with the water from his gourd he began to wipe him clean. When the gourd was empty, he shouldered the boy and carried him to the spring. There he washed him thoroughly. In his knapsack he had some of the ointments and underclothes Musajik had brought him. He rubbed the ointment all over Resul's body. Then he put on his underclothes and wrapped him up in the shepherd's cloak. Resul was breathing more easily, but his eyes were still closed. In a trice Mustan had lit a fire and pulled Resul as near to it as he could. Then he sat down beside him. 'Good for you, Resul,' he said. 'You didn't die. You're a lion, Resul. You stood it out. Well, you've deserved the right to do anything you like now, even to kill me. A lion!' he shouted. 'A lion, this Resul . . .'

Resul opened his eyes, then shut them again. Mustan jumped to his feet, almost dancing for joy. He rushed to the flock and, selecting a mauve sheep, he set to milking it. The milk of mauve sheep is said to have healing properties. Mustan knew this. The fresh milk was warm, steaming.

'Resul! Resul, brother, sit up, will you? Open your eyes again, my brave Resul, my lion. Come on, do.' He stroked Resul's hair, afraid to hurt him. 'Come Resul, sit up a little, please.'

Resul had regained consciousness for some time now. He could hear everything, but he wanted Mustan to go on and on in that warm comforting tone, so he kept his eyes shut. Mustan's voice grew more urgent, more caressing.

At last Resul looked up and smiled. His eyes had lost that nail-hard look. They were quite friendly now and Mustan laughed with glee. 'Drink this, Resul. It's still warm. I've only just milked it. I'm going away now to see Blind Ali about a friend of mine, Halil, who was to have met me here. I'll bring you back some salve and also grape-molasses. And sugar too.'

Resul's face was wreathed in smiles. He drained the brimming bowl of milk at one draught.

'I'll bring you a lamb too, a nice fat one. But who's going to mind the flock until I come back?'

'The dogs can mind the flock for a whole week all by themselves,' Resul said in a faint voice. 'Don't worry . . . Just go and come back quickly.'

Their eyes met and they laughed again. Mustan grasped Resul's hand and held it in his for a while. 'All right then. Keep well. I'll be back by tomorrow morning. If Halil should come, tell him to wait for me. But you won't tell him what happened, will you? What we did to each other.'

'I won't,' Resul replied softly.

Mustan went down the valley at a flying pace. By midnight he had already reached the village and was knocking on Blind Ali's door.

When Blind Ali saw who it was he was stricken with fear. 'I told Halil exactly where you were,' he said, 'and he set out to meet you yesterday. Don't tell me he hasn't come?'

'Well, he hasn't,' Mustan said.

'Perhaps he missed you,' Blind Ali said anxiously.

'He'll find me somehow, don't worry yourself about that, Ali,' Mustan said. He sat down and proceeded to tell Ali all that had passed between himself and the shepherd.

'You've made a mistake,' Ali said. 'You should have done away with him. That boy will bring trouble upon us all. It's too late now, you'll never find the chance to kill him.'

'But I don't want to kill him,' Mustan said. 'Look, you've got to get me some salve for his wounds, and also sugar and grape-molasses.'

'That's easily done,' Blind Ali said. 'But he's going to kill you. He'll smile to your face and at the first opportunity he'll kill you. Mark my words, I know the kind.'

'Let him,' Mustan laughed. He did not believe Blind Ali. He recalled how they had smiled at each other on parting and the handshake that had sealed their friendship and brotherhood. The strongest friendships were always born like this out of violent antagonisms.

'It's your business,' Blind Ali said. 'I'm just warning you. You don't know what he's like.'

But Mustan did know. When they had first met, Mustan's leg had not yet swollen. He was still able to walk, and it was then that Resul with tears in his eyes had told him about his life. His father had died and his mother had run away to live with some man from another village. So Resul was left to his father's brother who had eight sons already and was a very poor man. They made him sleep in a small stable with the calves. He was only three years old then, and it was there he ate and lived, with never a shred of clothing to his back, quite naked, until the age of five when a neighbour woman gave him some clothes that had belonged to her dead son. He was six when he first set foot in his uncle's house. It was a great event. They gave him some hot soup, and bulgur pilaff too. A year later he was allowed an onion with his pilaff. The onion was good to eat. He loved its taste and it made him belch too, three times, which was very agreeable. But the same year his uncle administered him his first beating, and afterwards they made a custom of it, not only the uncle, but the wife and sons too. They beat him every day, for no reason at all, just for the fun of it. When he was twelve he tasted something sweet for the first time, a spoonful of grape-molasses. He swore on his life that nothing more delicious than grape-molasses could exist in this world. At fourteen his uncle hired him out as a shepherd, and the first thing he did was to beat another shepherd boy senseless. Still, after a year he had made such a name for himself that the rich Davutoglus entrusted one of their largest flocks to his care. Not a wolf, jackal or fox, not a thief could get anywhere near the flock Resul kept and he never lost a single sheep. That same year he beat his uncle's second son black and blue and broke his arm. He did not stop at that, but also split open his uncle's skull causing him to be laid up for six months. For the first time he wore sandals to his feet and also handled money. He learned to play the flute too. He learned to fondle the breasts of shepherd girls and many other things besides. But for a long time he refused to talk to people. He shrank from human contacts. He was afraid, ashamed. He had a huge shepherd dog, and only to that dog would he open his mouth. Resul swore that the dog understood every word of what he said and that it even answered him.

'That boy will kill you,' Blind Ali said again. 'Even if you hide under the wing of a bird, in the ant's hole, he'll find you and kill you. Go back quickly and kill him while there's still time.'

Mustan was shaken, afraid all of a sudden. He knew Ali for

one of the shrewdest men in all these Taurus villages. 'Are you serious? You're not poking fun at me, are you?'

'That boy will kill you,' Ali repeated with emphasis.

'After all I did for him? After I spared his life?'

'He'll kill you. Go back and kill him first without wasting another minute.'

'But what if Halil's there? How can I kill him in front of Halil?'

'I don't know. All I know is that you've got to kill him.' He gave Mustan the salve he had asked for, a sack of sugar and a firkin of grape-molasses and set him on his way. 'Kill him,' was his last word as Mustan disappeared into the darkness.

So I'm to kill him, Mustan was thinking. But how, when I saved his life, when he would have died if I'd left him like that? How can I kill him now that he's like a brother, like a son to me? Ali's a clever man, but he's wrong this time. How can I bring myself to kill that brave little boy? Ali knows a lot, whatever he says turns out to be true, always, but . . . No, there's no getting out of it. I must kill him.

He spurted on up the mountain path, the fear in him growing stronger with every step.

What am I in such a stew about? After all, he's only a child. One bullet in his head, and then you throw him to the dogs and its over and done with. What matter if Halil does see you? I'll find a way to settle his account too, damn it.

All the way up to the cave he kept thinking of Halil and Jeren. And of himself too. All that had happened to him, everything was Halil's fault. If it wasn't for Halil he would have had Jeren all to himself. He would never have murdered the Agha's son or anyone else. He would never have come to this, dragging out the miserable existence of an outlaw in these mountains.

A policeman's bullet, that's the end for me, whatever I do. So why not kill Halil while I can? Then find Jeren where they'll have married her to that Chukurova fellow and carry her off . . . And after that, welcome death! Who cares? But as long as Halil's alive . . . He must die.

'Resul!' he shouted, exalted, full to the brim.

The shepherd was at the mouth of the cave, smiling. 'Did you bring me molasses?' he asked.

'Yes,' Mustan said. Resul threw himself at his neck. I must kill him at once, Mustan thought. It's now or never. And I must do it before he eats the molasses.

He shook himself free of Resul's embrace, jumped three steps away and levelled his rifle. He was pressing the trigger when he saw the look in the shepherd's eyes . . . Slowly he lowered the rifle. A burden was lifted off him. Resul had begged him at last, if only with his eyes.

'So you weren't going to beg, eh?'

Resul's eyes flashed. He was disgruntled, ashamed of himself, of Mustan, of the sheep, the dogs, the trees, the water, even of the flying bird. 'It's because I wanted those grape-molasses so very much,' he said sullenly. He sniffed at the firkin. 'Oooh, how good it smells . . .' He went to the mouth of the cave, took out the yufka-bread and fell to the molasses. He ate slowly, relishing every mouthful. 'Ooh,' he sighed when he had finished. 'A blessing on your dead dear ones, Mustan, brother, I've eaten my fill . . . Why d'you keep on wanting to kill me?'

'Forget it,' Mustan said sadly, helplessly. 'I'm not going to kill you now. I'll never do it.'

They sat down together under a pine-tree. Mustan could not look Resul in the face. Without lifting his head he began to tell Resul about Jeren and how he had got into trouble because of her. Then he told him about Halil and explained why he had to kill him. 'What do you think, Resul?'

'There's nothing you can do about it, brother. You've got to kill him as soon as he comes. If you like, give me your rifle and I'll do it for you.'

And so they decided to wait for Halil.

On the morning of the second day they saw him coming up the hill, and with him were two other men.

'He's not alone,' Mustan said, suddenly flustered. 'What shall we do now, Resul?'

'We'll deal with the three of them.'

'But we can't do that! The others have nothing to do with this business.'

'Well, I don't know,' Resul said. 'We'll see. Maybe we can get him away from them. Look! They're not armed, the other ones.'

'No, they're not,' Mustan said. 'Perhaps they'll go back . . .' He rose and shouted: 'Halil!'

'Mustaan!' Halil called back joyfully. 'I'm coming.' He was there in a minute, embracing Mustan. Then he sank to the ground and leaned against a tree. He was tired. His two companions, and Mustan too, waited standing for a word from him before they could sit down, and it was only after a while that Halil bethought himself of doing so. This did not escape Resul's notice. They sat down and Halil introduced the two men. 'These friends are from the Oymakli tribe,' he said. 'As you know, quarrels and fights are breaking out all the time between the tribes and the Chukurova people, and these friends here killed two men each in a fight about land. And then they came to me. They have no weapons. But they've got money, so we must get them some weapons and as quickly as possible. Tomorrow . . .'

We'll give one of them that rifle of yours, Mustan was thinking. As for the other, Allah is great . . .

'And do you know,' Halil went on, 'the news went to the tribe that I was dead! They took a blood-stained shirt and showed it to them, saying it was mine . . . You're supposed to be the one who killed me, Mustan.'

'They say that Jeren'll kill herself for sure,' the taller one of his two companions said. 'She believes you to be dead. And no one in the tribe will talk to her any more, or even look her in the face because she won't marry that Oktay Bey.'

'Didn't you know about this, Halil?' Mustan asked him.

'I knew, yes, but not that it was so bad . . .' Halil was in love with Jeren. He was mad about her, and as he listened to what was being said he felt faint with anxiety. A flame was burning in his heart. He tried to change the subject: 'They told me that the tribe is still wandering all over the Chukurova without being able to find some place to settle,' he said.

155

'We'd better go down, the two of us,' Mustan said. 'Maybe we can do something for them.'

'You're right,' Halil said. 'They're in a bad pass. And I must get there before Jeren does something. I know her. She's quite capable of killing herself.'

'I know Jeren too,' Mustan said. 'She'll kill herself.' But you're not going to see Jeren, my lion! No, if not tonight, then tomorrow you'll be pushing up the daisies, my lion.

He looked at Resul. Their eyes met and they both smiled.

15

*Somewhere below Fort Payas, Oktay Bey found the tribe at
last. They were wandering along the sea-coast in the direction
of Iskenderun. It was raining and they were all soaked to the
bone, men, women and children, horses, donkeys and camels.
Oktay Bey was just as wet as everyone else. He had been on
horseback for four days looking for them.*

The old fortress of Payas is like a massive square rock isolated
in the middle of the plain. To the east is the long range of the
Gavur Mountains, and the wind blows down from the mountains over Payas and on to the Mediterranean, wafting the scent
of pines. There are orange groves at Dörtyol, very old, but at
Payas always and always are the shades of the aged Turcoman
and Yörük beys bearing a heartbreaking longing for bygone
days. They are there always, the old beys, with their moss-
green eyes, their tapering beards, fettered in Payas dungeon,
heavy iron rings about their necks. The burden of their yearning laments can be heard yet. How long would they have lived
like that, chained in Payas dungeon? Not more than a year
surely. Dig anywhere in the ground about the fortress and you
will find it full of their bones. Like a cry of grief they pass along
this plain still, those prisoners, those exiles, bowed under the
weight of their iron collars, dragging their heavy clanging
chains. Their long laments ... Their long proud songs ... The
Ottoman has led us into captivity. The Ottoman has broken
and consumed us. The Ottoman has laid waste the tribes. They
have forced surrender upon us ... The long invocations, the
long, long imprecations.

In the Karachullu tribe, the children were dying like flies.
That morning again they buried a little boy at the foot of
Payas fortress and threw a few handfuls of that cruel Ottoman

earth over him, of that thankless earth that knows not benefits nor customs and traditions, nor even common humanity, that rejects stock and stem. As though the sword could reject its hilt.

The sheep were dying too. And passing by Erzin village, some people there shot three of the dogs point-blank, just for the fun of it. To Headman Süleyman the deaths of the children, the losses among the sheep, their miserable wanderings, everything was in the normal course of things, but the killing of those sheepdogs, each one as huge, as well-graced as a horse, and for no reason at all, was something he could not stomach. He stopped the caravan right there, on the shore of the great rolling Mediterranean, on the sands between the fields and the sea, and called for Fethullah.

'This is too much!' he roared. 'Go, find those who did this and bring them to me by hook or by crook.'

The Karachullu youths, who had been chafing angrily, did not have to be told twice. They made straight for the village, found the men sitting in the coffee-house and brought them by force to the Headman, taking care not to touch a hair of their heads on the way.

Süleyman's eyes swept over the village youths who stood before him smirking unconcernedly. 'Why did you kill those dogs?' he asked in a deadly voice. 'What did they do to you, you low-down bastards?'

The youths were taken aback. They quailed under the old man's cold fury.

'Speak!' Headman Süleyman thundered. But they only cowered still more.

He drew nearer, his steel-like eyes piercing into them. Then suddenly he spit on the first one's face. Then on the second, then on the third. 'Let them go now,' he said, 'the bastards. They're just brutes with nothing human left in them. Killing dogs . . . The skunks!'

That day they camped on the sea-shore, listening all night to the booming breakers and waiting for some retaliation from the villagers. But this time nothing happened at all. At dawn another child was dead and they buried him under the rain in a ditch beside a green-growing field. Then they packed up and left. They had no idea of where they were going to go, for here too, not a patch of land had been left unsown. Their clothes stuck to their bodies. The embroideries on their kilims and felt-rugs were blurred and faded, the colours running into each other, streaming down the legs of the camels, horses and donkeys. On and on the caravan trailed below Payas fortress in the driving rain, and that is how Oktay Bey found them. His boots were filled with water. His thoroughbred horse looked cold, its ears were drooping, shrivelled.

Oktay Bey was a sad-looking young man of about twenty-five, on the tall side, rather plump, balding already above the forehead, with large protuberant eyes and a black moustache.

He rushed up to Headman Süleyman. 'But this isn't possible,' he said. 'Like this, in the rain! Everyone will die. We must stop at some place. Look, I give up Jeren. I won't ask anything of you. Turn back the caravan and come and settle on our land. My father won't object. You'll spend this winter there, and afterwards . . . God is great.'

Not a word did the Headman reply. He remained quite silent. It was impossible to make out what he was thinking. Oktay Bey tried again, but could get no response at all from him. He walked his horse over to Old Müslüm and renewed his offer. Old Müslüm was breathing with difficulty. His face was a bilious green, but he still managed to keep on his feet. Oktay got nothing out of him either.

'Jeren, Jeren! What have you got against him?' It was Sultan Woman who spoke. She had drawn Jeren away from the others and was pressing her relentlessly.

Headman Süleyman called his son. 'We're moving to Dumlukalé,' he said. 'There are still some places that way where we haven't got into fights and made enemies. Maybe we can find some little strip of unoccupied land, some barren spot where they'll leave us in peace.' But his face was dark and hopeless, his cheeks hollow, his back hunched and his head sunk into his shoulders. His wet beard was stuck to his breast and the water trickled from it down his shirt.

159

'But Oktay Bey said . . .' Fethullah began. Then he checked himself. The look his father threw at him, the anguish, the deep despair in his eyes were enough to silence him. He did not mention Oktay Bey again.

And so the caravan was on the move once more in a fixed direction, north towards Dumlukalé, towards a new unknown. Dumlukalé was a long way away. It would take them at least four or five days to get there. The animals were dying in ever greater numbers as they proceeded. They skinned them and sold the meat and skins for almost nothing in the villages along the road.

'Jeren, daughter, think how deep his love for you must be! If it weren't so, would he have shared this wretched existence of ours all these years? Look at the presents he's brought you, look! Ten *beshibirliks*![1] A pair of gold earrings . . . And so many gold bracelets! Look, all for you . . .'

On the road Fethullah was forced to collect gold coins from the women's necklaces and headdresses. There was no money left at all in the tribe. He levied one gold coin from each woman. That night they camped in a derelict orchard just below the railway. Fethullah brought the gold to his father. How much more would they be able to give, the women of the tribe? Headman Süleyman counted the gold coins that lay before him gleaming in the light of the fire. So this was the last of their wealth, their women's ornaments . . . What was the use of it all? Would it not be better for the tribe to break up, for each to go his own way, to find some place to live? But they won't, he thought. Dispersion means death to them. They prefer to die this way, slowly but all together. And yet what about all those who have been leaving us all this time, gone to settle in some village or town, or simply vanished without a trace? It's that nobody can face the idea of a sudden wholesale break-up. They'll go on like this, splintering off one by one. There'll be less and less of us left and one day there'll be no Karachullu tribe any longer.

'One by one . . . One by one . . . Like Yeryurtoglu the other

[1] beshibirlik: Turkish gold five-lira coin used as an ornament.

day. He took his wife and children, he gathered up his sheep and just disappeared into the night. Yes, just like that . . .' Süleyman smiled bitterly. 'A whole world that is dying away . . . My world, yours . . . We are dying together, my brave old world. Even now perhaps, in this tribe the great Turcoman is breathing its last. The Turcoman race that has existed ever since the world began is dying out, agonizing right now before our very eyes.'

That night in his tent Headman Süleyman sat by the fire thinking these thoughts as he stared at the gleaming heap of gold before him.

'But Jeren, my dear, the lad's going to make you live in palaces, and if you don't want that, he's ready to live our life. We'll all spend the winters on his land and the summers in his highland pastures. Half the Chukurova is his . . .'

'What did Jeren say, my good aunt?'

'She wouldn't even touch the gold bracelets and necklaces you bought her . . . The only thing to do is to carry her off by force. I'd tell you to do that if it wasn't that she'd kill herself. She's that stubborn.'

She was like a shadow, a thing without a soul, never speaking a word, seeing nothing, nobody. She moved, she walked, she ate and drank without knowing it. She could not think. It was as if she existed no longer. But with her long lashes, the little hollows that marked her dimples, her lips redder now in the pallor of her thin drawn face, she was more beautiful than ever. Young and old, men and women were arrested before so much beauty. They could not take their eyes off her. There was an air about her, in her face, the curve of her lips, her proud graceful walk, her slender figure, something that cast a spell on people, that stirred the emotions, that grew stronger with the bitter agony of her face.

'Where,' Headman Süleyman thought, 'in what other race can one find such perfection? Such beauty . . . Like a stream that has flown underground for thousands of years and suddenly springs out of the earth, filtered, clear and pure . . . Ah, that young man Oktay knows what he's about. There's never been such a one as Jeren. He trusts in me, he thinks I'll help him obtain her, but that's one thing I could never do, not if every single one of the tribe were dying, agonizing before my very eyes, not if they told me, you are going to die, you, your children, all of you, and only Jeren can save you, and she's willing too, she only wants your consent . . . Even then I wouldn't give her away, I couldn't, I couldn't! I'd never give away Jeren. The most beautiful thing the human race has ever brought forth . . .' Then he was ashamed of himself. 'Am I in love with her?' He shrank from the very thought. 'At my age, in my declining years . . .' He smiled. 'Who wouldn't be in love with Jeren?' he mused indulgently. 'Anyone who sets eyes on her falls under her spell.'

'Aunt, aunt, my good aunt! Tell her again. I'm my father's only son. We own so much land in the Chukurova that five tribes like yours, even ten, could settle and live comfortably on it. Why is she doing this to me? Can't she love me just one little bit? And even if she can't, I love her. My heart can never forget her. Go to her, tell her that if she won't say yes today, I'll go away and never come back again, not even if I should be bursting, dying for the love of her.'

Yet even as he spoke he derided himself inwardly. How many times had he not sent such messages to Jeren! How many times had he not left the tribe in anger, swearing never to return, convinced he never would! The most he had been able to hold out had been a fortnight. He had always come back, complaining bitterly, yet trying again, his hopes growing stronger as time went by. 'This girl will be mine,' he kept saying fervently.

That morning in a burst of anger he mounted his horse and rode away. 'What do they take themselves for, these Yörüks? Let them drag on this miserable life, the wretches. They deserve it . . . The fools! They haven't seen half yet of what the Chukurova people can do to them. Let me see them find some place to settle this winter! I'll be watching, trailing them like death itself.'

But all the time he kept looking back at the caravan he was

leaving behind. There was a pain in his chest, a fire, a panic that grew stronger as he rode away. He felt as though his heart were being wrenched out of him. He cursed the day he had ever seen Jeren, he cursed the tribe, Jeren, his bad luck, he cursed everyone and everything. There wasn't a soul in all the Chukurova who hadn't heard of his attachment, and now, after all these years he would be branded forever as a rejected lover. What would he tell his parents, his friends? How could he face them? To be spurned by a Yörük girl! And the worst of it was that he would never be able to keep away. He would return to her and go on dragging himself after the tribe wherever they went, letting his pride, his manhood, his whole existence be trampled underfoot. Everyone in the tribe, even the children, looked on him with pity. But not Jeren. Not a single glance would she allow him. All these years she had never once lifted up her eyes to him. Perhaps she had never even seen him . . . He was hurting her too, just as much as he was hurting himself. Because of him, because they had nowhere to settle, they were taking it out on Jeren.

Swiftly he turned the horse and rode back. He had come a long way, but he caught up with the caravan in no time. Jeren was walking at the rear, holding her little brother by the hand. Her head was bent and she swayed as though in a waking trance. As soon as he saw her Oktay's breath failed him. His eyes went black and he held on with both hands to the pommel of his saddle. It was all he could do not to fall off. His heart was pounding so hard that it shook his whole body and even the horse under him.

He rode beside her for a while, but she walked on as though she had not noticed him, as though the world and everything around her never existed.

'Jeren . . .' he said and stopped. His voice was trembling. 'Jeren,' he began again, 'I have done you much injury. Forgive me. I couldn't help it. I have put you in a difficult position. And worse, I tried to buy you. I shouldn't have done this.' He blurted out the words with a great effort, breathing convulsively, as though he were choking. 'But now I'm going. I'll

163

never, never come back. This is the last time . . . The last, the last . . . I shall never see your face again. Only forgive me. Forgive me for all those despicable things I did, for all the harm I've done you.'

For the first time Jeren lifted her eyes and looked at him. There was kindliness in her eyes, even a little friendliness. Only an instant, and her lashes were lowered again, and she was walking on, indifferent as before. But this one look had unleashed a storm in Oktay's breast. What could he do, how could he tell her how happy, how proud she had made him? He tried, but in vain. He could not say a word. He would never be able to tell her. Quickly he rode on along the caravan. 'Farewell,' he told everyone. 'I have eaten your bread and salt all this time. Forgive me and farewell to you all.' He came to Headman Süleyman's side. Taking his hand he kissed it. 'Farewell, father,' he said. 'Forgive me.'

Then he galloped away so fast that the mud spurted from the horse's hooves spattering its rump. And the tribe watched him go, their last hope crumbling away, vanishing into the distance.

It was raining, a dense solid flood-like rain. They walked on, sinking to their ankles in the mud of the road, while the shepherds strove to keep the slow-moving sheep from straying into the bordering green fields of corn and bringing fresh troubles upon them. They were like a column of cranes, the sheep, one behind the other, spread all along the narrow road. The caravan was a very long one now, one end going back to the very outskirts of Payas and the other almost reaching to Erzin. The babies on the women's backs, on the camels and donkeys, were whining, their voices weak, tired with too much crying.

16

Kerem had taken up abode in Yalnizagach village and struck up an acquaintance with the village blacksmith, Sadi Demirtok. All day long he stood in the forge watching Sadi Demirtok as he beat the iron for ploughshares, fashioned tractor parts and repaired trucks, harvesters and combines. A passionate interest for iron work was stirring in his blood. Sadi Demirtok never once asked who he was, this boy who turned up at the forge every day and stood quietly watching the movements of his hands, nor what he wanted, nor where he came from. Kerem couldn't be happier. The villagers too never thought to question the boy's presence in the forge, nor to ask who he was. They took him for just a new apprentice of the blacksmith's.

The whole village was ringing with the sound of reed-pipes. Every child, boy or girl, had one, long or short, tongued or not, and played on it without respite from dawn to nightfall. Kerem was teaching Hassan and his new-found friends to play. And they, in their turn, taught him the songs of the plain. He was filled with admiration at the number of songs they knew, these village boys. They had kept their promise. They had not given away Kerem's identity and no one knew he was a Yörük boy. They had concealed their big secret from the grown-ups like a sacred trust, locking themselves firmly around Kerem. As for him, he had hidden his real reason for coming to the village from everyone except Hassan. Hassan was to be trusted, he knew this by now.

'It would be easy to steal the falcon, except for the Corporal,' Hassan told him. 'He sits up all night, his hand on the trigger. He's afraid, you see. He's beaten up so many people. And then he's hand-in-glove with the smugglers, but sometimes, when they won't pay him his share, he has them shot, so the smugglers too want to kill him. He's in a dead funk because of that. What can we do? Wait a bit, let's think.'

They had been thinking for days now, but with no success.

Kerem slept in a wattled shack in Muslu's melon-garden. It was as solid and rain-tight as a real house and the boys brought him food in plenty from their homes, eggs, cheese, everything. In exchange he gave them the pipes he made. If their parents asked where they had got these pipes from, they invariably replied: 'Hassan makes them.' Not one of them ever made a slip. It was always Hassan ... 'Hassan learnt how to make them from a gypsy boy. He learnt to play too, real well. He can make a pipe talk, even.' It was true. Hassan had quickly mastered what Kerem had taught him and could now play the pipe like a veteran piper.

The falcon was a great source of worry to Hassan and Kerem. The Corporal's son had taken it out three times, but then he must have smelt a rat, for they had never seen him with it again. The name of the Corporal's son was Selahattin. He was a skinny, sandy-haired, snub-nosed, silent little boy who was inclined to look down on the other boys. They in their turn kept him at a distance and never included him in their activities. When the news of the reed-pipes spread through the village, Selahattin began to try and make up to them and get into their good graces. But it was no use. The boys could not bring themselves to trust him.

'Why don't you like him?' Kerem asked. 'Are you afraid of him?'

'He's mean,' Kemal told him. 'His father caught a falcon for him up in the mountains and Selahattin never once showed it to us.'

At that Kerem gave a sigh.

'And then his father beats up everyone. He used to beat us too, like his father, and we could do nothing ...'

Süllü interrupted him. 'But one day Mustafa gave him back blow for blow. He went mad with rage, Mustafa did, and knocked him up well and good. Such a licking he gave him that

Selahattin was in bed for a week pissing blood and Mustafa had to make himself scarce. He fled and hid at his aunt's in another village. And the Corporal beat up Mustafa's father, who went and complained to the Vali. So the Corporal was forced to beg pardon from Mustafa's father. But after this Selahattin hardly ever came out of his house. He wouldn't play with us again, and when his father got that falcon for him he wouldn't even look at us.'

Kerem had emerged from his wattled shack by slow degrees. It had been done so quietly, so unobtrusively that the grown-ups never realized that a strange child had come and was mixing with their children. It was as though Kerem had lived there all his life. And then he discovered the forge and stood there for a whole day watching the blacksmith's huge dexterous hands and the flames leaping out of the furnace. The second day he drew a little nearer to the forge, and the third day he went right in. The blacksmith had seen him from the start but had made no move. Just like this child, he too had once crept into a black-smith's forge and then one day he had found himself with a hammer in his hand beating on the anvil.

Kerem and the blacksmith took to each other in no time. 'My grandfather's a blacksmith too,' Kerem confided to him, 'and so were all my ancestors. The great Master Haydar who was my grandfather's grandfather made swords for the Sultans. My grandfather says that the Bey of the Avshars waited a whole year at his door for a sword and then gave him a heap of gold for it.'

Sadi the blacksmith knew all this, and a lot more. He knew all the legends and traditions of the Turcomans about the hallowed hearths of the blacksmiths. For the Turcoman the blacksmith had always been a holy man. What Sadi could not understand was why this boy had strayed from his people. In the end Kerem gave himself away and blurted out his big secret, the story of the falcon. But no sooner had he spoken than he regretted it bitterly.

The blacksmith saw the consternation on the boy's face. 'Don't be afraid, Kerem,' he said. 'It's easy. We'll get that falcon out of there quickly enough.' He summoned Hassan and outlined his plan to the two boys. 'Tonight you two will climb on to Blind Ibrahim's roof and wait there. Mind no one sees you, though. I'll be waiting up too. Now, the Corporal's window is always open, so you'll just wait till it's midnight and everyone's fast asleep and then you, Hassan, will slip in through the window. You'll take the falcon and run. Kerem mustn't go in because if they catch him they'll beat him to death. But you, if you're caught, I can get you off, and in the meantime you'll say Selahattin told you to come, that you were going out hunting or to make pipes, anything.'

That night, according to their plan, Hassan slid along the roof and wriggled in through the window of the Corporal's house. But he was met by a volley of shots, and it was only in the nick of time that he jumped out and took to his heels. The Corporal burst out of the house, still firing into the darkness. 'They tried to kill me,' he kept shouting. Then the gendarmes came hurrying up from the police-station. 'That way!' the Corporal cried, pointing towards the mill. 'He went that way, the murderer.'

The whole village was roused. Men, women and children rushed up in their underclothes, still half asleep. As though they had nothing to do with it, Kerem, Hassan and the blacksmith joined the crowd that was gathering in the Corporal's yard. The hunt went on till morning, around the mill and all over the village, but there was no trace of the would-be murderer.

After this incident the Corporal got the wind up in earnest and had guards posted about his house day and night.

All the children came to know of Hassan's attempt to steal the falcon from the Corporal's house, and also that the falcon was in reality Kerem's very own. They also learnt how Allah himself had given this falcon to Kerem and how the Corporal had just come along and taken possession of Allah's gift. They were revolted at this injustice, and their rancour against the Corporal was whetted still more.

As for the villagers not one of them except Sadi the blacksmith ever knew that the much-hunted murderer on that night had been the boy Hassan, nor had they the slightest inkling about the falcon business. 'He'll be killed all right, never fear, this Corporal!' they said. 'Killed by the smugglers or the Yörüks or by anyone of those people he treats so cruelly . . . What a nerve the man had! Think of it, to break into the Corporal's house at midnight! Good for him!'

The children had only one thought, one aim now, to get hold of that falcon by hook or by crook. They would spend whole nights watching the Corporal's house. But the window was never opened and the door was always locked and bolted. Moreover there was a policeman pacing up and down the yard day and night.

'We'll never get anywhere this way,' Hassan said at last. 'It's no use trying to get in at night.' He went to the blacksmith. The two of them put their heads together and thought, and after a couple of days Hassan rushed triumphantly to the children who were waiting for him in the thicket of willows. 'It's in the bag, boys,' he said. 'And it's Kemal here who'll do the trick. His house is next to the Corporal's, and he's on good terms with Selahattin too. He'll go and persuade Selahattin to bring the falcon out hunting with all of us and we'll take him to the brake . . . See?'

'This is the best plan yet,' Kemal crowed. 'I'll go right away. Wait for me here. Anyway Selahattin's itching to show off his falcon to us, and to learn to play on the pipe too.'

'Selahattin mustn't see you,' Hassan said to Kerem. 'Go to the brake now with Memet and hide there among the reeds. We'll find you.'

Kemal was back in no time, bringing Selahattin along with him. All the boys swarmed up to them. Hassan stroked the falcon's feathers and inspected its beak and wings. 'This,' he announced knowingly, 'is a falcon of noble stock. Where did you find it, Selahattin?'

'My father caught it,' Selahattin replied, proud at finding himself the cynosure of all eyes. 'Up on the steep crags on the high mountains. My father says that falcons always make their nests up on the steep crags so that nothing can get at them, neither men, nor serpents, not even the other birds.'

'How did your father get there then?' one of the boys asked.

Selahattin waxed even prouder. 'My father,' he began. He was going to say, my father's a Yörük, but checked himself for fear the children would look down on him after that. 'My father's a Corporal,' he said. 'The government teaches all corporals to climb up the steepest crags.'

'That's true,' Hassan said. 'Only corporals can reach up to those high crags and find falcon's nests. This falcon here, there isn't another one like it in all the world. Look, its feathers are green . . . This falcon can catch not only birds, but hares and foxes too, and even wolves. My grandfather told me that the falcon perches itself on a wolf's back, and the wolf simply can't shake it off, however quickly it runs . . . And then the falcon with its sharp beak, see? It's like a knife . . . Well then, with its beak, it pecks at the wolf's eyes and at each peck it tears off a piece of its eye. The wolf tosses its head and twists its neck, it kicks and plunges, but it can't shake off the falcon that sticks fast to its back with these talons you see here. And so the falcon makes the wolf blind just by eating its eyes bit by bit. And when the wolf's blind it can't escape, never, it just spins round and round where it is. Round and round and round . . . And it's the same with the fox and the hare too.'

Hassan was really carried away by his tale. 'And my grand-father said . . .' he ran on excitedly. 'My grandfather comes from the highlands, he's not a Chukurova man. He comes from those steep high mountains where falcons make their nests, and he said: I've seen thousands of falcons up there, but I never saw one as beautiful as Selahattin's. He said no one can catch these noble falcons. He wondered how Selahattin's father caught it.'

Selahattin was carried away too. 'My father comes from those steep mountains too,' he cried out. 'From the land of the falcons, like your grandfather.'

'This falcon here,' Hassan went on, 'if you see a bird in the sky, flying as high as a bird can fly, just set this falcon at it . . . It'll catch it in a jiffy and bring it to you too. Why, with this falcon you can catch a hundred birds a day, francolins, wild pigeons, quails, hoopoes, bee-eaters, eagles, any bird you wish. It's enough that you should see the bird and let the falcon go . . .'

The children were listening to him, their eyes like saucers. They pressed around the falcon and touched it timidly with the tip of a finger.

'This won't do,' Hassan said in the end. 'Since we've got this wonderful falcon, let's go to the brake and have him hunt some francolins for us. Then we can roast them over a fire and have a feast of good fat meat.'

All the children began to lick their lips. 'Yes, let's,' they cried. 'Since we've got this wonderful falcon.'

Selahattin looked thoughtful.

'Come on, Selahattin,' Hassan urged. 'Let's go. Let's see the falcon hunting.'

'I must ask my father first,' Selahattin said.

'If you ask him, he won't let you. And you'll never see this wonderful, marvellous lion of a falcon streak like the lightning as he catches a bird. Isn't the falcon yours?'

'But what if it flies off when I let it go and doesn't come back?' Selahattin pleaded. 'What shall I do then? This falcon's still a baby.'

'But it's a genuine falcon, isn't it? My grandfather says that genuine falcons never get lost. Or isn't this falcon of yours genuine?'

Selahattin was silent.

'Why don't you speak? Isn't it genuine? If it isn't you'd better let it go anyway. What's the use of a falcon that isn't the real thing?'

'But it is, it is!' Selahattin cried. 'It's the best of falcons. Would my father have climbed those steep crags to catch it for me if it wasn't? He could have fallen and broken his neck. He wouldn't have risked death, would he, if the falcon wasn't a genuine noble falcon?'

'That's true,' Hassan agreed. He stroked the falcon gently. 'And it looks every bit a noble falcon. All right then, let's go to the brake and make it hunt.'

Selahattin hesitated, but Hassan felt he was wavering so he pressed on. 'You're afraid, my friend,' he said. 'You're afraid your falcon's not really a falcon but only a kestrel and that's why you won't put it to the test. And who knows, maybe it *is* only a kestrel that your father told his men to catch down in the ruins below the village and then passed off to you as a falcon. Come along, boys, let's go. Selahattin can stay away if he likes. We'll catch a kestrel too and parade it on our arm for a falcon.'

He began to lead the children away towards the brake, leaving Selahattin standing there by the willows, staring after them, the very picture of indecision. After he had gone a good way, Hassan turned and shouted: 'Look, Selahattin, if that bird you've got there on your arm is a real falcon, then come along and make it hunt. A falcon's not an ornament, it's for hunting. And if your father's from the mountain country, my grandfather's from mountains that are steep and craggy and seven times as high, and he says . . . But of course, if that bird of yours is only a kestrel then don't come with us. Stay just where you are.'

Selahattin was dying to join them. But suppose the falcon were to fly off and never returned? On the other hand, if he didn't go with the children they would soon have it all over the village that his falcon was only a common kestrel. All the glory of his wonderful falcon, all the beauty, would have been in vain . . .

'I'm coming!' he shouted out suddenly. 'You watch and see what a noble falcon it is, this falcon of mine.'

17

Old Haydar and Osman entered Adana a little before the early morning call to prayer. The city lights were still on. So many, many lights . . . They struck Old Haydar's eyes, heavy as lead. He had been to Jeyhan and to Osmaniyé, and once even to Adana, but he had never stayed the night and had never seen electric lights before. All those lamps! It was like daylight, as though they had splintered up the sun and hung a piece of it on to every single house in the city. This wasn't a town, it wasn't a city, it was a field of light. God, what a place! The tall, tall houses looming out of the night like spectres, like hundred-eyed giants, tall as three poplars, so huge you dared not look up at them. And even if you did you would not see the top. Old Haydar was afraid suddenly of these houses, of these lights, of these giants, of the moving shadows that waxed and waned, that wavered and struggled and dived, that vanished and started up again. There were only a few men in the empty streets. They wore strange blue sacks and hurried along at a running pace. Old Haydar fell in after them. They stopped at a large brightly-lit building that looked like a squat mountain. But, Lord protect us, what was this deafening din, this clanging and rattling and booming that came from the building? Hastily Old Haydar spurred his horse until he was well away from the noise. Then he reined in, breathing with relief, and waited for Osman who was sprinting up the pavement after him. Osman had been to military service and had seen many such buildings. A factory! God, so this was a factory! Eh, brother, but what a noise it made, enough to wake the dead! And so they wandered through the streets till daybreak. As the sun rose all the city-lights went out, just like that, at the same instant. But this time Old Haydar was not so startled. Now, which of these enormous buildings was the house of Ramazanoglu? It could only be the largest, the stateliest. Who else but the great

*Ramazanoglu would inhabit the loftiest one of all? They
had only to look for it. Old Haydar's hopes had been raised
at the sight of so many imposing houses. A man who owned all
this, a Bey, would surely not deny them a tiny little patch of
land . . .*

The streets and avenues were filling up. By mid-morning there
were such crowds milling around that Old Haydar could not
believe his eyes. This Ramazanoglu must be a very powerful
Bey, he thought. He felt hungry, but he did not want to eat
anywhere, for who knows what a wonderful meal the great
Ramazanoglu would offer him as Allah's guest and the last
descendant of the Blacksmith's Hearth? Who knows how many
generations of Ramazanoglus had girded themselves with the
holy swords of the Hearth and had taken courage from them?
Who knows how pleased the famed Ramazanoglu would be to
see him, with what marks of friendship he would greet him.

But why had this Ramazanoglu deserted them? And such a
great Bey too, whose family had always been the Turcoman's
principal friend. Why had he left them all alone on this plain,
why? A faint misgiving stirred in him. Could it be that the
Ramazanoglus, like the Ottomans, had turned against the
Turcomans? The sword denying the hilt, the axe sundering the
helve? The Ottomans had been bred out of the Turcomans, of
the same blood, their bonds were of the closest, and yet hadn't
they ruined the Turcomans, cut themselves from their own
stem? Much good it had done them, for in the end they had lost
all their vast empire. They had earned the curse of the poor
man, of the friend, of the father, the mother, the curse that is
worse than all, for it will take effect slowly but surely. The
great Ramazanoglu of name and fame would certainly have
pondered over the downfall of the Ottomans after they turned
traitor to their roots. No, no, the Ramazanoglus were not like
the Ottomans. Hadn't they stood fast by the Turcomans even
in that last great battle?

He had dismounted and was leading the horse. In his other hand he held the sword, and Osman walked beside him. People stared in wonder at the tall, red-bearded old man with those outlandish clothes and that sword in his hand, but Old Haydar took no notice of them at all. His self-confidence was unshakeable, and he pressed on, cleaving through the crowds like a great solid rock.

'Osman,' he said suddenly, breaking free of his thoughts, 'how are we going to find Ramazanoglu's mansion?'

'Well . . .' Osman hesitated. He knew the cities. He had spent four years in Istanbul during his military service. 'We'll have to ask somebody.'

'But whom shall we ask?'

They had stopped at a crossroads. Motor-cars, phaetons, tractors, buses whizzed by in a constant stream. People hurried about post-haste like ants scurrying from an ant-hole over which hot water has been poured.

This Ramazanoglu's done well for himself, Old Haydar thought, and his hopes rose. He has obviously added to his domains and is more powerful than ever. 'I'm glad, Osman,' he said. 'The great Ramazanoglu's grown even richer. Such a big wealthy Bey wouldn't grudge us a little bit of land, would he?'

Osman held Old Haydar in great respect. He dared not undeceive him, not now when he had worked on this sword for thirty years, when he had waited so long for this day . . .

The more Old Haydar looked at the crowds, the houses, the gardens, the more his face brightened. His beard was trembling with joy. 'Let's find some good man and ask him, Osman,' he said. 'Even the great Ramazanoglu's not so easy to find in this multitude of houses, all as large as palaces and reaching up to the sky. Let's ask somebody.'

A black-browed, toothbrush-moustached young man in a striped suit and brightly polished shoes was passing by. Osman made a move towards him.

'Wait!' Old Haydar stopped him. 'That's not the right man to ask.'

Osman drew back with deference, and after this he was careful not to take the initiative again.

Standing there at the crossroads with Osman by his side, his horse behind him, Old Haydar was like some very old Hittite deity that has broken off from its centuries-old resting place on the high sculptured rocks. He commanded a kind of wondering respect among the passers-by. Like some very old blood sublimated by the years, he moved through the veins of the new city.

A young man whistling a tune came to a stop beside them. His hair was as long as a girl's and he wore very tight trousers and a brightly chequered shirt. He looked as though he wanted to speak to them. Old Haydar gave him a sidelong glance. He had a clean innocent face and seemed friendly enough, but Old Haydar hesitated when it came to asking him the way. Something about the young man was repulsive to him. And then he had it. This wasn't a man nor a woman either. This was a hermaphrodite! He couldn't ask for Ramazanoglu of name and fame from a hermaphrodite! That wouldn't do at all. One had to be very careful whom one asked when it came to the great Ramazanoglu.

Then he spotted an elderly man in shalvar-trousers and was about to go to him. The man's hair and moustache were obviously dyed, and jet-black too, but there was something sad about his face. Suddenly the man walked over to a boy who was selling corn on the cob from a little cart, and slapped his face. He hit him again and again and not one of the passers-by interfered. They did not even stop to look. Old Haydar was pained that such a thing should happen in Ramazanoglu's domain. A grown man hitting a little boy! And look at him now, dragging the boy off by the ear! Old Haydar cast him a glance of aversion and turned away, feeling ever so slightly dashed. The great Ramazanoglu had grown so rich, his domains so large that he seemed to have lost control a little. He must be a very old man to have let things get out of hand like this. Look at that driver now, whipping up his horse so brutally he's going to kill it! And that youth, pinching a girl's bottom in broad daylight, in front of everyone! And the women! Half-naked in those dresses . . . A man was hurrying by, raging, cursing Allah and all the saints. You ought to be ashamed of yourself, man, Old Haydar muttered indignantly. He almost added, and so should you, great Ramazanoglu, but checked himself. Who knows, he thought, what worries that poor Bey has on his head, and he must be a hundred years old too.

Look at Old Müslüm, what he's come to, Müslüm who was like the eagle of the high mountains . . . Even little children make fun of him now.

He wanted to get away, to escape from this terrible hurly-burly. But his mind went to the sword. It was their one, their last hope. The world was changing, ah it was changing . . . And only they remained the same. How could one man, even if he was the great Ramazanoglu, cope with all this? Poor Ramaz-anoglu, old now, that mountain eagle, that refuge of the down-trodden.

Osman stood there without a word, watching the old man's every expression, pitying him from the bottom of his heart. The noonday sun beat hot upon them and still Old Haydar could not find someone to ask for Ramazanoglu, some open, friendly human face, some kindred spirit. Then suddenly he saw it. He looked across the street to his left and there in a shop, behind the counter was a large full dark-complexioned face with a drooping moustache smiling at them, a pleasant inviting smile.

'That man looks all right to me,' Old Haydar said to Osman. 'That shopkeeper . . . He's got a human face. Let's go and ask him.'

Osman had spotted the man long ago. They crossed the large avenue, dodging cars and trucks, phaetons and bicycles and stopped before the shop. He's got a good smile, this man, Old Haydar thought, like a real human being.

'He's smiling at us,' Osman said.

'Selam to you,' Old Haydar said in his strong deep con-fident voice. 'My name's Haydar. I'm a master blacksmith, the last of the Blacksmith's Hearth. I forge swords for Beys and Pashas. Perhaps you've heard of me.'

The man rose to his feet. His body was huge and tall, and as smiling as his face. 'What can I do for you, father?' he said. 'My name's Kerem Ali. Maybe you've heard of me too.'

'Kerem Ali,' Old Haydar said, 'I want you to show me the dwelling of the great Ramazanoglu of name and fame.' He laughed. 'His principality's grown so large, thanks be to Allah, that it's difficult to make out which is his palace.'

'Which Ramazanoglu is it you want, father?' Kerem Ali asked.

'The Bey,' Haydar replied. 'The big Bey . . . I have to see him.'

'There are many Beys among the Ramazanoglus. They're all of them Beys. Which one of them do you want?'

'The big Bey . . . Whoever's chief of the principality now.'

Kerem Ali bit back a mirthless smile. 'What is it you want him for?' he asked.

'I've got something to ask of him,' Haydar said, and he tightened his clasp on the sword.

Kerem Ali had grasped it all now. He began to think, and the more he thought, the sorrier he felt for the old man. His face had grown bitter as poison, and a sudden doubt seized Old Haydar. 'Has something happened to the Bey?' he asked. 'Is he dead and we didn't get the news?'

Kerem Ali shook his head. 'No, no. He's been dead these hundred years. The big Bey, I mean.'

'Yes, but show me the palace of the Bey who's taken his place.'

'No one's taken his place.'

'My good man,' Old Haydar thundered, 'are you playing with me? Ramazanoglu's place can't be left empty!'

'No,' Kerem Ali said. 'Yes, of course, but . . . You're right, but . . . There are so many Beys . . . Which one shall I send you to?' Suddenly, he thought of Hourshit Bey. 'I've got it,' he said. 'Hourshit Bey's the man you want. He'll listen to you and maybe he'll help you.' He called his young apprentice. 'Come here and take these beys to the house of Hourshit Bey.'

'Thank you,' Old Haydar said gratefully. 'God bless you.'

178

They followed the youth along garden walls, houses, apartment blocks and came to a little house set in the middle of a patch of garden. 'This is Hourshit Bey's house,' the youth said.

'Ramazanoglu's?' Old Haydar exclaimed. 'This, the Bey's mansion?' He stared in disbelief at the tiny house. Then he saw that there were several such houses, exact replicas, in similar small gardens all along the street. 'All those other houses are his too then?' he could not help himself from asking.

'No,' the youth answered. 'They belong to others. This is Ramazanoglu's house, Hourshit Bey's.'

'Aren't you making a mistake? I'm sorry, but are you sure it's here?'

'This is the house. And here's the bell,' the youth said. He turned and hurried off.

Osman pressed the bell and a little girl appeared at the door. Old Haydar was even more surprised. A little girl child opening the great Bey's door! Where were the soldiers, the men, the menials? He looked uncertainly at Osman and leaned to his ear. 'Osman,' he said, 'd'you think they've brought us to the wrong place?'

'I'll ask,' Osman said. 'Little sister, is this the house of Ramazanoglu?'

'Of name and fame?' Old Haydar added.

'It's Hourshit Bey's house,' the girl said.

'Hourshit Bey . . . All right then, we were looking for him. Go and tell him that Haydar, the Master Blacksmith from the Blacksmith's Hearth, is here, come to visit the great Ramazanoglu of name and fame, as Allah's guest . . .'

The girl ran in and was back in a moment. 'The Bey says won't you come in . . .'

Old Haydar turned the horse over to Osman. He smoothed down his clothes and followed the girl inside, holding the sword firmly in his hand, erect, the embodiment of hope itself.

The girl opened a door. In the room, sitting at a table was a diminutive man of uncertain age, perfectly bald, with a hairless washed-out face. Again the suspicion that there must be some mistake crossed Old Haydar's mind. The room too was such a

tiny one. A single armchair, a frayed old carpet . . . On the
table, books, pencils, papers all in a litter . . . Then his eyes took
in the walls. They were lined with books from top to bottom.
At the sight of so many books he felt reassured. 'Excuse me for
asking,' he said as he stopped in the doorway, 'but are you the
great Ramazanoglu?'

Hourshit Bey raised his head slowly, wearily. There were
pouches under his eyes. 'Yes,' he replied tonelessly.

Old Haydar stepped up and put his right knee to the ground
in homage to the Bey.

'Get up, father. Sit here.' Hourshit Bey pointed to the armchair.

Old Haydar stepped back respectfully and perched himself
on the edge of the armchair.

'Make yourself comfortable, father,' Hourshit Bey told him
courteously.

This couldn't possibly be the Bey! His voice had nothing of
the powerful tones of a Bey, nor did he talk like one. Haydar
laid his sword across his knees and folded his hands over it. He
lifted his tufty brows and fixed a steel-green questioning gaze on
him. 'You must forgive me, but are you really the great Ramazanoglu of name and fame?' he asked, sinking to the bottom of
the earth as he did so.

'Well . . . Yes,' Hourshit Bey said.

Old Haydar took the plunge. He began to speak of the tribe,
of their trials, how they were being persecuted by the Chukurova people, the Government, the police, the forestry guards,
how no one wanted them, how they had been bereft of their
wintering quarters, their summer pastures, decimated by
diseases and wanderings. All the time he spoke Hourshit Bey
kept muttering to himself. *'Intéressant, intéressant!'* was what
he said and his hand with the pencil flew over the paper before
him. Old Haydar was highly gratified at being taken so seriously.
After the initial surprise of seeing his words being noted down
as soon as they were out of his mouth, he forgot everything and
let himself go.

'And you should know, Bey,' he said in proud ringing tones,

that all the great Ramazanoglus for a thousand years have girded their swords at our hearth. Yes, we have forged swords for your noble family for a full thousand years.'

'*Intéressant, intéressant . . .*'

Old Haydar was puzzled by this word, but it had an encouraging sound. And he knew it was one of the quirks great Beys had, to use words no one else could understand. These sounds, intelligible only to themselves, only added to their glory.

'Yes, just as I tell you,' Haydar went on. 'And do you know of Rüstem, the Master Blacksmith of the Chebi tribe, who lived a hundred years ago? He wasn't even a blacksmith by descent. He didn't belong to a sacred hearth like us. He was just an apprentice who became a master only later on . . .'

'*Intéressant, intéressant . . .*'

'Well, this Rüstem made a sword and he worked on it for fifteen years. Fifteen years, my great noble Bey, fifteen years! And then he took his sword to the Padishah who was struck with wonder at this sight. "Wish me a wish, Rüstem, Master," he said. But the blacksmith only kneeled before him and said, "I wish your health, your majesty." "What use is my health to you?" the Padishah said. "Wish me a wish . . ." Rüstem was embarrassed. What could he ask in return for this sword? It had no price. But the Padishah understood. "I'm not asking you to put a price to this sword," he said. "It would be spurning the mastercraftsman who has fashioned such a beautiful thing. I just want to grant you a wish . . ." And so Rüstem said: "What we need is a place for our tribe to winter on. The peoples of the plain keep on harassing us to death." At once the Padishah roared out his firman: "The plain of Aydin is yours. Go with your tribe and settle there . . ." '

'*Intéressant, intéressant . . .*'

'Now there's no Padishah any more . . . So I've come to you, the great Ramazanoglu of name and fame, the Bey of the whole Chukurova plain, our Bey. You are our father, our whole race and blood and tradition. You are Ramazanoglu, who came with us all the long trek from Khorassan . . . I've come to you with

181

our complaint.' He raised his voice. His brow was pearled with sweat. 'They have ruined us. We were alone, defenceless on this Chukurova plain and so they trampled us underfoot, our honour, our sons, our daughters, our traditions, our integrity, all that is beautiful and pure in us they destroyed. They harried us from land to land. You or us, it's all the same, my noble Ramazanoglu. What's done to us, is done to you too. Aren't you our protector, the only one we can turn to? Find a remedy for our woes or issue the firman that will wipe us out for ever.'

'Intéressant, intéressant . . .'

'That's how it is with us, my noble Bey . . . I've made a sword too. Thirty years I worked on it, and I'm not like Rüstem an apprentice, initiated into the profession. I'm a true descendant of the Sacred Hearth. The swords we made . . .' He blushed, but forced himself to continue. 'There isn't a Bey or a Padishah from the time of Khorassan to this day who did not gird himself with the swords we made. Thirty years I worked on this sword, and now I've brought it to you . . . We have no land, nowhere to set foot on. Nobody asks for a huge place like the plain of Aydin. No, my great Ramazanoglu, nobody wants that. Just a little patch of land, enough to keep us alive. I've been forging this sword for thirty years and engraving it with holy words from the Koran. The Shah of Horzumlu would have given a whole realm to the maker of such a sword . . .'

'Intéressant, intéressant . . . I didn't know all this.'

'But you should know,' Old Haydar said severely. 'You should! They have finished us, my son, ruined us. Doesn't this touch you at all?'

'Intéressant, intéressant . . .'

'It should touch you, Bey. Our ruin, our end is yours too. Don't put too much trust in this huge city of yours though it is as bright as the sun. You're a very humble-minded Bey I see, but still you mustn't trust in all these worldly possessions of yours. Your real mainstay is your tribe, your people. Worldly possessions are here today and gone tomorrow, swept away by the wind, the flood, the stranger, the enemy . . . But your tribe, your people, they're for ever. No one can take them away from you, my great Ramazanoglu. No one.'

'*Intéressant, intéressant* . . . I didn't know all this.'

'Well, now you know,' Old Haydar cried triumphantly. 'It's a good thing I came and told you. I'm sorry, Bey, forgive me for saying this, it's not for me to give you advice, but you are a little to blame too. Doesn't a man take some interest in his tribe, doesn't he ask himself, what have they become, my people, how are they doing? D'you think a Bey's principality can survive this way? It can't. It will just go to rack and ruin, as yours is doing. Walk out of this house and see what's going on. True, your city's grown very large and the houses are like palaces, but the people are depraved, they haven't an ounce of human feeling left in them. Did anyone ever tell you that great huge men hit at weak defenceless little children in the streets and that whole crowds of people just stand by and watch?'

'No, nobody told me that,' Hourshit Bey said, his face a study of conflicting emotions.

'Well, I'm telling you! And when such things happen in a land, it means it's rotten, dying out.'

'*Intéressant, intéressant* . . .'

Old Haydar rose and drew the sword from its scabbard. 'Look at this, Bey,' he said. 'Thirty years! . . . That Rüstem worked only fifteen years at his sword, and him only a late initiate . . . Yet when the Padishah saw it, he cried, my God it dazzles my eyes . . . Ask me for anything . . . But I . . . Thirty years! A true smith of the Holy Hearth . . . Such a firman the Padishah roared out! The plain of Aydin is yours . . . But I . . . I've come to you, the great Ramazanoglu of name and fame . . . Take this sword!'

Hourshit Bey held the sword in his hands and gazed at it for a long while. There was admiration on his face and Old Haydar's exultation mounted. Then he began to speak. He did not lift his eyes from the sword and as he spoke, the world began to spin all around Old Haydar. The walls of the room caved in and swung back, the ceiling fell and rose. A pitch-black darkness in front of his eyes, then a blinding light . . .

Then darkness again . . . Then burst after burst of light.

At last Hourshit Bey sighed. 'So you see, my faithful old Turcoman, my good Haydar,' he said. 'You see. They have crippled us. They have created a new cruel world, a world that is a hell both for them and for us. Yes, that's how it is now. This huge town isn't ours any longer. It belongs to the rich, to the Aghas, to the Kayseri merchants. Everything belongs to them.'

A hand was at Haydar's throat, strangling him. He grasped at his beard with all his might and thought, thought with lightning speed, thought with his hands, his beard, his eyes, his conical coif, his feet, his sandals. He was trembling, drenched in sweat.

'So you are worse off even than us, my Ramazanoglu, is that so?' he said. 'So you too, like us, have lost the warm embrace of a friend, the sword to be girded, the very path of life? So they have destroyed you too, eh my Ramazanoglu, long before us?'

'They have destroyed us,' Hourshit Bey said. Old Haydar's defeat, his misery were slowly burning into him. 'The Aghas, the rich merchants . . . It's they who hold everything now. And their only god is money. Yes . . . *Intéressant, intéressant* . . .'

But the word had lost its magic for Old Haydar. He took the sword from the table and eased it into its scabbard with trembling hands. Then cradling it in his arms like a baby he was afraid of hurting, he took a step towards Hourshit Bey and bent down on his right knee. 'Keep well, my great and noble Ramazanoglu,' he said. But his voice held a faint intonation of self-mockery.

So, he thought, everything is changing and coming to an end. Things are happening, unfamiliar cruel things that we don't know, that we don't understand. Nothing can save our world from dying out. Nothing, nobody. We shall become like Ramazanoglu too. The generations after us will sit like him in a tiny room, pondering like barn-owls, with no other word on their tongue but '*Intéressant, intéressant.*' A room no bigger than a hoopoe's nest! And yet the great Ramazanoglu must count himself lucky. Our children won't find even that much.

Nothing . . . Not even a tiny strip of land.

He could not think any more. It was as though he were floating in some dense annihilating fog. When he came back to Osman he did not even look at him. He saw nothing as he lurched on with the sword pressed tightly to his breast. Osman could well imagine what had passed inside. He led the old man back towards the centre of the city.

But as Haydar walked he began to recover from his shock, to think again in disconnected snatches . . . He had said something, the great Ramazanoglu. What was it? Dead . . . Everything gone . . . But the Aghas . . . It was all over with the Beys . . . But the Aghas, those bastard offshoots of mankind . . . And yet Temir Agha . . . And what about Mad Memet Agha? Weren't they each one of them worth ten of these noble titled Beys? Weren't they wiser, more generous, more human? That Temir Agha, for instance, they said he was really a Kurdish Bey, but quite impoverished, who had come to the Chukurova where he soon became one of the richest Aghas there, with more land than even a Padishah's firman could have conferred on him. And all through the strength of his fist.

Gradually, Old Haydar's face cleared. Osman watched him with relief. He had thought the old man was going to die when he had emerged from Ramazanoglu's house.

'Osman, let's go to that good man. The one who's got the same name as our boy . . .'

'All right,' Osman said.

It was well into the afternoon when they came to Kerem Ali's shop. He was really glad to see this red-bearded giant again. 'Well!' he greeted them with a joyful smile. 'Did you find the great Ramazanoglu of name and fame?'

Old Haydar seemed to be awakening from a long sleep. 'I found him,' he said in injured tones, 'and I talked to him too. Look, brother, will you do me another favour?' What had hurt him most, what had made him really angry was that Hourshit Bey, who was after all a real Ramazanoglu, had never once asked to see the sword. Old Haydar had had the further humiliation of unsheathing it without being asked. But then, how amazed he had been, that Hourshit Bey . . . How his eyes had almost popped out of his head, like a frog's . . . Old Haydar was suddenly seized with a longing to show the sword to this good man, Kerem Ali.

'I'll do anything you wish,' Kerem Ali was saying. 'Just say it, uncle.'

'Thank you. God bless you for your goodness. Will you show me Temir Agha's house? I have to see him too. It's about this sword I made. Thirty years I worked on it . . .' He talked quickly as though afraid he might miss something. 'Our blacksmith's hearth is a holy hearth . . . Ever since the days we lived in Khorassan . . . They call me Haydar, the Master Blacksmith of the Holy Hearth. Shahs and Padishahs and proud powerful Beys all came to gird their swords at our hearth. Now, Rüstem, the blacksmith of the Chebi tribe who was not a true smith of the hearth, but merely an initiate . . . Well, he made a sword. It took him fifteen years to make it and then he brought it to the Padishah . . . And the Padishah . . . Tongue-tied with wonder . . . Wish me a wish . . . And I . . . I . . . this sword . . . A thousand years I've been forging it. A thousand, two thousand, ten thousand years . . . Ever since our hearth was founded. The Padishah gave Rüstem the whole of the plain of Aydin . . . Just for one sword! Look! Take it and look, good man . . .' He drew the sword from its scabbard and held it out to Kerem Ali. 'Like a drop of water it gleams in the sunlight! Ten thousand years it has taken me to forge this sword . . . Hold it and look . . . Hold it! You're a good man, let it touch your hand, it'll bring you luck.'

His red beard was quivering with excitement.

Kerem Ali was sincerely awed. He could not take his eyes off so much beauty. He gazed and gazed. He turned the sword over in his hands and stared again, spellbound.

A crowd was gathering about them. People stopped to look in wonder at the sword. They praised it, extolled it, and Old Haydar basked in the warm-hearted interest and admiration of the swelling crowd. At last Kerem Ali handed the sword to Old Haydar with a wealth of praise that could only come from such an honest man. 'Not in the hundred thousand years to come can such a sword be fashioned,' he said. 'Praise to your hands.'

'Send me to Temir Agha now,' Old Haydar said as he sheathed his sword.

'Temir Agha's dead,' Kerem Ali said. 'He's been dead a long time.'

'And Mad Memet Agha?'

'He's dead too.'

'There must be the sons, then. Or some other Agha like them.'

'Have nothing to do with the sons,' Kerem Ali said. 'Why don't you go to Hasip Bey? He's one of you, a Yörük . . . There may even be some kinship between you.'

'We're related to the Ramazanoglus and the Ottomans. Where does Hasip Bey come from?'

'That I don't know,' Kerem Ali answered. 'But he's of Yörük origin and one of the richest men in Adana city. The whole land of Yüregir from here to the Mediterranean belongs to him.'

'Maybe he's one of the Yüregir nomads . . .'

'Maybe,' Kerem Ali said. 'Perhaps you'd better see him.'

'All right,' Old Haydar said with renewed confidence. 'Let's go to him. Since he's a Yörük, and from Yüregir too, he'll know a man's worth.'

Kerem Ali turned to his apprentice. 'Look, go with this old man again and take him to Hasip Bey.'

The youth led the way and they came to Hasip Bey's dwelling. As soon as he saw the house Old Haydar was jubilant. There! he said to himself. This is what I call a mansion, a palace! It was a huge ornate building adorned with a wealth of coloured glass and gilt, occupying a large area in a wide garden. Like a fairy pavilion, Old Haydar thought, a thing of magic, all of crystal and beryl, of pearl and coral . . . That's how aghas should live, and pashas and sultans too. Poor Ramazanoglu, frustrated, spitting fire against the aghas. Yes, truly, the great Ramazanoglu of name and fame was no more. No wonder

Hourshit Bey had grown heated when he spoke of the aghas! He was dead and these people had taken his place for good. Old Haydar realized this as soon as he set eyes on the house. He was pleased and his hopes rose again. Hasip Bey, the owner of such a palace, would surely accept this bright sundrop of a sword. Master-craftsman, he would say, wish me a wish . . . Your health is all I wish, my sultan, my lion, my noble one. Of what use is my health to you, wish me a wish . . . A little patch of land, a tiny little patch . . . We have been beating swords such as this a thousand, ten thousand years . . . Ten thousand people, a hundred thousand, have fashioned these swords for generations in our holy hearths . . . And we shall go on beating them for thousands of years more. The world shall not be deprived of such a beautiful thing. There will always be men to realize its worth. Yes indeed, that's how it is, my noble Hasip Bey. Ramazanoglu was furious with you, he swore at you. But it's not his fault. After all, you've ruined him, you've taken his place. You mustn't mind him . . . Why, he never even asked to look at my sword! Not once! If I hadn't taken it out and shown it to him he'd never have seen it. This sword! Yes indeed, my noble Hasip Bey, it's just as I tell you.

He smiled at Osman, smiled with all his being, his long red sparkling beard, his tufty brows, his steel-green eyes, his golden conical coif and even the sword in his hand.

Kerem Ali's apprentice rang at the gate. 'Ask the man who opens for Hasip Bey,' he told them and went away.

The door of the house swung open and a footman in a shining silver-embroidered livery walked over to the gate and stood before them, stiff as a poker. 'What is it you want?'

His manner was stern and haughty, but Old Haydar was not disconcerted. It was just how the servant of a Bey or an Agha ought to behave. 'Is Hasip Agha at home?' he enquired in a bright ringing voice. 'If he is, tell him that an old Yörük, Haydar the Master of the Blacksmith's Hearth, has come to him as Allah's guest. An old Yörük, the master of the true hearth where genuine Egyptian swords are wrought . . . For shahs and padishahs . . .' Yes, ah yes indeed . . . That's how beys and

pashas, shahs and sultans should live. Yes, just like this. Ah my
poor Ramazanoglu, ah . . .

The footman turned away without a word and went into the
house, closing the door behind him.

Hasip Bey had been watching them from the window,
wondering what this outlandish old man, with his long coif,
his sandals, that sword in his hand, and an old jade in his wake,
could want with him. Could it be one of those Yörük relatives
of his, he thought, remnants from the age of the ancient
Hittites? He was annoyed. All the Yörüks of the earth, it seemed,
were bent on claiming kinship with him, such an invasion of
them there had been these past few years. 'Go back and see
what it is they want,' he ordered the footman. 'Are they
relatives or what?'

The footman went back and repeated all this to Old Haydar.

'We're not relatives,' the old man said. 'Our kinship is with
the Ramazanoglus and the Ottomans, not with the Yüregir
tribes. It's because we've heard of Hasip Bey's fame that we've
come. I am Haydar, the Master Blacksmith . . . Rüstem, the
Master Blacksmith of the Chebi tribe, not a real master at
all . . . Fifteen years it took him . . . But our hearth . . . For ten
thousand years . . .' And he recounted it all once more in great
detail.

The footman only half grasped what he was saying. 'They're
not related to you,' he told Hasip Bey, 'but to the Ramazanoglus and the Ottomans. This man is master of a holy
hearth. He's made a sword. A thousand years, he says, it took
him to make it. He wants to give it to you, and in return you'll
grant him a wish . . .'

Hasip Bey laughed. He thrust his hand into the right-hand
pocket of his trousers and drew out a sheaf of banknotes. 'Take
this,' he said, selecting a couple of ten-lira notes, 'and give it to
that old man. Tell him I don't want to see any swords or the
like.'

Old Haydar was waiting, his eyes on the door, holding his
breath. The footman appeared and held out the two banknotes.
'The Bey doesn't want to see swords or the like. He says you're

to take this money and go away.'

Caught unawares, Old Haydar took the money that was put into his hand. The footman turned and disappeared swiftly into the house. In an instant the door had closed fast behind him.

Old Haydar was quite paralysed. The ten-lira notes slipped from his fingers and were swept up by the strong west wind along the road and into a garden. Osman took his arm, and they walked away, the old man's feet weaving into each other. On and on they walked past houses and gardens, along the large avenues, but Haydar saw nothing at all now. Osman stopped at a grocer's to buy some bread and *halva* and they went on. As the sun was setting they found themselves on the bank of Jeyhan River. Old Haydar bent down and cupping up some water washed his face with great care. Had he been dreaming? Was he only just waking up? 'I'm hungry, Osman,' he said.

Osman opened the paper parcel and set the bread and *halva* before him. The old man ate quickly, hungrily. The last rays of the setting sun were playing ruddily on his beard. 'That Kerem Ali,' he said, looking up suddenly, 'what a good man he is, isn't he, Osman? Just that one man . . . So human his smile. Such a kind generous person.'

'Yes,' Osman agreed.

'Everything will have an end, everything will wane, will be corrupted, ways and customs will change, but human feelings will endure. In some place, in some corner, kindness, generosity will remain standing, like Kerem Ali, upright, a mainstay in this world.'

The day was fading into night, and with the darkness the lights of the city came on in a sudden burst. Old Haydar started. 'A thousand years, ten thousand years we fashioned this sword . . . Like a drop of water trembling brightly in the light . . . We will go on making it ten thousand years more . . . Ten thousand, a hundred thousand years . . .'

His mind's wandering, Osman thought. The poor man, it's been too much for him, all this.

'Ten thousand, ten thousand! A hundred thousand years more . . . Rüstem of the Chebi tribe . . . Not even from the true hearth . . . Only an apprentice, a late initiate . . . Fifteen years it took him . . . And I, thirty years . . . Ten thousand, a hundred thousand years . . . Wish me a wish . . .'

18

*When his father died Halil was still a child, Mustan re-
called. He had no one left but his mother. All the tribe had
taken turns to look after his flock. His tent was the first to be
set up, the first to be pulled down and loaded on to the
camels. At every bayram, as on Hidirellez day, the tribesmen
would come to Halil's tent to pray before the long faded
standard, the shrivelled drum, the old horsetail, the halberd.
What they stood for nobody knew, but they were relics of their
Turcoman forefathers, holy objects from old forgotten times.
They belonged to those happy days when the Yörüks were in
the prime of their glory, when under this very standard, bearing the horsetail in their hands, with long lances on their
shoulders, they had roamed the seven climes and the four
corners of the earth, bowing down to no one. Who was this
Halil, what was he? And Jeren, how she loved him, a love
unto death, a love that could make her trample over her own
people.*

A blasting raging north-easter was blowing that sent the trees
crashing into each other, strong enough to uproot the very
rocks, a crazy north-easter. Halil had gone to sleep. So had his
two companions, and Resul too. They lay on the dry grass in
the hollow of a huge rock, wrapped in their embroidered felt
cloaks, breathing deeply.

Even the serpent never touches a man in his sleep, even the
enemy. How can one kill a sleeping man? There on that spot
near the crest of Aladag, Mustan was consumed by the urge to
kill Halil right away.

What if I killed him now? he thought. I must. That man's
been a thorn in my flesh ever since I can remember. It's been
Halil, Halil all the time, no one ever saw or looked at anybody

else. He's still considered as some holy being, and even the old men, the women, children, sheiks and wise men are silent and rise to their feet before him. Who is he? What is he, this Halil? He's handsome, of course, with those blue eyes so strangely rimmed with black, deep as the far blue sky, pure as a child's . . . So tall too, and graceful . . . The whole tribe adores him, and the other tribes too. No, he must die, or I can't go on living. And what if I die too? . . . I don't care . . . I don't mind dying, so long as I know he's dead.

He crept up to the cave under the cover of darkness, drawing nearer and nearer to the sleeping Halil. The shadows, the starlight, the rocks and trees came rolling down like a torrent. The mountain rumbled. He held his breath.

Pull the trigger, Mustan.

Halil is setting fire to that Chukurova village . . . He has grown taller suddenly, formidable. A figure of dread, he sweeps through the village. Halil is a column of flame, a death-carrying blaze. In the tribe, among the other Yörüks, through the whole of that craven Chukurova plain his name spreads from tongue to tongue, a symbol of fear, of courage, of death, of friendship and beauty. There is only Halil in the world and no one else.

Pull the trigger, Mustan! The muzzle's just a finger from Halil's brow. Pull the trigger, Mustan, and let his head be smashed to smithereens . . . Pull, Mustan!

His hands went numb, his body was a mass of pins and needles. Strange shadows flitted by, striking him with fear. He took heart again, he went and came. Once more he aimed the muzzle straight at Halil's forehead.

Jeren will never be Halil's, nor anyone else's. She will marry Oktay Bey. The tribe needs that badly, they will give her to him . . . Wake up, Halil, sit up, brother! You must die.

When they were children Halil would never even deign to look at him. Like a wolf-cub he was, and all the children his slaves. How he would beat Mustan, and humiliate him too . . . And even now, when Mustan had taken to the mountains, an outlaw just like Halil, it was Halil, Halil all the time, his name on everyone's lips. Nobody ever spoke of Mustan . . .

Pull the trigger, Mustan!

He came and went like a caged creature in the raging wind.

Look sharp, Mustan, you must finish this business tonight or you'll never do it. Never . . . Pull the trigger . . .

The early morning call to prayer is sounding from a long minaret at Chukurköprü near Sumbas River in the Chukurova . . . Halil rides a bay horse, his rifle in his hand, but Mustan is on foot like a dog straggling behind him, and Halil never speaks to him, not once . . . They come to Dervish Bey's house. 'Wake up, Bey,' Halil calls in his strong deep voice. 'Your time has come.' Bold, fearless . . . 'Akmashat is our wintering place. Give it to us. What right have you to prevent us wintering there?' Dervish Bey's eyes are starting from their sockets. 'Don't kill me, Halil,' he implores. 'Noble men like you don't kill, not like this, not for a little matter of a wintering place. I know Akmashat is yours. Don't kill me, I have a wife and children to look after. Let the tribe come at once, tomorrow, and settle there.' And so they pitched their tents at Akmashat that winter, proudly, triumphantly. And so, even in the Chukurova, songs were sung in honour of Halil . . . Our people have no old songs. They don't sing, but their faces smile, sweet as a song. Nobody even looks at Mustan, nobody even remembers that he exists when Halil is there.

Pull the trigger, Mustan. Come on, pull and get it over with . . .

Halil's blood is spreading in a pool on the ground. A long hollow, and in it he lies, dead, his long body stretched out, handsome, not like a corpse at all, proud, haughty, confident, mocking. His dark-lashed eyes are closed, yet they live. He lies there in the hollow, myrtle branches strewed over him, heavy-scented. Heap earth and stones upon him . . . Halil is there, buried deep in the earth, but still smiling. His fresh red blood spurts out of the grave and over it thousands of golden bees are humming, bright, sparkling, shimmering-winged bees.

Haydar, the Master of the Blacksmith's Hearth, will never bow to anyone, not even to sheiks and saints . . . But before

Halil, he prostrates himself on the ground . . . Who is he, what is he, this Halil?

Pull the trigger, Mustan. Come on, get it over with!

His hands are not trembling now, nor is his heart fluttering like a bird in a cage. His mind is clear, made up. So long as Halil lives, the world is dead for him. Everyone is dead.

Pull the trigger, Mustan!

The north-easter chills him to the bone. It will be daylight soon, and still the muzzle is there on Halil's brow.

Halil embracing Jeren, swaying with her in his arms, this way, that way . . . Halil clasping all the most beautiful girls to his breast . . . All of them in love with him, Yörük girls, girls from the Chukurova, the towns, all gazing on him with adoration wherever he goes. Bright eyes . . . Tearful . . .

Mustan, Mustan, Mustan . . .

He went to Resul and roused him. 'Wake up, brother,' he said softly. 'Come this way a minute.'

Without a sound Resul slipped out of the hollow and followed him. They came to the spring.

'Wash your face to wake yourself.'

Resul did as he was told.

'Listen, it'll be day any minute now. I've tried and tried, but I haven't had the courage to kill Halil.'

'I wasn't asleep, I saw you,' Resul said. 'You came and went and came and went all the time.'

'Yes,' Mustan admitted. 'I couldn't do it. After all, we used to be friends . . . Halil's nothing to you. You don't know him at all. With me it's different, you're my very own brother now . . . Take this gun and pull the trigger for me. He mustn't live. I'm dead, you're dead, everyone's dead as long as he lives. All the young people are dead. He fills up the whole world. While he lives the whole world's dead.'

Resul could not understand why Mustan was so bent on killing Halil. Mustan had tried to explain it to him, but he simply could not understand. 'Give us that gun and let's kill him,' he said as coolly as though he were saying, let's kill that bird, or that ant, a fly or a bee.

Mustan handed over his rifle. He took the shepherd's felt cloak, wrapped himself up in it, and lay down at the mouth of the cave, waiting, his eyes closed, his whole being concentrated in his ears.

A wonderful sensation such as he had never known shook Resul through and through. It pierced him to the core of his heart. His hands were on fire and the stock of the rifle was red-hot too. Like a madman he whirled round and round, then stopped suddenly and pulled on the trigger. Mustan jumped, howling, and hurled himself back on the ground, writhing, clawing at the bushes and rocks. Resul fired again, twice. Halil was awake now, clutching at his gun. Resul rushed to cover behind a rock. 'Stop, Halil,' he shouted. 'Don't kill me. I shot Mustan.'

Mustan was rolling on the ground, biting at the earth and at his fingers. Halil tried to hold him. 'Brother, brother Mustan, why did they do this to you?' he cried. Mustan moaned. He screamed and struggled, his teeth gnashing at the blood-soaked earth, at the bushes and stones and tearing at his hands. 'I'll avenge you, I will. I will, brother Mustan. I'll not let you go like this.'

In the dawning light of day, he saw Mustan stretch himself taut three times as though his body would snap in two. His teeth were clamped together. The earth about him was steeped in blood, the space of a threshing-floor, clawed, uprooted all over. Then he stiffened and remained quite still. The flesh of his hands hung in shreds and the bones stood out, stark and white.

The two other men were waiting at a distance for Halil to rise. He sat on silent beside the corpse, his blood-steeped right hand resting on the ground, his eyes fixed on Mustan. Suddenly he looked up and saw Resul still standing beside the rock. He leapt to his feet with his gun pointed.

'Wait, Halil,' Resul said coolly as though nothing had happened. A smile hovered on the curve of his lips. Somehow his voice held such a commanding confidence that Halil was arrested. 'Wait, Halil, brother . . .'

19

The draggled broken caravan had come to a stop on the grass-less barrens of Saricham. In the grey dawn Headman Süleyman stood watching the tents being pitched. Everyone was weary, exhausted. Not a sound filled the air save the muffled rat-a-tat of tent pegs being driven in. Not a child cried. Not a dog barked. Light-hearted laughter had long deserted this tribe. The day glimmered. Headman Süleyman turned away. He could not bear to look at the torn faded tents, soiled with mud and hurriedly patched up, nor did he dare to count them. Old Tanish was beside him. His tiny lashless old eyes were blinking rapidly in the spreading sunlight. Steam rose from the crumpled bedraggled tents and from the mats and rugs and bedding laid out to dry in front of them. The milk had been drawn first thing and was boiling now in black cauldrons, wafting its odour gently through the air, above the smell of sweat and dank and decay. The baking sheets had been brought out too, and groups of women were hastily kneading the dough, rolling it out and baking layer after layer of the little flat yufka-breads. Others had taken their washing out to a distant runnel of water. A handful of small children, naked as the day they were born, paddled about them, but listlessly, with neither laughter nor play. The beat of laundry-staves could be heard, faint and far. Only one woman had not moved from her tent and that was Jeren. She sat there leaning against the central pole, heavy-hearted, spent, apathetic. The Headman asked Old Tanish if he had counted the tents. There had been sixty when they set out, and now there were only forty-nine. Sakarjali Ali had gathered up family and belongings at Dumlu and had disappeared without a word to anyone. Big Ali had broken from them at Anavarza. Kürdoglu Durmush had joined the Lek Kurds near Anavarza, taking with him Kepenekli Mustafa, Ayidögen Hidir and Azapoglu Haji . . . And Salman too, after they had crossed Hemité bridge, had turned off towards Bahché with all his family, weeping . . . Nobody felt like talking about this to the Headman, nobody even had the courage to tell him.

'And so we've come to this,' Headman Süleyman said with a deep long sigh. 'Shrunk down to almost nothing, Tanish Agha. From two thousand tents to one thousand. From one thousand to five hundred. From five hundred to a hundred. And then sixty. And now . . . And so like this, we'll dwindle to nothing. None of those who leave come back. We never hear a word from any of them ever again.'

'Not a word.'

'And so like this, one day there'll be nobody left at all.'

'Nobody,' Old Tanish said. 'That's clear as daylight.'

'It belongs to us, then, to bury the noble tribes of old, the days of glory, the great Turcoman, the Yörüks, the Aydins, the Horzumlus, to bury them like this, miserably, with no elegies, no words, no music, like dogs . . .'

'The glorious Turcoman is dying out with us, dying in our arms,' Old Tanish said.

'To what black days were we born! Would that our mothers had never given birth!'

On and on they talked, these two old men, like a funeral lament.

In the days of their glory the Turcomans had songs and legends and epics. They had traditions then, festivals, ceremonies. The ritual *semahs* and *mengis* were danced in large crowds. Solemn congregations were held that lasted three days and three nights. They had minstrels and flutists and great bards. Every household had an aged Turcoman grandmother who could tell all the ancient tales and ballads. There were sacred hearths then, and holy sages, and master-craftsmen who could fashion swords and beat the felt and weave carpets and kilims, and make soft leather saddles and precious silverware and vegetal dyes, master-craftsmen whose fame spread from Iran to Turan, from the land of the Rum to Arabia. And noble beys, each one like a powerful eagle. And when they descended into the plains they would be greeted with honours by valis and pashas . . . One by one, little by little everything had dwindled away. All was ended now. First the word had been lost, then the songs, the legends, the dances and rituals, Nasrettin Hoja, Yunus, the poet of all humankind, the *semah*, the solemn congregations . . . For forty years now the last remnants of the Turcomans had been agonizing all over the world. Everything had come to an end long ago.

'What are we striving for?' Headman Süleyman said. 'We've got a body on our hands, dead these hundred years, putrid, and still we persist in not burying it.'

'We'd have buried it long ago, Süleyman, if it'd been possible,' Old Tanish said. 'It's because we can't even find enough land for its grave that we've been carrying it on our backs these forty years.'

'Forty years . . . ' Headman Süleyman repeated. A bitter pain gripped him, and with it such anguish as made him tremble all over. This Saricham place was not auspicious. The people hereabouts were hard, greedy, unfriendly. Whenever a nomad tribe had tried to camp here, they had got into trouble. It was mid-morning already and no one had come yet, but . . .

He began to walk about the tents accompanied by Old Tanish, trying to joke with the tribespeople, to keep their spirits up. Down below, the flocks were confined on a bare stretch of land for what little grazing they could find there. Headman Süleyman was always cut to the quick to see the flocks like this, he felt something foul inside him that he could never cleanse and wipe away. All the way from Payas they had allowed the flocks to stray into the green sprouting crops of the Chukurova. Like a raging fire, like a plundering army had been the passage of the flocks from Payas to Saricham, devouring everything, destroying all on their way.

'Tanish Agha,' he moaned, 'think of what we're doing! Everywhere we pass we leave fields devastated as though by a fire. No wonder the Chukurova people turn into enemies. We let our flocks eat the portion of the poor and destitute. How can we blame them when we rob them of their crops? How can we expect them to be glad of that?'

'Now look here, Headman Süleyman,' Old Tanish protested, 'you know very well that where sheep graze the crops are always twice as bountiful. The sheep is a sacred creature. So it has been since the time of our father Adam. The Chukurova people don't know this. And besides they dare to sell us God's own grain.'

'Well, what do we do but steal it!'

Old Tanish was provoked. 'Then let them leave us a little space to step on. We've been wintering in this Chukurova for hundreds of years. Don't we have any right to this land at all?'

'Not any longer, it seems . . .'

'We gave their names to all the rivers, to all the mountains, to every single part of this plain. Every stone, every rock, every piece of earth bears the name of a Yörük tribe. Wasn't it all ours? How did they come to claim what is ours? Why? When? From whom did they buy it? How much money, how many sheep did they give to become the owners of our age-old wintering lands? Where were they when we lived in the Chukurova?'

Headman Süleyman laughed. 'They were with us. These people are our sons, our daughters, offsprings of the tribes. What became of the tribes, where did they go, do you think, as they grew smaller and poorer? Those people are us. We're doing nothing but oppress each other in this Chukurova. It's a matter of the sword hacking away at its own scabbard. Those who have gone from us are tearing at their own sheath. Take Sakarjali Ali. Five years hence, if we do last that long and pass by his village, he'll be the first to chase us away, stick in hand. And the first to strike at us too.'

Suddenly he stopped, transfixed, his eyes on a tent that lay on the ground, not yet put up, like a dead eagle with plucked wings and ruffled feathers, head and feet all in a heap.

'Why hasn't Halil's tent been put up?' he shouted angrily.

'Quick, let me not see the Bey's tent like this. Put it up, quick. I'm not dead yet.' Furiously he strode through the camp, majestic, the last desperate resurgence of some holy wrath. The young men rushed up to obey him. 'I'm not dead yet,' he thundered. 'Wait till I'm dead, and then you can leave the Bey's tent lying about, and throw away the horsetail, the drum and the standard that bears our emblem. Throw them into the river, together with my dead body. Or to the dogs . . .' At that moment he caught a glimpse of Jeren's head peeping from the tent as though from the mouth of a dark cavern. One instant, like a dream, and then it was gone. It drove him to fresh frenzy. 'And while I'm alive you'll leave Jeren in peace too. This tribe can't sink so low just for the sake of a little patch of land. Jeren's the most beautiful thing left to us, the last beautiful thing. We can't give her away to anyone against her will. So stop persecuting the girl. No one, no one is to touch Jeren as long as I'm alive. And as for that lad, that Oktay, just let him try and set foot in this tribe again! Just let him, that low, brazen, abject woman of a man! I'll kill him with my own hands, I will! Everyone is to talk with Jeren, everyone! I order you.' In all his many years as Headman of the Karachullu tribe, this was the first time Süleyman had ever said, I order you . . . 'Jeren is to dress in all her fine clothes, today, at once, and mix again with the tribe, like a rising sun.'

She was to him the last flash of brightness, the most perfect, to shine yet among the dying Yörüks. To end with Jeren, to die out with such a perfect brightness as Jeren.

He was tired. His legs trembled. He was going to fall, to be disgraced before all his people . . . Breathing heavily, he managed to reach his tent. Beads of sweat stood out on his forehead.

Everyone was astounded at the Headman's outburst. Never in forty years had they seen him in such a state. Old Tanish followed him into the tent. 'Now, take it easy, Süleyman,' he kept repeating. 'Take it easy brother . . .'. .

'Death! I want death . . .' Süleyman took a deep breath and his bright green eyes opened wide. 'O God almighty, grant me death! Death! I don't want to go on living after this. I don't want to watch this crumbling ruin. I don't want to see the stones tumbling down day after day. Every day a tent gone, every day! Wasting away with each passing day . . . Drained of all honour, pride and valour, of every human value . . .'

He closed his eyes. Old Tanish sat on there, watching over him as though at the wake of a dead child. He did not leave until he was sure that Süleyman had fallen asleep. Then he slipped quietly out of the tent.

The whole tribe, and Jeren too, were waiting outside, holding their breath.

'He's gone to sleep,' Old Tanish said. 'Anger tires old men. It makes them sleepy. It can even kill them . . . Don't disturb him.' He laughed. 'I'm going to get some sleep myself.'

A strange unaccountable gladness was spreading through the tribe, such as they had not known for a long time. A joy left over from the old days. It was as though the Yörüks were themselves again. And now Jeren was among them, dressed up in her fine clothes, and everyone was talking to her. Sheep were slaughtered and food was cooked, and they all settled down to eat as they had not done in a long time. The Headman slept on. They were careful to make no noise. Their joy, slow and restrained, flowed like a clear underground stream through their hearts.

And then the hunter Kamil brought a piece of news that added to their delight. 'I've heard it from a villager round here . . . He said Old Haydar took his sword to the great Ramazanoglu, who stared and marvelled and couldn't have his fill of looking at it for a whole day. So there are still people left on this god-forsaken earth to make such beautiful swords, he said, and went on his knees before Old Haydar. O Master of the Blacksmith's Hearth, he said, God bless your tribe, God bless you for bringing this sword to me and not to Ismet Pasha. This sword's worth more than all my lands, more than the whole land of the Ottomans. Go now and take your tribe to settle at Yüregir on the shores of the Mediterranean. I'm giving you a wintering place there that is grassy and fertile and well-watered . . . And then he killed sheep and lambs and a big calf too, and held a great feast in honour of Old Haydar, with drums and music. You're my guest, he said. Stay with me for a week, for it will bring my house good fortune and plenty to have the Master of the Blacksmith's Hearth under its roof.'

They listened, they repeated the story, and by evening other versions had taken shape. Each one made them tremble with joy.

'No, no, it wasn't Ramazanoglu he went to, but Temir Agha, the great rich agha, and Temir Agha was so lost in admiration at the sight of the sword that for three days and three nights he neither ate nor slept, but only gazed at it. Then he knelt down before Old Haydar and thanked him for not having taken the sword to Ramazanoglu, his arch-enemy. Thank you, he said, for bringing me this symbol of honour from the great Turcomans. Thank you for giving it to me and not to Ismet Pasha, that Ottoman. I'm only a poor Kurd, but our family have their roots in the holy land of Khorassan too, and if I've become an agha it doesn't mean I've lost all human feelings. The red and green banner has been upheld by us too, ever since the days of Khorassan. If I'd been in Ramazanoglu's place or the Ottoman's I'd have given you whole provinces and kingdoms. But as it is, I've got plenty of land too. So come and settle on it, wherever you choose.'

Little groups had formed and in each group a different story was told.

'No, no it was Ismet Pasha! And he said, if only this holy sword had come to me when I was fighting the Greeks and saving the fatherland! Then, together with Mustafa Kemal Pasha and our Padishah of the noble race of Kayihan and Khorassan who had the blessing of Hajibektashi Veli himself, I would have put to rout and conquered not only the Greeks, but all the lands of Arabia and India and China, and the English and French to boot. What crippled me then was that I didn't have such a sword in my hand. But still, you've come at a good time, Haydar, Master, for I'm planning a campaign against the Russians . . . So choose a place to settle, make your choice wherever you wish . . . And even the great Ismet Pasha bent down in homage before our Old Haydar.'

The rumours grew wilder and wilder, and nobody could tell any longer where they had started and who had said what. Most of the tribesmen did not believe a single word of all this, but they dared not open their mouths or do anything to dam the exuberant flood of joy. And even in the heart of the most incredulous, a little flame of hope had been kindled. 'There must be something to it,' they said. 'Considering Old Haydar's still not back, he must have obtained something. He's not mad, is he, to stay away so long if he hasn't had some success?'

Headman Süleyman woke up in the midst of all this excitement, but when he was told what had happened he only smiled and said nothing. So relieved was he to see them all in a good mood for once that he never gave their problems another thought.

Even Kerem's mother, who had been weeping bitterly ever since the boy's disappearance, now found some consolation. 'He left at the same time as his grandfather,' she said. 'They'll come back together.'

'Of course they will,' the other women encouraged her.

That night, everyone from seven to seventy slept quietly and peacefully, free of fear and full of bright dreams.

'Haydar, the Master of the Blacksmith's Hearth, our saviour, our hope . . . Old Haydar . . .'

Shepherd Ali was with the other shepherds grazing the flocks on the heath when he saw in the distance the shadowy figure of a horseman wandering about the mound where the tribe was camping. The shadow was going slowly round and round the encampment, but always at a good distance. After watching for some time Shepherd Ali began to be really curious. Now what could it be, this shadow circling the encampment like a blindfolded miller's horse? 'Boys,' he said to the other shepherds, 'I'm off to see what that horseman's doing or I'll die of curiosity. Is he mad or something, he's been going round and round like that for hours.' And he ran all the way to the circling man. 'Selam to you,' he called in his strong voice.

The horseman reined in. 'Selam to you too,' he replied, very low, very quiet, but obviously longing for companionship.

Shepherd Ali drew nearer. 'Who are you?' he asked. 'Why are you riding round and round this place in the dead of night?'

'Don't you recognize me, brother?' the horseman said with a sigh.

And then it dawned on Shepherd Ali. 'You're not Oktay Bey, are you?'

'Yes, I am. And who are you?'

'I'm Shepherd Ali . . . Look brother, I've got bad news for you. They're going to kill you. Headman Süleyman's very angry and he's given orders. Anyone who sees you is to kill you. But I won't. I like you. I pity you. So get away from here before anybody sees you. The tribe's had more than it can stand. If they see you they'll take it out on you. Don't stop here, brother. Get away quickly, or they'll kill you on the spot.'

'I don't care,' Oktay Bey moaned. 'I don't want to live on like this. I'll be glad to die and get it over with.'

'Don't stop a moment. Go away before you bring new troubles on our head. We've had more than our share. Run, I tell you. Run!' He lifted up his stick and took a step towards him. 'Run, man, don't stop. Run!'

'Don't shout, brother,' Oktay Bey said, his heart sinking. 'You'll wake them up and I'll be disgraced before everybody. I'm going.'

'Hurry up then,' Shepherd Ali said.

'Good-bye, brother. Keep well, all of you . . .' He spurred his horse down the slope and vanished into the night.

'Poor man,' Shepherd Ali thought. 'How he's suffering. It's worse than death this passion that's got hold of him. God preserve us . . .'

Day dawned and the little camp was soon bustling with life. Sheep were being milked and churns beaten. A fire was burning before every tent with milk boiling over it or *tarhana* soup cooking. Donkeys were braying, horses neighing and camels rumbling. The gay laughter of women rang from tent to tent. The steaming smell of milk and tarhana sank into the earth of

Saricham, warm and pleasant. The huge sheepdogs barked their long deep muffled bark, and from a neighbouring village came the sound of cocks crowing. Bells were tinkling and a long-drawn-out song was heard rolling over the flatness of the plain.

Headman Süleyman walked about the tents, erect, a smile on his lips as naïve as a child's. He watched the women patting the butter into the gaily decorated black firkins and eagerly breathed in the old familiar odour of the goatskin churns, redolent of the carefully thinned out pinebark with which they were finished. In the early morning light the tattered tents seemed beautiful to his eyes, as splendid as the tents of old, and at that moment he fancied himself back in the days of his youth, at the head of a thousand tents, wintering at Akmashat or at Narlikishla, and not waiting in fear on the barrens of Saricham for the dangers that threatened them.

'We've come to ourselves,' he thought. 'The tribe's back on its feet. Thanks to Old Haydar. And to Jeren . . . Or is it really because of that? Who knows . . . And who cares now! They'll see those Chukurova people, what's coming to them! So it's like cringing rabbits the Yörüks are? Well, they'll see now. Whatever happens . . .' He smiled proudly.

It was mid-morning when the shepherd came up, running. A warm gentle breeze was blowing from the south that stirred the blood in men's veins, the pleasant south wind of the Chukurova. 'They're coming!' he yelled.

Headman Süleyman laughed. 'Well, we were expecting them,' he said.

'They're from that village Halil had set fire to. I heard them talking. We'll burn them all, they were saying, at Saricham . . . Young and old . . .'

'Let's see them do it then,' Headman Süleyman's voice was steady, confident. 'Get ready. Find arms, sticks, knives, stones, anything. No running away this time. Let the Chukurova see what the Yörüks of Khorassan are made of!'

A horde of clamouring villagers were surging up to the camp, raising clouds of dust along the road. Some were on foot, others in tractors and trucks or riding donkeys and horses. They were

206

all armed with rifles, cudgels and hatchets. The two sides were like two armies in battle array. But the one was silent, holding its ground, while the other advanced in a furious vengeful mass. The Yörüks hardened by a thousand years of struggle stood calm and quiet before the yelling cursing villagers.

When the villagers came within a sling's throw of the Yörüks, their cries redoubled to the heavens at the hail of stones that assailed them. They howled, they ran, they fell wounded. Shots were fired, curses hurled all around, but they could not get any nearer the camp. At nightfall they retreated in disarray, carrying off their wounded to the hospital at Kozan. The weary sling-throwers celebrated their victory by drinking a bowl of milk but did not stir from their vantage point. Headman Süleyman went from the one to the other, triumphant as a general who has just won a pitched battle. 'We gave it to them this time,' he kept saying grimly. 'And we'll give it them again if they return.'

In the grey dawn, at the first glimmering of day, the villagers attacked again in greater numbers with a louder noise than before. They were met with a fresh hail of stones, but this time they all crowded into the trucks and tractor-trailers which moved straight into the tents. No sling-shots could stop them any longer. Fethullah flung himself on to the foremost tractors and dragged the drivers out of their seats. The tractors, together with their trailers, rolled down into the ditch and over-turned, spilling out the villagers all over the place. Then he rushed at the trucks and punctured the tyres of three of them with his knife. The villagers were surrounded now by an angry crowd of Yörüks. Women, children, old people, they all joined the fight which raged on violently till midday. From all the neighbouring villages people poured in to watch, and some even joined in on the side of the villagers.

Jeren had thrown herself into the thick of the fray. She and Fethullah were like wild tigers. Wielding heavy sticks they were here, there and everywhere, putting the flood of villagers to rout. But more and more of the Yörüks were dropping now, and among them were many women and children.

At last, just when the villagers had begun to fall back, the police arrived from Kozan town. The fighting stopped at once as the police swarmed into the tents of the Yörüks, confiscating all the sticks and slings and knives they could find. As for firearms they had all vanished. The attacking group was not even searched . . . On the contrary, the police helped them lift up their overturned tractors and repair their punctured tyres. Then the villagers got into the tractors and trucks and drove away shaking their fists at the Yörüks.

And now the Kaymakam himself made his appearance. Together with the captain of the police, they began to interrogate the Yörüks.

'Let those people stop attacking us wherever we go,' Headman Süleyman said, 'or this is what'll happen.'

'We won't wait for them to attack again. You're to leave this place at once.'

'We can't,' Headman Süleyman said, throwing all prudence to the winds. 'Not even if they kill us all, to the last man.'

'You'll go!' the police captain thundered. 'As if we've nothing better to do than bother with you people, year in year out! It's our job to maintain law and order here. If we'd been half an hour late today we'd have had five hundred casualties on our hands, both on your side and on theirs. I order you to leave. Are you resisting the law?'

'Of course not,' Headman Süleyman said. 'Never! We're all for the law. But where are we to go?'

'How should we know?' the Kaymakam intervened. 'It's not for us to find a place for you to stay. Go anywhere you like. You're free citizens in a free democratic state, free to go and come wherever you choose. But not to steal or kill, or knock people about. You're free citizens, but . . .'

'Then if we're free citizens . . .' the Headman began, but the police captain interrupted him sternly. 'I don't care what you are,' he said. 'You've disturbed the public peace here and I won't have you stay a minute longer. I'll pull down those tents of yours right over your heads.'

'You can pull them down,' Süleyman said, 'but where are we to go?'

'Turkey's a large country,' the captain cried in ringing tones. 'Huge! There are miles and miles of empty land where you can stay.'

'But this place is empty too,' the Headman said.

'It's empty, yes, but you've stirred up trouble here.'

'Did we start this fight? Did we attack them?'

'I don't care who started it. Come on, down with these tents. Now. This minute. Don't you hear me, man? If you don't obey me at once ... I ... I ... Sergeant!'

'Yes, captain?'

'Strike down all the tents. I want them loaded on to the camels as quickly as possible.'

The Kaymakam, the captain and the sergeant marched out of Süleyman's tent. He hurried after them, cradling a bandaged hand. 'But you haven't drunk our coffee yet,' he said. 'You can't leave my tent without having something, some milk, some *ayran*.' He was amazed at himself for having disregarded the age-old rules of hospitality. 'Stay and have a humble coffee at least ...' His voice was apologetic, ashamed. 'All this trouble has made me forget that I'm your host here.'

'That's enough talk,' the captain said. 'Are you going to take down those tents or not?'

'But where are we to go, my Pasha?'

The captain was exasperated. 'Go to hell,' he shouted. 'You're nothing but a thorn in the flesh for everybody. Nothing but trouble, trouble, trouble with you people ...'

'Nothing but trouble all these years,' the Kaymakam chimed in. 'We've had to leave off every other business in this paradise of Chukurova to deal with you people ...'

None of the Yörüks were to be seen anywhere. They had all crept into their tents which the police had already started pulling down. The Kaymakam and the captain stood at a distance, their hands thrust into their trouser-pockets, and watched as the tents dropped one by one over the people inside. And still no one appeared, not a sound or movement came from the fallen tents. It was an impossible job. The captain took the matter in hand.

'Fix your bayonets,' he ordered his men, 'and march on those tents. Pull those people out and make them collect their own tents.'

The men began hauling the Yörüks out of their tents. Women, children, men, old people, sick people, all were dragged to their feet, but sank down the minute they were left to themselves.

'All right, go on breaking up the tents,' the captain ordered. 'Some of you keep dragging these worms out and the others deal with the tents.'

Not a sound came from the Yörüks, neither a moan, nor a cry.

Suddenly the Kaymakam and the captain noticed that one of the tents was closely surrounded by a crowd of women and children who were preventing the policemen from getting inside. Not even the occasional thrust of a bayonet could break the tightly clamped ring of women.

Headman Süleyman's beard began to tremble. His eyes filmed over. 'Stop your men, captain,' he cried in anguish. 'Don't touch that tent. We'll leave at once.'

'Stand back,' the captain shouted to his men. 'What on earth is there in that tent?'

Süleyman went to the women. 'Go and load up the tents,' he said. 'We're leaving.'

'I must see what's inside,' the Kaymakam said.

'Yes, we must,' the captain said suspiciously.

Headman Süleyman led them in. The tent was quite empty, all tattered and worn. On the ground they saw an orange felt rug decorated with a sun emblem. It was in shreds and very old, but its colours still glowed undamaged, and the sun emblem stood out brightly. In a corner was a drum with shrivelled skin, and beside it stood a halberd. Near it a horsetail and also a long thing that looked like a banner. On the tent's central pole was hung a case of pure silk trimmed with beads. It contained the Holy Koran.

'What's all this?' the Kaymakam asked. 'Why is this tent so important to you? Is it something sacred?'

Süleyman felt like sinking to the bottom of the earth. 'These are the tokens of our tribe,' he answered. 'They have never left us ever since we came over from Khorassan. Nobody would touch them.'

The captain and the Kaymakam laughed heartily at this. Headman Süleyman tried to smile too as he followed them out of the tent. The Yörüks had finished pulling down the tents and were loading them on to the camels.

20

The banks of the long deep-set stream were overgrown with reeds all the way to the brake, and there the reeds spread out, thick as a wood, interspersed with blackthorn and jilpirti bushes and a few ash-trees. Far in the distance, to the west loomed the Anavarza crags with their crumbling ruins, swarming with snakes, haunted by the jinn and the peris, inhabited by large eagles, each one as huge as an aeroplane, and falcons and hawks and buzzards. And here too dwelt the immortal king of the eagles. They say he is a hundred times as big as any other eagle. His wings are of iron and he cannot fly, but whenever he feels like it a hundred eagles, five hundred even, get under his body and bear him off over the Chukurova plain, up above the Thousand Bulls Mountains, over the whole world. One month, two months, a thousand years . . . Then they carry him back to his palace on the Anavarza crags. Very wise he is, this king of the eagles, and his spittle is a sovereign remedy for every sickness . . . And when you think how small this falcon is, so tiny in the vast Chukurova plain . . . Is it really worth while? The palace of the king of the eagles is set so high on the steep crags that nobody can ever reach it. Only one person is known to have climbed up to it, and that is Gülenoglu Haji. But when he looked into the eyes of the king of the eagles he fell into a faint, and then the eagles carried him back unconscious down into the plain without ever hurting a hair of his head.

Hassan led the way into the reed-bed. Selahattin walked hesitantly after him, holding the falcon. The other children followed in silence. They were all thoughtful, on their guard. Selahattin was afraid. He did not want to go. His feet kept dragging him backwards. What if the falcon flew off and never came back? What if it did return, but without catching a single bird? After all this was only a raw falcon, untrained! How did one train falcons? Selahattin had no idea. He had never seen a falcon before in his life. What matter if it does escape? he thought. Isn't my father a Yörük? Isn't he from the land of the high crags where falcons make their nests? He'll get me another one. He'll get me ten falcons.

But he could not overcome his reluctance. It was such a beautiful falcon, this one. Such keen eyes it had. And then it understood every single thing you said to it and even answered you with those clever, almost human eyes. 'Hassan,' he called, 'wait a minute.' Hassan stopped and Selahattin caught up with him. 'Listen, this falcon's not trained yet and my father said . . . He said that if you let untrained falcons go like this, they never come back. What if we lose it? Let's train it first and then we can go hunting, the two of us, every day, and have it catch birds for us and roast them and eat them. Every day . . . But now, what if the falcon flies off into the Anavarza crags and doesn't come back? What shall we do then?'

He's right, Hassan thought, and for one moment he was tempted not to give the falcon back to Kerem. If they kept it and trained it, then they would have birds to eat every day. But Kerem would take his falcon and go away. They would never see him again, nor the falcon either . . . And then too, wouldn't the Corporal raise hell at the loss of the falcon and administer a sound beating to them all? Who knows, throw them into prison even . . . Wouldn't one of the boys spill the beans if laid under the rod and tell of the trap they had laid for Selahattin? Hassan's face clouded and he stood there wavering. Then Kerem rose before his eyes . . . All that he had gone through because of this falcon . . . And his father and mother burnt alive too . . . Kerem waiting now, hiding in the reeds since morning, his heart in his mouth . . . Pity for him took the upper hand. 'No, no Selahattin,' he said, 'my grandfather says that falcons are naturally trained. They always come back to perch themselves on their owner's arm. Think of it! We'll send it up now, how lovely! It'll soar high into the sky where the stars are, and there it'll catch some

213

beautiful big yellow-winged bird and bring it back to us.'

'Tomorrow,' Selahattin begged. 'Let's do it tomorrow. It'll be better, much better. D'you know what my father said? He said there'll be a whole crowd of birds flying in tomorrow . . . Hoopoes, bee-eaters, stock-doves, orioles, every kind of bird you can think of, all coming here . . . Today the falcon will only find us a couple of birds at the most, but tomorrow . . . It'll bring in a whole heap tomorrow. And then . . .' He smacked his mouth and licked his lips. 'We'll make a huge fire and roast all those birds over it and have a feast. Look, we've even forgotten to bring salt with us today, and we haven't any bread either. And there are so many of us. A couple of birds will never be enough. Tomorrow we'll be just the two of us.'

Hassan wavered again. His face was changing from minute to minute and this did not escape Selahattin's eye. He redoubled his efforts to convince him.

And all the while Kerem was crouching in a clump of reeds, watching them. 'Please Allah, don't let Hassan give way,' he prayed. 'Please holy Hizir, you who roam the seven seas on your beautiful roan horse . . . You gave me this falcon, remember? You caught it and gave it to me with your own hands. Who knows with what difficulty you climbed up the steep crags to get it, tearing your hands and feet on the rocks . . . Only to keep your word to me . . . Isn't it so? And the great Allah helped you too, didn't he? It isn't easy to catch a baby falcon, is it? And now they've taken this falcon away from me, that you went through so much to get! They've taken it away before I could set it flying even once, before I could have my fill of looking at its beautiful eyes . . . And look, I haven't told you this, they burnt my father and my mother, and my good grandfather, the Master of the Blacksmith's Hearth . . . They burnt our whole tribe to ashes . . . There's only me left, and my falcon . . .' He was angry suddenly. 'Why did you let them take it away from me? Why didn't you keep your word? All night long I waited for the waters to stop flowing and the stars to meet, and I didn't ask for much, not even for land, and now everybody's burnt to ashes because of me. Oh, how I wish I'd asked for a wintering place and not for that falcon. Oh dear, oh dear, what an ass I've been.'

His eyes filled with tears and he turned his head away to hide them from the boy at his side. Had he heard him arguing like this with the Lord Hizir? Muttering and shaking his hands, angrily moving this way and that.

'It's now or never, Lord Hizir. You must convince Selahattin and Hassan and get my falcon back for me. If you don't I'll tell the world you're someone who doesn't keep his word, and that's how people will know you till kingdom come. Nobody will ever wait for you again on Hidirellez night. They'll know that you don't really grant wishes and that, even if you do, you take them back again . . . Didn't I see the meeting of the stars? Of course I did! My eyes were quite dazzled. And didn't I wish for the falcon at once, that very instant? You know I did! Well then, give me my falcon. I want it now, this minute! Take it from them! Give it me! Give me my falcon!'

He caught a glimpse of a pair of eyes, grown huge with fear, fixed on him, but he did not care. 'Take it, take it! Bring it to me!' he went on admonishing Hizir excitedly. He wanted to let himself go and curse this Lord Hizir with all his might, this holy man who did not keep his word. But the fear in his heart was too strong.

The other children were standing in the distance, on the edge of the reed-bed, waiting for Selahattin and Hassan. They were devoured by curiosity.

'There's nothing to stop us flying it today as well as to-morrow . . .' Hassan was saying. 'It won't die before tomorrow, will it? Look, all the boys are waiting for us. They all expect it. If we don't fly this falcon today, they'll make no end of fun of us. Nobody'll believe in us or in the falcon again.'

'But what if it escapes?' Selahattin wailed again wretchedly. 'What shall I do then? My father'll kill me.'

For a moment Hassan was touched by Selahattin's obvious misery. Then he collected himself. 'It won't escape. How many times must I tell you that falcons don't ever run away. Look, the sky's full of birds!' He pointed to a lone bird fleeting by.

'The falcon would have got that one for us in a jiffy. We'd have had that huge bird here right now if we weren't wasting time talking.' He walked quickly into the thick of the reeds. Selahattin followed him, completely mesmerized, and all the children rushed up after them.

Hassan gave a shout. 'There it goes! Quick, give me the falcon, quick, the bird's flying away.'

'It's going! It's flying away,' all the children shrieked.

The falcon passed from Selahattin's hands to Hassan's, from Hassan's to the nearest boy's . . . On and on from hand to hand . . .

Hassan was pointing at the sky. 'Look, look! Look how the falcon's chasing the bird!'

Whoops and shrieks and cheers . . .

'It's drawing nearer . . . Look, it's attacking it! The bird's feathers are flying all about. What a falcon!'

Selahattin's eyes were wide open, glued to the sky. 'Catch it, catch it!' he shouted.

'What a blow it's given it! Ah, now it's got it!'

Selahattin was skipping about eagerly. 'Where? Where? I've lost sight of them. Where?'

Süllü grabbed his arm. 'There! Can't you see? There. The bird's only a jumble of feathers now. The falcon's plucking them off one after the other.'

Suddenly Hassan gave a cry. 'Oh dear, the falcon's let go!'

'No no, Hassan,' Süllü shouted. 'It's attacking again. It's trying to get three birds at one go.'

'Three birds at one go!' Selahattin rejoiced.

'It's chasing them! They're flying towards the Anavarza crags,' Hassan shouted. 'Come on, let's follow. We mustn't lose sight of the falcon.'

They all scampered out of the reeds and began to run in the direction of Anavarza, their eyes on the sky. A flight of birds was fleeting swiftly from the reed-bed towards Jeyhan River.

'It's attacking them, attacking a whole flock of birds!' Hassan shrieked clapping his hands in excitement. 'It's routed them, scattered them all over the sky. Look, it's caught one!

Look, look, Selahattin! What a falcon! What a falcon!'

Their eyes on the fleeting birds above them, the children giggled, then broke into laughter. They skipped and danced and split their sides. Peals of joy filled the plain. 'It's got it! It's bringing it down. Long live the falcon!'

They rushed back into the reeds. Then stopped, frozen in their tracks. Their eyes went from the sky to the ground, and then again to the sky.

'Where is it?' Hassan said in dismay. 'It was coming down right here with a bird in its beak, feathers flying . . .'

'It did come down,' Süllü said. 'I saw it. It went into that thicket. To eat the bird probably. Let's find it before it finishes it.'

They ran up to the thicket, Selahattin before all the others, his face clouded now, on the brink of tears, and fell to rummaging about. They searched for a long time, but there was no trace of the falcon, nor of any other bird. Not even the tiniest feather . . .

'Perhaps it's in that other thicket down there,' Mustafa suggested.

'I saw it come down here,' Hassan said.

'So did we, so did we!' the other boys cried.

The search went on till nightfall. No one spoke any more. In the end Selahattin broke into tears. 'Didn't I tell you this falcon was untrained? Didn't I? Now it's gone and my father's going to kill me.'

'Nonsense,' Hassan said. 'Don't cry. Perhaps the falcon's gone home. Perhaps it's taken that bird it caught straight to your house.'

Selahattin hung his head and wept on silently. The children took pity on him. 'Don't cry, Selahattin,' Memet said. 'We'll look for it again tomorrow, and the day after too. We'll search everywhere between here and Anavarza. We'll find your pure-bred falcon again.'

'Will we?' Selahattin asked wanly.

'Of course we will,' Hessan comforted him.

'Didn't you see how it flew?' Memet asked. 'Swift as the

wind. Like an arrow . . .'

'Like a bullet,' Mustafa said.

'How it grabbed that bird in the air! And it was three times as large as the falcon, wasn't it?'

'It's a very noble falcon,' Süllü said. 'How it attacked those birds. There were a thousand of them at least, weren't there? And they all fell rat-a-tat to the ground in fear.'

Selahattin was overcome with grief. What distressed him most was that he had not been able to catch even a glimpse of his falcon's prowesses, but he dared not confess this. If he'd only seen it once as it caught a bird, he wouldn't have felt his loss so badly.

They were drawing near the village and darkness had already fallen. And making away as fast as he could in quite the opposite direction was Kerem. He held his falcon tightly, stopping only to kiss and caress it joyfully.

'Look, Selahattin,' Hassan said, 'come to me tomorrow early, before dawn, and you too, children, and we'll all go and look for it. We'll never find such a noble falcon again. What a falcon! The lord of the skies . . .'

First thing in the morning Selahattin was in Hassan's yard and so were the other boys. All that day till nightfall they put heart and soul into the search for the falcon, forgetting everything, Kerem, Sadi the blacksmith and even the trap they themselves had laid to get the bird away from Selahattin. The next day and the next, the search continued unabated. They had convinced themselves that they would find the lost falcon one day. Such noble falcons never flew off and got lost. This one would certainly return to them one day . . .

21

It was raining over Adana town, a dark torrential rain that turned to steam the minute it touched the ground as though it were falling over red-hot tin plate. The streets and avenues and public squares were deserted. The rain had caught Old Haydar and Osman on the bank of Seyhan River at the first call to prayer. They had remained there all night, not knowing where to go, what to do. Old Haydar was crouching motionless, clasping his red beard, his eyes on the flowing river. At the first drop of rain he sat up and his bones cracked painfully. Never in all his life had he felt so weary, he who had toiled night and day unceasingly, year in year out, without a thought for his old age. My time is near, he thought, and so is the time of the Blacksmith's Hearth. This hearth, this anvil, this hammer will no more shower sparks on to the world, nor will these arms beat the anvil any longer . . . This huge town . . . There are no cocks here, no sound of crowing. No dogs, no barking. The people are either talking in a great hurry, or asleep, snoring noisily . . . A dark torrential rain is falling over Adana town, dirty, stifling, not like rain, not like water, murky . . . Never in all his life had Old Haydar seen such a rain, nor had he seen such a people, sallow-complexioned, shifty-eyed, underhand, slinking, dissatisfied, unpredictable, slippery. Even the great Ramazanoglu, he thought, even he never looked once into my face, frankly, openly, like a man. People here all turn away their eyes, like frightened deer. Nothing good can come of such a people, who can't look you straight in the eye. Nobody can do anything with them, not the great Ramazanoglu, nor the lord of pashas, Ismet Inönü, nor Mustafa Kemal even . . . He mounted his horse and Osman led him back along the wet slippery streets of the city. Even the houses were covering their faces with their hands here, and averting their eyes. They could not look

people in the face. What crimes they must have committed to
hide themselves like that.

Hourshit Bey was passing along the street with that trembling
gait and frail frame of his which had lost all trace of former
nobleness. He had a pile of books under his arm. Hourshit Bey
wrote books too. From his shop Kerem Ali could not resist the
impulse to call him. He was curious to find out what had taken
place between him and that old Yörük who held himself so
proudly, hiding the grief and sadness that was within him,
the hopelessness that had seeped into every hair of his thick
tawny beard.

'Hourshit Bey! Hourshit Bey . . .'

All of Adana knew Kerem Ali. He had ties of friendship,
warm and cordial, with almost every single person in the town.
Hourshit Bey's face brightened.

'What is it, Kerem Ali?'

'Come in, Bey. Come and have a cup of coffee with me.'

Hourshit Bey turned back. Gravely with pondering mien he
took the place Kerem Ali showed him. The shopkeeper's
capacious paunch quivered with pleasure as he dispatched his
apprentice for the coffees. He beamed at his guest with his
huge body, his large head, his moustache, his deferential eyes.
Then his face clouded. 'Yesterday,' he said, 'I sent an old
Yörük to you, a giant of a man, like an oak-tree. He had a
red beard, but he must have been a hundred years old.
Such a strange man . . . I was wondering what he wanted with
you.'

'So it was you sent him to me?' Hourshit Bey exclaimed.
'*Intéressant, intéressant* . . . Imagine, he was convinced that the
principality of Ramazanoglu still exists. And what's more, he
thought I owned all of Adana town! Very interesting, Kerem
Ali. He had a sword with him that he said it took him thirty
years to make . . .'

'I saw it,' Kerem Ali said. 'I was amazed at that old man's

craftsmanship. Nobody else could make such a sword nowadays, could they, Bey?'

'No, no one,' Hourshit Bey agreed. 'Nowhere in the whole world any more . . .'

'What did he want?'

'He offered me the sword, and in exchange he wanted some place for his tribe to settle on. It seems they're very hard-pressed, almost extinct those Yörüks. Any small patch of land will save them, but they can't find it.'

'What will happen to them then?' Kerem Ali asked. 'Will they simply perish off the face of the earth?'

'Like us,' Hourshit Bey said. 'They were doomed to end with us.'

'You Ramazanoglus are not ended yet though,' Kerem Ali said. 'When they pull you out of one place you soon take root somewhere else, and prosper there too.'

The coffees were brought in. They each lit a cigarette and took a few puffs in silence.

Hourshit Bey knew a lot about these old feudal families. He had read and studied their history very closely and it interested him to see that they had all dwindled into nothingness except for the Ramazanoglus, who still held positions of authority in Adana. They owned large farms, bank partnerships, import-export firms, factories, cinemas. They were influential in the province's politics and commanded members of parliament and even ministers in Ankara. But all the other great families were gone, the Jadioglus in Sivas, the Payaslioglus and the Kozanoglus in the Gavur Mountains, the Sunguroglus, the Aydinoglus, the Karamanoglus, the Danishmendoglus. Even the Chapanoglus yet so powerful only yesterday . . . And the Mentesheoglus, the Hamidoglus, the Dulkadiroglus . . . The last of the Dulkadiroglus, Haji, was actually plying a saddler's trade at Andirin, only a poor man now. But among the Ramazanoglus there was no one reduced to poverty as in the other families. Why was that? *Intéressant, intéressant*, Hourshit Bey muttered to himself. I must make a serious study of this. Only the Karaosmanoglus of Manisa are left standing like us, and indeed how very much alike are the histories of our two families.

The Ramazanoglus had transplanted their roots from the decadent, desiccated, sterile earth of the Seljuks to the new and thriving soil of the rising Ottomans. By the flick of a switch they had changed sides, becoming one with the Ottomans and sharing with them the good and the bad days that were to come. Then from Egypt came Mehmet Ali Pasha's son, Ibrahim Pasha, and his soldiers, raised on a foreign hardy earth. They occupied Adana, and it was not long before the Ramazanoglus transferred their roots to this new firm earth. How strange a quirk of fortune that the Karaosmanoglus should have done just the same. They too made a pact with Ibrahim Pasha. And then came the Republic, and the Popular Front was formed. Once again the Ramazanoglus planted their roots into this fresh soil, as though nothing were more natural, and once more they were on the forefront, members of parliament, secretaries-general for the young Republic. Then the new opposition, the Democratic Party was formed, and again the Ramazanoglus were there, roots firmly embedded in this new soil. Hourshit Bey felt a vicarious pride in considering how the land, the earth itself decayed, but not the roots of the Ramazanoglu family. And now a new storm was brewing, a fresh upheaval threatening. The workers had begun to mutter. Would the Ramazanoglus surmount this new change? Would their roots flourish even in a workers' soil? Who knows? He laughed. Their roots were so strong, so resilient, who knows? They might survive even this.

His laughter faded suddenly. What, he thought, was there left of the past glory of the Ramazanoglus? A single merchant from Kayseri, only yesterday a common *hamal*, a single one of the new agha landowners, only yesterday farmhands, could buy out all the Ramazanoglus left on earth.

'You're very thoughtful, Bey,' Kerem Ali observed.

'We're finished too, Kerem Ali. We seem to have survived, to be on our feet, but it's all over really. We're agonizing too, together with those Yörüks.'

'Oh no, Bey!' Kerem Ali was pained. 'What a thing to say!'

'It's the turn of the new rich merchants now,' Hourshit Bey pursued. 'Like the Has family. Like Talip Bey, Sabunju, Ömer Agha, Shadi Bey . . . It's their day now. We're dead, breathing our last. They will prosper until they too have exhausted their soil. But the soil they're stepping on is rotten, very rotten. It took us a thousand years to wear out our soil. They won't even last twenty years. That's obvious. They're swallowing up their soil much too quickly. Or is it that their roots are not quite firm? Yes, that's it. And they never will be, Kerem Ali. Look, already the flood is spreading, engulfing the whole world. Look at those workers, crowds of them, swarming like ants. They all want jobs, they want to make a living and live like men. D'you suppose they'll go on like this, poor and needy, helpless, powerless, always, Kerem Ali? Can you believe that? Oh no, and that's why the earth these new rich merchants are stepping on is rotten already.'

'So you think it's the writing on the wall, eh Bey?' Kerem Ali asked.

'Just so,' Hourshit Bey said. 'Just so, and ours too, together with them. Because we dragged our roots out from among the people and planted them into the earth where those merchants and new rich are thriving . . . Yes, Kerem Ali, ours too.'

'No, no, Bey,' Kerem Ali protested again. 'Not that, not that!'

Hourshit Bey gathered up his books. 'It's the writing on the wall for us too,' he said as he left. 'We'll perish with them, on their rotting earth. Good-bye.'

The rain had started in the night. His thoughts in a whirl, Kerem Ali sat on watching the pattering raindrops falling on the pavement. Suddenly, dreamlike in the rain he saw the old Yörük standing on the opposite side of the street. He was wet through, his red beard dripping, and so was his horse and the young man who accompanied him.

'Come in, father, come in,' Kerem Ali called, opening wide the door of his shop. 'You're wet. Come and drink a glass of tea. Come!'

Old Haydar crossed the asphalt street. Kerem Ali took his arm and drew him in out of the rain.

'You're drenched, father. Drenched! You'll catch your death at this rate.'

He invited Osman in too. They tied the horse to the padlock ring of the shop's shutters. Water was streaming down its rump and saddlecloth.

Old Haydar looked Kerem Ali full in the eye. 'Tell me, good man,' he said at last with difficulty, blushing like a child, 'how can I get to Ismet Pasha? Who can help me? How is it done? I must go to him. It's my last hope.'

Kerem Ali tried to speak. Don't go, he wanted to say to this old man, Ismet Pasha won't even glance at this sword of yours. Even if you go to Ankara, even if you do get to see him, he'll never be able to solve your problems. Ismet Pasha's no longer in the government. But he could not bring himself to do it. A pain such as he had never felt before gripped this good sensitive man and made him writhe. Then he collected himself and told Old Haydar to the best of his ability how to travel to Ankara and how to set about finding Ismet Pasha.

'May your road be easy, go with God,' he kept repeating as he saw the old man off. He simply could not believe it . . .

22

*Hemité Mountain is like a dagger thrust into the heart of the
Chukurova. Jeyhan River flows below it and afterwards the
plain stretches flat out to the Mediterranean Sea. Rising as it
does abruptly from the level plain, Hemité Mountain seems
tall and lofty. It is really only a small foothill leaning on the
Taurus range, quite barren with sparse growths of oak-shrubs,
medlars and arbutus among its rocks. Asphodel and narcissus flower all over Hemité Mountain. The narcissus here is
the most fragrant in all the Chukurova. And there are
pimpernels too, a brilliant red. The rocks are of sharp
granite almost as hard as flint, red-veined and speckled with
mauve and white and green. No springs gush forth from these
rocks. The mountain is dry, but for a thin trickle of water, a
finger's width, that oozes out of the crags overhanging
Hemité village. This tenuous source is said to date back to
the time of the Hittites. And so Mount Hemité stands there,
an arid block, of no use to anyone. Eagles used to nest there in
olden times. The steep crags would be black with swarming
wings. But now even the eagles have deserted this mountain,
gone no one knows where.*

In all the wide Chukurova plain the weary caravan had nowhere to go any more. Every village, every single man was an
enemy to them now. There was no village they had not quarrelled with, no field or open land they had not occupied and
been chased out of. And if not them, some other nomad
tribe . . .

Headman Süleyman, who knew the Chukurova like the palm
of his hand, could not think of a single place to camp, of any
village which would tolerate their presence. Where were they
to go? To whom could they appeal? Hard winter would soon

be upon them. And yesterday again Akcha Veli had gathered up his tent and family and left without a word to anyone. Only thirty-eight tents were left now. Last year the Karachullu tribe had counted a hundred. And the year before . . . And before that . . . When the Karachullu tribe descended into the Chukurova in those days, the plain was black with tents, ringing with life like a large city . . . Would they all dwindle out by the spring, the few remaining tents packing up and disappearing one by one, going God knows where? If only they would, Headman Süleyman thought. If only it could be over a moment sooner, this long-drawn-out misery.

They had been waiting in this field, through which the rice paddy irrigation canal flowed, since sunrise. They could not make up their minds what to do.

'Let's go to Akmashat or to Narlikishla and simply occupy the place,' Fethullah said. 'Let them kill us all and get it over with that way.'

Old Müslüm took his side. 'They've stolen our wintering lands, ours since all times, and we stand here cudgelling our brains about where we're to go! Straight to our age-old wintering quarters, that's where! And there to die or to kill. Look at us anyway, we're finished. Let's die on our own, our fathers' land at least. Let's put an end to all this.'

All the men of the tribe were of Fethullah's and Old Müslüm's opinion. They wanted to fight it out and settle down by force either at Akmashat or at Narlikishla. But Headman Süleyman still hesitated, splitting his head to think of a way out. His face grew darker, angrier.

'It's fifty years since Narlikishla's been settled by others, fifty years since villages have been growing there, and we never uttered a word of protest. D'you think they're going to listen to us now? And as for Akmashat, remember how Karadirgenoglu Dervish Bey urged us to settle there for good, to found a village? Remember? We never paid any attention to him at all. We thought the whole of the Chukurova would remain at our disposal forever, to go and come as we chose. And now that we're in dire straits, we talk of killing and dying.'

'Well, father, here we stand cornered,' Fethullah said. 'You tell us what to do.'

'Yes, you show us a way, Süleyman,' Old Müslüm said.

But Headman Süleyman was still hesitating. To go to Akmashat or Narlikishla with the tribe in this mood, excited, angry, would certainly result in trouble. He raised his head and looked at the mauve mountain in the distance. It was past noon already and they had been loitering in this place since dawn. He must make his decision quickly. The tribe was exhausted. They had to stop in some place for a few days at least. He pointed to Hemité Mountain. 'There,' he said. 'We'll stop there for a couple of days, and then . . .'

'Father!' Fethullah groaned. 'That place is nothing but rock. Not a green branch or blade of grass anywhere. No water, no nothing . . . Are we to die on that barren mountain?'

'We go there,' the Headman repeated, frowning sternly.

'Süleyman, son,' Old Müslüm pleaded, 'have you lost your senses? We can't settle there, and even if we do d'you think they'll leave us alone? They'll exact a toll from us even on those barren crags.'

'Some kind or other of mountain pass money,' Fethullah said.

'I won't pay it,' Headman Süleyman said. 'Come on, get moving. I know what I'm doing.'

Against their will they began to draw the caravan on towards the arid heights of Hemité Mountain.

'He's waiting for Old Haydar,' Fethullah raged. 'Let him wait! Old Haydar's going to give that sword to Ismet Pasha or to Ramazanoglu, and they'll give us land! God help us, what an idea, what an idea!'

'Ah, I think you're right,' Old Müslüm sighed. 'The bald man uses his nails to scratch his own pate first. If Ismet Pasha could get hold of land he'd keep it for winter-quarters himself. And the same goes for Ramazanoglu. He'd be the first to settle on any pasture-land and drink from the cool white-pebbled springs . . .'

'Shh,' Abdurrahman said. 'He can hear you . . .'

As the caravan proceeded on its way, the word passed among the women, the young girls, the children. 'We're going to Hemité Mountain, but only to wait for Old Haydar. He's got Ismet Pasha to give us land in the best part of Yüregir plain. He'll be back in three days and then we'll all go together to Yüregir . . .'

Sultan Woman held out her shrivelled claw-like hands to the sky. 'Quickly, come quickly, O my sage of sages, wise Haydar, Master . . .' she prayed. 'Come back quickly or we're lost. Please, O beautiful Allah, speed him to us with good tidings. Remove the obstacles on his path, strew roses before him all the way, send him to us quickly, O Allah . . . We need it so badly. They have turned us into animals. Look at the state we're in. He's our only hope, please Allah.'

They reached Hemité Mountain the next morning at dawn and stopped in a small valley overgrown with medlar bushes. Nobody had slept the whole night through, save for the little children on the camels. The loads were unpacked, the tents put up, and the shepherds herded the sheep down towards Jeyhan River. It was then that Headman Süleyman fully realized their losses. The flocks had been reduced by half. It struck him to the core. Swiftly, he summoned the whole tribe. 'Let everybody come, every man and woman, old and young. Everyone who's able to walk . . .'

When they were all assembled, he took out the pouch he kept always over his breast. 'This,' he said, 'is the gold you collected and gave to me. But it isn't enough. Old Haydar's gone, and he hasn't come back. So now I want you to give me all the gold you have left, your rings, your ornaments, noserings, necklaces, silver, money, everything. I shall go to Karadirgenoglu Dervish Bey. Here, I'll say, take this. It's all we have. Give us Akmashat in exchange. He's a good man. Who knows, when he sees that we have thrown in all our women's precious ornaments, he'll give us Akmashat without taking any of them.'

The women and young girls obeyed him at once. They collected all their finery and one by one they came to lay it on the kerchief that was spread before the Headman. Jeren came too, and gave up all she possessed. The other women cast black looks at her. Their mood had turned during the past three days and many of them refused to speak to her at all.

'Is that the lot?' Headman Süleyman asked.

They glanced at each other. No one answered. Then old Sultan Woman hobbled up, bent in two, and dropped a small pouch in front of him. 'There, Süleyman, take this too and find a wintering place for us. It's the money I was saving for my shroud. Maybe it'll come in useful to get us out of this mess. Haydar hasn't come back. Perhaps it's that Ismet Pasha didn't like the sword he made and clapped him into chains. You know what he's like our Haydar, his tongue runs away with him. Who knows what he said to that Ismet Pasha who then cast him into a dungeon. So take my shroud money, but if you get the land, you won't bury me without a shroud, will you, when I die? Aaah, it should have been me who took that sword to Ismet Pasha!'

The Headman opened the little pouch and emptied the handful of gold coins over the rest of the things. Then he folded up the kerchief and knotted it securely. His horse was ready. He mounted it quickly and rode off down the slope. The whole tribe followed him into the plain to see him off, and there they knelt down praying to God not to send him back empty-handed. Their prayers and invocations continued until he was lost to sight. At last, reluctantly, they rose and returned to their tents only to find that fifteen village youths were waiting for them there.

Fethullah went up to them. 'Welcome, brothers,' he said, and invited them into the tent to drink coffee and *ayran*.

The young men were pleased and surprised at Fethullah's hospitality. They hemmed and hawed, but in the end it was Greyhound Mehmet who took the plunge. 'Fethullah Agha, we've come so you should give us our dues too.'

'What dues?' Fethullah asked with a great show of amazement.

'The mountain dues,' Greyhound Mehmet insisted.

'Who ever heard of dues on a mountain?' Fethullah inquired

229

in mocking tones. This set the young men's back up. They had entertained great hopes of getting fabulous sums out of these nomads. 'Look, brother,' Fethullah went on earnestly, 'I swear to you with my hand on the Holy Koran that we have no money left. But nothing at all. Just before you came, my father collected it all, down to the last of the women's gold trinkets and the old people's shroud money, and he went away to buy back Akmashat, our old wintering place . . . If he can, that is . . . We are going to settle, just like you, and found a village.'

It was as if Greyhound Mehmet had not heard him. 'It's always the same story,' he grumbled. 'When it comes to us . . . nothing's left. Look here, my friend, we're the guardians of this mountain. It belongs to us, my friend . . . If it wasn't for us . . .'

'If it wasn't for you this mountain wouldn't be standing here, eh?' Fethullah laughed. 'Is that what you're trying to tell me, my friend?'

'So you're making fun of us, are you?' Greyhound Mehmet cried, leaping to his feet, his spindly bow-legged figure quivering with anger. 'Get up, boys! We'll get even with Fethullah Agha yet. Come, let's go now.'

With black resentful countenances, determined to get even for this humiliation, they started off down the hill.

'Stop, my friends!' Fethullah ran after them, regretting his joke a thousand times. 'Where are you going, my friends? I just made a little joke. What's there to be so offended about?'

But the others only pressed on, never stopping to speak or listen to him. You just wait, the looks they threw at him seemed to say, we know what we're going to do to you after this.

Fethullah tried to reason with them. He begged their pardon again and again, but in vain. They would not let themselves be conciliated. In the end he sank down on a stone and watched them march away with a swaggering air as though they were the lords of creation. 'Ah,' he said gritting his teeth, 'damn this nomad life . . . Whoever invented it, whatever forefather of ours, may he never rest in his grave! Look at them, those sparrows of men, look at those blustering braggarts.' His eyes filled as he

230

opened his hands to heaven. 'God,' he pleaded, 'put some mercy, some goodness into the heart of that Dervish Bey and make him sell Akmashat to my father, or if you will, kill us all this night, young and old. But put an end to our hardships. We've had too much.'

Down below in the plain the youths had stopped to hold a parley. Suddenly with a whoop of glee, as though to say, now we've got it, now we'll show you, they went on their way.

Fethullah could not move. He sat there on the stone till sunset, feeling as though his whole body had been beaten in a mortar.

It was evening and dusk already when he saw the horseman meandering on the road below at a slow shaky pace, cowering on the back of his horse. He knew him at once and a feeling of humiliation crept over him.

'The low-down brute,' he muttered. 'It's not love, this thing of his, it's downright infamy . . . Well, you won't get Jeren, you worm, not if you crawl there a thousand years, not if all the tribe drops dead before our eyes, one by one. If you really loved her, you wouldn't have tried to bank on the tribe's misfortunes. You'd have given us the land anyway, and then maybe she'd have been yours.'

But almost at once a wave of pity swept over him. He must be hopelessly in love that man, and love was a strange terrible thing when it got you. After all there were other girls in the world, more beautiful than Jeren even. So why did he keep on dragging himself miserably after her? Then Jeren rose before his eyes. Ah no, he thought, there can't be another in the whole world as beautiful as Jeren! Oktay Bey's right. I don't wonder if he keeps after her to the bitter end.

23

*Lambent shadows, red, green, blue, orange, played about the
pavements, shadows like beams of light. How bright this city
was, its lighted windows, its doors, its mountain-like buildings, its stars . . . The mausoleum of Mustafa Kemal Pasha
flooded with light the whole night through, massive, immobile
on its high ground . . . The giant shadows of the towering
buildings. Lights, shadows all mingling together, chasing
each other, joining, parting . . . Cars, buses, lorries. And
lights, always lights, crying, moaning, speaking . . . Ankara,
so huge, so illuminated . . . And every night the city moves . . .
It spreads out over the surrounding steppe. The tall buildings
weave into each other, separate and unite once more . . . The
lights, the huge shadows . . . Flashes of red, glittering,
sparkling, scattering, then fusing into large round bubbles,
only to sprinkle out again, red, blue, white, green, orange
spangles, swept up into the sky and showering to the ground.
Heavy as lead.*

Old Haydar stepped out of the bus one evening into Ankara
city. His road companion on the trip had been a nice young
man. They had talked all the way. He turned to his right to ask
him something. The young man had vanished. His eyes scanned
the crowd for him, but he was nowhere to be seen. 'They're all
the same, these young rascals,' he muttered wearily to himself.
'Alike as peas in a pod, pale-faced bloodless weaklings.'

He let himself flow with the crowd and presently he was out
of the vast noisy building and in the car-crowded street. He
stopped under a lamp-post, a strangely majestic figure with his
long bright orange coif, his ample coppery beard, his sandals,
his big tall body, his tapering hands, the tufty overhang of
brows hiding his eyes, and the sword that he held like a sacred

trust or like a new-born babe to be petted and handled with utmost care. People stopped and stared at him with curiosity. Old Haydar felt their gaze and it irritated him. Anyway he had been bursting with anger for days now. 'The fools!' he raged inwardly. 'Just look how they're staring. Just look! Like famished wolves, ready to eat me alive . . . Damn it, are you men? Damn it, if you'd been men, we wouldn't have been in this state . . .' He was looking to right and left, breathing fire and fury when he spotted his young travelling companion, but almost as soon lost sight of him again. 'It's not a town, not a city, it's a torrent of humanity that swallows up a man in an instant.'

He could not stand here much longer doing nothing. Should he go straight to Ismet Pasha's house this very evening? How long was it since he had left the tribe? Who knows what those vicious Chukurova people had made them suffer all this time. Or perhaps the tribe had forced Maid Jeren to marry that bald shameless good-for-nothing with hands as pink as a woman's.

No, he thought, they're still waiting for me. Poor things, for thirty years I led them on with the idea that when I finished making this sword some pasha or other would give us land in exchange for it . . . Like children I cheered them on with this hope. Some believed me, some did not. They argued over it for thirty years, but still it was something to look forward to. And now when there's no other hope left, it's the sword or nothing with them . . . Well, whether they believed it or not, this sword of his was the Karachullu tribe's last hope. And whether he believed it or not Ismet Pasha was his last hope. Ismet, the intrepid warrior who had trampled the Greeks underfoot, clever Ismet, sagacious, cunning, a match for not only one fox but a thousand foxes . . . What if he failed him too? There was nothing to go for beyond that. Some people had told him of a certain Menderes. Now who could that be? Ismet Pasha was an experienced man, not like that Hourshit Bey. He wouldn't hide behind his desk and gawk stupidly when a guest came to him, and what a guest! A hundred years old and paying obeisance to him too! Ismet Pasha's a veteran, he's seen war and death and bloodshed. He's beaten the Greeks. No he's not like Hourshit

Bey, he sits on the throne of the great holy Muhammed himself.

They have told Ismet Pasha . . . They've told him that Haydar the Master Blacksmith of the Holy Hearth has finished the sword he's been fashioning for him these last thirty years. How glad Ismet Pasha is! His white moustache twitches with pleasure. The Master of the Blacksmith's Hearth, the last, as the Hearth is dying out after ten thousand, a hundred thousand years, Haydar, the last sage of all, has made a sword for him with all the craftsmanship, the polished skill of a ten-thousand-year-old tradition . . . This sword has been forged not in thirty years, but in ten thousand, a hundred thousand. And it will never be made any more . . . Ever since iron exists this sword has been forged, and the last one of all falls to Ismet Pasha's lot. What more does he want! Kerem will never forge swords like this . . . Kerem will never forge swords at all . . . Never, never . . . A harrowing shudder racked his body. He winced as though a bee had stung him and all the blood drained out of his heart. A mad impulse to throw himself at these hurrying indifferent crowds . . . To shout at them, to shout and shout again . . . Don't you know, don't you see? Kerem will never make swords, never . . . Kerem has gone . . . Gone away for ever without a word of farewell to me . . . Kerem will never make swords, never! D'you hear me, O you people?

A blaze of light flared over the crowds, then all was shadowy again. The high buildings, the lights, red, blue, orange, green, mauve, the tall lamp-posts, the forest of lights, the forest of men, all was obscured, a flitting blurred mass of dim shadows. Shadows, long, short, alight, majestic, soaring into the sky, shrinking back, falling, heavy as stones . . . Whirling, swirling, eddying . . . Kerem will never make swords like us . . . Never, never will he beat the anvil like us. Never again . . . He lifted up the sword to the level of his eyes. This is the last one, the last, the last, Ismet. May you know it well, this is the last one of these beautiful sacred swords that the world will ever see. The last . . .

Oh, he'll be glad Ismet, when he sees the sword! 'Rise,

Haydar,' he'll cry. 'Rise at once. It's we who ought to kneel at your feet. Pashas like us, they come and go by the score, but Haydar, the Master Blacksmith, comes only once to this earth, and when he goes he never comes again . . . Since Kerem will never be a smith, since he doesn't even like swords . . . Now that this ancient hearth is ending in the person of Haydar the Blacksmith . . . Rise, rise and let us kneel to you instead.'

Sit down, sit near me, Master. What beautiful, what deft hands you have! So, for ten thousand years you've been forging these swords, straining them to pure perfection out of seas of fire? They're forged from fire, your swords, and not from iron, isn't that so? This sword you hold now, you've fashioned it out of the flames of ten thousand years, haven't you? For ten thousand, a hundred thousand years you have gathered all the flames in the world to strain out this one beautiful sword . . . Isn't that so, Master?'

Nobody knows since when the Blacksmith's Hearth has been kept burning. Its flames, its sparks are a torrent that has flowed out over all the world ever since it was created. And out of this fire our swords were made . . . Kerem's run away. He's gone. He'll never beat the iron, he'll never hammer out swords of pure-strained sparks, of lightning, of thunder. Kerem will never forge the light.

Overwrought, exhausted, drained of hope, yet hoping still against hope, turning death into life, Old Haydar stood there leaning against the lamp-post in front of the Ankara bus terminal, thinking of Ismet Pasha and of his grandson Kerem, clinging to those two as to his only bulwark against black despair. He knew the end, but would not recognize it. All thoughts of failure he drove from his mind. Obstinately he kept visualizing how warmly Ismet Pasha would greet him, and he glowed with anticipated pleasure.

Out of the light we strain the flames and beat them and forge a sword of flame. Ten thousand years, a hundred thousand years . . . Our swords are pure strained light.

The human flow was thinning out now. There was less hurry, less frantic running this way and that. Human beings in this city were like a swarm of bees at the mouth of their hive, a clinging sticky heap busy devouring each other, a frightened, quivering, glistening mass . . . How strange they are, these city people! They remind you of ants too. Yellow ants whose hole has been filled up with water and who are lying about drying in the sun, numb, yellow.

Old Haydar had always been wont to consider himself as a rather superior being. But now, conflicting emotions stirred in his heart. One minute he saw himself as some holy man, a half-god descended from the heights of the Taurus Mountains, and the next he felt as lonely and helpless as a babe in arms or a leaf that is trodden underfoot.

Aaah Kerem, ah!

A big man was passing in front of him. His long black moustache that had never known the clip of scissors added to the innocent expression of his child-like countenance instead of detracting from it. Without a moment's hesitation Old Haydar called to him: 'One minute, brother.'

The man stopped at once. 'What can I do for you, holy man?' he asked. 'Is there anything you need?'

They had understood each other. Old Haydar fell into step with him and together they walked up the street.

'Where are you from, holy man? Are you on a mission?'

Old Haydar told him all from the beginning to the end. When he had finished he took a deep breath. He was tired. They were walking in the direction of the Ministries now. 'So there you are, Hassan Hüseyin, brother. That's where life has brought us.'

'Let's sit somewhere,' Hassan Hüseyin suggested, 'and talk it over.' He led Old Haydar into a nearby coffee-house. 'It's going to be difficult to find the Pasha,' he said.

'But if we send news to him that it's the Master of the holy Blacksmith's Hearth who wants to see him?'

Hassan Hüseyin was silent. He could not bring himself to say outright that Ismet Pasha cared nothing for holy hearths and their masters. Besides, he too had begun to be infected by Old Haydar's enthusiasm. He tried to think.

'Holy man,' he observed, 'bless me if you're not just as on the day you came out from Khorassan. There's no difference. Just as you were a thousand years ago . . .'

Old Haydar was highly gratified. 'The just man strays not from the path of righteousness,' he thundered. This encounter with Hassan Hüseyin was restoring him to his old self.

'Let's go to my place tonight,' Hassan Hüseyin suggested. 'Tomorrow we'll find a way to see the Pasha. What do you say, holy man?'

'Morning brings counsel,' Old Haydar replied.

They climbed into a shared taxi in Kizilay Square and drove into the shantytown district. The word was soon passed among the shanties that a great sage from Khorassan had come to visit Hassan Hüseyin. That night his house overflowed with visitors who all paid obeisance to Old Haydar. There were so many of them that the blacksmith felt all of Ankara must have learnt of his presence here. Was it possible that Ismet Pasha should be the only one not to hear of it?

'The just man strays not from the path of righteousness . . .'

From Khorassan we came sweeping through the land. They have hounded us over the dusty roads . . .

That night Old Haydar's sleep was untroubled, feather-light as a child's. In the morning he rose brimful of energy like a youth of twenty. They offered him breakfast and he ate with appetite. Once again people began to flow into Hassan Hüseyin's house. It was already mid-morning before they saw the last of them.

'Hassan Hüseyin, my son,' Old Haydar cried in his deep ringing voice, 'it's time now. Take me to Ismet. A sage from Khorassan has come to see you, that's what you'll say. Come, let's go.'

They boarded a shared taxi again and got off at Ulus Square. Old Haydar was in high spirits. He was sure his luck had turned at last. Everything would be all right now, all their sufferings would be over and they would see happy days again. Patience, Karachullus, he prayed inwardly, there's only a little more to go. Patience. And you, Kerem, you didn't do right to run away my child, to desert the Blacksmith's Hearth.

237

Hassan Hüseyin took him to the People's Party centre and explained what they wanted. 'Just wait a little,' he was told. 'We're expecting the Pasha today.'

They waited. Noon came. Hassan Hüseyin went to buy some bread and cheese. They ate it up and waited again. At mid-afternoon they had a glass of tea and waited on.

Sallow-complexioned men were hurrying in and out of the rooms, stopping an instant to look at Old Haydar with expressionless faces, then walking away, their faces as frozen as ever.

It was getting on for evening.

'Did you tell them to say it's the Master of the Blacksmith's Hearth who wants to see Ismet Pasha? I'm giving you a lot of trouble, my good Hassan Hüseyin.'

'Not at all . . . Yes, I told them.' He got up and went into a room, then into another. When he came back his head was hanging. 'They made us wait for nothing,' he said. 'Now they say the Pasha won't come today. Nor tomorrow. Not even the day after.'

'We'll go to his house then,' Old Haydar decided.

'That's the only way,' Hassan Hüseyin agreed. 'You can't wait here for weeks.'

'God forbid!' Old Haydar's eyes flashed. 'What are you saying! Every minute I spend here spells death for them . . . Death. They're dying over there with every passing minute at the hands of those cruel Chukurova people. I must see the Pasha tomorrow without fail and get his firman.'

It was on the tip of Hassan Hüseyin's tongue to tell him the truth, but he could not bring himself to do so. And besides what difference would it make? The old man was bent on seeing the Pasha and no amount of persuasion would make him change his mind. One way or another he was bound to be hurt, so why should he, Hassan Hüseyin, do it?

'Master,' he said, 'I have to go away tomorrow, to Chorum on business. I'm going to give you two young men and they'll take you to the Pasha's house.'

'Good,' Old Haydar said. 'We'll go to him as Allah's guest.

238

It was a mistake to come and wait here. Maybe that's what offended him, and he's right. We should have gone straight to his house.'

Hassan Hüseyin said nothing. He took the old man back to his house, which filled with people again, even more than the night before, for by now the word had spread to all the believers of the sect in Ankara that a holy sage from the Blacksmith's Hearth of Khorassan was staying there.

The next morning Old Haydar woke up feeling even more vigorous than the day before. He set out at once with the two young men Hassan Hüseyin had assigned him. After they had changed three different shared taxis and walked another five hundred yards or so, they came at last to the Pink Villa, Ismet Pasha's dwelling. The young men stood by at attention. They were overwhelmed by this imposing old sage from Khorassan and did not know what to do to show their respect. Old Haydar walked up to the gate. He was intercepted by two soldiers and another man dressed in civilian clothes.

'What d'you want, father?'

'I want to see Ismet Pasha.'

'What for?'

'You'll say that a sage from Khorassan . . .' He had quite adopted this description by now. They had acknowledged him as such in Ankara and it had earned him no end of respect. '. . . a sage from Khorassan . . . Now listen to me carefully, son . . . Haydar, the Master of the Blacksmith's Hearth has come as Allah's guest . . . Mind well what I tell you, don't forget . . . The Master of the Blacksmith's Hearth has come as Allah's guest, and bringing with him a thousand-year-old holy keepsake . . .'

The man went away. Old Haydar waited and waited, but he did not appear again, nor anyone else for that matter. The young men were deeply mortified at this rebuff to their sage from Khorassan. They railed at Ismet Pasha in silence. Who was he, what was he to keep a sage from Khorassan waiting like this at his door? Ismet Pasha was only yesterday's man, while Old

Haydar was the Master of the ten-thousand-year-old Black-smith's Hearth! But for their deep respect they would have urged him away from this place. 'Come, holy father, come!' they wanted to say. 'Let's leave. Who does he think he is, that man!'

Old Haydar went up to the gate again. 'Soldier, son,' he called out courteously, 'that man has told Ismet that I'm here, hasn't he?'

'Look, father, don't wait here in vain,' one of the soldiers told him. 'I'll tell you frankly, a hundred people come to this gate every day, but the Pasha never sees anyone.'

'What's that?' Old Haydar thundered. 'What do you mean? I've been waiting thirty years to see him.'

It was mid-day by now. The young men bought a kebab sandwich for him. He squatted down at the foot of the wall and ate. Then he went back to the gate. Again and again he returned to enquire. Then, when it was already mid-afternoon a car stopped at the gate and out of it stepped a baldish, spectacled man with slanting bushy eyebrows and a determined jaw. At once the gate opened wide before him. Old Haydar was quick to seize this opportunity. He almost threw himself at the gate just as it was drawing to. 'Wait, brother, stop!' he cried. 'Are you going to see Ismet?'

'Yes,' the man said and waited. He was used to this kind of thing.

'I am Haydar, Master of the Blacksmith's Hearth of Khorassan . . .' Choking with excitement he proceeded to tell about the sword and why he had come, of how the faithful believers had greeted him in Ankara, and sheltered him and honoured him . . . 'Thirty years . . . Thirty long years . . . So I want to see him. And also I'm standing at his gate as Allah's guest.'

'All right,' the man said. 'You wait here. The Pasha's coming out with me anyway. You'll be able to talk to him then and offer him your sword. As for that business of land, that's not so easy. The Pasha's been battling for land reform all his life, but . . .' He turned and hurried away.

His words had warmed Old Haydar to the cockles of his

heart. So the Pasha had been concerned with them all this time, he knew about the problem of their wintering quarters! Normally, he would have been mortally offended at not being invited in at once when he said he came as Allah's guest. But it never occurred to him now to feel angry or insulted.

After a while Ismet Pasha appeared at last with the visitor at his heels. 'Good father,' one of the young men said, 'that one in front, that's Ismet Pasha.' And he retreated at once to the opposite pavement of the street. Oh dear, Old Haydar said to himself, as he stared in dismay at this frail shrivelled balding ancient who was hobbling up with tiny steps like a sparrow, that was how a man's face would wrinkle up when he'd been frustrated and cruel all his life, as ugly as an old leather-pouch. . . . The Pasha approached and stopped beside him. His eyes were flicking in their sockets, anxiously, warily. Old Haydar lifted the sword towards him as though offering a holy trust.

'Take it, Ismet,' he said. 'Thirty years I worked on it for you. And you know how it was with Rüstem, the blacksmith of the Chebi tribe . . . That was long ago . . . He went to the Padishah who was then in your place. Fifteen years it had taken him to make his sword, and what did the Padishah say? Now what, what did he say when he saw that sword? Wish me a wish, Rüstem, Master, he said . . . And the blacksmith asked for land for his tribe to winter on. At once the Padishah bestowed upon him the whole land of Aydin, all in return for one single sword. And Rüstem was not really a smith of the holy hearth. He was only an apprentice, a newcomer to the profession . . . But I . . . Thirty years! For thirty years I've been forging this sword . . . For you . . . It's agony what we're suffering in the Chukurova, agony . . . Take it . . . Take this sword.'

The Pasha's visitor took the sword from Old Haydar's extended hands and drew it out of its scabbard. Then his eyes lit up. It was obvious he could appreciate the value of such things. 'Look Pasha, look how beautiful it is,' he said. 'The Yörüks back in our Taurus Mountains still make swords like this . . . How right you were . . . Always right, always . . .'

He examined the sword turning it this way and that. The

Pasha only stood silently, his eyes blinking rapidly, flicking back and forth from the sword to Old Haydar, who was pouring out all the woes and tribulations of the tribe. It was impossible to tell whether the Pasha was glad, flattered or annoyed. In the end he took the sword from his spectacled companion and peered at it gravely. Then he smiled and handed it back to Old Haydar. 'Very beautiful,' he said. 'Very, very beautiful.' And he hobbled away quickly, hop hop, like a sparrow, and got into the car that was waiting for him. It drove away and Old Haydar was left holding the sword, stunned. He tried to move, to run after the car, to explain again, to tell the Pasha many many things, but he could not stir. He stood there, swaying to left and right like a poplar in the wind. And the sword he had been holding so tightly slipped from his hands on to the pavement and gave a loud clang.

'Very beautiful, very beautiful.'

Such is the well-tempered sword that has been quenched at just the right moment. When it hits a hard surface it sounds out, vibrant as a taut steel wire. And the pure voice rings on, dying in long slow waves.

'Very beautiful, very beautiful.'

The ground, the passing cars, window-panes, trees, spears, reds, greens, all were spinning madly, crashing down in shivers like hoarfrost from the skies, shattered, pulverized fragments flying, whirling through the air.

Old Haydar's legs caved in. He sank down on the pavement beside the sword. All blurred the lights, in broken fragments now, the shadows lengthening, contracting, swirling, breaking . . . Running wild, storm-like . . . The long long roads, the craggy mountains, buses smelling of feet, the Chukurova, flat, boundless . . . And blood, blood flowing everywhere, and Hassan Hüseyin, and the two young men crouching, shrinking, hiding their faces with their hands, and Kerem Ali . . . And trees and raging fires and dark dark shadows, and lights, frazzled, shredding, pulverized, scattering pell-mell through the air. With their two hands they have covered up their faces, hidden them . . . And Ismet Pasha is running away, his frail bent aged body, his legs growing longer and longer, Ismet Pasha in his pale suit, running, thinning out, about to break . . .

And swords are falling all over the pavements, clang, clang, clang . . .

'Very beautiful, very very beautiful . . .'

Such is the well-tempered sword. God forbid that it should hit a hard surface . . . Clang clang clang, it clamours out . . . And the sound lingers on, a long-drawn-out cry. Clang!

24

It was ten years ago, or maybe fifteen, that the Bey of Beydili tribe, Himmet Bey, came to see Sabit Agha one day. Sabit Agha owned so many acres of farmland that he himself did not know the exact figure. Himmet Bey dropped a huge bundle of gold at his feet. 'Take this,' he said. 'And give us land to settle on. You have so much that even if twenty tribes like ours come to settle, you'll still have enough left to set up a state on.' Sabit Agha said: 'You're right, Himmet Bey. Very true.' And he began to count the gold. It took him a long time and when he had finished he said: 'This is not enough.' And Himmet Bey answered him: 'It's all we have. The rest is up to your conscience.' And so they struck a bargain. The Beydili tribe would settle on the land, graze their flocks, sow and reap, and the remaining sum owed would be paid in equal amounts over the space of five years. Only then would they obtain the title-deeds to the land. Promissory notes were drawn up and signed before the notary-public in the town in the presence of witnesses, and the Beydili tribe settled down to found their village. Five years went by, and in the sixth year Sabit Agha produced another promissory note and exacted more money from them. The seventh year the same thing happened. They sold all they had to pay out. But in the eighth year they were unable to meet Sabit Agha's demands any longer. Thereupon the Agha laid a sequester over their crops and flocks. He removed truckfuls of grain from the threshing-floors and herded the flocks into his own land. It was a difficult time for the Beydilis. They almost died of hunger. Himmet Bey went to the courts only to discover that the promissory notes held by Sabit Agha were all in good order and that the yearly payments were due not for five years but fifty. There was no getting out of it. The ninth year brought a fresh sequestration on their goods. They had *nothing left now. The men hired themselves out as shepherds or farmhands, and they rued the day that they had ever attempted to settle on this land.*

Headman Süleyman got off his horse and handed the reins over to a lanky servant in ragged clothing. 'Is Dervish Bey at home?' he asked.

'Yes,' the servant said.

'Tell him Süleyman, Headman of the Karachullus, has come.'

The servant drew the horse into a stable and then ran up the stairs into the mansion. He was back in a minute. 'The Bey's waiting for you,' he shouted.

Headman Süleyman mounted the stairs and was met by Dervish Bey at the door. 'Selam to you,' he said.

'Welcome, welcome!' the Bey exclaimed and embraced him. 'How long, how many years is it since we've seen each other, Süleyman? You've gone and forgotten us! Aren't we brothers of the same blood? Didn't we lead the nomad life with you up to only fifty years ago?'

Though a nomad chief, Dervish Bey's father had been a learned man in his time. He was a graduate of the religious medresseh at Marash and had been awarded a teacher's certificate by the erudite scholars of that establishment. Then, with his tribe, he had joined the Bey of Kozanoglu. That was before the great rebellion, in which it was rumoured he had lent a helping hand. After the rebellion, from which he came out unscathed, he settled in that area of the Chukurova where his tribe had been accustomed to winter, and turned it into a large farm, including all the land that stretched right up to the foot of the Anavarza crags. He had no difficulty in drawing up the title-deeds. Later, as the Akchasaz swamp was being reclaimed, the farm grew in size. When the Armenians fled, their lands were quietly incorporated as well. And the present Bey, too, lost no opportunity in adding to his territory.

245

'The tribe's in a bad way,' Headman Süleyman said. 'We haven't yet been able to find a place to set foot on this winter . . .'

Dervish Bey led him to a sofa. There was a harsh, cruel, ruthless expression on his full-lipped, large-eyed face with the high cheekbones and drooping moustache. His white hair set off his dark, sunburnt copper complexion. He had a tic that made one side of his face twitch spasmodically.

'I've heard about it,' he said. 'You put up a good fight at Saricham. I was proud of you.'

'But all in vain, Bey, all in vain . . . Not even Mustafa Kemal or the Lord Ali himself could prevail. It's no use, they're killing us, Bey, wiping us out. I've come to you for help. We have nowhere else to turn to.'

Dervish Bey's large eyes grew larger still. He fingered his necktie and smoothed down the crease of his trousers. 'But what can I do? Of what possible help could I be to you?'

Headman Süleyman's hand went to his waist. He untied the bundled kerchief bulging with gold, and laid it humbly before Dervish Bey.

'What's this?' the Bey cried.

'This . . .' Headman Süleyman stopped. He was suddenly bathed in sweat. 'This . . . This is all we have, the last wealth of the tribe. I have collected it all and brought it to you. Give us just a portion of our old wintering place, Akmashat, and let us have a foot too on this earth . . .'

Dervish opened the bundle and emptied its contents over the carpet. There were bracelets, rings, anklets, necklaces . . . All of beautifully worked gold . . . Golden earrings, noserings . . . Headpieces of five gold coins in one . . . Gold money of Sultan Reshat's reign and of the Republic . . .

Headman Süleyman's hand went to his sash again. He produced a sheaf of banknotes. These too he placed beside the gold. Dervish glanced at the money from the corner of his eye and fell to thinking. He fidgeted with his tie, his moustache, his hair. His face was twitching convulsively. He rose and began to pace up and down the room. Süleyman never took his eyes off him, watching his every move anxiously, clinging to him with his eyes as though to a saviour. Dervish Bey's decision would spell life or death for them. On and on he paced the room, stopping now and then to lift his head and stare at the Headman with a long, searching, piercing gaze . . .

In the tenth year Sabit Agha was again sequestrating Beydili village. The people, reduced to naked poverty, had no prospect now but to go begging about the Chukurova. The men had grabbed pickaxes and shovels, scythes and sickles and rushed to the fields to prevent the police from seizing their crop that was waiting to be threshed. Not a man was left in the village, and the women waited with heavy hearts for the worst to happen. It was then that Sabit Agha made his appearance. 'Where are all the men?' he inquired as he got out of his car. 'They've gone to the threshing-floor,' the women replied. 'So they want to orphan your children, is that it?' the Agha shouted. 'It doesn't do to go against the police, to defy the law. Besides, you have only so little to wait now, only thirty-nine years and this village, this land will be all yours.' All of a sudden things began to happen. There was a change in the group of women, a swelling ferment. Sabit Agha made a dash for his car. A hail of stones rained down upon him and he found himself surrounded by the women. He drew out his pistol and fired. He fired all the bullets in the pistol. Five women fell. Black Melek, wounded as she was, grabbed him from behind and tripped him. Groggy from the hits he had received, Sabit Agha lurched to the ground. The stones came faster now, from all sides. On and on, in silence, all together, the women pitched stone after stone, hundreds of them, for how long nobody could tell. The heap of white stones that covered Sabit Agha was mounting, taller, larger, and still the women did not stop. Tirelessly, tenaciously, relentlessly they kept on hurling stones at the ever widening mound . . .

Dervish Bey raised his head and scanned Headman Süleyman again. 'Have you heard, Süleyman, about what happened to Sabit Agha? How the Yörük women . . . I saw it with my own eyes . . . The stones they heaped on Sabit Agha rose as high as this house.'

God, oh God, Headman Süleyman thought in silent dismay.

Curse them, did they have to kill that wretched Agha just now? This'll put the fear of Yörüks into every Agha's heart. They'll never get over it, not in a dozen years . . . 'I saw a truckful of policemen going that way as I was coming to you. I asked the villagers what had happened and they told me. It's bad, very bad.'

'Sabit Agha tyrannized them cruelly. The women were right. They did well, but . . . But where will it all end?'

'Aaah, ah Bey,' Headman Süleyman lamented. 'How can you say they did well, how? We've got a bad name as it is. But now . . . What did they do well, what?'

Dervish Bey sat down again. His hands ran through the gold. He glanced at the money. 'How much land can you get in Akmashat with this money, d'you think?' he said.

'I know, Bey. Very very little. But take this money and we'll give you promissory notes for the rest. We'll pay you back year by year, as we earn. Please do this for us, Bey. We are of the same blood, the same stock. No harm can ever come from us to you, nor from you to us. Every year we'll pay you a sum of money. We'll go on paying you for ever if you like, till the day of judgment. You see, we need that land so very badly . . .'

Dervish Bey's eyes were fixed on him thoughtfully. A long time passed.

'No, Süleyman,' he said at last. 'My heart burns for you, but I can't do this, brother. I'm not alone, you know. There are my sons, and they're frightened to death now. Sabit Bey's death has driven them out of their minds . . . I'd have given you some land, I swear it, if only you'd come a couple of days ago. But now it's impossible, not if you heap gold to the weight of the land itself in my yard here . . . The Chukurova Aghas would kill me if I did. My sons, all the Chukurova would turn against me. Aah Süleyman, aaah!'

Headman Süleyman heard nothing, saw nothing any longer. How he got on his horse and rode away, where he went, by what road or swamp, mountain or valley, whether it was night or day, how he made his way back to the tribe he never knew.

25

Three tall oaktrees grow out of the rocks on the very crest of Mount Hemité. Beneath these trees is a single earth grave, covered with roundish stones. And not far from the trees there is a little rock-well, one fathom deep and three span wide. At Hidirellez and on other feast days, the villagers come here with votive offerings or to make sacrifices, and they drink from this rock-well. In the solitary grave lies a holy man whose name is said to have been Hamit Dédé. Nothing is known about him, no legend, no miracle, either for good or for bad. He just rests there, at peace, beyond all care, under the lofty oaktrees on the summit of the mountain. There are days when clouds descend over Hemité, and then the oaktrees, that stand like a superimposed crest on the mountain, are hidden from sight. Narcissuses grow all around the grave of Hamit Dédé. Their scent is strong, intoxicating like all rock flowers.

Inquiring here and there Kerem had at last found out where the tribe was camping. He had left the Forsaken Graveyard down below and was making his way up Hemité Mountain towards the valley of medlars. He was brimming with joy and played with insects and birds, tortoises and bees as he went along. Once in a while he would send his falcon up in the air. The falcon would soar into the distance, but after a while it would return and circle above him, and when Kerem called to it, it would come and perch itself on his arm. And Kerem would always reward it with a sparrow, a skylark or a nightjar that he had struck down with a stone. He was deliriously happy to have trained the falcon to come back to him. He loved to watch it circling above him as he walked. Now when he came to the tribe he would be able to let the falcon go until it was out of sight and everybody had given it up for lost. And then it would come back to whirl above him. He would call to it and it would glide down gently into his hand . . .

He walked into the camp with studied unconcern. His mother let out a cry. His father, his brothers and sisters said nothing, nor did they ask him a single question. As soon as he could escape from his mother's embrace Kerem flew his falcon and it vanished into the sky. Soon it was back, swirling over the tents, swift as running water, and when he called to it, it came to him at once. Three times Kerem repeated his performance. A few children stood by and watched him for a while. Then they turned away and no one took any interest in him any more. The whole tribe was in a state of heart-stopping suspense, waiting on tenterhooks, with bated breath. They squatted about in front of their tents or perched on stones, their eyes all riveted on one spot, the last turn of the road that could be seen winding below. Down the slope the flocks, together with the shepherds and sheepdogs, had closed their ranks and cleaved to each other in huddled bunches. They were also waiting.

The autumn sun bathed the arid purple crags of Hemité Mountain in a stream of light. Strange bees, huge as a thumb, with hard iridescent blue wings, flashed through the air. They buzzed among the silent, waiting nomads with an incredible amount of noise.

Suddenly there was a stir. Headman Süleyman had been sighted in the distance. The Hunter Kamil rose and gazed out, shielding his eyes with his hand. 'Something's wrong,' he said. 'He's returning empty-handed, mark my words. If he'd pulled it off the horse's legs would have been dancing with joy.'

Black looks were cast at him.

'No horse whose rider is at peace would walk like that . . .'

'May your tongue wither, Hunter Kamil,' Old Sultan Woman cursed him.

'May your tongue wither . . . Wither away . . .' others echoed.

'How can you tell at this distance whether the horse is prancing or not, whether the rider's crying or not! May you live as long as your lie, damn you, Kamil!'

After that Kamil did not say another word.

Headman Süleyman was drawing nearer, always at the same pace. He was hunched over his saddle, and it was clear to everybody by now that this was an inauspicious coming, but still they clung obstinately to their hopes. As he was rounding the Forsaken Graveyard they moved and began to clamber down the rocks to meet him. They reached the plain and waited, and it was not long before he was among them. He reined in. They all raised their heads as he leaned over the pommel of his saddle to speak.

'He refused,' he said. 'Not even at the price of our gold, our money, our life would Dervish Bey give us Akmashat. He's afraid. Afraid that when we settle we'll chase him off his own land. The women of a Yörük village have just stoned an Agha to death over there.'

Wearily he got off his horse and climbed up the craggy slope towards the tents. The others followed after him. He went straight to his tent and threw himself down on a rug.

'Father,' Fethullah said, 'what shall we do? We're trapped here, on this barren mountain. There's no water, no grass . . . We're making do with rainwater from the rock-wells . . .'

'I don't know,' Süleyman groaned. 'Oh, I don't know, son.'

'If we stay here much longer all the sheep will die.'

'Dervish said to me . . . He said, Süleyman, you're my blood-brother. Let the tribe fend for itself and come to me. I'll give you a place for a house and as much land as you wish . . .'

Fethullah stared at his father suspiciously. 'And what did you say, father?'

'I said, thank you, but my place is with my tribe as long as it keeps together. I must be the last man. One day when I look about me and see there's no one left, then I'll think of myself. Then I'll try and find some place to go.'

'What are we to do now?'

But Headman Süleyman could think of nothing at all any more.

The tribe had been badly shaken at the news, but now they

were beginning to recover and to talk. Kerem was flying his falcon hoping that people would look, but no one paid any attention to him. In the end he grew tired of it. 'This falcon's only brought trouble to me,' he said. 'It's of no use to me at all. If only I'd wished for winter-quarters instead. The tribe wouldn't be in despair, stuck to this rock like so many flies . . .' He took the falcon and tied him to the picket in front of his tent. 'Stay here,' he said, 'you good-for-nothing. Because of you I nearly got burnt alive. And the whole tribe too . . . Stay right here, you unlucky bird.'

As he walked back among the tents he pricked up his ears. Everyone was talking about his grandfather.

'Is it possible? Is it possible Old Haydar would stay away so long if he didn't have some hope?'

'That's true! Look at Headman Süleyman. He didn't stay another day when there was nothing to be done.'

'That sword . . . That sword! Whoever sets eyes on it is struck with wonder, fascinated . . .'

'It's a magic sword. If they knew that they'd give the whole of the Chukurova for this sword, not just a little bit of land to winter on. A magic sword!'

'Don't worry. Old Haydar will explain it all to Ismet Pasha.'

'Ismet Pasha will look at the sword. He'll look and look and say, old man if you've made this sword yourself, may your hands be blessed for ever. If I'd had this sword in my hand when the war was on, if you'd brought it to me then, I'd have routed all our enemies and conquered vast large territories, and then you wouldn't have been wandering about miserably like this, look-ing for a little patch of land. Why, why, why didn't you bring this sword to me then so I could destroy the enemy at the root? Oh, you thoughtless Old Haydar!'

All through the night they talked about Old Haydar, torn between anxiety and exaltation, swinging from bright hope to black despair.

Three days later they observed a horseman crossing the bridge in the distance. The horse was being led by a man on foot.

Clearly it was Old Haydar. They all rushed down into the plain to meet him. Osman drew near tugging at the horse on which Old Haydar clung apathetically to the pommel, his red beard hiding the front of the saddle, his face pinched, a maze of wrinkles, tiny now, his long-fingered hands, his large shoulders, his broad brow shrunken, diminished. He looked very small on the back of the horse. His tufty eyebrows drooped lifelessly, hiding his eyes. The tall coif was rammed low on his head. His sword dangled behind him, strapped to the back of the saddle.

Only dimly conscious that the tribespeople had come to meet him, Old Haydar lifted his brows and let his eyes skim over the crowd with a vague hurt look. He waved his right hand three times as though chasing away a fly, then his brows hid his eyes again. His hand went to the pommel and clenched over it.

Osman led the horse up the rocky slope. Old Haydar's tent had been put up. Osman eased him off the saddle, took his arm and supported him into the tent. Headman Süleyman, Old Müslüm and the elders all trooped in after them.

'Welcome back,' they said.

Old Haydar mumbled something and withdrew into himself. They saw that knives would not open his mouth now. 'You're tired,' they said. 'Have some sleep. We'll talk tomorrow.'

Old Haydar was asleep the minute they left the tent. He had not slept for days.

'What happened is that Ismet Pasha sent him packing. Ah Haydar, he said, I won't give you a single stone, let alone land . . .'

'Because, he said, where were you hiding this sword when I was at war and the enemy breaking my bones? What need have I got for it now? So he threw the sword at Old Haydar's face. And Old Haydar, you know what he is, closed his eyes and opened his mouth and let fly at him.'

'Ramazanoglu, Temir Agha, Payaslioglu, Mursaoglu, Kozanoglu . . . All of them, all rejected the sword . . .'

'And Old Haydar got mad . . . It's not Allah you serve, he told them, but earth and stones . . .'

'Yes . . . And he stood up to them like a hawk.'

253

'And then he said, what d'you know of this sword, what d'you know of any human feeling? Nothing, you're just degenerates, lost to everything . . .'

'Such things he said to them as would make a dog wild . . .'

'This sword, he said . . . This sword is made to be girded by men, not by creatures like you. If I'd known how rotten you are, I wouldn't even have let you lay eyes on my sword, not if you offered me the whole of the Chukurova and all of Anatolia and Arabia as well . . .'

'And then he said . . .'

The next morning as the sun was rising, Kerem went to his grandfather. Old Haydar was trying to fix his anvil into the earth between two rocks. Kerem helped him to do it. Then, together, they shaped up the forge and placed in the bellows. No one but Kerem entered the old man's tent. They brought out the trough and Kerem carried water from the rock-wells and filled it up. By the afternoon the blacksmith's tent was all set.

Old Haydar piled the coal into the forge, struck a match and set fire to the kindling. 'Let's see you blow the bellows, Kerem,' he said. Kerem obeyed him and soon the coals were aflame.

'Come here, Kerem,' Old Haydar said. He took him in his arms and stroked his head. Then he kissed him and said: 'Run along now, Kerem. I'm going to work.' He smiled, and his red beard smiled too, bitterly, as he looked at his grandson. 'Did you find your falcon again, Kerem?' he asked.

Kerem was delighted that his grandfather had remembered the falcon. 'I did,' he said. 'And how it flies, grandfather, right up into the skies and then it comes back to me with all the birds it can get. It's turned out to be a marvellous stupendous falcon. The Lord Hizir's falcon . . .' Since the beginning he had wanted to confess to his grandfather about the falcon and how Hizir had given it to him on Hidirellez day, but he had never had the chance. He popped his head in through the flap of the tent. 'It's the Lord Hizir's falcon,' he said. 'The Lord Hizir gave it to me.'

But his grandfather was not listening to him any longer. He

had grasped the handle of the bellows and was heaving away with all his might. And as he blew the bellows he seemed to gain strength, to grow in size. His red beard shone with life, his tufty brows bristled. The muscles in his arms swelled. He was like a giant now. The weary shrunken defeated person who had come back to them from the city had disappeared and in his place was a beautiful vital powerful being. The most beautiful, the greatest of men . . . Kerem could have lingered on for days in the entrance to the tent, gazing with wondering eyes at that figure wreathed in flying sparks and grappling with the fire. But he was afraid. If his grandfather saw that he was being watched he would raise hell. So, for one last time, he looked at him as he stood there in the sea of sparks and reluctantly drew away.

Expertly, with all his strength, Old Haydar kept at the bellows until all the coals were aglow. The sparks subsided, drifting gently one by one about the tent. Then he drew his sword from its scabbard and held it to the light of the forge. He looked at it in wonder as the sparks shot up through the air with crepitating sounds. Then he planted it firmly into the soil and knelt before it. His head bowed in an attitude of complete surrender, a strange prayer rose to his lips, a prayer no one had ever heard, that he himself had forgotten he knew. He leaned forward, drew the sword out of the earth, kissed it three times and held it to his brow. Then he rose, the sword balanced on his open palm. Slowly, delicately, he let it slip on to the glowing coals of the forge and closed his eyes, muttering a prayer. It was a very ancient prayer this, a prayer for iron and fire and water. And in the end he sighed and fell to chanting. Suddenly, like a ravening tiger pouncing on his prey, he hurled himself at the bellows and pulled. Air streamed through the coals and the sparks flew. The forge turned white, then fiery red, and a cloud of sparks filled the whole tent. The glowing coals burned themselves out. Without a glance at the forge, Old Haydar heaped more coals over the embers, then clutched at the bellows again. It was getting on for midnight when he took the soft molten fiery sword from the fire and placed it on the anvil. He began to beat, and the sword changed shape. It folded once, then again and again, until it was rolled into a ball. Old Haydar took the sphere of molten iron and threw it quickly back on to the forge. Again he swung at the bellows and pulled savagely, expertly.

All the tribespeople were outside in front of their tents, their eyes fixed on the blacksmith's tent, waiting for some miracle they dared not hope for to be performed.

First a deep silence would settle on the blacksmith's tent, and in this silence the tent would come aglow and sparks shoot out into the night through the top and the flies. One moment the tent would fade into black darkness and the next it would be drowned in a blinding flash of light.

Then the sound of hammering would begin, deep and slow and rhythmic . . . And the valley of medlars, the whole of Hemité Mountain echoed and trembled and went mad with the frenzied relentless clang of the hammer. A formidable giant had alighted on the earth and was shaking it to its very foundations as he beat and forged what seemed to be all the swords, all the iron in the world. The hammering quickened, faster, faster, and merged into one long unbroken clangour. Inside, Old Haydar's hand that wielded the hammer whirred furiously. Then suddenly the tent went dark. The hammering stopped, but its sound rang on from rock to rock, the echoes receding and fainting far into the distance.

Then again the tent would be bathed in light. A dazzling brightness would pour out into the night and splash over the rocks. And once more the hammering, slow clear and even, sounding deep against the rocks, beating, beating, swelling, quicker, quicker. Then a pause, and the long-drawn-out vibrations ringing from crag to crag.

At break of day as the east began to pale, the mountain was shaken to its very depths. The hammering came faster now, harder, angrier. The tent glowed, an incandescent mass. Lights and sounds burst out of it, rising, swelling until they reached the topmost crest of Mount Hemité, there to freeze in one long lingering reverberation. Then a great stillness.

256

The tribespeople waited and waited, but no sound came from the blacksmith's tent again.

Day dawned and they crept up on tiptoe and lent a timorous ear. Not a breath, not the slightest movement inside the tent. No one had the heart to slip his head in and look. In the end Headman Süleyman nerved himself to walk in. Old Haydar was bent forward, his left cheek resting on the anvil which he had embraced with his broad arms. His red beard trailed to the ground like golden threads. He seemed to be asleep. The large heavy hammer had fallen at his feet. On the anvil close to the blacksmith's face lay a strange freshly-forged piece of iron with lightning-like spikes that resembled a wheel or a dial or perhaps the ancient emblem of the tribe, vaguely reminiscent of the sun-symbols imprinted on their orange felt rugs.

He retreated out of the tent to face the anxious crowd. 'Old Haydar is no more,' he said.

There was no sound, no cry, no lamenting. They all stood still, rooted to the spot. It was a long time before they could stir, and then one by one they filed into the tent. The Master Black-smith was smiling at them. Was it happily or sadly? . . . Perhaps a little angry? Hurt . . .

They did not separate him from his anvil. Just as he was, cleaving to it, they eased him on to a stretcher and carried the heavy load to the top of Hemité Mountain. They put him down near the earth tomb of the saint, Hamit Dédé. A little further, facing east, where the spreading branches of the oaktree ended, they dug a wide man-deep grave and lowered the blacksmith into it, still clinging to his anvil. Beside him they placed his hammer and the other tools from his forge. Then they strewed heavy-scented myrtle branches and leaves over him and filled in the earth, arranging white stones all around the grave. Old Haydar's body was not washed, because that is how it is with holy men when they die. No keening is held over them, no hymns are sung. There is no weeping. Old Haydar would not have wanted it. Holy men never require any of these funerary rites. Without waiting, they clambered down back to the camp and gathered up Old Haydar's tent, his clothes and all his earthly belongings and lit a big fire.

'Throw these in,' they told Kerem. 'It's your duty to burn all that remains of your grandfather. That's the custom.'

So Kerem threw his grandfather's things into the fire as he was told. Only the horse was left, and tradition decreed that it was Kerem who must kill it. Kerem loved the old horse more than anything in the world. 'Father,' he pleaded, 'don't make me kill the horse. You do it. Please!'

'You have to,' his father said. 'Don't disgrace us in the eyes of all the world.' And he thrust a pistol into Kerem's hand and gave him the halter.

Kerem looked at the horse. He looked at his father, at the waiting tribesmen. Then he drew the horse slowly down the valley and tied it behind a rock. He aimed the pistol straight at the horse's head, closed his eyes and pulled the trigger. The horse fell. Its body jerked twice, its legs and neck stretched out stiffly, then it was quite still. A pool of blood began to gather under its head.

Kerem wanted to vomit. His eyes were bloodshot. He went up to his father and handed back the pistol, never once looking him in the face. Perched on the picket in front of their tent, the falcon had grown restless. It flapped its wings and tried to fly. It pecked away angrily at its jesses and claws. It turned and tossed and tugged at its leash. All things he had never done before . . . Kerem looked at its eyes. They were as red as his own. He untied the falcon and holding it tightly, without a word to anyone, he set off down the slope of the valley of medlars. Once or twice he turned to look back, and each time the little cluster of tents stuck to the hill, clinging desperately to its slope, appeared more and more incongruous to him. He came to the plain and stopped again to look. The tents were old, dirty, weary, humbled . . . All through his last night his grandfather had been forging something. He had melted the sword and used the iron to fashion some strange thing with spikes, like a sun, like the emblem on their standard. But not quite. It looked like nothing he could think of. His grandfather had not had time to finish it. What could it be, this thing he had spoiled his wonderful sword to make? Some talisman? Some magic charm? But his grandfather had never liked charms and magic. He had meant it as an ultimate message to his fellow-men, but what was it, this word he had struggled so desperately to convey and had not been able to complete?

'My grandfather's gone too . . .' Kerem drew a deep sigh. He took one last look at the tents on the hill, then turned and walked away. When he came to the brake, he stopped. The tents were far behind. He looked at the falcon. It was quite calm now.

He touched the bird's head with his finger. 'D'you understand, my falcon?' he said. 'He's dead, my grandfather . . . Dead the great Haydar, Master of the Blacksmith's Hearth. Gone . . . I'm left alone. Alone . . . And I'm going away too. I'm leaving the tribe. So I say to you, be free, my little falcon, I release you . . .' But his heart ached even as he said the words. He stroked the falcon and looked into its eyes and kissed it. 'You've been a good brave companion to me, my falcon. Good luck to you. Don't tarry here, fly off straight into your mountains. You're still too young and even though you are a falcon some accident can happen to you in this alien land.' He kissed and caressed it, but could not bring himself to let it go. Slowly he unfastened the leash, opened the tiny button-size jesses and held the falcon up. They came eye to eye. Then he sent it flying. 'Go, my falcon, go now. My grandfather's dead and I'm going away too.'

The falcon soared up and Kerem hurried into the brake to hide in a bush, for he knew it would soon return, looking for him, wanting to perch on his arm. And so it was. The falcon circled once or twice high above, then shot like an arrow through the air towards Anavarza and vanished from sight. It was not long before it was back again, whirling over the brake, searching for Kerem. How he wished it would find him, would come back to him. But still he crouched there, while the falcon flew towards Jeyhan River and back again. Many times it came and went. At last, tracing wide circles it began to soar higher and higher until it was gliding through the sky and disappearing in the direction of Hemité Mountain.

For a long time Kerem waited there in the bush. But the falcon never came back. This hurt him more than he could tell. He began to cry. Crying, he fell to the road again, walking in the direction of Yalnizagach village. His eyes scanned the sky hopefully all the time, but there was nothing to be seen.

It was getting on for evening and the shadows were lengthening. Skylarks were warbling, bees buzzing. Flocks of birds passed through the sky, drowning the world in their loud twittering. Once more Kerem turned and looked at Hemité. The mountain was melting away, a pale blue mass, slowly fading into the night.

26

*By most people the owl is held to be an unlucky bird. If it
alights near a house or on its roof and hoots there, they know
that it bodes no good. Owls are said to come to a town or a
country as heralds of trouble. There are many different kinds of
owls, big and small. Some are long and dark brown, with huge
eyes that fill up both sides of the face leaving only a crooked
beak in the middle, and they stare out on to the world with a
gaping hungry gaze. The grey feathered owl is short and
squat, with even larger eyes and pointed ears, and it is more
rapacious. It cannot fly at all during the day, and if it does
it loses its way and flutters about confusedly until it smashes
down into some ruin. There are all kinds of owls on Hemité
Mountain. They nest in crevices on the crags. Some are as
large as eagles, others tiny as pigeons. It was three days now
that the owls had surrounded the Karachullu tribe's camp in
the valley of medlars. Their dismal hair-raising cries sowed
disquiet into everybody's heart. No one could sleep. All night
long with sticks and stones they chased them away. The owls
would glide off into the darkness with taut wide wings. But
next thing you knew, they were there again, perched on the
peak of the sharpest crags, their faces turned towards the
camp, hooting away worse than ever with their sinister
voices. Was there no way to get out of here, to escape from
this Hemité Mountain? All the roads were closed to them.
Try and go, try and break out if you can. Hunger is already
bringing sickness upon the flocks. Soon they will begin to die,
one after the other. If only, ah if only they could be let loose
to graze for just one night on those green fields stretching flat
out below, right up to Dumlu and the Mediterranean . . .
They would be saved then. But it would fare ill indeed for the
tribe afterwards. You're caught in pincers, my poor brave
people. You can strain and struggle, but there's no escape.
The end is death, my friends.*

That day, with a leather cask in her hand Jeren went to all the rock-wells she could discover and filled the cask to the brim. She had grown thin and this made her look even taller. Her eyes were larger than ever in her pale face and her hair thicker. She was like some still and stagnant water.

She cleared out a corner of her tent and strewed branches and leaves about the ground. Then she warmed the water in a cauldron over the fire and washed herself carefully using her precious soap. She had a dress in her bundle, an old dress that had been in her family for no one knew how long. It was of finespun silk velvet, pale mauve, trimmed with silver thread. She took it out and put it on. Then, discarding the rawhide sandals she wore every day, she slipped on a pair of shining shoes. She combed out her hair, letting a lock fall over her eyebrow. Her finery, the earrings, the necklace, the headpiece, she had all given to Headman Süleyman. She tied a green silk scarf over her head and went out.

All through the day she drifted from tent to tent talking pleasantly to everyone, kissing and caressing the little children. In the evening she went to bed, but without undressing. When everyone had retired, she slipped out of her tent and ran up the mountain.

A harrowing dread, fraught with pity, grew in her as she ran. The sweat gushed from her pores and her ears began to roar. The rocks, the whole mountain roared and throbbed, and all the owls fell in after her with loud hootings, thousands of them, and the sky was alive with flapping wings, with huge grisly open eyes and blood-dripping beaks. The sky rose and fell and heaved in a flurry of wings. She heard cries and rumblings, crackling sounds. The whole world was reeling about her. Dark horses were galloping by. Their hooves beat on the rocks and drew out sparks. The howling of wolves mingled with the beat of hooves and the hooting of the owls. Long shadows,

shadows of horses, lengthening, shortening, spreading and thinning, were sweeping up into the mountain from the plain below in an endless flow. Sparks flew from the rocks. And the white teeth of the wolves, sharp . . . A wolf carcass lying all stiff in the night, its white teeth bared like fangs, howling, a long deafening howl. And foxes, and eagles and falcons . . . And Kerems, thousands of Kerems, running, fleeing with a thousand falcons pecking away at their hands, the blood dripping, splashing down. A great rumbling . . . Stones are rolling down from the peak of the mountain, hundreds of large boulders . . . The horsemen, the eagles, the owls, the Kerems, the falcons, the dead wolves, the white pointed teeth, the scarlet snakes are suddenly wiped out. Boulders are hurtling down into the valley of medlars . . . The sound of men's voices, laughter and cursing, echoing from crag to crag. And still the boulders come crashing down with long reverberations that shake the mountain to its foundations. And then again the turmoil of wings in the sky, the rumblings, the beat of hooves . . .

Jeren clambered up the steep jagged crags to the very top of a rock that was tall as two minarets, the highest on Hemité Mountain. She flung out her arms. The rumbling, the noise died away and the world was empty and desolate, and Jeren heard herself breathe and her heart beat in her ears.

'Halil, Halil, Halil! You never came, Halil. I'll never see you again, Halil. I'm going, Halil, without ever ever seeing you again. Like this, Halil . . .'

Just as she was about to hurl herself down the precipice she shuddered violently. Her legs gave way and she dropped on to the rock. A light burst in front of her eyes and went out. Three times it flashed and faded. And then again the owls hooting, the flapping of eagles' wings, the long horsemen, the beat of hooves and the sparks . . . The sparks and Old Haydar's smiling body clutching the anvil, the howling dead wolf, its white bloody teeth extended sword-like. And the snakes, the snakes . . . The night running wild, whipped by the winds, the rocks wrenched out, tossed through the air. The huge mountain uprooted, wobbling, lurching into the plain . . .

Jeren rose. She opened her arms wide like the wings of a bird ready to cast itself into the void, but again all sounds died away and a desolate solitude encompassed her. 'I, Jeren, I! How did I come to this, how? I, Jeren . . .' And she wept tremblingly. Her arms fell to her sides and she folded down over the ground like a dead thing. But her mind was clear now, clearer and soberer than ever. An intimation of joy flickered within her, alike to hope and fear and death and awe. She tried to grasp its meaning but it eluded her. She was seeing Oktay Bey now, along with the horsemen, Halil, the owls . . . Stones were tumbling down the valley again, the bleating of sheep, men shouting . . . Long loud endless rumblings . . . The whole world was shaking. The lights below . . . And Jeyhan River flowing on . . . And wilder and wilder the north wind, the mad Boreas, sweeping up the very rocks . . . And fleeing before it a rustling endless flow of snakes. Hissing, whistling . . . Cold, blood-freezing gruesome whistles . . . Whistles that came from the earth, from every bush and plant and stone . . . That filled earth and sky . . . Jeren pressed her hands to her ears. Harder, desperately, but the whistling, the rumbling could not be shut off.

The darkness tossed, a frenzied tumult, a medley of arms and legs in the night, of horses, birds and snakes, of Jerens and Kerems and falcons. Villages, fires . . . And Oktay Bey, many Oktay Beys, many bulging eyes, many drooping horsy lips . . . Trees hurtling through the night, snails, red owls, red wolves, their eyes and claws and white teeth . . . And vultures, red-beaked . . . Thundering, blasting, swarming, the night streamed on.

She forced herself to her feet. But again the fevered night, the surging flood receded, subsided into silence, and all was clear again. There was no doubt, no confusion now in Jeren's mind. 'Halil isn't dead. He wasn't killed. They deceived me. He never even tried to see me once. The blood-stained shirt they showed me was a lie. A lie, a lie, a lie . . .' She spread out her arms. 'Halil, Halil, Halil . . .'

A noise rose from the camp below. Again the mountain shook from head to foot and large rocks rolled down the slopes one

264

after the other. Again the cries, the laughter, the cursing.

'Halil did this to me, Halil! He played this trick on me. Didn't he know how I mourned for him, how I wanted to kill myself, how the whole tribe turned against me? He played this trick on me . . .'

She flung her arms out wide. The north wind raged on madly and suddenly there was a flash of lightning. Again and again the lightning flashed, shedding light on everything. She clenched her teeth. 'Halil, Halil!' It came like a hiss out of her mouth. The thing that gleamed within her like some promised joy was there again, but still she could not capture it. She knew that if she caught it she would be saved. But if the rumbling and that tumult in the night started again, it would elude her for ever. Desperately she tried to think. It flickered once more and then she had it. The world was illuminated and a joyous tremor shook her to the core. The rumblings, the tumult, the confusion, all was gone, wiped away. Only the boom of great boulders rolling down into the valley persisted, and the screams and shouts that came from the encampment down below.

She clambered down the sheer face of the rock and walked on in the night with a song welling in her heart. The scent of sun-dried thyme and grass and of narcissus drifted to her nose. The rocks and earth too exhaled an acrid sweaty odour.

'Halil,' she was thinking, 'ah Halil if, as some say, you're alive . . . If ever my eyes look into yours again . . . If I see you Halil . . . You did this, Halil, you.' Just to say his name brought life into her, and warmed her blood, and filled her with love and dreams of togetherness.

On and on she lingered, listening to the night and the blowing north wind that was slowly subsiding as morning approached. She breathed in the smell of dried plants that crackled under her feet. She wandered from rock to rock, and the joy grew in her, wrapping her in a bright light. She hugged her breast tightly for fear joy would escape her again. She lay down full length at a rock-well and drank of the cold water. Then she found another well, a deep one, and washed her face. A dry yellow mountain flower was floating on the water. She took it and slipped it behind her ear.

Day was dawning. The night receded suddenly and light invaded the Chukurova, boring deep through the crust of the earth.

She saw Oktay Bey down in the plain. He was bent over his horse and riding toward Jeyhan River, still and motionless as the dead. Perhaps he was asleep on the horse. The very sight of this man had always made her shiver with loathing. Now she felt nothing. Maybe a little pity, some compassion, a grudging spark of admiration . . . 'He's better than I am,' she thought as she followed him with her eyes. 'I'm not worth his little finger. I let Halil go. I never followed him from mountain to mountain. I never shared his life of a fugitive. I did not hide with him, fleeing from cave to cave. I did not give him the proof of my love. Halil, O Halil, you're not to blame. I never proved my love to you. Forgive me, Halil! Forgive me for not letting these eyes of mine look on you even once with love, for forbidding my hands from ever touching you, for keeping all my beauty from you, my body, my lips . . .'

When she came to the camp she found everyone in a ferment. Fethullah was rushing about the tents like a mad bull, foaming, the veins in his neck swollen, a pistol in his hand. 'I'll kill them, I'll kill them! I'll kill them all. I'll set fire to their villages. I'll gouge their eyes out . . .' The women were gathered in a crowd, weeping. The men were silent. They sat about on stones, their heads hanging. Knives would not have opened their mouths. A great number of the tents were lying battered on the ground under huge rocks. And at the foot of a blood-spattered rock two children, a boy and a girl, eight to ten years old, were lying dead, steeped in blood, their heads crushed.

'What happened? What happened, oh what, what?'

Sultan Woman was beating her knees. 'Haven't you heard, haven't you seen? Weren't you here last night? Ah, you were well away, well away . . . All through the night rocks rolled down upon us from the mountain. The tents were crushed under them. And Musajik's children . . . See the poor mites . . . They could not get away in time. Stones rained upon us from heaven until dawn. Huge rocks . . . Look, look . . . All those rocks there came this night.'

The valley of medlars had turned into a heap of stone and rock.

'This can't be,' Fethullah kept repeating, beside himself, his eyes bloodshot. 'How can men turn into such bloodthirsty monsters just for a handful of money?'

Headman Süleyman was in his tent when Jeren entered it. But he never saw her. He sat there, bemused, crouching, with his arms around his legs and his chin on his knees. His beard was trembling.

'Uncle, uncle! Uncle Süleyman,' she called to him. Her voice was clear and firm. The Headman opened his eyes without moving. 'I've got something to tell you.'

Then he noticed the unusual brightness in her eyes. 'What is it, my daughter?' he said, surprised.

'I've decided that I shall marry Oktay Bey. Of my own free will. I've come to admire his goodness, his kindness. No one could have been as faithful as that man.'

'No one,' Headman Süleyman said as he rose to his feet. 'His is a wonderful constancy, a wonderful passion. May Allah grant you happiness, my Jeren.'

'He's down there wandering somewhere below in the plain. Tell them to call him.'

'I know. I see him every night,' the Headman said.

The news of Jeren's decision spread through the tribe in an instant. They forgot the dead children, the stones that had rained upon them from the sky, the broken-down tents, they forgot everything and a whirl of joy swept through the valley of medlars.

27

From Khorassan we rose and swept through the land, and bright shone our long lances on our shoulders. Like packs of wolves we overran the world, spreading out to east and west, riding our long-necked ruby-eyed horses to the confines of the Nile and the Indus, conquering forts and cities and countries, founding new nations. Like eagles we swooped down over the plain of Harran, Mesopotamia, the Arabian desert, Anatolia, the Caucasus, the vast steppes of Russia with ten thousand black tents, a hundred thousand . . . Our long seven-domed black tents of goatshair, each one a marvel of human craft, and inside the most delicate colours, the most beautiful designs . . . And our lances, our swords, our daggers . . . Our muskets with their gold-engraved ivory stocks . . . Our carved wooden mortars, our noserings and necklaces and coronets . . . Our rugs and kilims and cilices . . . In the plain of Harran we whirled in the ancient semah, thousands of us, and the gazelles of the plain whirled with us. Like proud falcons we were, and held great feasts and holy gatherings. From the shores of one great ocean to the shores of another we surged, wave after wave, and fortresses, cities, countries, races bowed down before us. A whole age we enthralled, and many cruel things we did to the men we subjugated. But never, never did we humble their pride. Our tradition forbade this always, to shame human beings. We never hurt the poor and the destitute, the women and children, whatever their race or country or religion. Friend or enemy, we held them in respect and treated them as we would treat our own fallen brothers, our children, our women, the aged of our tribe. And we touched not a hair of the head of the enemy who called for mercy. Our thick felt pavilions, embroidered and stamped with our many emblems, were warm and sturdy. No palace could ever compare with these pavilions in splendour. And so we moved over the earth,

sometimes free, sometimes captive, conquering and conquered
. . . And the centuries flowed past, and we broke apart and
shattered, and dwindled away, and the black tents faded . . .
We, who gave their names to great mountains and rivers, to
lands and countries, who beat our imprint into them . . . To
Anatolia we came, and before us rose Kayseri Mountain,
Ararat, Süphan, Nemrut, Binboga, Jilo Mountains . . .
And before us stretched great rivers, the Kizilirmak, the
Yeshilirmak, the Sakarya, the Seyhan, the Jeyhan . . .
And the vast Anatolian plateaux, Salt Lake and the
Aegean plains with their amber grapes . . . . And to all these
lakes and rivers, plains and mountains we gave their names.
In every corner of Anatolia we left our imprint, the names
and emblems of our tribes. So that we should not be forgotten.
So that in all these lands our race should take root and
prosper . . . They have driven us on to the dusty roads, they
have cast us up into the snow-capped mountains. We became
one with the land of Anatolia, intimate with its earth and
stones, its flowing waters and blowing winds, with its time-
weathered caravansaries and palaces, shrines and cities, with
the songs and traditions, the wisdom and lore that had sprouted
on this land, growing, greening, the process of thousands of
years. Soldered to each other like flesh and bone . . . Like rain
and earth . . . In every province we abandoned a part of us, in
every clime, in every tract of land. Discarded tents, forgotten,
left to rot away . . . From one single source we had gushed
forth, a mighty torrent, overpowering, inexhaustible. Into a
thousand sources we split and dispersed and shrunk and
drained away, sucked dry. And now perhaps, our songs will
never be sung any more. Brothers, disciples, sages will never
be of one heart again and join in whirling the ritual semah.
The moon, the sun will rise and set, but for other eyes. Buried
in oblivion will be our lore and customs and traditions. No
one will know what we thought, what we felt about the
burgeoning of the tree, the blowing of the wind, the birth and
growth and death of man. The budding of the flowers, the
roaring of the tiger, the falling of the rain, the greening of the

269

*earth . . . How the eagle lays its eggs, how to teach the un-
trained falcon, the long-necked unbroken steed . . . Nothing at
all will be known of our love for this world, our friendship
for its every creature, of that marvellous strength given to us
to become a part of every one of them. Our name will not be
spoken in the generations of men. Not all at once, but slowly
dissolving, wasting over thousands and thousands of years,
leaving a piece of us in every land, we have spent ourselves . . .
Like a bright water we flowed over this earth . . . And came
to Anatolia and saw Kayseri Mountain rising tall and clean
and beautiful, enchanting, bathed in light. Our long-necked
ruby-eyed horses . . . Our black cilice tents like a hundred
thousand mighty eagles alighting over Mesopotamia and
Harran Plain . . . A thousand souls whirling in the semah,
with a thousand gazelles, three days and three nights, forty
days, forty nights . . .*

Hassan Agha rose to meet Headman Süleyman. He was a tall
man with a sparse beard and a permanent look of wily cunning
on his face. Look, I'm laughing pleasantly with you now, he
seemed to say all the time, but you just wait, I'll soon be plant-
ing a dagger in your back. His pointed face was like a fox's, but
nasty, shrivelled, cringing, beaten, kneaded by bitter tribulations, a face that has triumphed in the end, but curses its very
triumph.

'Welcome, welcome, Süleyman brother! How glad I am to
see you,' he cried as he embraced the Headman at the door in
the old Turcoman fashion. His voice was that of an old woman,
a cracked, hoarse croak. 'What a good thing, what a good thing
this business! How pleased I am that my son should marry into
such a noble tribe as yours.' He took the Headman by the hand
and made him sit on the sofa. Then he settled down beside him
and put his hands on his knees. 'Yes indeed . . . And it's all
your work, I know. And I thank you for it, for the world has
never witnessed such a passionate attachment. Only the noble,

the brave man can love with such a love as this, beyond his own life even. Whoever heard of a base man in love? Large-hearted men always love like this, with a great overpowering passion. Yes, I admire Oktay. I respect him. He didn't become rotten, he didn't melt away in this Chukurova. He fell in love with a strong passion, worthy of his stock. And as for the girl, what a girl! Pardon me, my friend, but I say she's a lion that girl. And a she-tiger too.'

This was the third day now that Hassan Agha was inviting him to his mansion, greeting with great effusion and singing the praises first of his son and then of Jeren, quickly proceeding to relate to him every detail of his life.

'My mother is also a Yörük, a daughter of the famed Beys of Horzumlu. And my father belongs to that race of eagles, the fierce Lek Kurds, who swooped down on the Chukurova and ruled it for years. My mother's father was of the noble Avshar Turcomans who have subjugated the seven climes and the four corners of the earth ever since the time of Khorassan. For three hundred years they were castellans of the Sultan in nine hundred and sixty-six forts. That's the kind of race we come from, my friend. That's the kind of race that produces an Oktay, who can brave the years and misery and death for his great love . . .'

The tribe was camping on Hassan Agha's estate, near a clump of mulberry trees. They had pitched their long black tents in a neat orderly file, and this did not escape Hassan Agha's notice. Just as if they were founding a new village, he said to himself with growing anxiety.

Hassan Agha had held big festivities for the betrothal of his only son. He had invited the notables of all the neighbouring villages, the leaders and parliament members of both political parties, and all his friends in the town. Two camels, three young bulls and countless sheep and goats had been slaughtered. Such a feast it had to be that for years people would talk about it . . . The *raki* had flowed like water. Clothes had been ordered for Jeren from the most fashionable dressmakers in Adana. Had there been time, Hassan Agha would have had Jeren's clothes brought in from Istanbul itself. That day Jeren's beauty dawned on them like the morning star. Hassan Agha wanted everyone to see her, to stare in wonder, to stand amazed, dazzled by so much beauty and splendour.

'Yes, my brother Süleyman . . . I worked very hard to get this estate. Very hard. I am the son of a saddler. It was very difficult for me to make my way. If the earth here were to be watered with the sweat of my brow, as God's my witness it's mud it would be, mud these vast lands you see. Every particle contains a drop of my sweat. This land used to belong to a Turcoman Bey. He was a drinker and a regular spendthrift, a wild, pleasure-loving man who threw good money after bad. He fell into debt with me. And I worked hard, I didn't eat or drink, I didn't sleep, but I got him to be more and more indebted to me. I owned two shops, a grocery and a drapery, but I sold them both . . . Three motor-cars I sold too to get money for him. And a truck, and a threshing-machine . . . And God knows how many tractors. A wave of his hand, a nod of his head was enough. I gave him money, drink, food, honey, whatever he asked for. And all the time I worked, tirelessly, ceaselessly. Twenty years I laboured in this way, and then I slapped a mortgage on his estate . . . And then another, and another . . . But it still wasn't enough. A fourth mortgage, and at last it was all mine. But I did not drive him out. Oh no, I let him stay on in the farm till his death, and gave him *raki* whenever he wanted it, just as before, and even a little money. And so the Turcoman Bey ended his days here. He called me to his death-bed. Hassan, he said, you've made life easy for me on this earth and I thank you for it. Now I'm dying and I have one last wish. Say it, I said, it's my duty to fulfil your last desire. You know that big mulberry tree down there with great spreading branches? he said, I planted it myself with my own hands when they forced us to settle on the land. It was a frail sapling then. Now it's grown huge. It will live on and I'm dying. I want you to bury me there, beneath that tree. Of course I'll do it, I said. Thank you, he said, and breathed his last.'

Hassan Agha had taken the Turcoman Bey's widowed sister

as his third wife. She owned a great tract of farmland that bordered on the Turcoman Bey's estate and was almost as large. On the day of the wedding Hassan Agha incorporated the two estates into one. His present land was an amalgam of five different estates. And it was still growing.

He had something on the tip of his tongue, but somehow he could not come out with it. He talked and talked, beating about the bush endlessly, until his eyes gleamed as if he was about to say it at last. But then he would break into a cold sweat and humming and hawing would lapse into a sullen silence.

'This farm is my own flesh and blood. Its every stone is more precious than my own heart. This farm . . . This farm that I nursed like a baby in my arms, singing lullabies to it . . .' This farm, he kept saying, this farm! . . . And then he would stop and scowl. 'Yes, this farm is my sweat and toil, my blood, my soul . . .'

Headman Süleyman knew very well what he was driving at, but he waited patiently. All through the night this torture would go on, until the cocks began to crow and Hassan Agha's head dropped over his breast and he was snoring away as he sat there. If only he would come out with it and spare them both any further torment . . .

Again he heard the cocks crowing. Hassan Agha was nodding sleepily.

'Hassan Agha, Hassan Agha,' Süleyman burst out at last very loudly.

The Agha jumped. 'What is it, Headman?' he said.

'That's enough torturing yourself and me too. Come out with it. What have you got on your mind?'

Hassan Agha, a hard-bitten man, was not taken aback. His fox-like eyes gleamed with sly triumph. His voice was warm, stirring, charged with heartfelt emotion. 'I'm just wondering,' he said, 'what Oktay told you about your settling here on my land. You must know that Oktay's not entitled to give away one jot of it. That's one thing. And another is that he can't rent it away either. Nor can he sell any part of it. That's three. This farm belongs to me, all of it. Oktay could lease some of the land on a share-cropping basis, yes, but not to Yörüks who are relatives of ours and know nothing at all about farming. I won't have people who are related to me now, working on my land as share-croppers or mere labourers. That's four . . .'

Hassan Agha really felt for these Yörüks as he saw what a miserable downtrodden existence was theirs and learnt of all their sufferings and trials. How could it be, how, that men should have to put up with so much just because they could not find a little patch of land to set foot on? It was too much, too much . . . But as soon as they had come to the farm, they had looked around and taken stock of the place just as though it were their very own, and they had rejoiced. Like a cat entering a strange room they had peeped into every nook and cranny purring with pleasure as though they had bought up the whole place. They had let themselves go into transports of joy, and during the betrothal festivities they had capered and cavorted madly in the strangest dances imaginable. No, Hassan Agha resolved, whatever Oktay says or promises, not for any Jeren in the world, not even for the Virgin Mary herself will I allow the Yörüks to get a foot on my land. They'll grab it and never let go again. No force can remove them from the earth once they've stuck to it. Just let them drive their talons in, just let them! Ah, you fox of a Headman, you slyboots, you!

'I'm going to hold the wedding in the spring, Headman Süleyman. And the wedding festivities will last forty days and forty nights. Just like the old Turcoman weddings of yore it'll be, splendid, brilliant, worthy of our Turcoman fathers, and the Kurdish and Yörük ones too. Your tribe can camp here till then, that is until the spring. I will allow you to winter here this one year, and that only because of my son's marriage. In his honour. This land that I sweated blood to obtain can never be open to wintering nomads. It's out of the question . . . Whatever Oktay may have told you, this land is my very own, mine only. No one else can have a say in it. Not even my son, not even my own flesh and blood, my good, honest, brave Oktay, not even if he *is* engaged to such a girl as Jeren. No one, no one but me! So you can stay until the spring, but after the wedding you'll have to pack up your tents and go. Look, Süleyman, I'm not even exacting any payment from you for this winter . . .'

He slapped the Headman's knee and put his hand to his shoulder. He was relieved to be able to speak out at last and pleased that the Headman had given him an opening. 'Now look, my friend, light of my eyes . . . Listen, brother, you mustn't tell this to the tribe. Let them think they're here to stay or whatever our Oktay may have told them . . . Poor things, it'll be like a cup dashed from their lips . . . So I beg you, don't let on about this. It's a shame. My heart breaks for them, really. Let them spend at least one winter here in peace of mind. And next year . . . God is great. So it's understood, isn't it? I have your word, haven't I, that you won't speak of this to the tribespeople?'

'Very well,' the Headman answered with the dispassionate resignation of a man who has run the whole gamut of blighted hopes.

'And you, my friend, only for you and your son, I'm prepared to sell you some fifty dönüms off my land. And quite cheap too. Your son looks like a brave loyal fellow and I need men like him. People around here often try to stir up trouble against me . . . So next year you can leave the tribe and come and build yourself a house here on the land you've bought. As for Jeren's father, I've talked to him. He's going to sell everything he's got, his horse, camel, sheep, his rugs, and I'm going to give him a little place for a house there, where you see those mulberry trees . . .'

'Thank you,' the Headman said. 'It's very thoughtful of you, Hassan Agha. God bless you.'

He rose. They embraced, kissing each other on the shoulder In the old traditional manner, and then they parted. It was not iong before dawn and the last cocks crowed desultorily. He walked towards the tents through the darkness. There was something strange about the camp this night. Tiny lights flickered furtively in every one of the tents and as he drew nearer he heard whisperings, stealthy, barely audible, like a subterranean murmur of perfidy in the night.

His son was waiting for him in front of his tent. 'Father!' Fethullah's voice was fraught with a mixture of fear and anger. 'Have you heard? Halil is here.'

'Well, I'm glad,' Headman Süleyman answered in level tones. 'I've really been longing to see him . . . Where is he? Inside?'

Fethullah was nonplussed. 'He's in his own tent.'

'Well, go and bring him here.'

'No one spoke to him,' Fethullah said. 'No one even looked at him when he came. So he went straight to his own tent and hasn't come out since.'

'It was wrong of them. Halil's still the Bey of our tribe. Even though he doesn't act as the Bey any more, the drum, the horsetail and the halberd are always in his tent. How could you treat him so shamefully?'

'Well we did,' Fethullah said. 'What else could we do? He can only have come for Jeren. Doesn't he know she's engaged now?'

'Go and get him,' Headman Süleyman ordered him sternly. 'At once! No, wait . . . I'll go and you're coming with me. It's I who must go to him. He's still our Bey . . .'

He turned and walked away with long angry strides towards Halil's tent. Fethullah followed him. The barking of the sheepdogs filled the dawn, slow, deep-toned, seasoned.

28

Men of noble ancestry are like this, tall and slim. Halil's moustache, his beard were curly. His eyes dreamy. At itmes they lit up and flashed and turned into the eyes of a ravening wolf. They were eyes that altered every instant, changing from colour to colour, from light to light. A German carbine was slung over his shoulder. A bandolier hung from his right shoulder and another from his left, and from waist to breast, right up to the armpits, he had strapped four more bandoliers. His long silver-nielloed Circassian dagger swung over his left hip. His silver-embroidered Marash cloak was tightly clasped at the waist by a large cartridge-belt. On his head a plain fez . . . His shalvar-trousers were handwoven of thick brown wool, and over them, reaching up to his knees, he wore embroidered woollen stockings. Noble men like this have well-proportioned shoulders and a cleft in their chin. Halil had come riding on his white horse. A long-necked ruby-eyed horse . . .

Fethullah was foaming as he stalked about the tents. The men were grouped together spinning away irritably at their carved wooden spindles. The women were sullen, ready to burst. An ugly mad look was on everyone's face.

'What business has he to come? Tell me, Uncle Hidir, what business has this man, this bandit, with our tribe? It's not one month yet that we're settled here. Doesn't he know what we've gone through? Why does he come and spoil it all? It was him set fire to that village . . . Because of him those villagers almost killed us all. It's all his fault. What business has he to come, and a battalion of policemen at his heels too? In the very middle of the Chukurova plain too! Jeren was sick enough before he came, but now that she knows he's here, she's worse than ever . . .

What business had he to come?'

'No business at all,' Hidir said. 'None at all. If he's come for
Jeren, then the Karachullu tribe will die to the last man before
we let him take her away. Jeren's betrothed now, before God.
What business has he, and him an outlaw too, a bloodthirsty
bandit, to be snooping around a betrothed girl? And a girl who
rejected him, who decided to marry another man, and of her
own free will too . . . Fethullah, my son, you're quite right to be
angry. What if somebody goes and denounces him now to the
police? Eh, let me see him get out of this Chukurova plain then!
Let me see him escape! They'll kill him.'

'If somebody went and denounced him . . .'

'Informed the police . . .'

'. ∴. that Halil is here . . .'

'Halil . . .'

His name stuck in everyone's heart like a secret shameful act
of treason.

Old Müslüm flew into a rage. 'You miserable worms,' he
shouted. 'He's your own Bey. The horsetail is in his keeping,
the drum . . .'

'That's as may be,' Hidir retorted. 'But what is there left of
Beys or Pashas now? A shrivelled drum, a moth-eaten horsetail,
a tattered old standard . . .'

'Be quiet!' Old Müslüm thundered. 'Shut your wretched
mouth! Shut up, you vermin, shut up! The tribe's not dead yet
that you should speak like that of our standard.'

'Leave off, Hidir,' the others said. 'Don't go provoking the
old man.'

'But what if someone were to inform on him . . .'

'What would happen then?'

'The law would be here in a trice, with the police thick as
hail . . . And then . . . Then what?'

'What if he escaped them again? . . .'

'My two children died under those rocks, all because of
Halil.'

'It's all because of him they won't let us stop anywhere in the
Chukurova.'

278

'All because of Halil . . .'

It was evil faring for Halil. Almost every single member of the tribe was racking his brains secretly, thinking of what kind of trap could be laid to get rid of him.

'Tonight, when he's asleep in that tent of his . . . A heavy stone . . . Snuffed out like a candle he'll be! Who'll ever find out we did it? What d'you say, Kamil?'

'It could be done, Fethullah.'

'We could truss him up in his sleep and give him up to the police . . . After all he's only one man and we're a whole tribe. Couldn't we do that, Osman?'

'That's a good idea too, Rüstem. You know best when it comes to this sort of thing.'

Secretly, in the night, the debate went on. Then at midnight they made their decision. The three of them, Fethullah, Rüstem and Osman, would pounce on Halil in his sleep. They would bind him up securely and hand him over to the police. Why should they kill him? The police would see to that! After all, his was no petty crime. He had burned down a huge Chukurova village . . .

Halil was sitting up, wakeful, his hand on his pistol. Suddenly a shadow slipped into the tent. He leapt up. The shadow threw itself at his neck.

'Halil, Halil! . . . You're here! You're alive . . . They told me you were dead. They showed me a bloody shirt and said it was yours. Halil, no man's hand ever . . .'

'I know,' he said.

They fell silent. Jeren was all in a sweat, trembling as though she would fly. Her hand was in Halil's. She could not think. Fear scorched through her body. What would happen now? Her mind was numb. Everything, the whole world had been wiped out the minute she heard that Halil had come. Everything about her spelt Halil now. Her hands, her eyes, her ears, her hair, all had become Halil. Halil her thoughts, Halil her very breath.

'Jeren,' he said, 'I know all. What you've gone through, what

279

you did . . . Everything.' She clung to him more closely, trembling. 'We've got to be quick, Jeren. Some of the tribesmen are plotting to kill me. Headman Süleyman has warned me.'

'He warned me too,' Jeren said.

'What a good noble man he is,' Halil said.

He put his arm about the trembling Jeren and drew her out of the tent. Shadows shot out of the darkness. Quickly he flung Jeren on to the saddle, leapt up in front of her and spurred the horse. A burst of firing followed them. He reined about with a quick swerve and galloped on. They were lost if they could not make it to the mountains before dawn. The tribe would be up in arms by now, joining in the hunt with the police as if he were their bitterest enemy.

At break of dawn they had left Kirmajili behind and were making for Akyol. They passed Dikenli and began climbing the craggy slope of Karatepe. Halil half turned and looked back.

'Jeren,' he murmured. 'Jeren . . .'

29

This is the night that links the fifth to the sixth of May. On this night Hizir, the patron saint of land, and Ilyas, the patron saint of the seas, will meet. And at the same time two stars will join in the sky, one refulgent, rising from the west, and the other coruscating out of the east. The two stars will merge, waxing large and bright, and flashes of light will shoot forth over the earth. And at that very moment everything will stop in the world, everything will die. The blood will freeze in men's veins. The winds will cease to blow and the waters will hold their flow. The leaf will be still and the wings of birds and insects inert. Everything will be arrested. Sounds and sleep, the budding of flowers, the growing of the grass. All movement, all life will stop, will die. For just one instant. And if at that instant a man sees the meeting of the stars in the sky, their glowing radiance showering over the earth, if he can catch a glimpse of the flowing water frozen in its course, then, at that very instant, whatever he wishes for will come true . . . Let him wish for the most impossible thing, it will be granted him . . . If once on this night that links the fifth to the sixth of May Hizir and Ilyas should fail to meet, if the world did not die for that one instant, then the flowers would never bloom again, and all creatures on earth would cease to give birth. And the instant after the two saints meet and everything dies together, all life is renewed and gushes forth anew, stronger, more vigorous than ever before.

It was three days now that the Karachullu tribe had settled in the valley on Aladag Mountain. Last autumn when they had left for the Chukurova they had counted sixty tents. Only thirty-five had returned, a little more faded, a little more battered and worn. Today again it was the day of their big annual feast. From early morning the sheep had been slaughtered and put to boil in large cauldrons. Old women in white kerchiefs bustled about the cauldrons throwing in aromatic mountain herbs and dried vegetables. The rice-pilaffs too were simmering away gently. The orange felt rugs, embroidered with the sun and tree-of-life emblems, were spread out, ready, over the white marble-like stone.

This year old Koyun Dédé had come again, cradling his big *saz* beneath his long beard. And Dost Dédé too, that huge godlike man, a saint really, who walked shedding light into the darkness of the night, but did not know it himself . . . And Sümbül Dédé of the powerful voice that could be heard a three-day distance away . . . And young Ali Dédé who had come face to face with the Lord Hizir three times, and each time had said, go your way, O Lord Hizir, I have no wish to make of you. I am a human being and must bring about my own wishes myself . . . The pipers had come too and the famous drummer, Abdal Bayram of the holy drummers' hearth.

And so the feast began. When everyone had eaten and drunk their fill and the meal-cloths had been cleared away, the old Dédés entoned the *gülbenk* prayers and the valley of Aladag rang with the echo of their deep voices. Then hymns were sung to the accompaniment of the *saz*. And afterwards they all stood up for the *semah* dance, men and women, young and old. Their feet glided over the ancient earth with the fluidity of a rippling brook. Bodies swayed in harmonious unison, arms were raised wing-like and gently lowered.

And then, as the Dédés, rapt, were strumming away at their *sazes*, as the *semah* reached its highest pitch, flowing soft and swift over the immemorial earth like a bright water, Halil was seen coming down the mountain on his white horse with Jeren riding pillion behind him. They approached and Halil dismounted. He tethered the horse to a bush, then took Jeren by the hand and together they went to kneel before old Koyun Dédé. The sheikh blessed them both. They rose and joined the long line of dancers.

The *semah* dance came to an end and Abdal Bayram struck

up a very ancient rhythm on his drum. He began to spin round and round all by himself. The tall heap of wood was set alight and everyone joined the abdal in his whirling dance about the fire.

Then the sun set and the feast was over. Abdal Bayram picked up his drum and went away. Nobody looked at Halil and Jeren, nobody bid them welcome nor asked where they had been, what they had done all this time. They simply ignored them. But some there were who cast looks of hate and anger at them and even overtly spit on the ground.

Halil and Jeren made their way to the tents. The Bey's empty tent had been erected as usual. Leaving the horse at the entrance, they went in. Halil lit a piece of firewood. For a long while he stood looking about him. Nothing had been changed, nothing was missing. They went out again.

A fever of indignation was shaking the tribe. The valley of Aladag was alive with whisperings.

'This is too much,' Fethullah was saying. 'To come back like this after ruining all our plans, after making us the laughing-stock of all the Chukurova . . .'

'It's too much,' Hidir said.

'It's too much,' Musajik said.

'Too much,' the women said.

'Too much,' the children echoed.

Only two persons said nothing. One was Headman Süleyman and the other Old Müslüm.

'This can't be borne,' Abdurrahman said.

'No, it can't be borne,' Sultan Woman said.

'Never, never, never! . . .'

Rüstem rushed off to alert the police. Like a wind of death he flew down the slope of Aladag Mountain.

'Get your weapons all of you,' Fethullah said. 'If the police-men let him slip away, we'll have to do him in ourselves, tonight.'

'Why did he come?' Old Müslüm asked the Headman.

'He's still the Bey, even if only in name. He must be with the tribe on such a day, on Hidirellez day. That's why he's come,

283

Müslüm brother. And he did well.'

Headman Süleyman went up to Alagöz spring that spirted out
at the foot of the red flint rock. He took off his felt cloak and sat
down. There were stars in the water. The pool was all aglitter.
He was at peace now, his mind empty of all thought. He had no
wish to make of Hizir any more. He had come here simply
letting long habit take its course. So he watched the fish in the
little pool with a warped and bitter pleasure and thought how
strange it was that the air should be so warm and sweetly
scented. His large nostrils quivered like a bee's wings and
opened wide.

'Spring has come early,' he said, 'this year to the Binboga
Mountains. A fresh new spring bringing life to our souls. Ah,
my brothers . . .'

The fount beside which Old Müslüm had set up watch gushed
out from the body of a tree. If this water stops flowing, he
thought, I'll see it at once. It's splashing out so loudly, so fast,
that a blind man would know when it stops and a deaf man feel
the stillness.

'Look, Lord Hizir, time's running out, my sultan. If you
don't come to my help this year, then it's all over with me.
Look, even our Haydar's roared himself out of this world . . .
Wintering lands in the Chukurova? Land?' He was working
himself into a rage. 'Let the young people wish for that!' he
shouted out loud. 'Just let me see your stars, O Hizir, and I
shall wish only for Lokman the Physician's flower of immortality. Nothing else. Not even the whole wide world if you
offered it to me. Not even if you turned all these mountains
into gold, into land for the tribe to winter on. I wouldn't take
it. The flower, the flower! The flower of life, that's what I want.
Please Hizir, I've no time left. Please let me see those stars
meet, please. Let me see the waters stop just once, please. To
smell the flower and never die . . . I can't last another year, I
know, and then even if you swamp the world with flowers of
life after I'm gone of what use will it be to me? It'll never bring

284

me back to life once I'm dead . . .'

He stopped. A thought pricked at his heart. It made him angrier still. 'Certainly not,' he muttered. 'What's it to me? Wintering land? I want no wintering land from anyone!'

Then his face brightened again. 'Look my good Lord Hizir, that flower is here in Aladag Valley, ours to pick, I know. Tell me which flower it is. Please . . .'

He lay down on his back. His eyes were on the stars, his ear on the gurgling of the spring. It wouldn't do to be caught off his guard now. One moment of inattention, and it would be too late. The stars would have joined in the sky and passed on without his seeing them.

The three little boys, Hüsseyin, Veli and Dursun were watching for the stars too.

'I don't want any old wintering quarters,' Hüseyin declared. 'I'm not going to stay in this tribe anyway. I'm going to wish for something else.' But he had not yet decided. There were so many things he wanted this year . . .

Veli had long outgrown his last year's wish of sleeping one night in the big inn on the road. In the secret of his heart he nursed a wish, such a marvellous thing that he did not voice it, not even to himself. He would say it when he saw the star.

As for Dursun, it was the same for him as last year. 'What do I care about winter land?' he said. 'I just want my father to come out of prison. Then we'll have everything we could ever wish for, winter land and summer pastures, everything. The whole world will be ours, the whole world! Just let my father come . . .'

This year Bald Osman had not gone fishing for trout. He stood beside Fethullah, holding his gun . . . Many others of the tribe had also given up watching for the stars this year. They just waited in the night with their guns in their hands . . .

Women, children, old people were waiting, and young girls too, in a fever of suspense. The sick were waiting, the suffering, the sick at heart, the lonely.

Jeren and Halil had gone to the Tashbuyduran spring. Their

shadows fell on the mirror of the water. A long thin golden-coated greyhound was lying beside them. It was Halil's greyhound, and last year too it had waited with Jeren at this same spring. The stars were shining and under their frozen glitter Jeren and Halil linked hands and laughed. The stars, the water, the whole world was laved clean, pure and bright.

'We have nothing to wish for,' Jeren said. 'Come, Halil, let's go.'

'No wait,' Halil said quickly. 'There may be something. Something that'll come to our minds when we see the star.'

'All right,' Jeren said, and at that moment the greyhound at their feet pricked up its ears and rose.

'Careful, Jeren,' Halil whispered. 'Get into the hollow of this rock and don't move. Didn't I tell you that the tribe would never forgive us? They're there now. They've got us surrounded.'

They could hear sounds, feel stirrings about them, drawing nearer, louder in the night.

'Is it this night you've chosen?' Halil shouted out suddenly. 'Hidirellez night when not even a serpent, a monster, a blood-thirsty foe would attack a man?'

There was no answer, no breath. All was dead silence. And then suddenly volley after volley burst out from all sides. The skirmish lasted through the night. It was nearly dawn when Halil's gun fell still. The others stopped firing too. Jeren came out of the hollow where she had been hiding and went to Halil's side. He was lying face down on the ground. She gathered him up in her arms and vanished into the rocks, gliding like a bird through the air.

The sun was up the height of a poplar when the others moved into view at last and came to the spring. A pool of blood had clotted on the ground, and all about it were empty cartridge shells and green flies.

Jeren carried the dead body of Halil to the very peak of Aladag Mountain. There she took his knife and dug out a grave among the rocks. Her hand caressed the body gently. She kissed it and lowered it into the hollow. Then she shoved the earth back and placed a stone at the head of the grave, the largest she could lift. She turned away at once and went down the slope to the camp. The tribespeople rejoiced when they saw her return, even more than they had rejoiced at Halil's death. She went straight to Headman Süleyman.

'They have killed Halil, Headman . . . I have buried him and come to you.'

And she walked over to the Bey's tent. Halil's horse was still standing there before it. Raising the gun in her hand, she aimed it. The horse fell and as it still kicked and struggled she fired again.

'Bring some wood,' Headman Süleyman ordered the silent crowd, 'and heap it right here.' They moved and in an instant they had heaped up a tall mound of wood. The Headman went into the tent. First he brought the standard and cast it over the mound, then the horsetail, then the drum. He brought out all there was in the tent, the kilims, the felt rugs, the saddle-bags and threw everything on to the heap. 'Pull down that tent now . . .'

Jeren stood there quite still and calm, almost indifferent. There was not a tear in her eyes, not a sign of grief on her face. When they had laid the tent over the rest of the things, she stepped forward, but the Headman intercepted her.

'Stop, my daughter. This is the Bey's tent. It is for me to burn it.'

He struck a match. The wood caught fire and the flames leaped up. A musty odour of burning goatshair spread through the air. They all stood there, the whole tribe, mute and still, not once taking their eyes off the flaming pyre, until the wood, the tent, everything had been burned to ashes.

When there was nothing left, Headman Süleyman sank onto a stone and covered his face. A flood of tears flowed from under his hands. His beard was wet through in an instant.

Jeren's swan-like neck stretched out still more. Her eyes lingered awhile on the dead horse and went to the silent frozen crowd. She gave them a long deep look, then walked up to

Headman Süleyman and stood before him a moment as though she wanted to say something. But then she turned away. Slinging Halil's gun over her shoulder, she walked up the valley into the mountain and disappeared. The tribespeople stood riveted to the ground, not even daring to lift their heads to look after her.

And so it is each year. On the night that links the fifth to the sixth of May, Hizir and Ilyas meet somewhere on this earth. And the moment they join, all life is extinguished in this world, all living things die. But the next instant everything comes to life again, rejuvenated, stronger, more fruitful than ever before. And two stars come tearing through the sky, one from the west, the other from the east. They meet and merge, shedding a scintillating splendour over the earth.